"Why is it so important for ye to know any of this?"

"Because I live here," she said softly. "Because you and your clan are all I know."

He reached out to cup her cheek with his warm, calloused hand. "Do not be afraid, lass. Ye're safe here. I'll let nothing harm ye."

Then he slid his hand to the back of her head and drew her toward him for a long deep kiss.

She felt both desperate and overcome, frightened and at peace, all of those emotions jumbled up inside of her, emotions she only found in his arms. Somehow she found herself stumbling back against the vine-covered rock wall of the cliff as his body pressed into hers. She explored his mouth as if she could know everything about him . . .

By Gayle Callen

GAYLE CALLEN

LOVE
WITH A
SCOTTISH
OUTLAW

Highland Weddings

AVONBOOKS

An Imprint of HarperCollinsPublishers

HarperCollins
PUBLISHERS
Since 1817

LOVE WITH A SCOTTISH OUTLAW. Copyright © 2017 by Gayle Kloecker Callen. All rights reserved. Printed in the United States of America. No part of this book may be used or reproduced in any manner whatsoever without written permission except in the case of brief quotations embodied in critical articles and reviews. For information, address HarperCollins Publishers, 195 Broadway, New York, NY 10007.

First Avon Books mass market printing: July 2017

Print Edition ISBN: 978-0-06-246993-9
Digital Edition ISBN: 978-0-06-246994-6

Avon, Avon & logo, and Avon Books & logo are registered trademarks of HarperCollins Publishers in the United States of America and other countries.

HarperCollins is a registered trademark of HarperCollins Publishers in the United States of America and other countries.

FIRST EDITION

17 18 19 20 21   QGM   10 9 8 7 6 5 4 3 2 1

To Laura Lee Guhrke, my author buddy and dear friend: thanks for the brainstorming and the long phone calls where we can talk about everything and anything. Wish we didn't live almost a continent apart.

LOVE
WITH A
SCOTTISH
OUTLAW

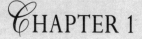CHAPTER 1

Scotland, 1727

The rain woke her first, hard and pelting against her face. For a long moment, she kept her eyes closed in confusion and uncertainty—and pain. God, her head hurt, the distant ache exploding as she came more and more to consciousness. The rain plopped on her eyelids and cheeks, and slid down into the wet mass of hair beneath her. Something was wrong, something beyond the rain, the aching head, and the sodden, uneven ground upon which she lay. Thinking about it only hurt more, so she tried to move, flexing her hands and feet, shrugging her shoulders. A wave of nausea roiled through her, but she couldn't let it overwhelm her. She shivered, teeth chattering, skull throbbing.

Why was she lying outside on the ground? Nothing came into her mind—nothing at all.

Surely it was because of the ache in her head, she told herself, fighting a growing feeling of anxiety. She needed warmth and release from the pain. Nothing would change if she just continued to lie there.

She crinkled her eyes, blinked several times, and opened them again. The sky was gray with patches of even darker clouds, letting loose a torrent upon the countryside. She forced herself to turn her head and saw a steep hillside above her, with the occasional bush clinging to the infertile ground. There were marks etched in the earth, like a giant had taken its fingers and gouged downward, leading right toward her.

With a groan, she rolled to the side, feeling every muscle protest like little screams erupting inside her.

And then she saw the blank stare of a dead man.

She screamed aloud, hoarse and choked, unable to look away. There was blood on his face, and his neck was at an unnatural angle.

She had to cover her mouth with both hands to stop the sobs from leaking out. Though she wanted to look away, she couldn't let herself. He was dead, poor soul, but he was also a stranger. He was lying at the foot of a hillside, right beside her, and his face meant nothing.

She meant nothing.

She had to accept it now—there was nothing inside her head about who she was or why she was lying next to a dead man. Nothing existed before the moment she'd been awakened by the rain.

As she rolled away from the body, she told herself that she knew what things *were*—that hadn't left her. There was the sky and rain and mud. She had hands that shook, a head that pounded, hips that ached as she arched away from a rock beneath her.

With a groan, she leveraged her hands beneath her and pushed until, trembling, she was in a sitting position. And then she saw another crumpled, unmoving body. She let out a moan of fear, looking around as if for the enemy who'd done this. But she was alone, with only the vastness of barren hills and wild water.

The person behind her was dead, but maybe not this one. On her hands and knees, she crawled the short distance, rocks cutting her palms, mud oozing between her fingers.

"Sir? Are you well?"

But when she touched his sodden coat, she knew; he was hard and cold and very dead. She forced herself to look into his face, eyes half-closed and staring at nothing. He was a stranger, too.

She sank back on her heels and hugged herself as despair washed over her, the feeling as wet and miserable as the rain itself. But she could not let herself surrender to fear. She wouldn't die out here, alone. Looking around, she saw water flowing down the ravine, overrunning its banks. The uneven, rocky ground stretched downhill, away from her, rising into the slopes of barren brown hillsides, and between them, the darker green of valleys, dotted with the occasional copse of trees. There was nothing else in the world but the forlorn emptiness of countryside, no houses, no villages, no roads.

Turning her neck, she looked back up the ravine. She must have come from up there with these men, fallen down, maybe caused those gouges in the earth. But if they'd been riding horses, they were long gone, taking with them any belongings that might have explained who she was or where they were going.

She wasn't sure when night might fall, but she needed to find help or at least shelter, before the cold killed her as the fall had killed these men.

Staggering to her feet, she began to walk downhill, away from the dangerously high river. Each step jarred her bruises, but at least nothing seemed broken—except her head, which pounded so hard she could only keep her eyes half open. Her soaked gown and cloak weighed her down, making each step an uneven lurch.

DUNCAN Carlyle, outlawed chief of the Clan Carlyle, rode his chestnut gelding, Arran, slowly through the rain along the narrow dirt path that wound between the hillsides of the southern Highlands. A fast-flowing burn overflowed its banks from the deluge, sending a rush of water on its way to the sea. It was a cold September day, nothing unusual for the Highlands. His wool plaid kept some of the heat in, and his horse's flanks steamed against his bare thighs. He still had an hour's journey back to his encampment, but he didn't let his mind drift. He was ever alert for enemies. There'd been a close call when he'd almost been captured six weeks ago. It had taken two days of hard riding to elude his pursuers. Since then, he and all his men had stayed close to their encampment and avoided outsiders.

As the path took a turn, Arran's ears went back, and Duncan felt the tension in the reins. A woman walked toward him, her hood draped back from her shoulders, her bare head dark with rain—and something else? Standing in the stirrups, he looked about, but saw nothing but the harsh Highland hills scattered with drooping purple heather. She was far too close to his encampment for comfort, and he wondered where the rest of her party was.

He urged his horse into a trot until he approached her. Her uneven gait came to a halt as her lowered gaze took in first the legs of his horse, then rose slowly. He inhaled at the sight of the ugly bruise on her forehead, and the wound beside it that streamed with blood. Her eyes were rimmed with blue shadows of distress, her face blanched white. She stared up at him unseeing, allowing him only a glimpse of her golden eyes before they rolled back in her head as she collapsed.

Swearing, Duncan swung down from his horse and hovered over her still form, years of wariness guiding his actions. "Mistress? Can ye hear me?"

As he touched her shoulders, he felt the fine material of her cloak. After straightening her limbs, he lifted her upper body into his left arm, cradling her head so that he blocked the rain. He probed near her wound gingerly with his right hand, and she frowned and weakly tried to turn away.

His wariness deepened. There was something about her, a familiarity that echoed inside his head but refused to take shape.

"Where am I?" she whispered, her accent English. "What happened?"

An English lady in the Highlands? He chose to answer the second question rather than the first. "Ye've a nasty wound to your head, mistress. Did ye fall?"

She blinked as if she might lose consciousness. "Where am I? What happened?"

Now it was his turn to blink, but he remembered that wounds of the head could cause confusion. He knew he had to stop the blood loss.

"Mistress, can ye stand?"

She opened those eyes again, large and golden, in a delicate face. Her dark hair streamed back from her forehead, her hairline coming to a peak.

He recognized her, a flash of memory from Stirling several years ago, when he'd glared his hatred at the Earl of Aberfoyle, a haughty old man on horseback, forcing aside a poor lass heavy with child to make way for him. The earl's family was seldom in Scotland, so their arrival in the Highlands had caused a stir. Duncan had seen this woman riding just behind, wearing the fine gown and jaunty hat that marked her a noble lady. At least she'd looked distressed at her father's actions.

Catriona Duff was the daughter of Aberfoyle, the chief of the Clan Duff and Duncan's bitter enemy. Aberfoyle was one of the main reasons that

Duncan was an outlaw who had to protect and feed his people while on the run.

He lifted his head and looked about, as if the earl and his entire retinue were somewhere nearby, waiting to attack him. "Where are your men?" he demanded.

"What happened?" she asked weakly.

"Ye've hit your head. Where are your men?"

"My—men?"

Her hand fluttered toward her forehead, but he didn't allow her to touch the wound.

A spasm of pain narrowed her eyes. "I found them . . . dead," she whispered. "What happened to me?"

"I don't know." He would just have to hope she was telling the truth. Six weeks after almost being captured, he was still wary of anything unusual in his part of the Highlands. Dead men would prove her story true, but he couldn't deal with them now.

"I—I can't remember—I can't remember anything!" Though her cry was feeble, it was full of helplessness and fear.

"Ye don't remember the accident?"

"Not . . . the accident, not even . . . my name."

He frowned down at her, wondering at what intrigue she was playing—or what her father had set in motion. He wouldn't put it past the bastard.

She clutched his plaid. "What happened to me?" she cried in despair.

"I do not ken. I must clean that wound. Can ye stand? I can pull ye up on my horse."

He rose, lifting her up with him until she could

clutch the saddle for support. After mounting, he reached down for her. He would have preferred she ride astride behind him, but she seemed so weak that he ended up cradling her across his thighs. She leaned into him, her head lolling onto his chest, her blood staining his black, red, and yellow plaid.

It didn't take long to reach the rocky overhang he'd used for shelter several other times. Once out of the rain, he searched his saddle pack but found nothing that would do for a clean bandage. He ended up cutting several strips from the end of his shirt with his dirk. The wound seemed clean enough after all the rain, so he wrapped the improvised bandages around her head and hoped they stopped the bleeding.

She looked at him helplessly the whole time, and he felt like she was memorizing his features. He studied her, too. Her high cheekbones emphasized the hollows beneath, and her full lips hinted at an expressive mouth. Her pale face was as remote and beautiful as a statue, making her appeal to him on a primitive level that he would never acknowledge.

Why was she in the remote Highlands? According to gossip he'd heard long ago, she rarely visited her father's castles. Was she the advance of a larger party headed right for Duncan's unsuspecting people? She was so close to his hidden encampment. If he let her go, she could bring men to hunt the area, risking his people—risking the good he was trying to do. He couldn't release her until he knew all the facts.

As he stared down at her, her eyes closed, her

waxen complexion and flickering frown betraying the presence of pain. But now he saw more—the brooch that decorated her shoulder, marking her: the insignia of the Duff clan. He pulled it off her and hid it away in his saddlebag. It would be safer if no one knew who she was. There were too many desperate clansmen who might react with violence.

"Time to go," he said gruffly, helping her to a sitting position.

He saw the panic in her anguished eyes and barely had time to help her turn her head aside before she retched. Much as he despised her father, he pitied her condition. She was almost boneless as he lifted her to her feet. He covered her bandaged head with the hood of her cloak, hoping for some protection. His gelding, which had been grazing patiently in the rain, accepted both their weight and turned for home without Duncan's guidance. He pulled his excess plaid around her for warmth and protection from the rain, but couldn't stop glancing at her pale face.

She represented everything he despised, daughter of the man who cared so little about the Scottish people that he allowed children to be stolen and sold as indentured servants, practically slavery, in the American colonies and the Caribbean plantations. When Duncan had tried to call attention to what was happening, the sheriff and other magistrates in Glasgow along with their sponsor, her father, the Earl of Aberfoyle, had boldly threatened to imprison him. They'd rationalized that they were taking care of the problem of the poor

and orphaned. After the childhood he'd endured,
Duncan couldn't tolerate seeing children abused.
Perhaps there could have been more subtle ways
for him to go about it, but subtlety also meant
going slow, letting even more children be abandoned.

He'd sworn he would be a better chief than his
father had been, but instead, he'd made everything
worse. He'd brought his complaint to the Court of
Session, and the magistrates hadn't even allowed
witnesses to be brought forth. Duncan had been
imprisoned in a thief's hole, and was about to be
sold himself, leaving his clan defenseless, if he
hadn't escaped. In these last five years, he'd become a wanted man, an outlaw with a price on his
head. The Earl of Aberfoyle and the magistrates
continued to profit from the misery of others.

Since that day, the Carlyles skirted starvation,
while the Duffs enjoyed the fruits of an earldom
that spanned greater Britain. Catriona's garments
were expensive and London-purchased, while
his sisters wore coarse cloth they'd woven themselves. Duff children had warm beds and full bellies at night, while Carlyle children huddled with
their parents in the dark, fearing being dragged
from their beds.

Duncan had begun his own campaign against
his enemies, and he'd learned patience. When a
pack train of horses carrying casks of Duff whisky
through the Highlands had come to Duncan's notice, it had been easy to steal it, sending the Duff
guards fleeing through the hills on foot. He'd begun smuggling the whisky into the Lowlands,

or onto a boat in the River Clyde on the way to the Atlantic. That money had bought new seedlings after a famine had nearly starved his people. He never stole too much whisky, and never from the same route. He let the guards grow lax before he struck again. It wasn't solving his main problems—how to get the warrant on his head rescinded and end the kidnappings—but it was the start of his retribution.

And now into his path had come Catriona Duff. If he kept her for a while—and how could he not, with her injuries?—he would make the Duffs suffer as the Carlyles had all these years. This could be the culmination of his vengeance. Let the old earl wonder where his daughter was. Duncan wouldn't harm her, and if she wasn't a spy, she'd get a firsthand look at what her father had allowed to happen to an entire clan.

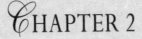HAPTER 2

She came awake to the slow rocking of a horse's gait. For just a moment, she felt safe and almost warm. Hard arms supported her, held her close, and the ache in her head had dulled a bit, after resting against the warm masculine chest. Beneath her ear, she heard the steady beating of a strong heart.

Slowly, she opened her eyes and stared up at the man who'd rescued her. Everything about him was dark—hair drawn back in a queue beneath his cap, the stubble shadowing his strong jaw, even his eyes, so dark she could barely see his pupils. She wasn't sure why she felt safe—he was a stranger after all. He could have left her behind, could have robbed and beaten her, but instead, he was helping her. And as for being a stranger—well, she was a stranger to herself.

She had hoped sleep would bring back her memory, but it hadn't. It hurt to search through what seemed like cobwebbed corners of her mind.

It was easier to think about this man she was utterly dependent on. He spoke gruffly, as few words as necessary, it seemed. But to her surprise, his touch had been gentle as he'd bandaged her head. Though his clothes were plain and sturdy, he talked as someone who'd been educated. He seemed . . . noble to her, a man down on his luck. Her own clothing was far finer than his; apparently she came from a wealthier family.

Keeping his gaze straight ahead, he said, "Ye're studying me hard."

She was so close to his neck that she could see the movement of his Adam's apple above his neck cloth. Her cheeks felt suddenly hot as she grew all too aware of the intimate way he held her.

He glanced down at her, those dark eyes piercing. "Do ye remember something?"

She shook her head. "No, nothing. Where am I?"

"Scotland."

"I . . . am I Scottish? I speak differently than you do."

"Ye sound English to me."

"Oh, I see. The English and the Scots do not always get along."

He arched a brow.

"I remembered that!" she cried, then winced again. "This is the strangest feeling, to know unimportant things—"

"The animosity between England and Scotland is unimportant?" he asked, his voice growing colder.

"No, I wasn't talking about that," she said swiftly.

"I meant I know the proper names of things, but absolutely nothing about myself, not even *my* proper name. Do you think it will all return?"

She searched his face, looking for comfort, but finding none at all. He only shrugged and said nothing. She imagined that he would probably leave her in the nearest village—and she wouldn't blame him.

"Where are you taking me?" she asked, her voice sounding small and hesitant.

He looked at her again. "To my clan."

For a moment, gratitude made her feel weak. "I—I don't even know your name."

"Duncan Carlyle."

As he said his surname, he eyed her closely, obviously awaiting a response. But it meant nothing to her. The blankness inside her brain made her feel helpless and dependent, and she sensed that she wasn't used to feeling that way.

"Thank you for your help, Mr. Carlyle."

She could not let her fears rule her. Her memory would return; she just needed to be patient.

There were so many questions she wanted to ask, but she stifled them at the forbidding expression he wore. He was obviously not a man of idle chatter. If he was taking her to his clan, there would be plenty of people to question.

Gradually, she drifted into a doze, but twinges of pain kept her from deep unconsciousness. She must have truly slept, however, because the next thing she knew, she felt him lower her to the side and release her into other arms. She came awake with a gasp, but she couldn't quite open her eyes.

Another man spoke in an unfamiliar language, but she understood none of it.

"Let me go!" She felt panicky that Mr. Carlyle had changed his mind and meant to abandon her.

The man tightened his grip, and suddenly he was speaking English. "Eh, listen to that fine voice."

It didn't sound like a compliment.

"Laird Carlyle, what are your orders for this Sassenach?"

Sassenach? She stiffened, knowing that word meant an Englishman. For some reason it offended her. She opened her eyes to face the man who would decide her future.

But it was Duncan Carlyle standing there, hands on his hips, eyeing her. He was so broad through the chest, as she well knew, his muscled arms evident in the form-fitting coat he wore over shirt, waistcoat, and plaid. Above his stockings, his knees were bare and powerful-looking. She didn't think she was used to seeing a man's naked legs.

"Do ye feel well enough to stand, mistress?" he asked.

"You're Laird Carlyle?" she asked. "Why did you not say so?"

Laird Carlyle arched a dark brow. "I didn't think it necessary." He looked at the man who held her in a stiff, awkward grip. "Try setting the lass on her feet, Ivor. But hold tight. The head wound is serious."

When her feet touched the ground, her legs felt shaky, and she kept her grip on the man's coat. She turned her head, expecting to see a cottage

or manor or something near the trees that now
protected her from the rain. But instead, she saw
an uneven wall of a rock, extending above her
head and toward the sky. Directly in front of them
was a dark opening that looked like a mouth into
the side of the mountain. She didn't know what
to make of any of this. She glanced at Ivor, the
bearded man who steadied her, his hair a dark
blond and nearly touching his shoulders. No neat
queue for him. But he wore the same black, red,
and yellow plaid as Laird Carlyle did.

"This is Ivor, my war chief," Laird Carlyle said.

Ivor winked at her. "And who might ye be, lass?"

She opened her mouth, but nothing came out.
A name was the first thing you granted a stranger,
and she had nothing to give.

"She's taken a blow to the head," Laird Carlyle
said, "leaving her confused."

Ivor's bushy eyebrows lowered; he stared at her
as if she were on display. All she could do was
raise her chin and force a pleasant expression.
But it was difficult. Now that she was standing,
the mild ache in her head was beginning to throb
again. Ivor tightened his hold on her arm just as
she realized she'd begun to sway.

And then her world spun again as Laird Carlyle swept her into his arms. She didn't protest—
after all, his embrace was the only safety she had
known in this world that seemed so new to her.
He walked directly to the hole in the cliff and went
inside. She gave a little gasp, expecting complete
darkness, but to her surprise, the cave opened
up, with a ceiling she couldn't even see. Torches

lined the rough walls, illuminating a little community of people. There were several small fires, with roasting spits or cauldrons suspended over them. Rough wooden tables were encircled by flat tree stumps in place of chairs. To the right, pallets and blankets were stacked, in the rear, trunks and crates. Along the wall to the left, she saw a small stream running the length of the cave. There was even a flat, wooden bridge crossing it, leading into another dark entranceway.

It was in that direction that Laird Carlyle strode, carrying her as if she were a feather. The half-dozen or so people, mostly women, stared at them in surprise. Her cheeks blushed with heat at being carried in front of people, but what else could be done?

"Laird Carlyle?" called a woman.

He didn't pause, only spoke over his shoulder. "Maeve, bring your healing potions. The lass is injured."

He crossed the flat bridge, which bounced with his steps. The water beneath gave off the smell of damp earth. The cave passageway continued to the right, but he took her left, into a small, rough chamber. There was a pallet on the floor, two trunks, and a chair at a table stacked neatly with books and papers. Pegs had been driven into the stone and were hung with a man's clothing.

Laird Carlyle bent to lay her down on the pallet, and she felt the comfort of a stuffed mattress.

"Where are we?" she asked as he straightened.

"Scotland," he answered briskly.

She would have thought he teased her, but he

was so serious, she wasn't certain. "You know what I mean."

There was someone in the passageway behind him, but he didn't turn. His narrow-eyed gaze studied her. He had the darkest eyes she'd ever seen; the pupil seemed to disappear within.

"This is a place of safety my people use when necessary."

"It looks well used," she said. "Is there a war I've forgotten, one you need to hide from?"

"Nay. Stop asking questions and allow Maeve to see to ye. We'll talk in the morning after I've buried your men."

She drew in a sharp breath. "That is kind of you. Those poor men—I can't even offer them true mourning without knowing who they are. Their poor families . . ." She broke off, feeling tears threaten.

"Mistress, ye were in a tragic accident through no fault of your own," he said gruffly. "When your memory clears, we'll see to their families."

She sniffed. "I'll never be able to thank you enough for your kindness."

He looked away as if her gratitude made him uncomfortable.

"I don't know enough to even tell you where they are," she said.

"Ye couldn't have walked far. I'll find them." With a nod of the head, he left the little cave.

Maeve entered, wearing a woolen gown with a fichu draped about her neck and tucked into the laces at her bodice. The edge of her linen cap dipped, but didn't hide the wide, disfiguring scar that rippled down the left side of her face, just missing her eye, as if her skin had been melted in a fire. The other half of her face showed that she couldn't be more than thirty years old.

Before she could embarrass herself by asking about Maeve's injuries, Laird Carlyle returned, carrying a brazier piled with peat. As he worked to start a fire, the two women waited. At last, with a brusque nod, he departed again.

Maeve's smile was lopsided because of her injury, but it was still friendly, as she set a tray on the table and laid an armful of clothing on the chair. "Good day, mistress. Ye've heard that I'm Maeve. And what are ye called?"

She looked over the woman's shoulder, wishing Laird Carlyle would return and explain it all as easily as he had to Ivor. "This will sound foolish, but . . . I don't know my name. I woke up in the rain, with a pounding head and . . . that's all I know. Your laird found me wandering down the road." She gave another shiver.

Maeve's expression faded from interest to deep concern. "How terrible for ye, mistress. Wounded, and now soaked—ye'll catch yer death. Don't fash about anythin' but feelin' better. That will help yer memory. Let's get ye out of these garments."

It took far too long to unpin, unlace, and untie all of her clothes, for the wet strings proved difficult. But at last, she was dressed in a clean nightshift, her head poulticed and bandaged, the scratches on her palms cleaned. She'd wanted to dress in a gown for the day, but Maeve had insisted she needed her rest after such a terrible wound, and she hadn't protested all that much.

They'd found a small pouch of coins hidden within her skirt, and without saying anything, Maeve tucked it beneath her pillow, out of sight. If Laird Carlyle had been a dishonest man, he would have looked for such a thing and left her to die. But he'd helped her, brought her to safety—in a cave, she reminded herself. There had to be a story behind that.

When at last she lay on the pallet, a blanket pulled up around her, she felt almost peaceful, warm for the first time in hours. Her head continued to throb, but it had dulled. She had a bowl of soup warming her from the inside, and she tried to tell herself to be content that she wasn't alone, that a kind man had found her.

She drowsily watched Maeve put away her healing supplies, then said, "It feels so strange not to know myself. I must have a name, a family, maybe even a husband."

"Ye wear no ring, nor is there a mark of one," Maeve pointed out.

"True. I *could* be newly married. But regardless . . . I need to be called something, even if it's only temporary."

"Should I just suggest names and ye can pick the one that seems to speak to ye?"

"Just . . . name myself?" She blinked again, feeling the distant call of sleep. "Very well, what kind of person do I look like, Maeve? A Mary? An

Elizabeth? No, those just don't . . . *mean* anything
to me."

Maeve studied her with narrowed eyes.

"Fiona?" Maeve asked. "Margaret? Catherine?"

"Catherine!" she cried. "I like it."

"Do ye think 'tis your name?"

"I—I don't know. But I need to call myself something."

"Mistress Catherine ye'll be then," Maeve said,
rising up from the chair. She placed a cup of water
at the edge of the table, within easy reach, then
made sure that the lantern had a fresh candle. "I'll
check on ye later, Mistress Catherine," she said,
emphasizing the new name. "And I'll try to keep
the voices down out in the great hall."

"The great hall?"

Maeve chuckled. "Our private joke. Sleep well,
Mistress Catherine."

Catherine.

After Maeve pulled the curtain across the
opening and left, Catherine turned the name over
and over in her mind, even as her eyelids grew
heavier. It was a good name, solid, respectable.
She hoped she was a woman who deserved it. But
she worried that if she was traveling by herself,
with only two men, what kind of woman was she?
Or had one of those men been the husband she
couldn't remember?

THE rain had stopped, the sun was setting, yet
Duncan lingered in the small paddock, curry-
ing his horse with a comb to loosen the dirt and

sweat. The animal asked no questions, unlike the people he was going to face when he went back inside. The wind picked up, and Duncan lifted his head at the eerie wail emanating from high above him. Though the sound was part of his everyday life, others thought the castle was haunted. Even the majority of his clan crossed themselves and kept their distance, which proved beneficial, since they couldn't know where he was hiding. He'd handpicked the couple dozen men who lived with him in the caves, choosing the strongest, the most talented—the ones without close family who depended on them. The rest of Clan Carlyle lived in several nearby villages, farming their meager lands, raising a few precious head of cattle. The outlaw status of their chief had meant few people wanted to trade with them. The whisky smuggling was the only thing keeping his people from starving. But his clan couldn't know about that, though he imagined many suspected. They probably thought he was reiving cattle, too, but he preferred stealing from the Earl of Aberfoyle.

And now he'd stolen the man's daughter to show him the reality of losing a child.

Duncan tipped his head back and could just see the turret of his ancestral home, rising on the mountain high above the glen. From miles away it could be seen, a testament to the greatness the Carlyles had once taken for granted—or a reminder of how far they'd fallen. Oh, the fall had started long before he was born, but for a man who'd vowed to raise his clan up again, he'd done a poor job of it.

No one had lived in the Carlyle castle for several

generations; who would think to look for Duncan in such an obvious place? Yet he'd brought Catriona Duff here—the daughter of his enemy. She'd been unconscious and hadn't seen the hidden path. He would just have to make certain she stayed within the cave until he knew if she was lying to him. If she caught a glimpse of the castle, she'd be able to guide her clansmen here, and he couldn't allow that. He was endangering his people just by bringing her to the cave.

Taking a deep breath of resignation, Duncan followed the path along the mountainside until he reached the entrance to the cave. He'd passed several hidden men guarding the encampment. Inside, he found his people eating supper, seated on logs or stone, all eyeing him warily. These were the only clansmen allowed close to him, the ones he trusted most to aid his whisky smuggling, and on rarer occasions, to help find the stolen children before they could be taken onto ships for the colonies. But he could never relax and be one of them, was always conscious of the danger he'd put them in—like when he'd nearly been captured last month. He was their chief, the reason their lives were hard, and it was his responsibility to give them a better life.

Maeve brought him a plate of fried trout and someone cleared a place for him at one of the tables. They were all unnaturally quiet, and he knew why.

"The stranger is not hungry?" he asked in Gaelic, in case Catriona was eavesdropping.

"She needs to stay abed," Maeve said. "I brought her soup."

The four women continued to serve the men, but the men eyed him curiously. Most were young and unmarried. They were plain-speaking and rough, used to the hardships of the Highlands, which suited Duncan well. One of the men, Angus, had a wife but no children, Melville had a grown daughter he refused to leave alone at their cottage, and Mrs. Skinner, a widow with a son in Duncan's camp, wanted to cook their meals. The women had come to live with them and help, for which Duncan was grateful. And then there was Maeve, unmarried and likely to remain so since she kept herself distant with men because of her disfigurement. But she'd been a friend since his youth, and he would not deny her the chance to help the rescued children.

"So ye've brought a wench to yer room," Angus called from his place at the table.

There was some chuckling, but most were probably concerned that he'd broken the rules he'd given them. No one was to bring anyone to the encampment without a discussion. Much as Duncan had final approval, he knew his men appreciated being consulted.

"I've not brought the lass for myself," Duncan said. "Ye saw the bandages on her head. She was badly wounded, and I couldn't leave her wandering the road. She was unconscious for the journey here—have no fear she knows anything that can harm us." And he would keep it that way.

"Ye could have brought her to the village," Melville mumbled into his drink.

Duncan wasn't certain that comment was

meant to be heard by him, but he answered it anyway. "I could have, but I didn't. She claimed there are two dead men near where I found her. I'll go look for them in the morn, and then I'll know more of her situation. She was too near the cave for my comfort."

Maeve gave the clansmen a frown, and Duncan knew she would not remain silent. She was the mother hen of this encampment, and everyone respected her. Sometimes he felt like the two of them oversaw this little pocket of the clan together. He appreciated her help, common sense, and companionship. He could never make right what his family owed her, much as his father had tried.

"The lass is lost and wounded," Maeve explained. "Laird Carlyle did the right thing."

Duncan eyed Maeve. "Did she remember anything else?"

"Nothin', not even her name."

More murmurings floated through the group. Duncan felt a touch of guilt for lying to his clan about Catriona's identity, but he wouldn't make them complicit in his crime. Because it *was* a crime, holding a noblewoman captive, even though she didn't realize it, even though her father deserved whatever anxiety Duncan caused him.

After swallowing a bit of trout and a mouthful of ale, he said, "Until we know more, Ivor, I'd like ye to see to extra patrols, in case someone is looking for the woman. If ye see them, don't approach. Return to me." He let his gaze take in the rest of his people. "And when ye speak to the woman, tell her nothing of our purpose here."

"How long will she stay?" Ivor asked.

Duncan regarded his war chief impassively. He deserved as much truth as Duncan could give. "I know not. She's injured, and needs to heal. And there is the problem of her memory loss. We'll take it day by day." Then he glanced at Maeve. "Do ye have an extra pallet for me to sleep on out here?"

Angus snickered. "Ye don't want to share yer room with the lass?"

Duncan was glad to give his men something to laugh about, but it wasn't easy for him to join in. He arched his brow and said dryly, "None here would force themselves on an injured woman—and that includes me."

He went back to his fish, and let the conversation swirl around him. He'd leave at dawn to go find the dead men she'd told him about, and if he was lucky he'd know more about why she'd been traveling so near his encampment.

He thought about Catriona, asleep in his chamber, and wondered where her father thought she was. Would the man pace over his frustration, his helplessness, his fear? Duncan had spent many an evening with a grieving woman who'd lost her child forever to the kidnappers. The earl would never suffer that unending pain he'd caused so many families; his daughter would eventually be returned to him. Though Duncan seldom allowed himself to feel content, he did so now at the thought of the earl's worry.

CHAPTER 3

It had been awkward for Duncan to leave the encampment alone to deal with burying bodies. Ivor had seemed skeptical when Duncan had turned down his offer of help and asked the war chief to oversee a hunt for fresh game. But Ivor was a loyal man and had made no protest.

Because Catriona couldn't have walked far in her condition, it only took an hour or so for Duncan to find the place she had described—a steep ravine, a burn overflowing its banks. The two dead men were still there, their bodies broken in the fall. They were plainly dressed, obviously guards rather than a new husband or betrothed. Though they had died tragically, he could not alert their families. Eventually, when Catriona returned to the Duff clan, he'd make sure she knew where her guards were buried.

He stared up at the path they must have taken in their fall, shrubs uprooted, earth gouged. It was amazing that Catriona had lived. The storm the previous day had been ferocious, and horses could have flung off their riders in a panic—but all three of them? He couldn't believe that. More likely they'd come too close to the edge of the hilltop in the storm, slid down themselves, then bolted in fear. But the steepness of the drop made him think the horses had certainly not gone unscathed. And if they had run off, it wouldn't be long before they were found and people came looking for Catriona—something he didn't want, not until he figured out why she had been so close to his encampment.

It wasn't difficult to find and follow the bloody trail of wounded animals. None of them had gone far, and he was able to put them all out of their misery, though he wouldn't be able to bury them. The tragedy was a waste of good horseflesh.

It was the baggage that gave him the most consternation. The men's needs had been few, a clean shirt, weapons, ammunition, food for the journey. They'd been dressed in breeches for traveling, not a clan-revealing plaid. But Catriona had obviously meant to be gone for a while, as there were gowns and shoes and undergarments. He didn't want all of this found—it would cause too many questions and could lead right back to the Duff clan—but he wanted to be able to get his hands on it when needed. So Duncan buried it with the spade he'd brought, marked with an unusual rock so that he could find everything again. Next he turned to the men themselves and did the same. During the backbreaking work, he planned what he would tell Catriona.

CATHERINE awoke in near darkness, but for the guttering of a candle. She didn't know what had awakened her, or if it was even morning. She lay still, tense, until she heard the sound she'd thought was only in her dreams—a high, keening wail that didn't sound human. It raised gooseflesh on her arms. She came up on her elbows, wincing as her muscles protested, but the sound was already so distant, muffled by rock and earth. Or she'd imagined it. After all, she could hardly claim that her mind was acting soundly.

Because much as she'd gone to bed hopeful, this morning she still had the same blank slate in her mind. Her memories only started yesterday, when she'd awakened in the rain beside two dead men. *Her* men, she assumed, and she wasn't even able to mourn them properly. She didn't know what had happened, except somehow they'd ended up in the bottom of a ravine. Had it been an accident? Or had someone forced them over and left them for dead?

Now she was being ridiculous, inventing enemies to explain an accident. She closed her eyes and lay back again, and the terrible ache in her head eased somewhat. The rest of her body felt bruised and sore. She glanced at the clothes Maeve had left, but she wasn't sure she could dress herself, considering how weak she felt. The urge to use the chamber pot only grew stronger. She had to brace herself on the table to combat the dizziness, and her head pounded so hard she closed her eyes. But she was able to take care of her needs. Rising back to her feet, she swayed again, grabbing the chair, just as she heard footsteps in the passageway.

Maeve swept the curtain aside and entered, carrying a tray. She took one look at Catherine—who was so weak that black spots were floating in her sight—then put the tray on the table and a bracing arm around Catherine's waist. Together they made it the couple steps back to the pallet, where Catherine collapsed with relief. The two women smiled at each other.

Maeve put her hands on her hips. "Good mornin', Mistress Catherine. I see ye felt up to gettin' out of bed yerself."

"Well I had to," she insisted, "but perhaps I'll take things slowly."

"Aye, see that ye do," Maeve said good-naturedly. "Do ye still like the name?"

"I think I do, thank you. I hope you don't grow too tired of hearing me offer my thanks for all of this." She gestured with her hand, encompassing the tray and all of Maeve's work. "I'm determined to be on my feet soon, and then I can repay you all for your hospitality and do my part."

"Think nothin' of it, mistress. Here in Scotland, we always help strangers in need. And ye're our guest—even if 'tis only in a cave. Now, how do ye feel about breakin' yer fast?"

Catherine sniffed appreciatively. "It smells good."

"I thought it best to start ye on somethin' plain as ye're healin', so 'tis only porridge, but I've added honey to sweeten it."

Catherine imagined such an encampment didn't

have many luxuries to spare, and surely honey was one of them. "That was kind of you."

"Do ye need help sittin' up?"

Between the two of them, they put an extra pillow behind Catherine, and she was able to sit with the tray across her lap. She found herself starving, and the porridge tasted delicious.

"I cannot believe how lucky I was to be found by your chief," Catherine said, after finishing her bowl and wishing there was more. "I was so confused I could have wandered right into a river. But Laird Carlyle was kind and gentle with me."

Maeve sent her a startled look, then smiled. "Glad I am to hear that. There are not many who'd use those words to describe him. I've known him since we were bairns together, and beneath that gruff behavior is a good man, one he doesn't often let show."

"Why not?"

Maeve hesitated. "His life has not been an easy one."

Catherine thought it strange that a woman with such a devastating scar could say such a thing, but she was obviously loyal.

"It can't be easy, if his clan is living in this cave," Catherine said gently. She was far too curious, even though it was none of her business.

"Not the whole clan, of course," Maeve said, then winced. "'Tis not my story to tell, mistress."

"I didn't mean to pry. I have no memory of my life, no idea where to go or what to do next. Asking questions is the only way I can learn anything."

Maeve sat down in the room's only chair. "I cannot imagine such a thing. I'll answer what I can, but there is little I can say about his lairdship."

"How many people live in this cave?"

"'Tis not our regular home, but right now over twenty people are stayin' here."

"Why?"

Maeve didn't answer.

"More things I cannot know," Catherine said, hiding her frustration. "Surely Laird Carlyle can tell me something. Where is he?"

"Gone to bury your men, mistress."

"I cannot just lie here," Catherine finally said, fisting the blanket with frustration.

"Ye must, for at least another day. Let me look at yer injury."

Maeve was efficient as she worked, and as she regarded Catherine's uncovered wound, she gave a critical nod. "It seems to be healin' well. 'Twill probably leave no scar at all."

Maeve applied a healing salve before beginning to wrap a clean bandage around Catherine's head.

"Would you mind telling me what happened with your scar?" Catherine ventured with hesitation. "Only if you wish to, of course."

"There is nothin' much to say." Maeve continued to work, not meeting her eyes. "I was deliberately burned by a cruel person when I was a child."

Catherine gasped, and laid a hand on Maeve's arm. "I'm so sorry."

"'Twas a long time ago and best forgotten." Maeve finished tying the bandage in place and rose. "I think ye should sleep some more. I'll check back on ye later."

Because Maeve's smile was as friendly as always, Catherine hoped she hadn't been offended by her curiosity. The woman left a fresh candle in the lantern and departed. Hearing a boisterous laugh from the "great hall," Catherine found herself wanting to be out there, but dreading it as well. Everyone would stare at her with suspicion, with pity, maybe even with hatred, since she seemed to be English—at least her accent was.

Then why had she been traveling through the Highlands? Wouldn't she have visited Edinburgh, perhaps, in the Lowlands?

And that made her think about Laird Carlyle. Had he been of age to fight during the rebellion, when the Jacobites had claimed victory on the field, but hadn't won their cause? Could that be part of the reason he and his people hid in caves?

She seemed to know historical things, but not her own name, which was very frustrating.

Aloud, she whispered, "My name is . . ." and hoped the right words would fall from her lips. "My name is . . ." Nothing.

Her mind was spinning, and that wasn't helping the throbbing behind her eyes. Taking a deep breath, she tried to wipe away her doubts, her very thoughts, to let sleep claim her. It wasn't easy, but at last she escaped the pain down the dark well of unconsciousness.

DURING a meeting of the men before supper, Duncan gradually lost their attention as, one by one, they went silent, staring past him. He turned around to see Maeve helping Catriona across the footbridge. Even the women cooking over their cauldrons looked up, before whispering among themselves.

Though Catriona still had a bandage wrapped around her head, the fall of her dark hair hid some of it. He could see that he was not the only man to realize her beauty. Even in the simple garb of his people, she was riveting, her waist slim, her breasts pressed up to overflowing by the stays, though she did try to cover herself with a fichu. Her expression showed determination, even as she allowed Maeve to steady her arm.

Not all of his people's expressions toward Catriona were admiring or curious. They'd heard her speak with her English accent, and he saw Melville wearing a skeptical frown. But Duncan was their chief, and his word was law.

Maeve brought her to the first table and helped her find a seat on the end of a bench. One man got up and left; another slid to the far end. All watched her warily.

Catriona only gave a brief wounded look, before raising her chin with an arrogance that was inbred in her, a subconscious memory—unless of course she was feigning her memory loss, a possibility Duncan had not yet dismissed. She'd only been with them for a day.

"Mistress Catherine requests permission to eat with the clan, Laird Carlyle," Maeve said.

Duncan hid his startled response to that name. "She has remembered who she is?"

"You don't have to talk as if I'm not here," Catriona said.

She spoke politely, but the men murmured regardless, most likely at the way her English accent made her seem foreign. No one but he knew that she was Scottish.

"I have remembered nothing," she continued. "But I had to have a name."

Yet she'd chosen to use one that was the English version of her own name, Catriona? It seemed suspicious. His men, abused by the English for too long, could see that she was no ordinary lass; Duncan hoped he wouldn't have to guard her from their justified anger.

"We discussed many names," Maeve said, giving the group of men a frown.

"And I liked the sound of Catherine," Catriona said. "You also should know I have no memory of Gaelic either. I assume that is the language in which you speak to your men."

He nodded. He couldn't even take reassurance in that. She could be lying, or if she was telling the truth, why would an earl's daughter, who spent most of her time in London, know any Gaelic at all? Still, he would be careful to reveal nothing too important in her hearing, regardless of which language he used.

She looked around. "Might I wash up before eating?"

"We wash in the burn." He nodded his head at the little stream. "Wash just where it leaves the cave, beyond where we take our drinking water."

"But I'll bring ye a basin while ye're recoverin'," Maeve called, giving him a stern look Catriona couldn't see.

Duncan crossed his arms over his chest. He wanted Catriona to know the rules and abide by them like everyone else—but he didn't mean to be unsympathetic to her injuries.

"I can do it," Catriona insisted.

"And so ye will—eventually," Duncan said. "Maeve is right."

Maeve brought a pot of soap and the basin, then helped her wash.

"Ye look pale, Mistress Catherine," Duncan said, emphasizing the name she'd chosen for herself. She didn't react as if she remembered she *had* another name. "Should ye not be abed?"

Her smile was faint. "Perhaps, Laird Carlyle, but it was a long day there. I hoped you wouldn't mind if I shared supper with your clansmen." She lowered her voice. "And I hoped to hear what you found at the sight of my accident."

As if on cue, the last four men at her table got up and left, making an exaggerated show of handing their empty plates to the women before leaving the cave.

Catriona's troubled gaze followed them, as Duncan sat down opposite her. He took a drink of ale from his tankard.

"I did not wish to drive anyone away," she said quietly.

"They saw that ye wished to speak with me," he answered. "The way we live, they've learned to be discreet."

She looked around with interest, as if she would question him more about that, but instead, her golden eyes found his and focused with determination. "What did you find, Laird Carlyle? Was the scene as I remembered?"

"'Twas just so, mistress. Two poor souls dead. I buried them, then marked their graves so they could be found again."

Her expression was solemn. "So you found nothing to indicate who they were?"

Or who *she* was—the unspoken question was vivid.

"Nothing," he answered. "Your horses had been injured in the fall. I tracked them and found that none could be saved."

She inhaled sharply, murmured, "Poor beasts," before saying, "And my baggage? Surely there were packs or . . . something."

"Stolen, mistress," he replied, the lie coming easily.

She gasped. "Someone stole my goods but left the horses to suffer?"

She was quick—he hadn't even considered that he should have claimed the horses had already been killed. "The thieves might have been in a rush, fearing to be discovered. Many Highlanders are desperate for a way to feed their families."

Though she nodded, she studied him too closely. "I imagine your people know all about desperation."

He glowered. "Are ye accusing us of—"

"No, don't misunderstand me." Wide-eyed, she put up a hand. "I simply meant that because you live here, in a cave, things cannot be good for your clan."

"This is not all of my clan."

"So Maeve told me, but when one doesn't re-member even the most basic facts, it's difficult to believe one can make judgments about anything." She smiled when Maeve approached with a platter of salted herring and boiled leeks and cabbage.

"Eat slowly, mistress," Maeve said. "I still think ye should be havin' soup."

"I had it for luncheon, Maeve. I need something more, or my stomach will gnaw through my back-bone."

Maeve nodded and moved away. Catriona glanced around, noticing that several men smirked with disdain. "What did I say?" she asked softly.

"Luncheon. 'Tis for ladies of fine birth. We have dinner at midday."

"Oh."

She stared down at her plate, her shoulders lowered as if in defeat. He found himself feeling sorry for her, something he hadn't expected.

"I understand your people have no cause to think kindly of the wealthy," she said softly. "I do not know how I came by my fine clothes. For all I know, I could be some man's mistress."

Duncan shook his head. "With your fine way with words? More likely some man's wife."

Her expression twisted. "If so, I am causing him and the rest of my family much pain." She looked down at her plate, using the small knife to disturb the cabbage, but not eating.

"Ye wear no ring, mistress. Do not fret about what ye do not know. My patrols will be looking for anyone searching for ye. Be at peace."

She took a deep breath and let it out, attempting a smile as she cut a piece of fish and ate it. She chewed for a moment, then ate another bite, more quickly.

"I am trying to be at peace. I will admit I'm surprised I don't feel hysterical. To know nothing about myself, I should feel panicked. But . . . in some ways, it's a challenge, like figuring out a child's puzzle. I know things I might have learned or heard as a young girl, history for instance." She gestured toward her plate. "But every time Maeve has given me something to eat, I've had no idea if I'll like it or not, whether it might be a favorite I have no memory of."

He had to admire her fortitude. Many in her situation would be reduced to cowering, afraid to face the world. "Do ye remember faces of people ye might know?" he asked.

She shook her head. "Nothing. I feel alone in the world, but for your clan's kindness. I imagine I should be grateful that I know how to talk or even dress myself."

And that made him glance again at her cleavage, obscured by the fichu. He looked back down at his plate. He was noticing too frequently that she was a beautiful woman, with sincere eyes that could make a man feel as if he could lose himself. But if there was a plan against him by her father, that would have been part of it. It was difficult not to notice a woman as striking as Catriona.

Maeve approached. "Mistress Catherine, I think ye should rest now."

Catriona sighed. "Very well. I do feel tired." She gave Duncan a faint smile. "You've allowed me to use your chamber while I recover, Laird Carlyle. I am grateful."

"I was being practical."

Maeve rolled her eyes.

He added, "But I should retrieve some items before ye go to sleep."

"Of course, please do," Catriona said.

He followed the two women through the great hall and into the passageway. Catriona sat down heavily in the single chair, on top of several feminine garments, and let out a sigh.

He almost asked if she was in pain, then stopped himself. It wouldn't do to seem too curious about everything she did. Maeve excused herself to fetch hot water, leaving Duncan alone with Catriona—and the mess. He was surprised to see items of women's clothing scattered about, her ruined shoes where they could trip her, a hairbrush and pins spread out on the table, garments on the chair instead of hung on pegs, forcing her to sit on them. It was none of his business how she wanted to live. Under her curious gaze, he found a fresh shirt in his trunk and gathered his shaving items.

"There is room in the trunk if ye wish to put any clothing away," he offered.

"Thank you," Catriona said, then looked around with a rueful smile. "I'm sorry your chamber isn't more tidy. I confess I don't even realize there's a problem until I see it through someone else's eyes."

The amusement with which she regarded her flaws should have bothered him, but he found himself impressed that she didn't try to blame Maeve or use her illness as an excuse.

"I asked Maeve why you all live in this cave," she continued, "and she said it was your place to tell me, not hers."

He straightened and regarded her warily.

"You said most of your clan lives elsewhere."

"In their own homes, aye."

"But a select group lives here, because . . ." She trailed off expectantly.

"I cannot be answering all your questions, mistress."

She blinked up at him, before nodding. "Of course not. I was simply curious."

"Were ye? How can I know that?" When she flinched, he held up a hand and spoke with quiet determination. "I am responsible for everyone here, and we live in this cave for a reason. There are people looking for us. How am I to know if ye're not lying to me about your lost memory?"

"You think I'm lying?" she said in a cooler voice. "Why would I do that?"

"I've heard of men addled from a blow to the head, but never this complete loss of memory. Ye seem to function well in every other way, which makes me curious. I know nothing about ye, do I?"

"And I know nothing about *you*," she retorted. "Of course I would ask questions—I am at your mercy, after all. You could want . . . anything from me."

White with strain, she was all prickly and stiff, and he admired her defiance, especially considering he held the upper hand. It felt strange to admire the daughter of Aberfoyle.

"I brought ye here because ye needed help," he

said. "And now I'm offering ye as much honesty as I can. I hope ye offer the same."

Maeve entered the chamber carrying a steaming basin and towels, eyes downcast as if she'd heard every word,

Duncan sighed. "Please show Mistress Catherine where we bathe."

"I hope you're not saying that I smell," Catriona said tiredly, her defensiveness melting away.

He bit back a smile. "I offer ye a kind gesture, not an insult. Good night, Mistress Catherine."

As he left his chamber, he realized it was dangerously easy to sympathize with her, injured and alone amidst strangers, but still trying to defend herself. Wouldn't he do the same?

He couldn't relax his guard. He needed to be wary, to remember who she was.

He trusted few people, a lesson formed in childhood, beaten into him by a mother who hated her life and made certain her family suffered for it. He'd been a frightened boy whom his father should have protected, but his father had waited until it was too late.

CHAPTER 4

After Laird Carlyle had gone, Catherine distract-
edly pushed aside the things on the table to make
room for the basin and towels. Maeve didn't meet
her gaze, and Catherine couldn't help wondering
if the woman thought she was lying, too.

At first Catherine had been at ease in his presence, this man who'd saved her life. She'd been
foolishly admiring his hair, how she could now
see that it was auburn, and thinking what a handsome man he might be if he smiled. He exuded
a powerful, yet leashed strength that affected her
far too much.

But his words of distrust had shaken her, reminded her that she was an outsider. She really
knew nothing about him at all, except that he and
this small band of people were in hiding. They
could be thieves, for all she knew.

She glanced at Maeve, who was laying out towels and the nightshift. Catherine stopped her questions in her throat, knowing that trusting Maeve
was probably a mistake, too. With her memory

gone, trapped in a cave, Catherine shouldn't trust anyone.

But she smiled tiredly at the servant, who was only trying to help her. "Apparently, I need to bathe."

"Och, his lairdship doesn't know how to be tactful."

"So I gathered," she said dryly. With a sigh, she stood up. "But I am curious. I take it the water pools somewhere within the caves?"

Maeve grinned. "'Tis better than that. But I think ye should wait until another time. Ye're tired, and 'twouldn't do to slip."

"But—"

"And perhaps ye should wait for the men to be gone."

"Oh." Catherine let out a sigh. "Very well, I bow to your expertise. But please show me where it is tonight?"

She followed the maidservant out into the passage and turned away from the great hall. Maeve carried the lantern, which glimmered on rock walls that were smooth and damp. A chill wind rippled across them, and Catherine shuddered. She couldn't imagine being in these caves in the dead of winter.

Over her shoulder, Maeve said, "There are no other little caves like the one ye sleep in. But up ahead, the burn that enters the caves from the mountains above separates into two paths. The one runs into our great hall, and we can use that for drinkin' water."

"How wonderfully convenient." Catherine had

begun to hear the sound of running water growing louder with every step.

Maeve smiled. "The second travels deeper into the caves and ends up . . ." She trailed off as she stepped through another uneven entry way. ". . . here."

Catherine gasped as she followed Maeve into another cave. The lantern light glittered on a pool of water that churned from a waterfall not much taller than a man. The water seemed to burst out of the cave wall.

"This is incredible," Catherine said with awe.

"Och, don't be deceived—it looks beautiful, but the water is . . . brisk."

Catherine laughed. "I'll remember that."

"And if ye decide to bathe, the signal for privacy is a shoe left in the passageway. Ye shouldn't be disturbed."

"I appreciate that, thank you. For now I'll use the hot water basin you brought me."

Catherine took one last look at the natural beauty of the waterfall, before Maeve and her lantern started down the passageway. Catherine paused. Inside the waterfall cave, it was completely black, an inky stillness that hid danger to the unwary.

It was a reminder of everything that had happened to her since she'd woken up.

In the morning, Catherine awoke and dressed in the dark before Maeve even arrived. She could hear male voices echo along the rock, but decided not to face them alone. She was still irritated by Laird Carlyle's accusation that she could be lying.

Lying! Why would she lie about losing her memory?

She'd been wearing fine clothes, yes, and that marked her as someone from a wealthy family. Apparently, he had something against wealthy people.

Well, he *was* a chief who lived in a cave, she reminded herself, wincing. It was all such a mystery, one he didn't want to talk about, and had obviously instructed Maeve not to discuss either. Figuring it all out would at least give her a purpose.

Because otherwise, she had nothing at all except the struggle to regain her memory. She felt like she was floating in a boat without oars, with no idea where she was or how to get somewhere else. She was stuck.

But she didn't have to feel sorry for herself or be a burden. She wasn't an invalid; surely she had some sort of skills to help. She'd remembered how to dress herself, after all, she thought dryly. And then perhaps, if she didn't panic, her memories would come back on their own as her wound healed.

She was sitting in the chair, waiting patiently, when a glow bobbed down the passageway, and the curtain was drawn aside. Catherine narrowed her eyes at the sudden light.

Maeve came to an abrupt halt. "A good morn to ye, mistress. I assumed ye'd still be abed."

Catherine slapped her hands on her thighs as she came to her feet. "No, I'm feeling much better. It's time for me to do something to earn my stay here."

"Earn your stay? Ye're our guest, mistress," Maeve insisted.

"That is kind of you, but I simply cannot sit around waiting for my memory to return. Assign me something to do. I'm a quick learner—I think."

They shared a smile. Catherine was grateful for the other woman's presence. Maeve made her feel at ease, made her think that at least she had one friend here amidst Clan Carlyle.

"Let me look at your wound first," Maeve said, guiding her back into the chair by the shoulders.

Catherine waited patiently, only wincing once as the bandage seemed stuck to her forehead. "Is it inflamed?"

"Nay, ye were lucky." She met Catherine's gaze. "It must have been terrible."

Catherine shrugged. "It was mostly just the pain and confusion that I remember. I don't think I wandered long before your laird found me." She put a hand to her forehead tentatively. "There is a giant lump, though."

"It already looks better. Except for your eyes, o' course."

"My eyes?" Catherine said, aghast. "But they don't hurt!"

"They look like someone took a fist to both o' them. Purple, blue, green—very attractive," she teased.

Catherine winced. "Maybe I'm vain, because I don't like the sound of that."

"We all want to look our best. No shame in that." Maeve applied more salve, then began to wrap a clean bandage around Catherine's head.

"We still need the bandage?" Catherine asked.

"We're in a cave, mistress. Surely ye don't want bat droppings falling in it."

"What!"

Maeve gave a hearty laugh. "I be teasin', mistress. We chased out the bats long ago."

Grinning, Catherine shook her head. "How long have you lived here?"

Maeve sighed. "Ye know I cannot speak of it."

"Do you have your own home somewhere else?"

"I did."

"Meaning . . . you don't anymore?"

Maeve didn't answer.

"I'm sorry if I'm prying," Catherine said with a sigh. "When you don't remember anything, you're filled with questions about . . . everything. I hope something I ask will trigger my own memories. I imagine where I lived, see myself going through a door, or looking out a window, or turning down a bed."

"Is it workin'?"

"Not yet. So if I keep asking questions you aren't allowed to answer, just tell me to stop."

"'Tisn't that I'm not allowed, mistress," Maeve explained. "Laird Carlyle is not a tyrant whose fist we live beneath. I made me own decision to support him and what he's doin'. Perhaps he will answer your questions."

"That won't happen," Catherine said with faint bitterness. "He thinks I'm lying about my memory loss." She hesitated. "Do you?"

"Nay," Maeve said kindly. "But his lairdship has had reason in his life not to trust most people."

Catherine shook her head. "Then he must live a very miserable, lonely life."

"Aye, that he does," Maeve said. "He trusts us with most things, but his inner thoughts and feelings? Nay."

Catherine could believe that. She remained silent as the woman tied off the bandage and helped pull her hair back to secure it in a simple knot at her neck.

Maeve stepped back and examined her.

"I'm presentable?" Catherine asked.

"I believe so."

"Please thank whoever loaned me their gown," she said, spreading wide the plain brown skirt. It was tied over a stiffened petticoat. She knew she'd been wearing a hooped petticoat when she'd arrived, but it had probably been damaged beyond repair.

"'Tis mine," Maeve said almost shyly. "I made it meself, so 'tis not as fine as ye're used to."

"It is perfect, and all the better because you worked on it yourself. Thank you. I'll take good care of it."

Maeve blushed and bobbed her head, the edge of her cap dipping to cover her eyes.

"And who knows what I'm used to?" Catherine added. "For all I know, I'm a thief who stole that gown."

"Och, that is certainly not true!"

"We don't know that, do we?" Catherine asked bitterly. She took a deep breath. "But thank you for your belief in me. I cannot dwell on my hidden past. All I have is the present. Let me find a way to be of assistance. You'll be helping me fill my day, as well."

"If ye insist," Maeve said doubtfully.

She was staring at Catherine's hands.

Catherine held them up. She'd scrubbed them as well as she could in the basin. "Is something wrong?"

Maeve shrugged. "Those are delicate hands, mistress, not used to hard work."

"Then it's time they were of use."

Maeve bowed her head and held her lantern to lead the way back down the passage. The "great hall" opened up before her, the ceiling dark above, with a haze of smoke from the several fires. The entrance to the cave was the only natural light, so the torches were surely kept lit most of the day. The odors were a mix of charred wood smoke, too many bodies, and something cooking.

A few men still lingered over their breakfasts, eyeing her suspiciously as Maeve made her sit down at an empty table to eat. An older woman, her bosom big, her hands well worn, slapped a plate down in front of Maeve, said something in Gaelic, then went back to the girdle on the fire to put on more oatcakes.

Catherine watched her go, then asked Maeve, "Does she know I don't speak Gaelic?"

"I'm sure she does. But Mrs. Skinner does not speak English."

Catherine's eyebrows lifted. "Oh, I see."

"She's the mother of one of our youngest clansmen, and is a widow, come to make sure her laddie eats well."

Catherine took a bite of her oatcake. "And I appreciate it."

She stiffened when she saw Laird Carlyle enter the cave, his impassive gaze focusing immediately on her. She remembered his accusation that she could be lying, and as much as she was offended, the objective part of her understood his concern was for his people.

Laird Carlyle strode toward her, looking intimidatingly large and powerful. He wore a dark green coat over his shirt and belted plaid, with the excess plaid up over his shoulder and held in place with a brooch. A sword hung at his side, a pistol tucked into his belt. His knees were bare above muddy boots, his auburn hair tied back in a messy queue, and his brows lowered in a frown. With his dark, dark eyes, he seemed menacing, and as he came to a stop right in front of her, she had to force herself not to back away.

She wasn't going to show him any fear. She might be alone in the world, with nowhere to go, but she wasn't going to cower.

"You are well enough to be out of bed?" he asked.

"I wouldn't exactly call it a bed." She was attempting a light, dry tone, but his lip didn't even quirk with the hint of a smile. "But, yes, I am feeling better. I wish to be of help, to earn my keep."

"I've told the lass she's our guest," Maeve said, "but—"

Catherine interrupted. "And that's kind of you all, but I need to do *something*."

Laird Carlyle took a hold of her hand and held

it palm up. Her soft skin seemed somehow embarrassing within his big, rough hand. She rose to her feet and tried to pull back, but he didn't release her, and she faced him over their joined hands.

"I doubt ye've worked a day in your life," he said.

A voice came from a group of men near the entrance. "Unless 'tis on her back."

Maeve gasped, Catherine inhaled sharply, but before she could defend herself, Laird Carlyle spoke.

"Melville, I will not have Mistress Catherine disrespected," he said coldly.

One of the men turned on his heel and left the cave, and Catherine thought she remembered that same man glaring at her the day before.

For Laird Carlyle's ears only, she said, "Didn't you disrespect me by accusing me of lying?"

"I told ye the truth about my suspicions," he answered impassively. "Surely ye don't want things hidden from ye."

"Like you're hiding in these caves?" she whispered back, feeling suddenly reckless. Perhaps she was a bold sort of woman.

He arched a dark brow. "Ye know nothing about us."

"And neither of us knows anything about me. Let us not assume the worst, shall we? I want to help, and that's all."

He let her hand go. "Aye, ye can do that, and 'twill be appreciated."

"But there are rules in this encampment," he added, "and ye shall follow them. Ye'll do whatever Maeve or Mrs. Skinner tells ye to do. And ye're not to leave this cave."

She blinked at him. "I beg your pardon?"

"Ye could be a danger to yourself or to us. No one can know we're here, so if ye don't know our location, then ye can't tell anyone."

"Why can no one know you're here?" she asked.

"That is none of your concern, mistress. But these people are *my* concern, and I will protect them however I can."

He leaned over her, all broad shoulders and threateningly male. She was surprised and confused to feel a flutter of excitement at his nearness. She reminded herself that he was not a suitor, but a man who was trying to intimidate her, and he was succeeding. If she didn't find a way to ease their concerns, she'd be miserable, as well as trapped in the cave.

And a small part of her, like a tiny child curled in the corner of her mind, was afraid to go outside into the world. She didn't like that part of herself. "Very well, I accept your terms," she said coolly. "For now."

"For now?" he echoed with suspicion.

"I reserve the right to discuss changing these rules later, when you and your clan learn that I don't mean anyone any harm."

Don't cast me out, the little girl in her head pleaded.

He locked his gaze with hers, as if sizing her up. Catherine let him look his fill, and looked back, telling herself he was just a man, a man with secrets he had to protect. Though he had all the power right now, those secrets made him vulnerable. Perhaps he knew that and didn't like it, and used all this bluster to hide it.

Or perhaps he was just a man who needed to have his own way.

She hoped her memory returned soon, so she didn't have to linger and find out.

Catherine spent the morning preparing vegetables for the midday meal, cauliflower, cabbage, and onions. It was far easier than the butchering Mrs. Skinner was doing. Catherine eyed the bloody mess uneasily, where it was skewered above various fires. None of this seemed familiar to her.

But something did seem familiar—telling others what to do. More than once, she had to bite her tongue before sending one of the women off to fetch something for her, as if she wasn't capable of getting it herself. It was simply natural for her to give orders. That might be appropriate in whatever life she had—scandalous or proper or otherwise—but it wasn't her place here.

Mrs. Skinner occasionally said something to her in Gaelic, then rolled her eyes and sighed loudly when Catherine didn't understand. When Maeve was absent, a timid young woman named Janet translated. When Catherine smiled her gratitude, the woman only blushed and ducked away, as if afraid to be seen with a Sassenach.

All morning, Laird Carlyle returned occasionally to the cave and just looked at her—which didn't help her popularity. Did he think she was going to use the tiny dirk and threaten her way out of the cave? He had to know she had nowhere to go.

A young clansman came near the cooking fires and stole a bannock and then a kiss from the young woman who must be his sweetheart.

Catherine didn't realize she was still watching them until Maeve said softly, "Janet and Angus only married earlier this year."

The girl was so thin and petite, Catherine wouldn't have thought she was old enough to marry. She gathered the pile of turnips together and eyed Maeve. "She followed him . . . here?"

Maeve shrugged. "They wished to be together. 'Tis not quite the same with Sheena." She gestured with her chin toward the other woman, more buxom and full of confidence. "She's here because her da wouldn't leave her behind."

"I imagine Laird Carlyle allowed it because the women help keep his men fed," Catherine said.

"As if the men don't know how to feed themselves? Ye assume much, mistress," Maeve chided gently.

Catherine sighed. "Forgive me. I don't like being accused of lying, and it makes me irritable."

"Ye don't like not being trusted. 'Tis how we all feel."

Catherine couldn't help staring at the two young women who now spoke to each other quietly as they worked. Though one was married, Catherine felt older than they were. Could she herself be married, or a spinster? Or might she have chosen not to marry, because she wouldn't settle for less than love? There were so many kinds of women she could be, and to not know herself was incredibly frustrating. As she cut vegetables, she thought hard about marriage, tried to picture the image of a man at her side, a man in her bed, someone to share a discussion of the day, someone who understood her. She was annoyed when Laird Carlyle flashed into her brain, and she immediately shoved that thought away. She was only thinking about him because he'd saved her life, and now he controlled everything she was doing.

But her brain seemed a vast emptiness, where no faces surfaced except those she'd met since she arrived at the cave. She would keep trying to find a memory somewhere within her.

When the laird returned the next time, it was with all his men. They were a rough bunch, their clothes well mended, their hair needing to be brushed, their beards untrimmed. Most carried wood to be stacked against the wall.

Many looked at her with both curiosity and skepticism, but she was growing used to it. She wasn't to be trusted, she understood that, but at least the women had tolerated her while she helped them. Even gruff old Mrs. Skinner had made a point of showing Catherine how to arrange the mutton pieces on spits over the fire.

When all the men were seated at the tables, talking loudly, Janet and Sheena serving ale from pitchers, Mrs. Skinner handed Catherine a full plate and gestured toward their laird. So now Catherine was to serve this man who thought her a liar.

But Catherine had wanted to be of use. And this is what women did, served their men, much as she chafed at the role.

He wasn't her man—none of them were. And

by the distrust on many of their faces, they were glad of it. Did she have a man somewhere who was desperately searching for her? Or parents who feared she was dead? For a moment, she tried to imagine a childhood, tried to see a mother and a father standing over her. Were they stern and strict, or might they have been tolerant of a little girl's foibles? Had she been held on her mother's knee at night—and now that woman might think her dead? The grief of losing such memories threatened to overwhelm her.

Mrs. Skinner snapped her fingers in Catherine's face and gestured impatiently at the chief. It was obvious "Himself"—as she'd heard more than one of the clan refer to Laird Carlyle—was to be served his meal first.

All the men watched her approach, including the laird.

He searched her face as she set the plate before him. "Should ye be working so hard? Ye don't look recovered."

She didn't want him to be able to see the grief that had been so hard to suppress. "Maeve told me I have two black eyes."

"That's only one of the colors," he said. "I thought ye'd just hit your head, but could ye have been beaten?"

Her lips twisted. "I don't think so. Nothing feels bruised but my forehead."

Then to her surprise, he reached up and touched her upper cheek with warm callused fingers. After a shocked moment, she ducked her head away. Why had he touched her in front of all of his men?

"Did that hurt?" he demanded.

If he was concerned, she couldn't tell by his expression, with the perpetual frown he always wore. But his touch had been gentle . . . she didn't know what to think, couldn't trust herself to interpret anything at all.

"I am fine," she said. "Now eat, so your men can."

He glanced around, then lifted up a bannock, and sure enough, his men fell on their food ravenously.

But Laird Carlyle didn't take a bite. Instead he took her hand before she could leave. Catherine inhaled, stiffened to pull away, but he did nothing more than stare at the couple of blisters on her palm.

"So now we know I haven't been cooking to earn a living," she said dryly.

"Have Maeve see to those," he said, letting her go.

Catherine turned away from him stiffly. So he cared about her health. Probably because he didn't want her dying on him.

But she surreptitiously watched him. He was there with his men, participating in their discussion, but he never smiled, never really looked like he was a part of them. Of course, he was their chief, their leader, so perhaps all men were careful about such a boundary. She didn't know. All she knew was that she was far too interested in him.

But how could she not be interested in the man who held her fate in his hands?

CHAPTER 5

Duncan told himself that he needed to keep an eye on Catriona, and he'd had a difficult time outside that morning seeing to the new foal because he'd kept returning to check on her. He didn't know what he'd expected to find, since she was working with the women. She hadn't given up in frustration at being ignorant of the hard work necessary to prepare a meal—even after blisters marred her delicate hands.

She was still angry with him for saying she might be lying about her memory loss. Perhaps stubbornness was the reason she'd worked so hard all morning. He continued to watch her from beneath his lowered brows, as if he expected her to do something that revealed she knew that cooking was beneath her. Instead, she carried plates for his men and ignored their open stares. One of the men grabbed her skirt. Duncan was about to toss the table out of his way to reach them, but Catriona turned back unperturbed, then handed the man the bannock he'd apparently asked for. It was

Melville again, who obviously didn't approve of having a stranger in their midst. He had a daughter here, so perhaps he was allowed to be wary. But harm Catriona?

Duncan was being ridiculous. None of his men would harm a woman he'd brought to the encampment. She was under his protection, and he took that seriously.

A little while later, he was seated alone at his table, finishing up the last bit of mutton as he watched Catriona receive her first lesson in washing dishes. Ivor sat down across from him.

His war chief eyed him silently for a moment, then began to speak in Gaelic. "The patrols returned while ye were eating. They found no strangers, no one looking for a missing woman."

Duncan nodded, relieved.

"Ye've kept us close to the encampment these last weeks after the attack on ye," Ivor said. "Should we spread out farther, because of the lass?"

"Aye, do that. Be careful."

Duncan knew his time hiding Catriona was limited, but he hoped to make her father suffer as long as he could.

Duncan glanced at her, saw her smile at Maeve, and felt the shock of it. He hadn't yet seen her relaxed, with pleasure in her expression. Her golden eyes were alight, her full lips tilted up, her teeth near blinding with whiteness. Except for her head injury, she exuded health and vitality, a woman whose every need had been tended to. He tried to tell himself that of course she'd been able to take care of herself—she had access to her father's blood money.

"Ye watch the lass more than ye should," Ivor said quietly.

Duncan focused his gaze on his war chief. "I brought her here. I feel responsible."

"For her, or for your people, because I cannot tell exactly who."

"Ye damn well know whom I've spent my life protecting," Duncan said, trying to stifle his rising anger. "I want no danger brought to them."

"I know why ye couldn't leave her on the side of the road to die, but in some ways, 'twould have been easier."

Duncan arched a brow at Ivor.

"Nay, I'd not have let the lass die, either," Ivor said tiredly. "But she's a vulnerability I don't like. We don't know who she is, who her people are."

Duncan did, and it magnified the vulnerability tenfold.

Ivor squinted at him. "But there's something ye're not telling me."

Duncan couldn't lie outright to the man he considered closest to him, a friend. "When I can tell ye my plan, I promise I will."

"There's a plan, is there? I think the best plan would be to leave her in the nearest village, where people might know her."

"Nay, I cannot do that. That would be abandoning her. We're all she knows."

"Ye aren't responsible for every person in the world, Duncan Carlyle." Ivor let out a tired breath, his mouth crooking up on one side within his bushy beard. "And if ye just wanted a woman, I don't believe ye'd have slept out here with the men last night."

"That's not what this is about." But he could not lie to himself—he found Catriona Duff far too desirable. His body didn't care that she was the daughter of his enemy—he had a cock-stand every time she got too close. He wasn't helping himself by touching her, even to examine the blisters on her hand. Was he using concern to stay close to her? She'd be wise to be wary—*he'd* be wise to never let himself be alone with her. This weakness was something he hadn't imagined he'd feel, not after all these years of trying to protect and support his people.

"Laird Carlyle!"

Duncan rose to his feet as young Torcall rushed toward him from the cave entrance. His men's easy smiles died, their voices quieted to hear what Torcall had to say.

"There's a shipment, yer lairdship," he said, his breath coming fast as if he'd ridden hard.

"Say nothing more," Duncan ordered. He wanted details, but not in front of Catriona Duff. Raising his voice, he said, "Let us go."

As if choreographed, the men spread out to their respective corners of the cave to arm themselves and prepare for whatever might be needed. Duncan was proud of how well trained they were, how seriously they took this mission.

He glanced at the women, who were frozen, solemn, and concerned, forgotten towels or dirty plates in their hands. Catriona's wide-eyed gaze went from the women to the hurrying men, and at last to Duncan. He saw her questions, knew he had no time to make excuses. He simply assigned two men to stay behind and guard the encampment, and the rest saddled and mounted their horses to follow Torcall.

No one would speak to Catherine about where the men were going. The easy camaraderie between the Carlyle women changed to a tense silence only broken when orders were given by Mrs. Skinner or Maeve. Many glances were cast at the entrance to the cave, outside which Catherine assumed the two guards stood at the ready.

They prepared a simple meal that could be offered at whatever hour the men returned. Then the women sat beside the cooking fire and sewed silently, mending clothing that had been well worn. Catherine asked for a chance, figuring every woman learned to sew; surely she knew how. None of the women looked confident in her abilities, but to her relief, she was able to mend a frayed cuff and attach a torn sleeve at the shoulder. Who had she sewn for in her past life? She concentrated hard on the needle going in and out, trying to imagine sewing in a different room, with different people. Nothing.

"Mistress Catherine," Janet began tentatively, "ye truly have no memory of a time before?"

Catherine looked up in time to see Maeve frowning at the girl.

"I don't mind answering questions," Catherine

hastily said. Surely by being open, she would put the women at ease enough so that they'd eventually return the favor. "Please, ladies, call me Catherine."

Janet and Sheena exchanged a smile as Sheena said in a false whisper, "She even sounds like a highborn lady."

Catherine tried to relax—at least they were teasing her with good nature. "I have no idea if I'm a lady."

"Yer mind," Janet began, eager curiosity shining through her words, "'tis just . . . blank?"

Catherine nodded. "It's obvious I know what things are called, how to talk and sew, but . . . when I try to imagine my life before I woke up next to those two dead men"—Janet and Sheena gave twin shudders—"there's nothing but emptiness. I should know the men I was traveling with. Their poor faces keep coming back to me, but they are still strangers to me."

The women were silent, barely moving, their sewing forgotten in their laps.

"Perhaps . . . they died trying to protect me," Catherine whispered. Was one of them her husband? She shivered. Her mind shied away from that idea. How could one mourn a man one didn't remember?

"Or perhaps they were villains who'd kidnapped ye!" Sheena said enthusiastically; then, eyes suddenly wide, she clapped a hand over her mouth.

Maeve had been quietly translating for Mrs. Skinner, and now both older women gave the younger one thunderous frowns.

"I only meant," Sheena continued weakly, "that without any memories, it can almost be like a story that ye can make up as ye please."

Catherine cocked her head. "You mean . . . create something for myself?"

"Why not?"

After Maeve whispered in Gaelic, Mrs. Skinner looked at Catherine with grudging compassion.

"I don't know if making up the past would help me, but I'll remember your kind advice, Sheena." Catherine attempted to sound positive as she said, "It could have been worse. Imagine what would have happened if your laird had not found me."

"He's a good man," Janet said solemnly. "He cares about even the lowliest of people."

"And I am certainly one of those," Catherine agreed.

Janet blushed. "I didn't mean—"

"But it's true." Catherine reached to touch the young woman's hand, then changed her mind. "I am not a Carlyle. He could have left me to fend for myself."

"He would never have done that," Sheena insisted.

Janet and Maeve exchanged a sympathetic smile, as if they understood Sheena's adoration.

"Surely you need to take care of yourselves, not feed another mouth," Catherine continued.

Sheena set her sewing in her lap. "We don't see it that way. We help people. 'Tis what we're here for and what our men are riskin' their lives for."

"Sheena," Maeve scolded gently.

Catherine had been hoping Sheena would keep

going, reveal more of the Carlyles' secrets. But Maeve was in control. Catherine would probably find more answers by approaching Sheena or Janet alone.

"'Tis time for bed." Maeve got to her feet, and the other three women followed her lead.

The women set up the screens that separated their pallets from the men's.

"Might I wash myself at the pool?" Catherine asked. "I haven't had a chance since I arrived."

Maeve searched her face worriedly. "Are ye feelin' steady enough? I should go with ye."

"No, I don't need to inconvenience you. I promise I won't go in deep. I just need to feel clean."

Maeve hesitated, then sighed. "Let me find ye soap and towels. And call if ye need me. With the men gone, I should be able to hear ye from here."

"Thank you."

After Maeve had given her what she'd promised, as well as a fresh chemise and nightshift—and admonished her not to wash her hair until she no longer needed a bandage on her head—Catherine wished the women a good night and left. She felt a little guilty still being the only one with her own chamber. She'd lingered in the passageway to peer back into the great hall, watching as Sheena and Janet removed pallets from the stacks to lie beside one another, continuing to talk quietly. Catherine ducked away, and knew that she'd probably keep the private chamber until Laird Carlyle demanded it back. Did that make her a selfish woman?

After remembering to leave her shoe outside the waterfall cave, Catherine undressed by the light of a single lantern. Now that she was alone, the water seemed dark and mysterious. She couldn't see the depths. The rock face where the water fell glistened blackly. Catherine didn't know if she was a superstitious woman, but if so, this cave would scare her.

She was exceedingly careful stepping down from the ledge into the pool. The water only reached mid-calf, but she gasped at the chill that was surely left over from winter. She realized she didn't even know what month it was. For a moment her head spun. She felt . . . unmoored, adrift, as if time was a current dragging her to an unfamiliar land.

Then she shook herself free of such fanciful musings. Since she had no idea when the men would return, perhaps filthy from their ride and desperate to bathe, it was best to hurry. She felt carefully with her foot, realized there was another rock ledge deeper, and stood on that one, up to mid-thigh, to quickly wash her body with the facecloth. She couldn't imagine immersing herself into the unknown depths—could she even swim?—so she squatted to rinse herself off, shivering all the while.

Only when she was wearing the clean nightshift did she tiptoe down the passageway, slip past the curtain, and into her little chamber. It felt safe, as if it cocooned her, though she knew that could never be true. It was her mind trying to find a way to accept what had happened to her.

She crawled onto her pallet and pulled the blankets up over her head. Where were the men, and what was involved in this particular shipment?

IN Catherine's dreams the rain was falling, soaking her, seeping into her skin. The dead men were moving about as if desperate for her notice, for her to remember them. The sound of male voices shocked her awake. For a moment, she huddled beneath her blankets, forlorn that her dream hadn't told her who the men were.

She realized she'd never really fallen into a deep sleep, anxious about what might happen. Without a dressing gown to wear, she was forced to pull on her petticoats and skirt, along with sliding into the bodice and lacing herself in. All the while she hurried, she kept expecting the men to settle into sleep, frustrating her ability to find out where they'd been.

She froze as she moved aside her curtain. Was someone crying?

At the entrance to the great hall, she paused to take in the scene before anyone saw her. All of the men had returned, and the women had stoked fires and were boiling water and heating cold food.

But not Maeve; with a shawl wrapped around her shoulders, she was standing with Laird Carlyle and the other men, all of them gathered around . . . children. Catherine gaped. There were five or six of them, and the youngest boy, perhaps five years old, was the one who was crying. Maeve bent and put her arms around the child, who resisted, obviously frightened by the strange surroundings, and perhaps by Maeve herself.

The oldest boy, who could have only been ten

or so, rested his hands on the little one's shoulders and said something near his ear. The little one nodded, put a thumb in his mouth and tried to settle his heaving shoulders.

And then another child sobbed.

Catherine couldn't just hide away and do nothing. The children were obviously frightened and in shock. She swept out of the passageway, ignored Laird Carlyle's frown and boldly approached them.

The men looked at her with wary distrust. Two moved to the cave entrance, as if she'd make a dash for freedom. Freedom to go where? Didn't they understand she was helpless, dependent on them for everything? Just like these children.

She spoke directly to Maeve. "What can I do?"

"Mistress Catherine, ye should return to your bed," Laird Carlyle said in his deep, gruff voice.

Ignoring him, she took a cup from Maeve, got down on her knees, and offered it to the boy who stood apart from the others, hugging himself, chin to his chest. He wouldn't meet her eyes, and he was biting his lip so hard she expected to see blood. Every exposed bit of skin was covered in dirt, but at his wrists, she couldn't mistake the raw marks of rope burn. Who could do such a thing to a child?

"Have something to drink," she said gently.

His wild gaze darted from the other children to Laird Carlyle to the cave itself. But Catherine remained patient, until at last he stared briefly into her face. She offered only a kind smile, but didn't pressure him.

When he took the cup, it was with shaking

hands. Greedily, he drank the water, then lowered the cup and stared at her as if he could read her face like a map. She felt embarrassed, remembering her bruises, but she let him look as long as he needed. When he said something in Gaelic, Catherine looked around for Maeve to translate, but instead saw the plaid and bare knees of Laird Carlyle. She looked up to see him frowning down at her, hands on his hips.

"What did he say?" she asked.

"He gave ye his thanks," Laird Carlyle said.

Maeve set platters of oatcakes out on a table. Several of the children rushed forward to begin eating. The little boy beside her waited, looking around with the wary intelligence of one who'd had to survive by his wits. At last, he took slow steps toward the table, reached out for an oatcake and nibbled cautiously, looking about as if someone might snatch it from him.

Catherine rose and continued to watch the children. "They're starving," she murmured to Laird Carlyle. "Where did you find them? They can't possibly be your 'shipment.'" She emphasized the word.

At first the chief said nothing, causing impatience and frustration to build up inside her. Was she never to know anything about these people who'd taken her in?

He cleared his throat. "Scotland's own poor and orphaned bairns are being sold as indentured servants to the colonies and West Indies plantations. But 'indentured servant' is just another word for slave, when 'tis done for no reason beyond filling greedy men's purses."

Though the words he spoke shocked and appalled her, the ugly bitterness in his voice made it sound incredibly personal, beyond righting an injustice. She tucked that idea away to consider later.

She put a hand to her chest, staring at the five children who ate oatcakes as if they hadn't seen food in a long time. She shuddered with nausea. "These children . . . they are the shipment your man warned you about?"

He nodded.

"And you rescued them."

He nodded again, without filling in any details. Was he a man who downplayed his own bravery, or was he simply protecting his methods and his men from the danger she might present?

"How did you learn about this barbaric practice?" she asked.

From beneath lowered brows, he watched the children guzzle cider and cram more oatcakes into their mouths before being gently admonished to take their time. Then he looked to Catherine, and she saw the way he studied her, took her measure. She lifted her chin, and though she wanted to babble something, anything, to prove herself to him, she said nothing. He either trusted her, or he didn't. There was a connection between them, a pull of awareness that seemed so very foreign to her— but then, how would she know? Yet she felt caught in this intimacy with him, though they were surrounded by people.

And as if he felt the need for privacy, he gestured toward the little stream, away from the people gathered to tend to the children. Catherine followed, and though they were on display, it felt as if they shared confidences all alone. They stood beside the footbridge but didn't cross it.

"It happened to one of my own clan," he said heavily. "A poor farmer came to me, complaining that his son had been abducted. I thought surely the lad had simply run away, but the father actually saw, far down the glen, two men take up his child and ride off with him."

"How terrifying," Catherine whispered, searching his eyes, which seemed to see far away.

"He went to the nearest villages, but no one had heard anything like it. So he came to me, his chief, because I should be able to help."

She said nothing, fearing that this particular story did not end well.

"By the time I found a trail to follow, 'twas too late. The boy was gone, hidden away somewhere, and there was no proof as to what had happened. The Lowlanders thought we were simply telling tales to cover our negligence. They usually side with the English, and think we're but savages," he added harshly.

Catherine flinched. Was she one of the English he so obviously despised?

"I discovered that other children had gone missing, one or two every month or so, always the ones with no families, or ones too poor for their families to do anything about it. It started with orphans on the streets of Glasgow where the children could easily be sold to agents from the colonies. But when that supply wasn't enough, poor children were chosen, stolen away from their parents' arms. 'Tis far more difficult a crime to hide. But the magistrates—with the sheriff's support—paid them no heed, were silenced with coin by the wealthy who only gained riches as those poor lads and their families suffered."

Catherine's mouth had sagged open the more he talked, and now felt so dry it was difficult to swallow. The suffering of the children seemed unimaginable. Stolen from the only place they'd ever known, sent on a dangerous voyage across the ocean, forced to work—and she imagined the conditions under which they toiled would be foul. She shuddered and placed a hand over her mouth, struggling to control her nausea.

Laird Carlyle took her elbow as if to steady her, and with relief she let herself consider him for a moment, rather than the fate that was befalling innocent children. This was the most she'd ever heard the man speak, and his words rang with disgust and hatred. She was forced to reevaluate what she'd been thinking about him. He'd confessed his suspicions about her, and she'd been offended, but he didn't know her—she didn't know herself. And what were his suspicions, compared to the fact that he'd rescued her, just like he'd rescued these poor children from a terrible fate? "Laird Carlyle," she said, "have you been rescuing children for long?"

He shrugged. "Several years now. 'Tis why we're living in these caves. I spoke out, tried to bring the case to the Court of Session, and they had me imprisoned."

She gasped. "Imprisoned for speaking the truth?"

"To the wrong people. They wanted me silenced before word could become widespread. They wanted their gold. When I escaped, the sheriff and the magistrates had me outlawed and punished my clan." He looked at his people, many of whom were trying to make the children feel at ease. His voice hoarse, he said, "My people supported what I was trying to do; some of them followed me. And I led them into a hard life, and caused their families to suffer. Only recently I was almost captured again, which could have harmed them even more. We have to be so very wary of the outside world."

She heard the self-recrimination he couldn't hide, and she wanted to comfort him. "No wonder you live apart from the rest of your clan. But they obviously believe as you do that children should be protected."

He narrowed his eyes at her. "And Carlyle children are suffering for it, their parents shunned because of my outlawed status, their cattle selling at prices too low if they sell at all."

"I know that this is terrible, but surely it's better than losing their children to such evil men."

He exhaled a deep sigh. "Aye."

"Why would the sheriff go along with this? He's a man who represents the law."

"Aye, but he's also a man who knew poverty himself, who raised himself up by whatever means he could so he'd not know deprivation again. Every coin he accumulates keeps him further away from that poverty he can't forget, that I swear he must see when he looks over his shoulder, because he's running away from it fast enough. He has several fine horses and a flat in an elegant townhouse, with furniture gilt enough to entertain an earl." And then he broke off.

Catherine glanced at the little boy she'd tried to help. He sat with his head bowed, away from the other children. He didn't speak to them, or show any excitement about being rescued. Now that the other four had their bellies filled, she could hear the torrent of questions being thrown at Ivor and Maeve. But the little boy acted like it didn't concern him. He pushed away Janet, who tried to scrub his filthy face. Catherine wanted to gather him into her arms and rock him as if she could help him feel safe from the world.

"You have done something brave and important, Laird Carlyle," she said softly. "And your clan's willingness to support you, regardless of the hardship, speaks to their kindness and fortitude. But now that you've rescued these children, what happens next?"

She wondered if he'd even answer, if he thought her too bold. But that intimate spell around them held. Though most of the clan was only yards away, the two of them stood close together, speaking softly, absorbed as if in their own world.

"Gathering evidence to bring to a higher court is proving difficult. The children's tales hold no sway with the magistrates, who are sharing the spoils with the sheriff. We have yet to find something in writing as evidence of their villainy; they are far too clever for that. But we keep looking. Every time we rescue a child, those villains who aren't killed in the attack, we return with broken bones or other injuries, removing them from this foul duty. Eventually they'll have to run out of men willing to kidnap children, forcing the sheriff to do his own work, or lose the money he's promised to a nobleman too smart to dirty his hands."

Catherine frowned, wondering at how his tone had changed when he discussed this nobleman.

"Until then, we return the children to their families, who are now on guard. Four of these newest children have families to return to. We've begun to keep track of how many children are in the area, so that we have the numbers to use against the sheriff when he's caught. I know we cannot solve the problem across all of Scotland, but we damn well can do something about our corner of it. But the boy ye spoke with, and others like him, can't be easily kept track of. On the journey here, he admitted he has no one, and lived on the streets. His Christian name is Finn, but he might not even have a surname."

"What will happen to him?" she asked nervously.

"We hope to find him a family. Highlanders are a generous people, but times are difficult, and the famine too recent. We will be patient."

"Until then he stays here?"

Laird Carlyle eyed her impassively, and when she would have gotten her feathers ruffled, she reminded herself of the good he was doing, even at risk to himself and his clan. She knew she was asking too many questions, but she couldn't help herself. She wasn't much different than Finn, both needing a place to stay, desperate to find a home.

"Aye, he'll stay," Laird Carlyle said.

She smiled at him with relief. "Excellent."

For a long moment, he studied her face, as if he'd never seen her happy before. Now that she knew the secret he was protecting—one of the secrets anyway—she couldn't help but feel kinder toward him.

"'Twould seem I am in your good graces again, mistress," he murmured.

Without a second thought, she put a comforting hand on his arm. She noticed the way his muscular body seemed to take up too much room, take up all the air, leaving her light-headed. As he tensed beneath her hand, she suddenly realized that people were watching them, that they stood too close, talked too intimately—and now she'd touched him, as if flirting with him.

Goodness, was she actually blushing?

She stepped back so quickly that she stumbled. When he reached out, she put up a hand to stop him from touching her again.

"I'll return to help Maeve." Turning away, Catherine added over her shoulder, "My thanks for the explanation, Laird Carlyle. I appreciate the trust."

"See that I don't regret it."

She rolled her eyes and said with mild exasperation, "Must you ruin every honest discussion between us?"

Well, she assumed it was honest. Did she really know?

He stared at her with those black, mysterious eyes, and for just a moment they lingered on her lips, before he abruptly walked away.

Her mouth went dry. Low in her stomach she felt a tension she couldn't understand, though she knew it had to do with him. Maybe she was the one who'd ruined their discussion by thinking too much about him as a desirable man, when she had no right to do such a thing.

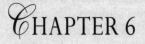

CHAPTER 6

Duncan watched highborn Lady Catriona Duff help to serve grimy, defensive children, who didn't have money or fine manners. He didn't know what to think as she cleaned up a cup of spilled ale without complaint, sliced apples into pieces for the children to devour, smiled at them with the confidence of a woman assuring them that all would be well.

He was relieved by the thaw that had occurred between her and the other women. The cave was already so small that any arguments would distress every resident. Catriona was different, and there was no hiding that fact. She scrubbed her hands repeatedly as if she wasn't used to dirt under her nails. She even questioned the translation of Mrs. Skinner's orders. Catriona was a woman used to being in charge, even if she didn't remember that.

But she'd blended in quickly, just by being willing to work and help the children. The women had accepted her, and soon the men would, following his own lead. He'd confided in her more than he meant to. But the rescued children couldn't be explained any other way. Detail after detail had poured out of him, lured by her sympathy. Those golden eyes had shone with approval.

And she'd touched him, and he'd had the over-powering desire to pull her into his arms. He hadn't been able to stop watching her mouth, had imagined kissing her, caressing her, laying her down on his pallet and taking her.

What kind of chief was he, to let the daughter of his enemy affect him so? He shouldn't want her understanding, just her acquiescence.

But she bustled about almost authoritatively, asking for whatever food she thought the children needed. He knew she wasn't used to being sub-servient. Anyone could see that she was a woman who'd been trained to run a household; she was a lady.

He suddenly had a sobering thought—would behaving in her old manner trigger her elusive memories? He studied her too closely, looking for a sign that her mind was releasing the truth, a sign that she didn't belong here.

But it didn't happen. She seemed lit by an in-ner fire of resolve, of determination to help the abused children. She treated them with gentle-ness and good nature, and when their steps grew weary, their heads drooping, she worked with the other women to find them pallets to lie upon near a warm fire.

She did not leave their care until all were asleep, including the silent orphan who spoke not at all, but whose eyes were windows of both wariness and fear. Catriona sat beside him until he fell asleep, and only then did she speak a soft goodnight to Maeve.

He continued watching her until she was at the entrance to the passageway into the next cave. She looked over her shoulder one last time and saw him staring, then blushed and turned away. What had she read in his expression? He'd worked so hard to overcome his impetuous youth, to become a leader to be trusted, a man who expressed impassivity, not emotion.

But he wasn't thinking with his brain when he looked at Catriona.

CATHERINE didn't sleep well, unable to shake her concern for the children. She rose and dressed swiftly, this time in a dark plaid gown, with her chemise apparent at her neckline and shoulders and at the laces that attached her sleeves. She wasn't wearing a fichu, and trusted that the chemise distracted from her cleavage. She hardly wanted to display herself before the men.

Unwillingly, she remembered the way Duncan Carlyle had watched her when she'd retired for the night—retired to *his* chamber, his bed. She had no memories of any bed at all, she reminded herself with sarcasm, but that didn't matter. She hadn't been able to gauge his expression, but she'd felt . . . hot, as if it were high summer instead of sliding into autumn. Her legs had felt weak, and between them—good God, she could not let herself remember how restless and yearning she'd felt in his bed.

She scolded herself for such weakness. He'd rescued her, been kind to her, even as he'd harbored natural suspicions about something so outlandish as losing all of one's memories. This was gratitude she was feeling, nothing more.

It didn't help that he was handsome in a rough, masculine way, with his unruly auburn hair that seemed to want to escape his queue, high cheekbones, the stubble of a day's growth of beard, and dark eyes that hid the weight of the world.

No, she was done thinking about him. There were helpless, lost children to focus on. She entered the great hall when the cave entrance was still awash with gray light. Without thinking, she crossed to look out upon the dawn, only to find one of Laird Carlyle's men silently stepping into her path, blocking her.

"Oh, my apologies," she murmured, giving him an embarrassed smile before turning away.

He didn't smile back. But she was starting to learn people's names. He was Melville, Sheena's father, and it was obvious he didn't like her—and trying to go outside had probably increased his suspicion.

But she'd almost forgotten what the outdoors even looked like. There were few men in the cave, and she imagined the rest were outside, feeding animals, gathering wood, or hunting.

After washing her hands in the burn, Catherine walked to the cooking fires and greeted the four women. "Good morning to you." She glanced past them to see the five little boys, all still sleeping soundly, some wrapped tightly in their blankets, others sprawled with abandon. "At least some of them feel safe at last," she said wryly.

Maeve translated for Mrs. Skinner, then smiled. "Some had nightmares, but I was able to console them."

Catherine stiffened. "Oh, I could have been helping you."

"Nay, 'twas an easy task."

"Then at least allow me to help with breakfast."

Soon they had cauldrons of porridge and boiling eggs to be consumed with fresh buttermilk, and Catherine's mouth watered. The scents awakened the children, who looked frightened again, as if they hadn't remembered the rescue. While the clanswomen set a table for the children, she guided them to wash up in the stream. The little orphan boy, Finn, seemed frightened of the water—of perhaps everything. He resisted much washing, and since she didn't want to push him, she settled for making certain that at least his hands were clean. When Maeve announced breakfast, and the children rushed to the table, Finn hung back.

"Are you not hungry?" Catherine asked gently.

Eyes downcast, he only shrugged. So he did speak English, she thought with relief.

"I am Catherine. I understand you're Finn."

He mumbled something, but she didn't call him on it.

"Finn, that's a good strong name," she said. "Come and taste the porridge. Do you like eggs?"

Another shrug. But she made certain the children shared the meal, and that no one with quick fingers ate more than another. Then she just sat back and listened. The children recounted being tied together in a cart, covered over by a tarpaulin, fed blackened oatcakes over several days, seldom even allowed to stretch their legs except at night, when they'd be locked into an old barn. The other four women listened with sympathy, but it was obvious they'd heard this before, after other rescues. To Catherine, it was fresh and appalling, and her chest ached without the release of tears she couldn't shed.

Finn said nothing, of course, just ate steadily, his eyes downcast. He stared at the eggs on his plate in curiosity, poking them with his finger before finally eating one, gingerly at first, then with more enthusiasm. Catherine suspected he'd just had his first egg, and her throat grew tight at withholding her emotions. The poor boy.

"What do we do now?" the eldest asked, while the youngest put his thumb in his mouth and looked around with interest.

"I want to go home," whispered another, his voice wobbly.

"We're contactin' yer parents, as Laird Carlyle said," Maeve responded. "Ye know it may take several days until we can bring ye to them. Until then, ye remain in the cave, helpin' with chores as best ye can and waitin' for his lairdship to give permission to go outside."

"Chores!" the oldest said in dismay.

"Busy minds cannot dwell on things best forgotten," Maeve said.

That seemed reasonable, Catherine grudgingly

admitted to herself. She almost asked about tutoring, but stopped herself. The boys would only be there for a few days—she glanced at Finn—she hoped.

And then she had a sudden horrible thought. What about her? Could she read? Could she *remember* how to read? She tried to remember words, but in her panic, everything stayed a blank. She only grew more and more fearful, wondering what else she had forgotten she even knew.

"But for now," Maeve was saying, "there are sticks near the burn. Build yerselves some boats."

And they were off, even young Finn, though he trailed them and stood back while the other boys flung themselves on the embankment, grabbed the sticks and string, and began to build.

Catherine and the other women prepared even more food for the men, who would be returning for dinner at midday. In between, she watched over the children until they grew tired of boats and turned to marbles. Finn continued to hang back, and soon the other boys didn't even bother to include him in their games. Catherine almost interceded, until Maeve suggested that boys should learn to solve their own small problems, so they'd eventually be prepared for the big ones.

For the first time, Catherine had some time where she had absolutely nothing to do—and she was in a cave. She glanced at the entrance with longing, seeing light and imagining the sun on her face. She would give almost anything to step outside and simply inhale something fresh that wasn't smoke and men's body odor. But she knew that wasn't going to happen until people began to trust her.

Someone sighed loudly right next to her, and with a start, she turned to see Janet, watching the boys and shaking her head.

"What is it?" Catherine asked.

"I tried to interest the boys in chess with Angus, and they would have none of it. Splashin' and gettin' wet and dirty was all they wanted."

Catherine barely heard anything after "chess." "You have a chessboard?" she asked excitedly.

Janet eyed her. "Ye remember how to play?"

That stopped Catherine, who closed her eyes and imagined the board and all the pieces. In her mind she saw them move. Opening her eyes, she said excitedly, "Yes! I believe I do. Where is the board?"

Janet found the board on an upturned crate along the rough stone wall. The game pieces were in a plain wooden box on top—no wonder Catherine hadn't seen it. When she lifted the lid and saw the delicately carved ivory pieces, she gave a little gasp.

"'Tis Himself's set. Few use it."

"He has forbidden it?"

"Nay, but . . .'tis from his family's past, when things were better, aye?"

Catherine nodded. "I understand. No one wants to risk damaging it. I'll be careful." And the act of mental exercise might help regain her memories, she realized with excitement. "Do you play?"

Janet shook her head.

"I could teach you."

But Janet was already glancing at the other women as if she couldn't wait to escape.

"Go on then, I won't keep you."

Smiling with relief, the young woman darted away. Catherine gently touched the king, surprised to see three crowns, one on top of the other. But she imagined every artist had their own particular style. These pieces, with their stacked rounded disks, were tall and slender, as if they'd tip over if one became too excited during the game.

Who could she play with? She looked around and saw the women talking quietly near the children. The only other person was the guard at the door—the one keeping her from stepping outside. It was Angus, the young man newly married to Janet who had said he played chess. Catherine could tell he was trying to focus on keeping them all safe, but he kept watching his wife with longing. There was a man who needed to be distracted, and whom she needed to befriend if she was ever going to be trusted to see the last heather on the moor before autumn chased it away.

When she marched up to Angus, he stiffened and eyed her warily.

"Angus, I've been told you play chess."

He looked around as if for moral support before giving a tiny nod. "Aye, I do, but—"

"Will you play with me? Your wife just showed me the chessboard."

"Laird Carlyle's board?"

"Is that a problem? Has he forbidden its use,

considering he left it out in the open?" As if there were cupboards in a cave where he could have tucked it away.

"Nay, but—"

"Have pity on me, Angus. It's something I remember knowing how to do. We won't even leave the entrance. I'll bring the board to you, and you can even stand while we play."

She didn't wait for a reply, just returned for the crate, and then the game board, setting them along the cave wall near the entrance. She caught a whiff of the outdoors, of heather, earthy and herb-like, and could have swooned.

Angus still eyed the women and then the entrance, like a small boy who worried about being caught doing something naughty. But she ignored him, sat down on a stump, and lifted the first piece, a horse's head, from the box.

"The knight is lovely," she breathed, the ivory so translucent she could see the carving strokes.

But she couldn't waste time admiring the set when Angus might balk at any moment. She set up the pieces without even thinking about it, then stared in wonder at what she'd remembered. She tried to think of playing the game before, of who might have been across the board from her, but nothing came into her damaged brain. She was growing accustomed to feeling defeated where her memory was concerned.

She moved a white pawn two squares, then looked up at Angus expectantly. "Your turn," she said brightly.

He glanced away again, and she saw that Janet was regarding them curiously. But when his wife nodded, Angus reached down and moved a black pawn, before standing up straight next to the entrance again.

By his first move, Catherine could see he was not an advanced player—how did she know this? she wondered—and adjusted her strategy accordingly. It didn't take long before she let him win, and he actually smiled at her with happy triumph. She smiled back. Maybe it wouldn't be that long before she could gain a few minutes' freedom outside. It wasn't like she would run from her escort; she was just starting to feel closed in, as if the ceiling sank lower every day. And it had only been a few days! She couldn't imagine the months and years Laird Carlyle had been here.

And then the chief himself walked through the entrance and right past them. Angus stiffened and shot her a frown. She quietly pulled the little crate away from him along the wall, to keep from implicating him. Laird Carlyle's gaze swept over the cave and settled on her, making her blush. She wasn't going to feel guilty for playing a game. More men arrived, milling between her and him, so she quickly put the pieces back in the box and left them on top of the game board. She didn't bother moving the crate back where it had been— she had plans to play with every guard she could. But for now, there were hungry men to be fed and they all sat down, waiting to be served.

She took up a pitcher to fill the men's tankards

with ale. Many spoke in their own language at first, then switched to English when she was near. Had she finally earned their reluctant respect?

When she leaned past his lairdship's shoulder to serve him, feeling all embarrassed as if she'd never been near a man before—and for all she knew, she'd been raised by nuns—he met her gaze and didn't look away. She didn't want to give him a chance to ask about the chess game.

She took a deep breath. "Shall I bring you something else, Laird Carlyle?"

"Nay, the ale is fine," he said, his manner full of his usual gruffness. "How were the bairns this morn?"

She tried to will the tension from her shoulders. Everything was fine. "They wanted to be outside, of course, but since they couldn't, Maeve was quite ingenious suggesting they build boats in the burn."

"She's had practice," he said dryly.

Her smile faltered. "It's a shame she has had so many stolen children to help. Or do you mean having children of her own?" she added, frowning.

"Nay, she's never married."

Catherine glanced at Maeve, whose gentle manner made her a favorite among the clan. Did no one see past her scar to court her? Or did living in a cave make one put off marriage? she guessed.

"How long does it usually take to return the boys to their parents?" Catherine asked.

"Anywhere from days to weeks, depending on how much information the child is able to supply. We're lucky that the youngest is brother to the second oldest. Their parents' village is relatively close. We'll return them on the morrow, making less work for ye ladies."

"We don't mind," she said absently, then frowned as she looked for Finn, who was sitting at the children's table, staring at one of the fires rather than talking with the others. She lowered her voice. "I'm worried about Finn, the one who rarely socializes."

"Och, the quiet one, aye. Once rescued, some of the bairns forget quickly what happened to them. Others . . . 'tis some time before they move on."

"Who can blame them?" she murmured sadly. "I saw the rope marks on their little wrists."

"Aye, they're tied up day and night so they don't escape." His voice grew thick. "I'll not see that done to a child. I understand too well how it works on the mind."

She stared at him in surprise, but he said nothing else. Ivor called for more ale, and she went back to work. Had something been done to Laird Carlyle as a child?

She continued to think on it as the women ate their own meal and cleaned up. Catherine watched the laird say something to Ivor, then head down the passageway, she assumed to his chamber, the one he'd not yet taken back from her.

The women settled into sewing, while Maeve spun wool from a handheld distaff to a spindle. Catherine chose a rather large shirt, with embroidery on a torn cuff. She set about repairing it without even thinking about it.

"Ye know fine embroidery work," Maeve commented.

Catherine looked up, then glanced at the cuff in surprise. "And so I do! I hadn't even realized."

"'Tis the shirt of Himself," Maeve said.

"How did he damage such a fine piece?"

"He wears what he has to wear, like all of us do," Sheena said.

Catherine held it up, and noticed the strained shoulder seams.

"'Tis many years old," Maeve said. "Take it to Laird Carlyle for fittin'."

Janet and Sheena glanced at each other, wide-eyed, and Janet smothered a giggle. Sheena only frowned.

Catherine willed herself not to blush. "I'll return quickly," she said, and took the shirt to the passageway.

Outside the curtained-off chamber, she hesitated, but there was no wooden door upon which to knock. She leaned closer, wondering if she could time her disturbance, but all she heard was the shuffling of paper.

"Ye're breathing mighty loud," he said from the other side of the curtain.

She jumped. "Forgive me, Laird Carlyle, I didn't know if it was a good time to interrupt."

He swept back the curtain so suddenly that she started. She found herself looking up into his shadowed face, the lantern behind him making his features even more remote and intriguing.

"What do ye need?" he asked.

She held up the linen. "I'm mending your shirt, where you've strained the shoulder seams."

He stepped back and motioned her inside. "Come in."

The chamber looked different and it took her a moment to realize why—he'd folded all of her clothing and set them in piles on the pallet. It had all been in his way, of course. She never thought about *why* she left things about; it was just something she did, something natural. She wondered if she was simply messy, or used to servants. And if she had servants—which she might, wearing such a fine gown—she seemed to have no problem giving them a reason to do their job. She flushed with embarrassment.

She could see papers set in neat piles across the table, a book nearby, and for a moment, she panicked, before saying faintly, "I don't even know if I can read."

He eyed her. "Pick up the book and see."

She opened the leather cover and gave a sigh of relief when she read, "*The Defects and Remedies of English Husbandry*, by Robert Child. Oh, thank goodness."

"'Tis hard to fake that kind of relief," he said dryly.

It was her turn to eye him. "I don't understand." Then she stiffened. "Ah, back to my supposed lying again."

Folding his arms across his broad chest, he leaned casually against the rock wall. "For what it's worth, if I didn't believe ye were telling the truth, I wouldn't have told ye about our mission."

"Well, aren't I grateful I've suddenly become

trustworthy." She didn't bother to hide her sarcasm.

He caught her upper arm and pulled her toward him, saying quietly, "And I'm supposed to take your word for it, for something so unbelievable as a loss of memory, when my people's safety depends on my judgment?"

He was leaning over her, far too close. She could *smell* him, manly scents of the outdoors that were far too attractive. The black depths of his eyes might as well have been mirrors, for all she could understand there. But she did see anger and frustration lining his forehead, bracketing his mouth.

And then his gaze left hers and slid lower, to *her* mouth, and that first sense of attraction blossomed into heat that spread from her chest up to her cheeks, then down, lower, feeling like it burned between her thighs. She gave a little gasp, feeling every imprint of his fingers on her arm, especially his thumbs against the side of her breast. She should tell him to let her go, but words wouldn't come. All she could think about was how much she liked his hand on her body, on her breast.

He lowered his head, and she could barely breathe. She felt his hair brush hers, the heat of his cheek so near, but not touching. His breath on her lips made a moan escape her. If she turned her head, just the slightest bit, their lips would meet. And she desperately wanted that, needed to feel close to someone—to him, this man full of contradictions: anger and righteousness, intensity and reserve, empathy and wariness.

"I want to kiss ye," he said, his soft voice husky. "But I'd be taking advantage of ye."

They were still so close, but she lifted her gaze and met his. The black depths of his eyes were coal with a spark of fire down deep.

"Not if I give you permission," she whispered.

His lips touched hers with a gentle exploration that surprised and moved her. With another moan, she leaned up to him, tilting her head to give him more access. He pressed kisses against her mouth, like petting a fragile butterfly—but she was not so delicate. She kissed him back, harder, and it was his turn to groan, even as he opened his mouth, slanting it across hers until she did the same. The rasp of his tongue along hers made her shudder with both shock and dark passion. She'd never felt anything like it. It made her feel desperate and reckless; it made all her concerns recede. The only thing that mattered was his mouth bringing hers to life.

She wanted to be closer, and as if he read her mind, he let her arm go and drew her up hard against him. Her breasts against his chest made her gasp; his arms wrapping about her made her feel like a woman, not a victim. She was able to touch him at last, wind her arms around his neck, then tangle her hands in his wild hair. The queue came undone and she felt brazen as she held his face to her by his hair.

At last he lifted his head, and both of them breathed hard as they stared at each other. She would have pulled him to her again, but he suddenly stepped back, forcing her to let go. The silence between them seemed loud as her mind cleared, and she remembered why she should never have kissed him. She didn't know who she was, what she was: wife, fiancée, mistress? When she regained her memories, would she be horrified by her behavior? Because she'd have regrets if she allowed this to go any further.

And then there was how he'd feel when he found out who she was. She didn't want him to have his own regrets about helping her, or to think she'd used this attraction between them to benefit herself.

"I should not have done that," he said, eyes narrowed.

"You did not do it alone."

"'Twill not happen again."

"No, it cannot." Her words sounded weak, so she cleared her throat and straightened her back. "We don't know who I am, *what* I am." She glanced down at the book on the table. "I don't even know what I'm capable of. This memory of mine could come back any moment, or not at all. I have to find some kind of future for myself."

Here, among these kind, generous people? a voice whispered slyly inside her. But that would be safe, and far too easy. And she knew little about him, she reminded herself.

Tentatively, she said, "Do you . . . is there a woman—"

"Am I married?" he interrupted brusquely. "Nay, there is no one."

Relief moved warmly through her.

"I will never commit to a woman when all I can offer is this."

When he put out a hand, she knew he meant not just the cave, but the life he led.

"Surely you will not do this forever. You deserve happiness, too."

He looked at her for far too long, and she couldn't read his expression. Was he punishing himself?

"'Tis nothing I think about," he said. "Right now I am concerned with those children, and stopping what is happening to them. But I have not forgotten your plight, mistress."

Catherine, she thought. *My name is Catherine*. But she realized he rarely said the name she'd chosen, as if he could not forget that it and her whole identity was a fraud. She knew it, too.

"My men will keep visiting the surrounding villages to ask about a lost woman. It has only been a few days."

"But they've heard nothing," she said, trying not to be disheartened when he nodded. It was early yet. "Maybe I'm not from here, and I was simply traveling through." With just two guards? she wondered. Through the horse paths of the Highlands?

"Even if that is true, someone will look for ye eventually."

Sometimes she felt like such an inconvenience to him, and other times closer than she could ever have felt for another man. It seemed too raw, too rare, this desire that made her watch him whenever she could. But it wasn't just desire. She hugged herself. "I don't like feeling so helpless and dependent. I *know* this about myself."

He said nothing.

"And I don't want to be yet another person you have to take care of," she added bitterly. "You believe I'm telling the truth about my memory now. Maybe it will help if you let me go outside occasionally."

"'Tis dangerous."

"So it's dangerous for all these people you care for, but *too* dangerous for me?"

His frown deepened. "They know what they're doing and how to protect themselves."

She felt a touch of fear. She didn't know anything at all about herself. But . . . maybe it was more than what he was saying. After all, most women had to be protected.

"Your camp is well guarded, I assume, so it can't be just that," she mused, then met his gaze decisively. "You don't want me to know where we are. You're in hiding, and you can't trust a stranger in your midst with your secrets."

He said nothing, but he didn't need to. It was too obvious.

"I want to be angry with you, but I can't," she said tiredly. "I'm an unknown risk. I could have family worried about me, searching for me, risking your encampment. Or maybe I don't," she added with frustration.

"I am certain you have people who care about your welfare," he said. "You were finely dressed."

"That means nothing. I could be wealthy and be totally alone in the world."

She paused, and another uncomfortable silence settled between them, full of possibilities and danger and yearning. She saw him glance at his paper and discarded quill, knew he wanted to finish whatever he'd been doing—that he wanted to be rid of her and this . . . feeling between them that could not be.

Then she saw the shirt on his bed, and suddenly fitting it to him seemed far too intimate and uncomfortable a task. But how could she return to the women with it unfinished, especially after all this time had passed with him alone? She might not remember much, but she remembered how a woman's reputation could be so important.

She picked up the shirt. "If you give me your back, I'll hold this up and do a rough measurement."

He eyed the shirt dubiously.

"It is a fine piece of workmanship," she said, letting her fingers brush the embroidery at the cuffs. "A woman who cared about you sewed this."

"A long time ago."

"Which is probably why it no longer fits."

He turned around, presenting her with his wide shoulders beneath his coat and the excess plaid. She held the shirt up, attempting to match the seams where she guessed his shirt was.

With a muffled sound of impatience, he let down his excess plaid, leaving it to hang from his belt, as he removed his coat. She felt another thrill of both anxiety and eagerness. But he left his shirt on, and she should be relieved, she told herself.

Beneath the shirt, his flesh was warm, the muscles hard. She tried to concentrate on how much she needed to let out the seams, but she kept imagining him removing the shirt, touching him, tasting him—

Tasting him! Where had such a shocking thing come from? She was so glad he wasn't looking at her scarlet face.

Clearing her throat, she tried to speak normally. "Did your mother make this shirt for you? Or perhaps a sister?"

"My mother died many years ago, and my sisters are older and married with their own households."

"Aunts? Grandmothers?"

"None I saw frequently."

"Brothers?"

"Just me." He looked over his shoulder at her. "Is that a problem?"

"No! Not at all, it just sounds lonely."

"Perhaps ye know from experience."

She sighed. "Maybe I do, but it's just a feeling, not an actual memory."

"Although my clanswomen are competent seamstresses, I believe this was a gift several years ago from a Carlyle chieftain's wife. If it is irreparable, then use it for rags." He shrugged her off.

"I didn't say that." She draped the shirt over her arm. "I'll leave you to your letter, Laird Carlyle."

He gave her a quick look, as if he might say something. Did he want her to call him by his Christian name? *Duncan.* But all he did was wave her off, as if she were his servant rather than a woman he'd just passionately kissed.

She pulled the curtain shut behind her and held back a groan at her behavior.

CHAPTER 7

When Catherine retired to the little cave bed-chamber that night, she saw that Duncan had left the table with only a neat stack of papers and the book to one side. Her garments—the ones he'd picked up from the floor and folded, she thought with a wince—were still on the pallet. She had to make more of an attempt to keep the chamber as neat as he preferred, so she opened the lid of the large trunk he'd told her to use. There were folded shirts, stockings, and another length of plaid, and it felt far too intimate to be touching them. She carefully stacked them on one side of the trunk, and was surprised to uncover a sheaf of papers.

Frowning, she lifted them up. Though very old and brittle, the top paper opened easily, and she realized it was a letter addressed to the laird, but the inscribed date had to be for Duncan's father. It was simply business, discussions of crops and cattle and seed. Feeling curious, she read the second letter referring to a land dispute from a generation ago. It was a window into a world where the chief wasn't an outlaw, where the Carlyles were average Scotsmen with the normal problems of farmers and landowners everywhere. She was touched by the thought of Duncan keeping them as a memento of his father. Knowing she shouldn't be reading something so personal, she was about to fold the third letter away when the words leapt out at her in a strong hand, with a bold "A" as the only signature. This man seemed to be threatening Duncan's father to keep silent about . . . something. Threats? She frowned, confused, then read closer.

"A". assured Duncan's father that a missing child he'd asked about had died. Had the old laird been looking into the missing children, too? Rifling through the rest of the letters, she found more correspondence from chieftains about the kidnappings. It hurt her to think that this had been going on so long.

She was glad to know that Duncan was going to make sure such evil stopped. He'd dedicated his life to this, risked everything to keep the children of his clan safe. His father would be proud.

But this was none of her business. She was starting to feel guilty for even having read the letters. She was at the mercy of Clan Carlyle; she didn't want them to think she snooped where she didn't belong. She quickly folded away the letters, then put her clothing on top, before someone discovered her.

For the next three days, Catherine couldn't help noticing that Duncan was avoiding her. Oh, he didn't leave the great hall when she came out of her chamber, but he avoided speaking with her unless he had to, avoided eye contact. It wasn't that he was a social charmer with anyone else either, of course. When he was with his men, he often spoke in Gaelic, another way he was reminding her to stay away. She knew he had a lot on his mind, and she felt guilty that she'd added to his worries. Here he was, taking her in, providing for her, and now the kiss had made things terribly awkward between them.

And caused her to toss and turn far too often in his bed each night. She kept waiting for him to ask for his privacy back, had tried to keep the chamber neat for him. More than once she'd quietly asked Maeve if she should offer to give it up, but Maeve had continued to insist that Catherine was a guest of the clan.

So Catherine was left to lie awake and imagine the laird sneaking into her chamber and wondering what she'd do. She didn't like feeling so . . . obsessed. Did other women have this problem? Thankfully, her days did not leave much time for eyeing the chief of Clan Carlyle. Two of the rescued children had been returned home, and one more had his family contacted. The fourth child had given enough details that Maeve was confident the men would find his family soon.

And that left Finn. Catherine felt an affinity for the boy from Glasgow who protected himself by keeping his distance. He seldom spoke, didn't know the most basic of manners, resisted cleanliness as if it were a threat. Once he realized people said "thank you" for receiving something, he be-

gan to mumble those words. Although the other
boys had been talked into a bath in the cave pool,
Finn utterly refused to join them, and Catherine
worried what terrible scars from his life on the
streets he might be hiding. They did persuade
him to change out of his filthy clothing by offering him privacy at the pool. Catherine stood in the
passageway and listened to make sure he was all
right, since she assumed he couldn't swim. Except
for the occasional splash, he was utterly silent, obviously unable to enjoy being clean. She brought
his filthy clothing to Maeve, who took them outside to boil, holding them far in front of her with
only two fingers. Maeve later confided that she
was surprised she didn't discover lice.

But when he emerged, Finn looked even more
fragile without all the dirt, his skin pale, his clean
hair hanging ragged to his neck. For a day, he retreated even more into himself, turning his face
away from people, as if he was naked without all
his dirt. Catherine kept trying to draw him out
with offers to teach him chess but he was uninter-
ested. Hoping Finn would watch the game while
she befriended another clansman, she challenged
the guard, Torcall, when most of the men were
away. Torcall shifted from foot to foot with uncertainty, looking past her.

She glanced over her shoulder but saw no one
but Finn nearby. Finn squatted on the ground,
playing with stones, acting as if he was ignoring
them. She didn't believe it.

"Do you play chess or not, Torcall?" she repeated.

He opened his mouth, but before he could say

anything, Angus strode by, on his way outside. He looked at them both, and at the box of chess pieces she held in her hand, and said, "Aye, go on and play her, Torcall. She could use the practice."

Catherine held back her amusement. She'd apparently succeeded in making Angus believe she was a terrible chess player.

So Torcall nodded and pulled over the crate with the chessboard on top. Soon they were hunched over it, eyeing each other competitively. Finn crept closer to watch, still pretending he was more interested in his rocks than what they were doing. Again, Catherine could tell immediately that she was the better player, and found herself enjoying the challenge of outwitting the poor man by losing to him. How had she learned the game so well? As was her habit lately, she kept trying to form a mental image of herself in some other place, learning from a chess expert. Nothing.

"Checkmate," Torcall said with satisfaction.

She didn't have to pretend surprise—she'd let her thoughts briefly drift away, after all. "Well done," she said, smiling up at him.

He smiled back with good nature, then seemed to recollect his duties, and glanced at the cave entrance with guilt.

"No one slipped through, I promise," she whispered.

"'Tis not your duty but mine," he growled.

She didn't take offense. She only hoped she'd begun to win him over, she thought, glancing outside with longing.

Apparently she hadn't hid it well, for Torcall

said gruffly, "'Tis dangerous in the wilds of the Highlands, Mistress Catherine. Ye're safer here."

She nodded as demurely as she could. Glancing at Finn, she said, "Did you understand some of the game, Finn? I could teach you more."

But without a word, he ran to the stream, keeping his back to the cave.

She sighed. "That poor boy has been through so much."

"Sad it is," Torcall murmured. "But he's safe now, aye?"

As she pushed the crate back against the wall, she didn't think Finn felt all that safe.

It was a good thing Catherine was still paying attention to him an hour later, because only she noticed when he slipped through the cave entrance and outside. She didn't want to call attention to him, so she took advantage of Torcall's focus on sharpening his dirk, just as Finn had, and followed the little boy.

The shock of sunlight made her falter and shield her eyes, but her sight adjusted enough to see the boy disappear to the left. She followed the rock wall and came upon Finn at a paddock, leaning on the wooden rail and watching the horses. When she came to a stop beside him, he flinched, his shoulders coming up like a turtle retreating into its shell from the world.

And inside her chest, her heart felt like it shattered for him. She may be alone in the world right now, but knew she hadn't always been so. This little boy had only known the streets of Glasgow.

Though Catherine wanted to gather him against

her, promise she'd keep him safe from the world, she could do none of that. She had no power except in the offer of understanding. She knelt down beside him, watching as he eyed her suspiciously, but he didn't try to run away.

"I just needed to see the sky," he said in his quiet little voice.

She glanced up at the blue, dotted with puffy white clouds. "If I remember correctly, it's usually quite rainy in the Highlands. We're lucky today."

Finn put his hands on the paddock rail and simply nodded. They spent a quiet few minutes watching the horses graze. They were big, majestic animals, content with their lot. Catherine wanted to be content in the moment too, to know that agonizing over what she was missing was wasted effort. She could learn from these horses. Perhaps Finn could, too.

"Have you ever ridden one?" she asked.

Finn shook his head solemnly. "Almost run down by more than one."

Catherine inhaled sharply, then realized that Finn was watching her, the faintest amusement in his blue eyes.

"Are you teasing me?"

"Nay, mistress."

But she thought he'd enjoyed startling her, and perhaps that was a good sign.

"Did you come out here to run away, Finn?"

His eyes widened. "Nay, where would I go? Look at all these mountains and the glens between. I'd be lost or swallowed up by a bog, so His Lairdship said."

So Laird Carlyle had had to scare the children for their own safety. She wanted to disapprove, but it had obviously succeeded—and he'd had practice knowing what worked best with frightened children.

"But I don't know where I'll go when 'tis time to leave," Finn finished on a whisper.

"We could decide together," Catherine said. "I don't know where I belong either."

He frowned at her. "I heard ye lost yer mind."

Giving him a gentle smile, she said, "Not my mind, but my memory. I don't know who I am or where I'm from. Laird Carlyle took me in, just like he's taken you in."

"Maybe 'tis good ye cannot remember," he said solemnly.

She hadn't thought of it that way. It made her sad to think that the boy might not want to remember what he knew. "Regardless of what I wish, I have no memory beyond waking up a few days ago in the rain, just before Laird Carlyle found me."

Finn regarded her directly, for once not lowering his eyes. He appeared about to say something, but then pressed his lips together and turned back to the horses.

"I imagine you could ride one if you ask," Catherine said.

He shot her a wide-eyed look. "I never learned."

"You could learn now."

He bit his fingernail, and she noticed it was already down to the quick.

She let her suggestion linger there, and at last realized she was outdoors for the first time in almost a week. She inhaled deeply, realizing how long she'd smelled only the scents of men in too close quarters, peat smoke, and cabbage. Now the air was redolent with the earthy scent of heather, leaves just beginning to turn toward autumn majesty—and horses, of course, she thought, eyeing those great beasts with amusement. Rising, she stared around her and saw that the cave was up a hillside, and that the green, rocky glen stretched out before her between barren-brown mountains. She saw shaggy cattle—each too thin—and the occasional herd of sheep. There was a village far down the glen, but the only reason she knew that was by a collection of rising smoke from home fires.

"I cannot stay here forever," Finn suddenly said, his voice low and angry. "Himself won't let me."

"Finn—"

"They'll foist me off on strangers."

"They want to find you a family," she said earnestly, putting a hand on his shoulder.

He shrugged away her touch. When he ran back toward the cave entrance, she let him go, but turned to gaze after him—

And saw Laird Carlyle, his legs planted in a wide stance, arms folded across his chest, barring her way.

DUNCAN couldn't miss the way Catriona flushed with guilt. She'd known his order to remain in the cave, and she'd broken it. He wasn't going to be swayed by the pretty blush of her cheek, or the way the wind tugged loose a stray curl beside her ear. But hard as he tried to ignore how she made him feel, he looked at her in the sun and remembered the shadows of his room, and the way she'd come willingly into his arms and opened her mouth to him so eagerly, so innocently.

While he'd kissed her under false pretenses, knowing the truth of who she was, and denying her that comfort.

He didn't like himself for it, but what her father had done—what he'd allowed—was bigger than both of them and this attraction that couldn't mean anything.

And yet . . . he'd kissed her, unable to stop himself, unable to deny the dark hunger he felt for this woman.

Linking her hands behind her back as if trying to appear casual, Catriona said, "You have a beautiful glen, Laird Carlyle. I was relieved to discover that I remember the names of plants and trees. It's so frustrating to remember such mundane things and not—"

"Ye know I said 'twas dangerous for ye to be outside." He made himself sound cold and harsh.

She flinched, but met his gaze boldly. "I know. But would you have preferred that I let Finn go? I'm the only one who saw him run out."

"If it happens again, alert the guard."

"And frighten the boy even more than he already is?"

"He knows he need not be frightened here."

"He knows you'll give him over to a family whenever you choose. Of course he's frightened. Who wouldn't be?"

"And the two of ye commiserate, because ye think I'll send ye off, too?"

Her shoulders sank, and she said softly, "No, I think I might have more say than Finn. But maybe I won't."

"Ye're trying your best to wheedle your way into friendship with my men, to give yourself a say."

She stiffened.

"Do ye think I don't know ye've been attempting to befriend every guard with your pretense at bad chess?"

"I didn't see you watching me," she answered, with a trace of defiance.

"I'm always watching ye." He held back a grimace, knowing he revealed too much.

She blinked at him, then a wash of color painted her cheeks. She was remembering the kiss, too.

"I'm sorry my chess skills are not up to your standards," she said, speaking too quickly as if to distract them both.

"Och, we both know your chess skills haven't even begun to be challenged."

She shot him a taunting sideways look. "And you saw all that from wherever you hid to spy on me?"

"I was not spying on ye. Ye made no attempt to conceal what ye were doing."

She cocked her head, but didn't respond, just looked away from him and toward the glen, mostly hidden from them by trees. They could see glimpses of purple heather on distant hillsides, but the villages were obscured. He watched her study his land and people, the ones he'd broken the law for, the ones he'd been banished for protecting. Inevitably, she looked up—and gasped.

He knew what she'd seen, but he looked up, too. The castle tower, far above as if in the clouds, jutted out over the cliff, the sentinel of Carlyle lands. The walls on either side were crumbling inward, but that proud tower held on.

Almost breathless, she said, "That is . . . amazing. It is yours?"

"The ancient birthplace of my ancestors. But 'tis a ruin now. Rather an ironic symbol of my chiefdom, aye?"

"I disagree," she insisted. "You may be outlawed, but it's a brave, valiant thing you're doing, and your ancestors would be proud."

She could have punched him in the gut and it might have wounded him less. Brave and valiant? He wanted to laugh his disgust at himself. If she only knew what he was capable of, what he'd done to her in the name of family pride and vengeance. And he would change none of it. Her father had to understand what the parents of those stolen boys felt like. It might help stop the kidnappings.

The wind picked up, and the familiar wail began.

She stared upward. "It's coming from up there, isn't it? At night it seems quite frightening."

And that was the point. He shrugged. "I'm so used to it I don't even hear it anymore."

"I had wondered if my head wound was making me hear things," she admitted, her mouth twisted in wry amusement. "What is it?"

He looked up, even as he realized he didn't want to meet her eyes as he lied to her yet again. "'Tis just the way the wind moves through the ruins."

"Could we go up?"

"Nay, did I not just say there is danger there?"

She blinked at him. "Oh, very well. Did you grow up there?"

"We had a manor in a nearby village."

"And your father ruled from there."

"If ye call what he did ruling."

She eyed him with curiosity, and he didn't like having revealed too much with his sarcasm.

"He'd be proud of you," she said quietly, "whatever your relationship used to be."

"Nay, he would not. I vowed to be a better chief than he, thought I could not possibly be worse. I was wrong."

Frowning, she opened her mouth as if to contradict him.

"I'm not an honorable man," he warned her. "Ye already know that."

Color bloomed in her cheeks again. "I don't know what you've done, or why you punish yourself, but you can't stop me from thinking well of you. You rescued me; you rescued those children. You've given me a place to stay when I have no one. And Finn will see that you can be trusted."

He didn't think his guilt could keep growing, not after everything her father had done in the name of her family, but grow it did, until he felt cut by it.

But still, he wanted her. The green-and-yellow bruises beneath her eyes only reminded him that her beauty was not solely what he desired. It was her, the woman who'd lost everything, yet served his men with patience and gratitude. She could have reacted to her trauma in fear and neediness; instead she'd tried to do her part, had given herself over to their mission.

Every second he watched her mouth as she spoke only reminded him that he wanted to take it, invade it, claim it. Every graceful movement of her body as she walked past him, sending a little glance sideways at him, made him want to drag her beneath him, made him want to show her the power he could wield over her with passion. She would feel as helpless and desperate as he did.

Instead, after she'd gone, he stood immobile for far too long, seeking to master himself, to remember what was at stake.

Two days later, Finn was the last boy left, and before breakfast, he watched Catherine try to cook oatcakes on the girdle. Maeve had given her her own cook fire to practice, and the women left her alone, giggling whenever they glanced her way. Not Sheena, however. Catherine had not won her over, and her disdain was less and less hidden. Catherine didn't know what she'd done to offend her.

When Catherine burned her second batch, Finn chuckled, and it was so difficult to act like his briefly amused expression wasn't the best thing she'd seen from him in days. He seemed to be opening up under her attention, and she knew that if he learned to relax with people, he would eventually accept and appreciate having a new family.

Looking at the girdle, which seemed to mock her with its hot black surface, she gave a frustrated sigh. "I am a woman. I should know how to cook. I know how to *sew*."

"I thought everybody knew how to cook," he offered amiably.

She almost laughed aloud. They were both in the same position, waiting for a new start to life—and apparently he felt better thinking she was worse off than he was.

Or maybe he just liked to be of help, for he flattened the next ball of dough, and did a better job watching over it than she did. For an hour they worked together companionably. He'd become her little shadow, the two of them stuck there together.

Until Duncan came over. Then Finn seemed to shrink as he scuttled away.

The laird eyed the boy, frowning. "I've not beaten the lad," he said gruffly.

"But other men have." She spoke quietly, and he stepped closer to hear her. "Perhaps the men who kidnapped him, or simply the men who lived on the streets with him."

"And he's said nothing about family to ye?"

She shook her head. "I honestly don't think he has any. Sort of like me, for surely your men would have encountered people looking for me by now."

She tried to keep her voice expressionless, because she didn't want him to see how it kept her awake at night, at first wondering if her family was missing her, and now dreading that she had no one out there at all. Perhaps those men who'd died had been her only family.

"It's been eight days," Duncan said quietly. "Ye were traveling. If 'twas a fair distance, ye're not likely to be missed yet, aye?"

She shrugged, glanced down at the girdle, and gave an unladylike curse. "Oh, I've burned them again."

When she removed the blackened cakes from the heat, she glanced up to see him watching her, unsmiling. But his eyes seemed a bit less shadowed, as if she amused him. Or maybe she was reading too much into this inscrutable man.

"Ye've picked up the language of a cave-dwelling clansman," he said dryly.

She ignored his teasing. "I can serve the food, stir it even, but I will never rival Mrs. Skinner. Surely there's something else I can do. Laundry, perhaps? You trust me outside now."

He took her hand and lifted it, as if pointing out how white and useless it was.

She practically forced her thumb near his face. "See, I'm developing calluses, aren't I?"

They were standing too close again, and she realized that seemed to happen too often. She glanced about and saw more than one pair of eyes watching them speculatively, most without rancor. They were a source of interest, but only Melville seemed to care what they did with each other.

Lowering her voice, she said, "Do you have any idea why Melville dislikes me so?"

Duncan grunted. "I've been told he hopes I will marry his daughter."

Catherine's mouth dropped open, and it took everything in her not to look Sheena's way. "What does that have to do with me?"

He cocked his head. "I've never kissed his daughter."

She felt her face flame scarlet. "Oh. But . . . he doesn't know we've kissed. I promise I've not told anyone."

"He's not a stupid man."

"It's my fault," she murmured, not knowing where to look anymore. "I'll try to be more careful. I don't know if I've ever kissed a man before, and it seems pretty wonderful. Perhaps my face showed too much . . ." She trailed off in distress.

When he didn't say anything, she risked a glance up, only to find him staring at her mouth with a hunger he didn't bother to hide.

Maeve interceded, bustling her away with the women to begin clearing the breakfast dishes and shooing the men off to their day's chores, which eventually left Catherine and Duncan even more alone.

Catherine stayed where she was, embarrassed and grateful as she hovered near him as tentatively as a bird. He didn't move away either; she could hear him breathing, knew it had quickened, just as hers had—here, in front of too many people.

"What happened to Maeve's face?" she asked quietly, trying to distract herself.

He studied his friend's face impassively, and

then said the last words Catherine expected. "My mother did that."

Her eyes went wide, her lips parted in shock, but he wore no expression at all.

"Surely an accident," she began faintly.

"Nay, very deliberate."

Her stomach roiled with nausea at the thought of someone burning another's flesh. No, not "someone"—his mother. "But . . . why?"

Duncan glanced at Maeve, still out of hearing range. "It wasn't because of Maeve, but her mother, our housekeeper. My mother felt threatened by the woman."

"But Lady Carlyle was the wife of the laird, the most powerful woman in the clan. Why would she be threatened?"

"She was a selfish woman who'd been forced to marry by her family. And she could not let anyone forget it. She wanted a husband with more power and ambition. My father was a weak man, who tended to retreat rather than confront. He wasn't much respected, most especially by her."

Though he disparaged his father, his mother's conduct was far worse, in Catherine's opinion.

"He and our housekeeper had a bond of friendship. To this day, I don't believe it was more than that. She was a sympathetic, friendly woman. Her daughter Maeve was one of the companions of my childhood. Everyone doted on her, and her mother loved her. To punish our housekeeper—and my father—my mother burned Maeve's face with a clothing iron fresh from the fire."

Catherine gasped—she couldn't help it. She

hadn't wanted to draw his attention, stop that far-off look in his eyes as he remembered and confided in her. Now he shot her an impassive glance.

"Aye, that was the kind of woman she was. And 'twas the final cruelty for my father, who'd put up with her abuse of the servants, her children, and himself."

Her children? Catherine thought. Did he understand the plight of the children he rescued because he'd been treated badly himself?

"What did your father do?" she asked faintly.

"He killed her."

CHAPTER 8

That night, all was silent as Catherine slowly swam up out of the inky blackness of sleep. Confused, still dazed, she was suddenly vaulted into awareness by the rush of air, of movement.

Suppressing a gasp, she came up on her elbow but could see nothing.

Someone was there.

Her heart slamming against her ribs, she was mentally cataloging everything on the table that could be used as a weapon, when a man said, "I didn't mean to disturb ye."

Duncan. Letting her breath out in a rush, she lay back and tried to breathe normally, but it was hard to be normal around the man who held her life in his hands, who made her remember their arousing kiss every time she simply looked at him.

And now they were alone in the darkness.

"You have every right to be here," she murmured. "This is your chamber."

"I'm not taking it back. The men and I are leaving, and I needed something from my trunk. I'd have brought the trunk out before now, but space is tight in the great hall."

"You're leaving? In the middle of the night?" She hated how vulnerable she sounded.

"'Tis just before dawn, hardly the middle of the night."

His voice out of the darkness seemed close, intimate—especially since she was lying in his bed, wearing nothing but a nightshift. She'd never thought of clothing as protection, but the layers of chemise, petticoats, stays, and gown had always served that purpose.

And there was that kiss. Oh yes, they'd kissed. She probably should not lie here in the dark, listening to his breathing, remembering. But her awareness of him was becoming so thick it felt like she couldn't take a deep breath.

"You can light a candle from the brazier," she said. "I don't want you to trip. I've tried to keep things neat for you, but it seems to be . . . difficult for me."

He lit a candle, and the flare of light illuminated the harsh, handsome lines of his face, stark cheekbones and grim mouth. He set the candle on the table and didn't look at her.

"Is it another shipment?" she asked.

"Perhaps." He bent over his trunk, lifted the lid and rummaged within.

More children stolen away from all they knew. She shivered and prayed that Duncan and his men rescued them with great success and no loss of life.

"How long will you be gone?" There was that foolish vulnerability again.

He glanced over his shoulder at her. "Ye may be sleeping in my bed, but ye shouldn't ask me such things as a wife would."

Arousal curled warm within her at the thought of being a wife to this man. The feeling was heightened because he seemed to be thinking the same thing. By candlelight, she could see the set of his jaw, the way his fists clenched and his breathing increased. She reminded herself that he was obviously fighting such thoughts. But they were alone in the shadows, and the kiss hovered between them with a tension she'd never imagined.

It was wrong to want to kiss him, when she could not offer him a single detail about herself.

He let out a breath and straightened after closing the trunk. She could see his big body turning toward her out of the shadow.

His voice soft, he said, "I cannot blame ye for thinking we are more intimate than we should be. I've told ye things about my family that I never speak of."

The tension that had been growing between them dissolved into sorrow. She shivered, remembering the revelation that his father had killed his mother. She'd spent all day imagining his childhood with parents who hated each other, a mother so vindictive she took out her jealousy on a child, and then that terrible crime. No wonder he was so sympathetic to the children he rescued—he'd want to protect them from what he'd gone through.

"Perhaps you needed to say it aloud," she said. "I was grateful to help you in some way after all you've done for me. I will not abuse the knowledge."

"Everyone here already knows."

"Was your father arrested?"

"Perhaps ye don't remember the way of the Highland clans. My father was chief. He could decide life or death for his people, even his wife. She'd committed a grave sin, harming a child. None challenged his right to decide her punishment."

She didn't ask for details—it must have been terribly painful for him. She couldn't imagine the horror of one parent killing another, regardless of the justification.

Reaching out, she touched his arm. He was in his shirtsleeves, and he felt so warm against her palm. "I'm so sorry for what you suffered."

His muscle tensed beneath her hand. "I do not need your pity."

"You have my sympathy, Laird Carlyle. Or may I call you Duncan? 'Mistress' and 'laird' are so awkward between two people who've"—she was about to say "kissed," but realized it would be best not to bring it up—"discussed what we've discussed."

He moved his arm away from her. "We should remain formal."

She knew that was for the best, but in her mind he was already "Duncan." "Yes, I suppose you're right."

At the door, he paused with his hand on the curtain. "We will return when we can. I'll not leave the cave unprotected. Ye're safe here."

Then he was gone. Safe? How could she feel safe when she didn't know who she was, when every attempt to regain her memory had failed? She blew out the candle, then rolled over on her stomach, hugging the pillow against her cheek. He cared about her, though he didn't want to show it. Were all men like that, trying to be so gruff and imposing, hiding any softer feelings?

He didn't want to care about her—she couldn't fail to realize that. He was an outlawed chief, doing his best to protect his clan. He didn't have time to dally with a woman he could never have.

But she could imagine being held in those strong arms, feeling safe and desired.

With a groan, she rolled onto her back and put the pillow over her face, as if she could smother such fantasies. What man could ever risk caring about someone like her, when every important detail of her life was unknown?

THE pack train of horses seemed to appear out of the predawn mist, one after the other. Casks roped across their backs juggled inelegantly as they found their footing down the hillside and the narrow dirt path. Duncan and his men waited silently, until he had a rough estimate of two dozen whisky-laden horses, and a half-dozen mounted guards. The Duffs had added two more guards to this shipment's journey, had planned a new route south, but the earl or his men obviously underestimated Duncan's determination. Duncan had let several shipments go unharmed, until once again the Duffs were lax about the danger, as if Duncan might have abandoned this enterprise. That wouldn't happen. He wanted the earl to know that another batch of whisky would bring him no illegal profits.

The mist sank low in the glen as the pack train descended, the packhorses picking their way down a sloping path. Duncan and his men hid beneath a fall of rock, and at his whistled signal, they rose up, the mist swirling off them. The packhorses in the lead reared, and one man fell from the saddle, while Ivor knocked the other to the ground. Duncan took care of the first with a blow to the head with the hilt of his claymore. The lead horses tried to run, their neighs like screams, but they were all tied in a long line. One horse fell on the uneven path; a cask of whisky cracked open and splashed across the rocks in a pungent explosion.

Several mounted guards on either side raced toward them. Two dozen Carlyle men used swords and cudgels to bring a half-dozen men down, overwhelming them with no loss of life.

Only when the men lay groaning along the path did Duncan wipe down his claymore, sheath it, and say to his men, "Bandage the worst of the wounds and then tie them together."

They left the Duff men without horses, where they'd eventually help untie each other and have to wander for help.

But the whisky—the whisky and its profits were for the Carlyles. As Duncan led the pack train south toward the River Clyde and their hiding place, in his mind he was already making plans to signal the ship captain, who regularly came into the Firth of Clyde, and unload this cargo.

And Duncan realized he would continue thinking about these things he'd done a dozen times, anything to keep from thinking about Catriona, whom he'd left sleepy and warm in his bed.

Damn his traitorous body. He should have been focused on retrieving his clothing, but instead, he'd had to grasp every ounce of control just hearing her breathe. And when he'd lit the candle, her gold eyes had looked so ethereal and luminous. Much as she'd kept herself covered, just *knowing* she wore so little had been erotic. He'd wanted to draw her up against him, free her long plait of hair and spread it through his hands.

To make matters worse, she might welcome his attention. He'd hoped that telling her ugly details about his past might make her keep her distance, but it had only encouraged her. He kept reminding himself that she was the daughter of his enemy. She could regain her memory any day. He knew it would change everything.

But what if she didn't? What happened if she stayed this way forever? She wouldn't remember her family, her friends—she would only have him and his clan. Keeping her from the earl could only last so long, he reminded himself sternly. He hadn't meant to keep her away from them forever. Yet he'd found no clue that anyone was looking for her, which was so suspicious he couldn't keep ignoring it.

And yet . . . here he was, focused on her rather

than on the whisky shipment. Ivor gave him a frown and Duncan put Catriona from his mind.

IT had been a day and a half of fear. Catherine's constant worry for Duncan and his clan preyed on her thoughts, hour after hour. She hoped to distract herself by helping with the laundry in cauldrons outside the cave, or learning Gaelic from Maeve, but such measures proved useless. Mid-morning the second day, Catherine felt a need to escape, to be alone with her fears and confusion, as if she'd climb out of her skin trying to keep calm and expressionless. She left the cave, and to her surprise no one stopped her. Angus did follow along behind, at a distance that fooled no one. What did it matter, as long as she could breathe fresh air, feel the wind in her face?

She couldn't just hide in the cave and pray for her memories to return, so she took the only path she knew, along the cliff wall to the horse paddock. There was a three-sided stable where the horses could escape the weather. Inside she found grooming equipment, a currycomb and brush. These felt right and good in her hands, and when one of the friendly geldings nudged her, she began to curry him. She crooned softly, not paying attention to her words, just basking in the sun and the breeze and letting her worried thoughts drift away.

"Do ye hear yourself?"

Duncan. Catherine whirled about, the currycomb clutched tightly to her chest, as if to stop herself from flinging her arms around him in relief. He looked well, whole, leaning his forearms on the top rail of the paddock, watching her with those dark, arresting eyes.

"Hear myself?" she repeated. "I don't think I was saying anything important."

"Ye spoke with a faint Scottish accent."

Her eyebrows went up. "I did? I didn't do it deliberately."

He shrugged. "I heard it."

"I'm not disagreeing." Eyeing him, she continued to pet the horse, who put his head over her shoulder as if he wanted her attention. She glanced at the gelding, so close, and smiled.

"Ye're good with animals."

It almost sounded begrudging.

"Good with animals, and possibly Scottish. Those are two clues I didn't have before."

"You were riding a horse when ye fell down the ravine, and ye're in Scotland. These two new 'clues' aren't all that unexpected."

She rolled her eyes. "Ye don't understand how important it is to know something about myself." She let the silence grow a bit, eyeing him. "Did ye bring home any kidnapped children?"

He shook his head.

Her chest tightened uncomfortably. "You were too late?"

"Nay, there were no children to be found. 'Tis rather soon, considering we just rescued Finn's group a week ago. 'Twill take them a while to come up with new men. We made certain that the ones holding Finn and the other boys won't be capable of riding a horse, let alone stealing children, for a long time. Eventually the sheriff will run out of men and be forced to show himself. Just not last night."

After nodding her approval, Catherine leaned her head along the horse's neck, and the great animal allowed it.

"So I'm good with horses," she began. "Might I go riding?"

She thought he might have stiffened, just a bit.

"Nay."

"There's a village nearby. I saw the smoke from it. What's its name?"

"Nothing ye've heard of."

"How do you know?"

"Because if ye lived so close, or had visited, I'd already know about ye and I'd ken where ye're from." His gaze slid away from her.

"So I'm still not to know where I am."

He frowned. "'Tis better this way."

"I would never reveal anything that would jeopardize your clan," she said softly.

He didn't answer, and she got a faint tingle of premonition, as if there was another reason he was being so vague with her. She studied him closely as if she could read something in his expression— but she was only kidding herself. He might as well be wearing a mask.

"Mistress Catherine!"

Finn came racing down the path from the cave and skidded to a halt when he saw Duncan. The boy's blue eyes, momentarily full of excitement, now shuttered as he murmured, "Beggin' yer pardon, yer lairdship."

"No apology necessary," Duncan said, leading his own horse into the paddock.

"We'll unsaddle him for you." Catherine stepped forward to take the reins. "It'll be a good lesson for Finn. Riding a horse can be fun, but taking care of the animal is an important obligation."

Duncan didn't release the reins immediately.

"Do you not trust me to see to your prized possession?" she teased in a quiet voice.

"My horse is far more important than that," he said, then let go of the reins. "I trust ye."

Was she supposed to thank him for the great honor? she thought wryly. But perhaps it was an honor to him—his horse was his constant companion, his means of transport. So instead of smiling, she simply nodded.

"I think I should take the saddle off," he began.

"No. We can take care of it."

He arched a brow. "Call one of the men if you have need."

"We won't, but thank you."

Duncan turned and walked out of the paddock. Finn didn't move, but Catherine thought he shrank into himself when the chief walked by. Duncan had rescued him, had proven himself— why was Finn still so afraid?

Once Duncan was out of sight, Catherine gestured for Finn to come closer. The little boy stared up at the massive horse, wide-eyed.

"He won't hurt you," she said.

"He might step on me by accident," Finn insisted.

Some of the bad things that had happened to Finn hadn't been deliberate, but he'd been wounded anyway. She didn't blame him for being cautious.

"Do you want to sit on his back before we remove the saddle?"

"Nay!" He gasped and backed away.

"I won't force you. It's your choice. But come closer so I don't have to shout."

For at least an hour, she talked about horses, their equipment and care. Finn never seemed bored, but more than once he gave her a glance that seemed skeptical.

"Go ahead and ask whatever's on your mind," she said patiently.

"Well, ye're a lady," Finn said with solemn logic. "Ye must have had servants. But ye know all about horses."

"If you're going to ride one, you need to be able to care for it when you're traveling."

Suddenly, she had a flash of memory, saw a chestnut horse in a fine stable and felt a deep love for the animal as she'd tended it. And then it was gone, and she was left to wonder if that had been her first glimpse of her old life. She wanted to be excited and hopeful—maybe her memories would return after all—but she also felt the deep sadness of knowing that if the memory had truly been her old horse, that horse had suffered in the fall down the ravine and been put out of its misery.

She comforted herself by teaching Finn what she knew. Perhaps she could instill a love of horses in the boy, so that he could find pride in being accomplished—and it would give him something

to do besides sit apart from everyone else and
brood.

FOR a few moments, Duncan watched Catriona
and Finn. Studying her seemed like all he wanted
to do lately. She offered gentle kindness to the boy,
and Duncan couldn't understand her easy tem-
perament. She'd come from a terrible father, a man
who profited off selling innocent children.

For all Duncan knew, losing her memory had
changed Catriona's entire personality. She was
the wealthy, pampered daughter of an earl, and
if she knew what Duncan was doing to her, she'd
hate him. He had to remind himself at all times
that they were enemies.

Because watching her with the little boy un-
nerved him, twisted things inside him, made him
feel too soft and warm. He prided himself on ex-
amining everything he did with objective eyes.

He couldn't be objective about Catriona.

And he couldn't stop watching her. Instead
of retreating to her chamber—his chamber—as
usual that night, she stayed out with the men
gathered around one of the fires. They were celebrating the success of their smuggling raid, toast-
ing each other with Duff whisky, but she didn't
know that. Duncan knew she only saw their high
spirits, and now that she was no longer quite the
prisoner within the cave, perhaps she felt free to
enjoy herself.

But it made everything worse for him. He was
forced to watch her smile at Ivor, at Angus, at Torcall. Even Melville's glower couldn't douse her

good mood. She listened to them tease her to try some whisky, until she finally did. The sight of her face going red sent the men into gales of laughter, and when she wheezed in a breath, Duncan saw even Finn giggling.

To his surprise, she motioned for another dram, the men hooted their encouragement, and this time, she sipped it with more decorum. She listened to their stories of life in the Highlands, the freezing mornings bathing in a loch, the cattle they'd stolen, the redcoats they'd outraced.

She grew tipsy enough that she was all set to learn the bawdiest song the men knew. When she stood up to lift her glass, she teetered and caught herself on Ivor's shoulder.

Duncan rose up. "I believe that will be all, laddies."

They protested halfheartedly.

"Don't stop our fun," Catriona begged.

"I'll not stop *their* fun, only yours. Ye'll not be happy if ye're puking through the night."

She twisted her face into something so funny, that even he almost smiled amid the roaring laughter of his clan.

"Aye, well, men, I be off," she said, her Scottish accent perfect.

That caused even more laughter. She took a step toward the passageway at the back of the cave, and reeled to one side, where Ivor caught her arm. Duncan strode forward and lifted Catriona into his arms. She was warm and curved in all the right places. He'd held her like this before, when she'd been a stranger, but now—now he knew too much about her. Now she made him feel a yearning that bordered on desperate, and not just for her body.

"Whee!" she cried, kicking her feet, even as her head fell back.

When she flung her arms over her head, he dipped to keep her securely against his chest. This was not the same as holding the dazed, sodden woman he'd held the first day they'd met. She literally squirmed to get comfortable against him, and he was glad his plaid hid his reaction. The women stood together and watched him curiously, but he could have sworn Maeve smiled with approval.

Maeve made no secret that she thought he needed to find a wife, to "settle him down." As if he could ever bring a "Lady Carlyle" to live in a cave. And choosing Catriona? He was using her for revenge, and lately it seemed as if his punishment would be never having her, the sweet, intelligent, and compassionate woman that she was. If Maeve only knew . . .

Someone had already lit a candle in his bedchamber, and the curtain made the flame dance on the rough stone walls.

"'Tis like the spirits, dancing in the night," she murmured, then chuckled.

That accent again. He wondered if other things would begin coming back to her.

As if she read his mind, she said, "I remembered something today."

He froze just before laying her on the pallet. He stared down at her flushed face, his gut clenching, and waited, even as he told himself that if she'd remembered anything significant, she would not have been enjoying the evening with her captors.

She tugged the hair just above his ear and grinned. "Nothing important, silly, just a horse that might have been mine in a fine stable."

He didn't think a woman had playfully tugged his hair before. The women he'd known intimately had been brief moments in the dark, satisfying a need in them both, and little else.

But Catriona, drunk though she was, felt comfortable enough to tease him, even as she devastated him with hints that her memory might slowly be returning. This woman who mischievously lounged in his arms would then turn into a she-devil, and instead of tugging his hair, might rake his face with her nails.

"What do you think of my memory?" she asked lightly.

When he would have risen, she caught the front of his coat and held him there, until he put a knee down to balance himself.

"Duncan?"

His Christian name on her tongue felt as intimate as he had feared it would, but he didn't correct her. "'Tis a random memory, to be sure."

Her smile fading, she said, "I fear that mare was the one ye had to kill. I even had a dream about her last moments alive, as the earth gave way beneath us in a storm. Just that frozen moment, not the actual . . . fall. I thought it just a dream, a memory I'd created, but the horse was the same."

That was two more memories she'd had, and her brogue had only broadened. Was her time with him growing short? He was surprised at the surge of melancholy such thoughts brought forth. Though at first her presence in their encampment had made things awkward, now she was a lovely helper, whose smiles and enthusiasm had won over many a cynical clansman—perhaps even him. Seeing her with Finn only made him think about the family he had denied himself. He was too eager to see her every time he entered the cave, too aware of her presence, too full of longing for her touch.

"I am sorry for your pain," he said hoarsely, then cleared his throat.

He was still bent over her, and he knew he should rise and step away, but she was all languid and prettily blushing. Her lacings and stomacher pressed her breasts above the neckline, and he longed to lean over and explore the valley between them with his lips and tongue.

"You have nothing to be sorry for," she said, cupping his cheek.

Her touch sent a jolt of urgent need through his aching body. He felt poised on the edge of control.

"You have done all you can to help me," she whispered. "If I never remember anything else, I will have to be content."

"Content?" he echoed in surprise. "How could ye be content to never find your family?"

"Because I've realized that family is what I make of it, and who I choose to be with."

Those golden eyes searched his with a yearning he could no longer resist. He bent his head and kissed her, exploring the softness of her lips, tasting the sweetness that was her mouth. Her hands clutched his garments, pulling him closer, and with a groan he deepened the kiss, letting his tongue enter and mate with hers. His chest against the softness of hers, one arm beneath her neck, he let his other hand roam her side and hip, feeling the round fullness beneath skirt and petticoats. Back up he traced his hand, where the swell at the side of her bodice taunted him.

Was he the sort of man who'd grope a woman who'd been addled by whisky? He seemed to be the sort of man who took advantage of a woman with no memory. He broke off the kiss, resting his forehead against hers, trying to catch his breath.

"Duncan."

The sound of his name on her lips made him shiver.

"Don't stop." She turned up her face, grazing his chin with a kiss.

"I must—*we* must."

"But it feels so good to be in your arms."

She moaned and squirmed, and it was all he could do to remember his honor, the little he had left.

He straightened, and her hands fell away from him as he rose stiffly to his feet. "Good night," he said, giving her a nod, almost a bow, of respect.

Her hands fell back to her chest; her eyes watched him with a yearning he couldn't face.

Turning aside, he asked, "Shall I send Maeve in to help ye undress?"

Unspoken was his belief that Catriona might have wanted *him* to perform those deeds.

She shook her head. "I'll be fine. Good night."

He marched his unwilling legs down the passageway and into the cave. Most were so engrossed in merriment that they didn't notice his arrival, except for some knowing and even amused glances. He ignored them.

His whisky was waiting on the table where he'd left it, and he downed it in one gulp, letting the fire burn him. He had to face the fact that he didn't want her to remember her life before he'd found her, that he thought they could somehow be together. It was a ridiculous fantasy, and he should have known better, but apparently his body did not. She made him feel alive, beyond duty and anger and vengeance. Being with her reminded him of families, of children, of a wife who might wait only for him.

He was a fool. He could never have her, for if he did, he'd spend the rest of his life waiting for her to remember the truth of how he'd tricked her, how he'd used her in vengeance against her own father.

And that look of desire, maybe even someday love, would turn to hatred.

CHAPTER 9

At the first sounds of voices in the great hall, Catherine opened her eyes—and groaned. Her head pounded, and she knew the oncoming day wouldn't be pleasant.

As memories of her drunken behavior flooded back, she clapped her arm to her forehead and winced with embarrassment. She'd practically thrown herself into Duncan's arms. If he hadn't shown restraint, they might have been entwined naked together right now.

For a moment, she couldn't think what was wrong with that. This was Scotland; she knew there were trial marriages, where people could change their minds at the end of a year.

She shot upright in disbelief at where her thoughts were going. Marriage? She'd known the man less than a fortnight! And considering that was still better than how little she knew about herself, she had to be crazed. She dropped her face into her hands. Very well, she was crazed—with lust. And she was rationalizing how she could protect her reputation and still be with him.

Be with a clan chief in exile, who was encamped in a cave.

This was ridiculous; she had to go speak with Duncan, apologize, come to some kind of understanding.

After she lit a candle, she washed and began the process of dressing. To distract herself, she remembered last evening, and the way the men had seemed to accept her in their midst, making her feel totally comfortable for the first time. They'd spoken some English, and some Gaelic. Since Maeve had been teaching Catherine, she'd begun to recognize a few words now and then. But something about the men's discussion seemed . . . off. It was something about the whisky itself. She knew most of the whisky distilled in the Highlands was illegal, to avoid the high taxes on malt. It was so common that everyone knew about it. The British didn't often come to do anything about it. So the men were probably just hiding knowledge of their illicit stills.

There was something more important she needed to do. After she finished dressing, she went to the great hall. Many men were still rolled up in their plaids or beneath blankets on their pallets. Naturally, the women were awake, gathered near cauldrons and at the work tables. Catherine looked but didn't see Duncan anywhere, so she left the cave. The sun had just risen above the horizon, though mist still obscured it in the glen. Duncan wasn't at the paddock, and with Angus watching her, she knew she dared not go anywhere else.

As she approached the cave entrance again, she saw Duncan coming from the opposite way, bare-chested and damp, but for the plaid wrapped around him. His wet chestnut curls dripped to his shoulders. He must have bathed outdoors, instead of using the cave pool. Had he not wanted to awaken her? When he saw her, he came up short, face freshly shaven, his brows deep in a frown. She tried to keep her gaze on his face, but it was difficult, with so much glistening skin.

"There you are," she said with determination.

"Ye've been looking for me?"

"I needed to talk to you about last evening." She glanced at Angus, who stiffened and hurried back inside the cave.

"Do ye want me to apologize?" he asked.

Her lips parted. "Of course not! If anyone should apologize, it's I. I know we're attracted to each other, but that doesn't give me the right to encourage you."

The faintest of smiles touched his lips. "I'm not certain I've ever heard a woman speak so boldly."

"Women should say what's on their minds, just like men."

He came closer, eyeing her with interest. "And what do ye feel ye must say?"

"Why . . . what I just said. There's something between us, but I believe it's best not to complicate things by acting upon it—right now."

He cocked his head. "Right now? So there'll be a time when ye snap your fingers, and I'll understand we're to start courting?"

"Yes—no! That sounds so cold-blooded."

To her surprise, he boldly looked down her body, then said, "I'm no feeling exactly cold-blooded about ye."

Flustered, she tried to look anywhere but at his wet chest, where the hair grew in damp swirls, and made her want to . . . touch it. Touch him. She took a deep breath. "I understand feeling . . . heated. But . . . we don't know who I am," she finished softly.

Her life was a void stretching out behind her. To not know oneself was frightening and over-whelming. It took all of her mental strength to keep her anxieties at bay. But every time she kissed him, those anxieties later rose up as if to drown her with all she did not know about herself, all she could not offer him.

The warm look in his eyes disappeared so fast, she almost thought she imagined it.

"Aye, ye have the right of it," he said, beginning to move past her into the cave.

And all she could think was that she didn't want to be wise or sober. She wanted to be young and wild, testing her wiles on a tall, handsome Scottish outlaw.

AFTER Catriona's confession, Duncan's day only got worse. His messenger returned with missives from two different noblemen from whom he'd re-quested help convincing the magistrates to end the bounty on his head. But the two men had no wish to associate with Clan Carlyle, and had re-jected him. Disgruntled, he went to the one place where he knew he'd never be rejected—his sister's home.

His oldest sister, Winifred, had married a lawyer who'd been raised in Clan Carlyle and moved to Glasgow. His second, Muriel, lived nearby, in the village of Ardyle, married to a clansman who owned cattle and a bit of farmland.

When he arrived, Muriel was working in her vegetable garden, her youngest on a blanket in the shade. Duncan casually sat on a bench near the blanket, and eyed the sleeping babe as if it might jump at him like a spider.

When Muriel still didn't notice him, he said, "Where are your other terrors, sister?"

She gave a little shriek, came off her knees, and collapsed onto her backside when she saw him. "Duncan Carlyle, why must ye give me a fright every time ye visit?"

He gave her a faint smile. "Because 'tis so easy to do."

Muriel looked around with a frown. "I told Robby to fetch a pitcher of water to drink, but that was some time ago. Robby!" she called.

The four-year-old appeared out of the bushes as if awaiting a summons. His face was filthy, his dark hair wet with sweat. "Aye, mum? I was followin' a worm."

"The water?" she said patiently. "Perhaps your uncle would like some, too."

Robby blinked at Duncan. "Good day, uncle," he said politely.

Duncan nodded. "A good day to ye, too, nephew. And water sounds refreshing."

Muriel rose to check on the sleeping bairn, then came to sit beside Duncan on the bench. She gravely took the pitcher and ladle, offering some to Robby first, then Duncan, then took a deep draft herself.

"Ah. Thank ye, lad. Now ye may go back to your worm-chasing. But don't jump over—"

Robby vaulted right over the blanket and the baby, who slept on.

"—Alice," Muriel finished weakly. Glancing at Duncan, she said, "The lad does not walk if he can run. He'll wear me out before Alice is his age."

"His da was never one to sit still himself."

"Stop saying I told ye so."

Duncan raised both hands. "I didn't. Ye said such a man would always work hard rather than sit around on his arse."

"And he does," Muriel said tiredly. She took another dipper full of water, then eyed Duncan. "So I hear ye have a guest up in the caves."

He grimaced. "I figured ye'd hear about her from Maeve."

"Maeve might be my closest friend, but I actually heard from Ivor, when he came to visit his mum."

"Traitor," he grumbled. "I hope he didn't gossip with anyone else."

"He didn't, only to me. So ye didn't want us to know ye have a fine lady trapped in a cave?" she said, with both amusement and curiosity in her voice.

"I'm here, aren't I?"

"So ye planned to tell me." Her look was full of skepticism. "Mmph. No wonder ye haven't visited much—although 'tis nothing new."

"Ye know why I don't come often," he said in a low voice.

"Aye, we need to be protected, so ye've told us." Muriel rolled her eyes. "We are not outlawed, Duncan, only you."

"But I don't want the clan punished for what I've done, any more than it already has been. So I'll continue to avoid ye as much as I can."

"No one but Carlyles even travel to our remote village."

"They could track the cattle your husband has thieved."

She pretended outrage. "James is a law-abiding man. But if the English and the Lowlanders insist on making it difficult for us to feed our families, then they get what they deserve."

For several minutes, they said nothing, just studied the barren mountaintops that surrounded their glen, and their silence gradually turned companionable once again. When he was a wee bairn, Muriel had tried to soften the blow of their mother's wrath, even though she was often the target herself. Their older sister, Winifred, was far better at staying on Mother's good side, saying just what the woman wanted to hear. When their father had killed their mother, Winifred had already been married and living far away. Muriel and Duncan had only had each other as their father succumbed to guilt.

Now she regarded him with obvious determination. "Aye, I'll take your fine lady in for ye. I was wondering when ye'd come ask me."

"That's not why I'm here."

Her determination changed to astonishment. "What? She's to stay in that cave with your rough men?"

"And women. Maeve is taking good care of her."

"Of course no one knows better than Maeve how to make a guest feel at home. But . . ." Astonishment changed to curiosity. "Ye don't want to rid yourself of a woman who has no memories of her past?"

Duncan hesitated, and then realized he could not lie to his sister, even to protect her. "I cannot rid myself of her because I know who she is."

He thought Muriel might exclaim in disbelief, but she only narrowed her eyes and studied him as if he was one of Robby's worms.

"Go on," she said coolly.

Releasing a sigh, he told her about finding Catriona and recognizing her as the daughter of the Earl of Aberfoyle.

Muriel threw her arms wide. "But ye did not feel it right to tell her—or anyone else?"

"At first I thought she was lying about the memory loss, that if returned to her father, she might reveal our location."

"But when ye knew she'd truly lost her memory . . ."

"Now her father is discovering what it's like to be missing a daughter, just as the poor parents of Clan Carlyle have had to do because of that man's evil and greed."

He knew his voice had grown cold, because his sister looked away from him and hugged herself.

"Och, Duncan, what have ye done." She bowed her head.

"What had to be done. I saved her life. She doesn't know anything about being a Duff. When I think her father has suffered enough, I'll return her."

"I think ye're making a mistake that will haunt ye."

"It won't be the first. But ye must swear to tell no one. I should not have told ye, nor made ye bear the burden of silence, but I couldn't lie, not to you."

"But ye've lied to everyone else who believes in ye."

"They'd understand," he said stubbornly. "Now ye know why I have to refuse your offer of housing the lass. She feels safe with us, and I need to keep an eye on her."

"Duncan Carlyle, when she regains her memory and kens what ye've done . . ."

"I'll deal with it when it happens—*if* it happens."

Muriel stretched out her legs and leaned back on the bench. Her eyes closed a bit, but she never lost sight of Robby, who was now moving on his knees through the grass, following the progress of his worm.

"Is the poor lass not afraid with all of ye?" she said quietly.

"She was uncertain and afraid at first. But she's settled in well."

Muriel rolled her eyes. "What is she doing all day?"

"Working with the women."

She shot upright with a gasp. "Ye're treating her like a servant?"

"Aye," he said with sarcasm, "'twas my exact thought when I found her bleeding in the rain— look, another serving woman to help the cause."

She folded her arms across her chest and grumbled, "Well, how am I to know. 'Tis your first kidnapping, after all."

He grimaced. "She insisted upon helping, claimed that she owed us for taking her in. I told her she's a guest, gave her the only bedchamber—"

"*Your* bedchamber?"

He deliberately kept his gaze on the sleeping bairn, so Muriel couldn't uncannily read his mind about the night's excursion into that chamber and what had happened. "Aye, 'tis not as if I don't sleep beside my men when we're on the road."

"Hmm."

Alice began to fret, and with a cooing sound, Muriel picked her up and put the babe on her shoulder. She looked at Duncan over the little bonneted head. "I understand that ye've taken responsibility for her. But what happens if her memory never returns? Are ye going to return her so that all believe her reputation destroyed? Ye'd have to marry her then."

Duncan stiffened. Much as he desired Catriona, nothing beyond unrequited lust was ever going to happen. "Nay, I will not. There are over two dozen people with us at all times, proof that she's been safe." Now he really was lying to his sister. "And even if she wanted to, I would never allow a woman to be with me when I have so little to offer."

Her expression crumpled into sorrow. "Oh, Duncan, don't say such things. Ye're chief of the Clan Carlyle. Ye'll find a way to reverse the ruling against ye. Those noblemen ye wrote to—"

"Already told me they will not help."

"Then another way will present itself." Her eyes focused on Robby, who'd disappeared behind the well. She held out Alice, her little blanket drooping, her head still tipped forward in sleep.

Duncan leaned back on the bench as Muriel put the babe on his chest.

She lifted her skirts and strode to where her son had disappeared. "Robby! Stop right there!"

Alice barely felt like any weight at all, as if Duncan lifted even one hand, she could blow away in a light breeze. Tilting his head down, he watched her yawn with those tiny, perfectly formed lips, then settle right back against his chest into a deeper sleep.

For several long minutes, he could hear Muriel giving a low scolding to Robby, but Duncan was alone with Alice. The bairn was as needy of her mum as his clan was of him. He felt the responsibility of that position—did the Earl of Aberfoyle feel the same for Catriona? Then why wasn't the man looking for her?

CHAPTER 10

It had been easy for Catherine to go for a stroll, to stretch her legs and escape the smell of so many bodies, cooking fires, and a recent batch of meat that had gone bad. Angus, her shadow, was still with her, but after she promised she would only roam the area around the cave, he didn't protest when she walked past the paddock and found a path heading up the cliff side, to the castle, she hoped. When he called her name, she paused, her mind scrambling for a way to persuade him, but all he said was that the way was steep.

"I'm ready for the challenge," she called back.

She heard him telling another man where they were going, but she only lengthened her stride before Ivor or someone had second thoughts about letting her walk alone.

The way was steep, but Cat felt energized using her muscles and breathing deeply of the heather-scented air. Though the castle above was deserted, someone walked this path regularly, and she guessed that it was probably Duncan. He felt powerfully responsible for his clan, and she imagined he felt a duty to the castle as well. He was an honorable man, the kind any woman would be proud to be with.

Soon her rambling thoughts faded as her breath huffed and sweat broke out on her forehead. She tripped over a rock once and came down hard on one knee, but she didn't let that stop her. It was a rare blue-sky day, and the sun beat down on her mercilessly.

She turned a rocky corner, and the castle seemed to rise up as if by magic. It was made of uneven-sized stone, fit together by a master mason. The outer walls were square in shape, with towers at each corner. The walls had been breached in several places, and there was no gate lowered in the gatehouse. The road leading up to it was high with weeds, and Catherine picked her way up it, trying to watch her footing and still gape at the romantic reminder of a wealthier time for Clan Carlyle.

She was just approaching the gates when someone called her name. She looked back and saw Duncan coming toward her, his expression ominous. She caught a final glimpse of Angus giving her a pained look of sympathy as he headed back down the path.

Catherine stopped and waited for Duncan to approach.

"I did not give ye permission to roam the countryside," he said coldly.

A week ago, she might have been afraid of that voice, but not anymore. The chief would be hard on his enemies, but not her.

She gave him her happiest smile. "I know," she said, with conciliation in her voice. "But you allowed me to walk around the cave area, and this is . . . *around* the cave. Angus was with me as well."

He scowled down at her. "Ye dragged the man into your misbehavior."

"It just felt so good to be moving about, using my legs, breathing the country air. Plus, I'd had a revelation, and could hardly contain myself."

"What revelation?" he asked dubiously.

"When Ivor told me you'd gone to visit your sister, I had a sudden memory. I have a brother!"

His expression turned blank.

"I know, it's shocking," she said happily. "I remember nothing about him, can't even picture him, but I know in my heart I have a brother." She put a hand on his arm. "This is more proof that my memory is slowly returning. I feel so much better, although I remind myself that at this pace, it might take a year to remember everything. But I hope not," she added, feeling wistful.

Duncan said nothing.

"How is your sister?"

"Well, thank ye."

"Well? It sounds as if it's only duty that keeps you visiting. I'm sorry to hear that."

"'Tis not duty. I appreciate that she offers wise counsel. Sometimes."

He added that last word in a tone she couldn't quite read.

"And do you offer the same to her?"

He arched a brow. "She's a married woman with

a husband and three bairns. I don't think there's much I can aid her with."

"That's not true. You're a wanted man, and yet you make time to see her, risking your freedom. I'm sure she appreciates that."

He shrugged.

He was obviously uncomfortable with the subject, so she turned to face the castle. "I'm here, so I'd like to go in."

"And if I say no?"

"You won't, will you? I'm fascinated by history."

"Ye've remembered that, too?" he asked dryly.

She lifted her chin, sensing victory. "I'm fascinated right now, so no memory is involved. When was it built? If you know, that is."

"Of course I know. 'Twas finished in 1230."

"That's almost—" And then her voice caught, as she realized she didn't know what year it was.

His voice sounded just a bit softer as he said, "In three years, 'twill be five hundred years."

"Ah, so it's 1727." She tried to sound matter-of-fact, but the sadness came through. "At least mathematics hasn't failed me."

He let out his breath. "Very well, we'll enter the courtyard, but when I tell ye 'tis too dangerous, ye'll listen or I'll throw ye over my shoulder and carry ye out."

She eyed his broad shoulders and thought, *You promise?* But it wouldn't be fair to say those words aloud. "I'll obey your every command."

He rolled his eyes.

She put a hand to her chest in mock outrage. "Do you doubt my honesty?"

He didn't say anything, only strode past her toward the gatehouse. Excitedly, she fell in behind him. Within the gatehouse, the darkness smelled dank and unused, perhaps with even the remains of a dead animal.

She looked up at the black hole that was above her. "No one let the portcullis down?"

"With the walls breached, it matters little."

She winced, hating to appear stupid. Apparently she could suffer the sin of pride about some things. They came out into the courtyard, where weeds and grass grew as high as her waist. The towerhouse, the main building, was part of the wall opposite her, and there were lower buildings along other walls. Everywhere doors were missing, and the weeds seemed to continue right inside.

"How was it damaged?"

"In the war between the Royalists and the Covenanters almost a century ago. After the walls were breeched, my family tried to remain, but a civil war involving Scotland, England, and Ireland made it dangerous to be so unprotected. When the war had ended, my grandfather moved to a manor home in the nearest village, and there we've been ever since."

Left unsaid was that there had obviously not been enough funds to repair the castle.

She eyed the towerhouse again. "You must have kept watch here, since there doesn't seem to be much damage."

"It helps that there are rumors of ghosts."

She shot him an astonished look. "Ghosts? How intriguing."

The wind picked up, and the wail she'd heard from the caves was so much louder, warbling and eerie.

"Ah, I see now. You did that deliberately."

He said nothing.

"How did you do it?"

She didn't wait for an answer, only walked quickly toward the towerhouse's main entrance.

"Catherine, stop—"

But she pretended not to hear, ducking inside. The windows had no glass, but they let in enough light. Broken furniture was scattered across the floor through rubble, and the dirt from her passing rose up and made her sneeze. And yet the wailing continued, and she realized it wasn't just one sound, but a combination of many, a jarring disharmony. She headed for the circular stairs in one corner.

"I said stop!" Duncan's voice reverberated like thunder through the stone great hall.

She stopped on the first step, turning to face him. "Then tell me what it is."

"Reeds."

"What?"

"Dried, hollowed reeds as thick across as my thumb."

He came toward her and she realized that the stair put her face-to-face with him. She was suddenly distracted by the thought of being free to rest her arms on his shoulders, to lean into him, to let him sweep her into his embrace—

All of this, after her vow to stay away from him? She shook herself out of his spell and heard him finish.

". . . in each window upstairs."

"Uh . . . the reeds are in each window?"

He frowned. "'Twas what I just said. They're well fastened, and then when the wind picks up, it whistles through them in that strange, eerie manner."

"Quite clever." She caught herself staring at his mouth and forced herself to look into his dark eyes. "Did you come up with it yourself?"

"My sister and I used to play with them."

"The sister you visited today?"

She found even his nod fascinating. Had she ever been so distracted by a man? She wished she knew. The weak part of her said to take what she wanted, that he wanted it too, that she couldn't stop living—she might never remember anything.

She could never dishonor him that way, especially if they discovered she was married. As always, the thought made her heart begin to race with the fear that she might never know herself at all. But . . . she'd remembered a brother. Instead of taking comfort in that, it suddenly made her almost dizzy. If she had a husband, shouldn't she have remembered that first?

She needed to distract herself. "Why can I not go higher?"

"'Tis far too dangerous."

"What about the battlements?"

"Most certainly not."

"You just don't want me to see the lay of the land."

"There are many ruined castles on hillsides— 'tis more of a concern for your safety."

She didn't believe him but she understood his need to protect his clan. It made it difficult to disobey him, however much she wished to.

"Very well. But take me through the towerhouse."

"It cannot be that ye've been living in a cave too long," he said dryly.

She smiled at his humor, although he did not. She tried to imagine a broad grin on his face, but she couldn't. He was a stoic, serious man. It would be a rare and wonderful gift to be able to make such a man laugh.

"I admit, it's good to get away and see something different." She gave him her winningest smile.

For a long moment he simply frowned at her. She thought all was lost until he suddenly spoke.

"Very well. But I lead, and we won't be going near windows."

That ended up being easier said than done. But grateful that he'd given in, she didn't push her luck much. They wandered through several floors of empty rooms that had been stripped of everything long ago. The longer they looked, the sadder she became. She felt like she could see the ghosts of children running through these corridors, mothers chasing them, fathers looking on with pride and love. The eerie wailing only increased her mournfulness. No wonder people stayed away.

It must be far worse for Duncan, knowing his ancestors built this castle, and he and his clan could no longer live here. She didn't ask if he'd considered restoring it—of course he had. She imagined being an outlaw didn't allow for such funds. She'd heard the men talking, knew how difficult it could be to survive in the Highlands. And Duncan was unable to speak on behalf of his people without risking gaol.

Instead, he helped the most vulnerable, the children, when he could have remained safe in this glen. She looked at his impassive face, as he studied the remains of a dais down below them in the great hall, where once his ancestors had reigned. He was not a man who dwelled on the past, which she thought a very noble trait.

She had to be careful, or she could feel too much for this lonely man.

MOVING from ghost room to ghost room, Duncan felt a sense of unreality. This castle had been made for the Clan Carlyle, to house them, protect them, bring them together in joyous celebration and to console them through the trials of life. A woman like Catriona was made to oversee such a place—he knew her father the earl must surely have plans to marry her to another nobleman with lands and castles and thousands of dependents.

Would she remember that soon? He'd actually felt a chill when she excitedly told him about having a brother. Every day was one day closer to her memory returning, one day closer to her eventual departure. His plan to teach the earl the lesson of a child's absence was backfiring on Duncan— someone he himself would know the loss of her bright spirit in his life.

Ever since his sister had mentioned marriage, he'd been able to think of little else, even though he knew it could never happen with Catriona. Here in this castle, a symbol of the wreckage of Clan Carlyle, she seemed lovely and ethereal, a ghost of all that might have been.

When at last they began the descent down the steep path, Duncan was forced to touch her, though he'd been doing his best to keep his hands to himself. He reached back and helped her down a particularly rocky slope. Once she lost her balance and slid right into him. The tangle of their limbs, even impeded by her skirts, preyed on the weakness of his desire, harming his resolve to remain unaffected. Though she began the descent in cheerful spirits, by the end even she seemed strained and couldn't meet his eyes. All this touching obviously did not lend itself to *her* vow either.

At the bottom, she took a deep breath and said, "Well, I thought that would be easier going down than it had been going up. It's a good thing you were here."

She smiled up at him, and for a long moment their gazes met and held. The unusual golden color of hers kept him captive. He didn't know what he was looking for but he knew he could never find it with her.

CHAPTER 11

Over the next couple days, Catherine tried to honor her promise to keep her distance from Duncan, grooming horses, making soap as she learned Gaelic, trying to draw Finn out. She and Duncan were doing a dance of avoidance, and she worried it was becoming so obvious that it would focus even more attention on their attraction. She had to treat him like everyone else.

One evening, while he was drinking a dram of whisky and frowning as he watched Finn playing alone with his rocks, Catherine set the chessboard on the table next to him.

"Shall we play, Laird Carlyle?" Calling him by his Christian name in front of his clan seemed far too intimate.

He seemed to take a long time to lift his gaze from Finn. She wanted to talk to him about the boy, about the absence of any new memories, all of her frustrations. He wasn't her confidant, she reminded herself sternly.

Duncan eyed the chessboard and spoke dryly. "Ye wish to let another man defeat ye at chess?"

"Perhaps I shall win," she said with confidence, even as she knew she wouldn't do that. It would unravel all her efforts to win the acceptance of his clan.

"Ye can certainly try."

He set up the black pieces, while she set up the white. Several people eyed them with interest, but no one came too near, for which she was grateful.

She held up the king. "Why does this have three crowns?"

He picked up the black king and studied it. "Some say it represents James Stuart, the rightful heir of both England and Scotland until almost forty years ago."

"I may not remember the personal details of my life, but I seem to remember the animosity between England and Scotland—although we're supposed to be one country now." She hesitated. "I know that part of the reason King James was denied the throne was because he was Catholic. Are you?"

"Aye."

"Do you believe in the Stuart right to the throne, and call yourself a Jacobite?"

"Not aloud, if I value my neck." His mouth quirked in half a smile as he moved a pawn. "But I already risk my death in other ways—such beliefs can hardly make it worse."

She moved her own pawn. "I believe there was an uprising against England when I was younger.

And don't ask why I can recall history but not my own name."

"The Fifteen, aye, named for the year."

"Were you part of it?"

He frowned and moved his bishop. "Nay, I was too young."

"You seem to regret that."

"I do. After the Union, England denied vows they'd made, refused Scottish peerages in the House of Lords when they'd promised otherwise, taxed the citizens more than they could bear. A man has to stand up for his country."

They remained silent for several moves, testing each other in the game. She deliberately made a mistake or two, wondering if he noticed.

"For a woman without personal memories," he said, sitting back, "ye seem to remember much of history."

"I told you not to ask about that," she said wryly. "And what does it matter, when I know not which side of the war my family belonged to. In my mind, history is as if I've read about it, not lived it or even heard mention of it. I try to picture a father telling me his experiences with the Fifteen, but there's . . . nothing. I don't know if I'm English or Scottish. But of course, there's my accent, which might indicate the truth."

"Perhaps. Or perhaps it shows ye were educated in England."

She smiled even as she shook her head. Concentrating on the board again, she realized she had him in check. Damn. She would have to move away before he noticed.

"Ye have me beat, lass," he said.

She glanced at him, wide-eyed, trying not to stare at his full mouth as he smiled. "That can't be true. It must be an accident."

He stood up. "Never sell yourself short. And I'm not a man who minds losing to a beautiful woman."

He walked out of the cave and she watched him go, unable to take her eyes off the sway of his perfectly pleated plaid, his strong calves, the breadth of his shoulders. She dropped her forehead to her palm and groaned.

THE next day, a redheaded stranger appeared in the mouth of the cave, a woman who seemed known to everyone, Catherine thought. The woman and Maeve embraced and talked together softly, excitedly, as if long parted.

Maeve motioned for Catherine to join them. Catherine had been sewing a new shirt for Finn, but she put it aside and came forward, curtsying to the stranger, who looked her over with open interest, even as she herself curtsied.

"Mistress Catherine," Maeve said, "this is Mistress Muriel, sister to Himself."

Catherine studied her with far more interest. This woman had been at Duncan's side through a terrible childhood, had known the same sorrows. Now she smiled at Catherine with all the warmth and joy that Duncan could never show.

"Mistress Catherine, Duncan has told me all about your plight," Muriel said. "I thought ye should know that right away, since I came to meet ye."

Duncan had talked about her, Catherine thought in surprise. She didn't know whether to be flattered or intrigued. "I hope he didn't bore you to tears with my travails."

"I confess to the utmost curiosity. I've never met anyone who lost their memory."

"Me neither—oh, wait, I don't know if that's true."

They smiled at each other.

Catherine glanced around the cave. "I feel that my first instinct would be to invite you for tea in the parlor, but . . ." She trailed off, feeling embarrassed.

"I can bring ye both some tea," Maeve said. "Go sit outside on the bench."

"Make sure to bring yourself a cup to join us," Muriel said with mock severity.

Catherine thought it was going to be easy to like Duncan's sister.

As they waited for Maeve on a hand-hewn bench under the shade of a tree, Muriel studied her.

"For such a great blow to the head that ye received, glad I am to see that the worst of it has faded."

Catherine put a hand to her head, where she was still tender. "There's but a small bump."

"And the lovely shade of green still rimming your eyes."

Catherine winced and touched her cheeks. "I didn't realize. Everyone here is kind enough not to mention it. They're very good people—as you must know."

"These are some of the younger, wilder men of the clan, anxious to spite the redcoats and defend their laird. I wasn't certain how they'd treat a lady."

"We don't know that I'm a lady, do we?" Catherine asked wryly.

"Of course we do." Muriel's gaze quickly dropped from hers. "Even in your plain wool gown, ye walk and speak and behave in a way that sets ye apart. I can tell that from just meeting ye."

"Oh, dear." Catherine hated to think it was obvious that she felt . . . different from the other women.

"Ye can't help yourself, of course, and I'm thinking no one is offended. Ye've just seen and experienced more of the world than this wee glen."

Had she? Catherine was growing used to not dwelling on what she couldn't change. That strategy had brought her the memory of her brother, after all. She put a smile firmly back in place. "The men have been quite considerate to me."

"I hear ye help serve them—they'd *better* be kind to ye." Muriel shook her head.

"I don't mind. What else should I do, sit in a corner and do nothing while others work? If I'm a lady, perhaps I do too much of that. Although I do seem to know how to take care of a horse, so that's helpful."

"What are your plans?"

Catherine took a deep breath, and let it out slowly. "I have none. Your brother has patrols looking for signs that someone is searching for me, and so far . . . nothing."

Muriel set her hand gently on Catherine's arm. "I'm sorry. Try not to worry. When ye discover the truth, it'll all make sense."

"I tell myself you're right."

Muriel's sympathy and comforting words made her feel like a friend. With perfect timing, Maeve arrived with a plain tea set on a tray.

"You have everything in that cave," Catherine said in disbelief.

"We've lived here for a while now."

Maeve and Muriel glanced at each other and back at the teapot as Maeve poured. They had the ease of friends, and Catherine imagined there was a wealth of unsaid things between them. She'd try not to pry, but she couldn't let this opportunity go.

"How long has it actually been?" she asked.

Maeve stirred her tea. "I've been here with his lairdship for three years, but Himself has been an outlaw for five."

"Duncan was alone here for two years?" Catherine asked, aghast.

"Duncan, is it?" Muriel said. "Quite informal of ye."

Catherine felt her face growing heated. "'Laird Carlyle' just seemed so long, after a while. It was my idea; he did not give me leave."

The two other women actually smiled at each other, and Catherine was on fire with embarrassment.

"Ye're bold," Muriel said. "I like that." Her smile faded. "For almost a year after he escaped gaol, they hunted for him in large numbers. He moved about constantly, and certainly never came near his own land, for fear of risking the lives of his clan. I hated to think of him alone night after night, never letting himself trust anyone."

"How did he end up here?" Catherine asked.

"He became ill," Maeve said. "At the time, he'd only been in the next glen. In the middle of the night, I found him at my cottage door, near dead of fever."

"He was thinking of my children," Muriel said solemnly, "and refused to come to me, foolish man."

"Considerate man," Catherine insisted. "He has such a fondness for children, he'd never forgive himself if something happened to yours."

Both women eyed her, Maeve with amusement, Muriel with speculation. Could Catherine not think well of the chief, without giving them ideas of an impossible relationship?

"Laird Carlyle only remained in me barn for a night," Maeve continued. "He retreated to the caves to finish healin', and eventually he just . . . stayed. One by one, the men followed him in their quest to aid the children."

"He has spoken to me of his childhood," Catherine said. "Mistress Muriel, do you believe he feels so strongly about helpless children because your own mother was not kind to you both?"

"'Not kind' is quite a polite thing to call our mother. And it's Muriel, please. If we're all mistressing each other to death, we'll never finish a conversation."

"That is generous of you," Catherine said.

"Nothing generous about it. If Duncan has told

ye such secrets from our past, then it seems I can feel comfortable enough to answer your questions. Aye, we were all scarred by our mother's hatred of her life. She had not wanted to marry Father, and never let him or anyone else forget it. She was cruel, impatient, sharp-tempered, and miserable. Ye could almost feel sorry for her, if she wasn't so uncaring about anyone but herself. Father . . . now he was a pitiful soul, just as miserable as Mother in his own way."

"Though he'd never take it out on anyone," Maeve said solemnly.

"But he also never stood up to her—or to anyone," Muriel said. "And *that,* Duncan could not forgive. Father didn't lead our clan into battle against the British in the Fifteen, and Duncan was too young to go himself. Mother caught him trying to sneak off once to join the other clans and . . . let me just say that he couldn't sit for a week. Duncan could never see beyond his disappointment that Father wasn't a warrior, a bold leader of men. He couldn't see that Father had his own strengths: intelligence, compassion. Or if Duncan saw them, he cared little."

"He was young and headstrong then," Maeve said.

Muriel nudged Catherine. "Wild, they called him."

Catherine looked from one woman to the other, wide-eyed and intrigued.

"Many thought he'd never make a good chief, he rebelled so much," Muriel continued. "He kissed the maids, played pranks, rode about the country-side with the other lads. But after Father died, he had the scare of his life."

She made no mention of their father killing their mother, but Catherine wasn't surprised.

"They almost did not elect him chief," Maeve said quietly. "The fact that he hadn't earned their respect, that they only gave him the honor be-cause he was the only son of the chief, changed him, forced him to become a man quickly."

"And he was so young," Catherine said sadly.

"But he proved himself," Muriel said with pride in her voice, "as those of us who knew him best, knew he would. He stood up to the magistrates and sheriff on behalf of the most helpless of our people, and even now he continues to provide for the Carlyle villages, so that we do not starve in the winter."

Catherine perked up. "He provides for the villages—from here? How does he do that?"

Muriel wouldn't meet her eyes. She pressed a hand to the upper slope of her breast. "Oh, dear, I've been away from my bairn too long, and she surely needs to nurse. I'd best be on my way. 'Twas such a pleasure to meet ye, Catherine."

Baffled and growing more curious by the min-ute, Catherine said, "But didn't you want to wait to see your brother?"

"Nay, I came to meet *you*." Muriel smiled, then gave Catherine's hand a squeeze. "And I'm glad I did. I know we'll see each other again soon."

Muriel kissed Maeve on the cheek, then took the

reins of the horse Torcall brought her and mounted. She waved good-bye as she trotted away down the narrow path.

Catherine eyed Maeve, who continued to smile long after they could no longer see Muriel. "You're close to her, I can see."

As if startled out of her thoughts, Maeve blinked and turned to look at Catherine. "Aye. I worked in their home my whole life. She started out as my mistress and became my friend."

"And Laird Carlyle is your friend."

Maeve's gaze turned penetrating. "Nay, not in the same way. He is my laird, my chief."

"And yet the two of you are close like friends," Catherine persisted.

Smiling, Maeve shook her head. "If ye have a question, ask, mistress."

"Catherine."

"Catherine."

It suddenly seemed so important that Catherine have friends too, that she find a way to not feel so alone.

"Maeve, how does Laird Carlyle provide for the villages?"

Maeve didn't look stricken, as Muriel had. "Ye'll have to talk to Himself for those answers."

Catherine sighed. "I thought you might say that."

It was a long day until the men returned from hunting just before supper, and then there were hours of preparing the meat, some to eat soon, some preserved in salt brine for later. It wasn't until the exhausted men had a brief meal, and settled around their fires to retell stories of their hunting adventures, that Catherine was able to take Duncan aside and then lead him outside for privacy.

"Now everyone thinks ye have nefarious plans for me." Duncan folded his arms across his chest, while behind him, the sun had disappeared, leaving a golden halo on the mountains.

"No, if that were true, I would have taken you to the bedchamber."

"In front of everyone? Nay, ye're too shy for that."

"Am I?" she countered.

They looked at each other, and the faint buzz of insects suddenly seemed too loud within the charged silence that stretched between them. His face was shadowed in the growing darkness, but his eyes gleamed.

She cleared her throat. "Your sister visited today."

He took a deep breath. "Impressive change of subject."

"I thought so."

"What did she want?"

"To meet me."

She thought he might have grimaced.

"Of course she did," he said tiredly. "She's incredibly curious."

"A good trait."

"Not necessarily."

"In women?" she demanded with annoyance.

"In anyone. Curiosity can cause too much trouble, and Muriel has always gotten into her share."

Catherine winced. "I'm glad you weren't going

to say that curious women are in the wrong. I find that women are treated very differently from men, and that is unfair."

He arched a brow. "And ye remember examples of that?"

"Why . . . no, I guess not. It's simply something I believe deep inside me. And of course, I don't see any of the men helping the women cook," she added with a pointed frown.

"And I don't see any of the women riding on the hunt," he responded dryly.

She put her hands on her hips and leaned toward him. "Did you ask any of them?"

As she suspected, there was nothing he could say.

"I imagine Carlyle women would be happy to help support the clan in any way they can. In fact, they'd probably accompany you when you . . ." She trailed off and gave him an expectant look.

Impassively, he said, "When I what?"

"Do whatever you do to support your people," she said throwing her hands wide.

"My people farm and raise cattle."

"No, what do *you* do to support them?"

"What do ye mean? My men and I protect them, and we hunt for them. Some of today's meat will be distributed."

She dramatically rolled her eyes. "Your sister said you support the Carlyle villages and keep them from starving, and I don't think it's by hunting alone. When she realized what she'd said, she couldn't bid me good-bye quickly enough. And Maeve said I should talk to you about it."

"Another example of too much curiosity."

"It's something you do at night," she mused, remembering when the men had returned without any rescued children.

"There are many things I do at night."

His voice had dropped into a deep range that seemed to slide across her skin with a promise of sin.

"You're doing that on purpose," she accused.

"What?"

Those dark, gleaming eyes dropped lower, and she felt as if he could see right through her fichu.

She crossed her arms over her breasts. "You're trying to distract me."

"Is it working?"

"Yes—no! Your men were celebrating your big secret that night when I drank too much. They were speaking in Gaelic, and Maeve is teaching me your language. It was something about the whisky we were drinking . . ." She trailed off, frowning.

Though it was near dark, the impassive expression on his face told her enough.

"It's the whisky itself, isn't it?" she mused. "You're smuggling whisky to avoid the British taxes."

He seemed to search her face. "Why is it so important for ye to know any of this?"

She opened her mouth, and nothing came out right away. Why *was* it so important to know everything about the Carlyles—everything about Duncan?

"Because I live here," she said softly. "Because you and your clan are all I know."

He reached out to cup her cheek with his warm,

calloused hand. "Do not be afraid, lass. Ye're safe here. I'll let nothing harm ye."

That wasn't what she was worried about, but she forgot when he slid his hand to the back of her head and drew her toward him for a long deep kiss. She felt both desperate and overcome, frightened and at peace, all those emotions jumbled up inside her, emotions she only found in his arms. He backed her up against the vine-covered rock wall of the cliff with his body, while she explored his mouth as if she could know everything about him.

Cupping her face in his hands, he kissed her forehead, her cheeks, the curve of her jaw, the slope of her throat. Her heart raced at the intimate contact, at the groan he made when he nipped the skin beneath her ear. She dropped her head to one side as he kissed his way down her throat, then lingered at the hollow, with a lick.

To her surprise, he fell to his knees, hands on her hips, and continued his exploration of her collarbones. She clutched his head to her, gasped when he pulled the fichu away, and then his mouth was on the upper slopes of her breasts. His dark hair gleamed under the first touch of moonlight as it peaked over the mountain. When he reached the neckline of her gown and could go no farther, her regret and frustration were sudden and surprising.

Raggedly, she began, "I wish—" and then stopped. She didn't know what she wanted.

And then he licked a gentle line into her cleavage. She shuddered.

"I want ye."

The words were hoarse and quiet, and his breath light across the dampness of her skin.

"Duncan . . ." She didn't know what to say.

"But I won't take ye."

He was right but oh, she wished he wasn't.

"But I can make ye feel such pleasure."

He slid his hands to the front of her hips and up over her bodice. Above her stays, her breasts were only covered by her chemise and the gown. When his hands covered there, squeezed gently, it was as if she'd been shocked by lightning. When his fingers gently squeezed her nipples, she jerked in his arms, feeling a stab of pleasure that shot down within her body.

"Duncan!" his name was an agonized whisper into the darkness. "What are you—" But she couldn't ask, didn't want it to stop.

For a long moment, he buried his face into her neck and kissed her skin, while his fingers played a dance across her breasts that she'd never imagined. She desperately wanted to undo the front laces of her gown, feel his touch on her bare skin, and as if he read her mind, she felt him tugging the front laces loose. She wanted this, but she was afraid to want too much, when nothing could ever be normal between them.

But she wasn't going to marry him, wasn't going to sleep with him, they were just . . . touching.

"Open your eyes," he whispered huskily.

She did so, and in the moonlight, she watched in awe as he slid her chemise down, baring her breasts, which seemed presented to him by the up-thrust of her stays. She should be embarrassed—

but she wasn't. She felt both proud and humble, to affect him, to know how they could make each other feel. Her nipples tightened into points as an evening breeze caressed her.

"My God," he breathed.

Instead of touching her with his fingers, as she'd been silently begging, he leaned forward and touched her with his tongue, a lick across her nipple which made her skin come alive with overwhelming pleasure. She moaned and clutched him to her, and to her astonishment, he sucked her nipple deep into his mouth. Gasping, she arched her body, desperate for him to do more.

Then they heard voices at the entrance of the cave.

They both froze. Oh, God, she would never be able to face the men again. They'd think she was a—

"They cannot see us," Duncan whispered. "Just hold still."

"I can't. When you do—that, my body no longer seems my own."

He inhaled deeply, then said her name with a reverence that surprised her. She was afraid to move, utterly bare to him, even as his men were talking. Then their voices stopped.

"Where are they?" she whispered.

Duncan placed a kiss between her breasts. "The guards changed. One went back inside and the new guard went to the paddock. We're alone now."

And sinner that she was, she wanted him to touch her again. For a long silent moment, neither of them moved or spoke. Her hands were still on his shoulders, and seemingly without her volition, she slid them into the hair at his neck.

With a heavy sigh he rose to his feet. Pressing his cheek to hers, he whispered, "Everything in me cries out for ye, lass. But I—we—cannot."

She nodded, turning away from him to draw her chemise and gown back in place. Her fingers were trembling as she tightened the laces and re-arranged the stomacher. When she was done, she was afraid to face him, but he pulled her against him and rested his cheek against her hair. All the reasons why she couldn't have this life were crowding around her, making her feel embar-rassed and ashamed and sad.

But she put her hands on his arms and they stood there in the moonlight.

"Duncan," she said quietly.

"Hmm?"

The sound of him vibrated against her back, and it seemed almost as intimate as his mouth upon her skin.

"If you were only smuggling your own whisky, I don't believe you would have hidden it from me."

She thought he tensed behind her.

"I'm right, aren't I?"

After a long moment when she thought he would ignore her once again, he said, "Aye."

"So you're stealing whisky, smuggling it, and sharing the profits with your people."

"Aye, and I'm not ashamed of it. We steal it from the nobleman who supports the sheriff and magistrates in their evil deeds, the man who allowed me to be outlawed rather than end the theft of children. So indirectly, he also finances my men and our search to stop him."

"That makes sense to me," she said. "Thank you for explaining it, even though you didn't have to."

He rubbed his cheek slowly against her hair. "What he and the sheriff have done to my clan and to innocent children has to be punished somehow. Right now this is the only means I have."

"Who buys the whisky?"

"Lowlanders, and some is smuggled south by sea. We don't harm the nobleman's men—we steal their horses and tie them up, so their return home is delayed."

"Aren't the casks marked?"

She glanced up and over her shoulder to find him staring down at her in surprise.

"Ye know something about whisky, do ye?" he asked.

She shrugged. "I—don't know. Perhaps I simply assumed."

"These casks aren't marked, which means his lordship is smuggling his own whisky."

"Well, he deserves whatever he gets," Catherine said firmly, then turned around within his arms and faced him. "What can I do to help?"

He seemed to search her gaze. "Catherine—"

"I, too, want to fight against the man who'd condone selling children. It's not fair how you've been treated just for caring deeply about your people."

He briefly closed his eyes, before saying tiredly,

"By helping my men, ye're helping our cause. 'Tis enough."

She wanted to disagree, but couldn't after he'd been so honest with her. "Thank you for trusting me," she whispered. "I never thought anyone would risk telling me the truth after my memory loss."

"Catherine—"

She put a hand to his lips to silence him. "At night, when I try to fall asleep, the enormity of what I've lost stretches before me. But to have your clan accept me, to have you trust me—I am content."

She went up on tiptoes to kiss his cheek, then hurried back inside the cave before she could embarrass herself by crying. Most of the men had found their pallets and were rolled up on the floor in snoring lumps. Maeve was the only one who gave her a worried look, but Catherine offered a shaky smile and crossed the footbridge over the burn and ducked into the passageway. Only when she had drawn the curtain and closed herself into her chamber, lit thoughtfully with a candle by Maeve no doubt, did Catherine sink to the floor and cover her mouth, stifling a sob. She might not have her memories, but she no longer felt alone. The relief was overwhelming.

CHAPTER 12

$\mathcal{D}$azed, his chest tight with pain, Duncan stumbled away from the cave, uncaring of where he might go. The darkness wrapped around him, and the night sky wheeled overhead like a thousand pairs of bright eyes, watching him.

What was he doing? Catriona was a lost innocent and he continued to take advantage of her. It wasn't enough that he'd kidnapped her, but now he was making her depend upon him—hell, he'd told her he wanted her. He was letting her think she had a home with them, and a place in his own life. He might even have taken things further if they hadn't been interrupted. He leaned against the rock cliff and shuddered. As if he could ever offer a woman—especially the daughter of his enemy—any kind of life with a price on his head.

But that didn't seem to matter when he held her in his arms. She was eager and loving; perhaps that let him delude himself for those brief moments. She knew he hadn't told her everything about the smuggling, and he hadn't been able to lie to her anymore, when he was lying about so much else. He'd told her what her father had done, without mentioning the earl's actual name. He hadn't wanted it to spark her memory. But if she got her memories back, she'd damn well put the clues together, and could betray him. And how could he blame her?

And to make things worse, she'd asked how she could help—against her own father. After everything the earl had done, how he'd encouraged the stealing of children, Duncan should be glad to turn Catriona against him. It would be the ultimate revenge.

But it only made Duncan ill to contemplate it. He couldn't—wouldn't do that to her.

But apparently he was willing to hurt her in other ways, and he had to stop himself. And the only way to do that was to find out why no one had been looking for her. Waiting around was making him risk everything to be with her, and he had to get back to being objective, to understanding and accepting that she wasn't for him.

It was time to find out the truth.

Though she'd fallen asleep with eyes wet from weeping, Catherine woke up feeling at peace. She'd cried from relief, and the knowledge that she was not alone in the world, that Duncan would never allow her to be. She didn't know what her future held, but she was content to let it happen, and to cease her constant worrying, to accept that she could be like other women.

As she helped to serve the men breakfast, she

didn't see Duncan, and after a while, she quietly asked Ivor where he'd gone.

The war chief eyed her for a long moment. "He had business to attend to, mistress. He has no need to clear his plans with anyone."

Catherine blinked at the prick of embarrassment his words caused. "I know that, sir. I was simply curious."

Several men chuckled, and worse, Sheena didn't bother to hide a superior grin. Catherine stiffened, annoyed with herself for feeling defensive toward Sheena. She felt a tug on her elbow, and turned to find Finn watching her earnestly.

"Come to the horses with me, mistress," the boy said, tugging her hand.

She had to smile at him—did he see that she needed to be distracted? He was a clever boy, quiet most of the time, but it was obvious he noticed and evaluated everything.

She spent much of the day with him, either at the paddock, or teaching him his letters. She heard nothing about Duncan, and didn't ask any more questions, knowing it wasn't her place.

But that night after supper a rider came with news. Catherine felt a sick twist of fear that something had happened to Duncan. It wasn't her place to stand beside Ivor waiting for the news—she wasn't the lady of the clan, after all. So she stood with the women, hands on Finn's shoulders, and watched with apprehension as Ivor spoke quietly to the rider. All around her, the men muttered and waited.

At last Ivor faced the gathering. "We have word of a shipment tonight."

Tension and excitement moved from person to person. Catherine felt Finn tense beneath her hands. Many glances of skepticism were cast her way, and she knew most didn't know she knew all of the truth.

She raised her voice. "Children or whisky?" she demanded.

Maeve stared at her wide-eyed, as did many of the men. Ivor frowned.

"Laird Carlyle told me about the whisky smuggling," she admitted.

That turned Ivor's frown fiercer. "'Tis none of your concern, mistress."

"If children are to be rescued, we have preparations to make," Maeve said calmly.

If the woman was trying to smooth things after Catherine's inappropriate questions, Catherine didn't think it was working.

But Ivor nodded to Maeve. "Children, 'tis believed, perhaps several of them on their way from Stirling to the coast. Prepare to leave," he announced to his men.

As the men dispersed to prepare, Finn broke away from Catherine and hurried toward Ivor. She followed in time to hear the boy plead.

"Let me come with ye."

"Nay," Ivor said brusquely. "Skilled men are needed, not boys."

"But who will convince the lads that ye mean them no harm?" Finn asked softly. "When ye rescued me, I didn't believe ye any better than the other men. They might feel the same. I could help."

Ivor's expression softened and he put a hand on Finn's head. "Lad, yer bravery is to be commended. But we've been doin' this for years without ye. No need to go riskin' yer life."

Finn said nothing, just fisted his hands in his coat and watched the men. When Catherine bent to speak to him, he ducked away and raced outside. She couldn't find him right away, and as more and more of the men saddled their horses and gathered to leave, she began to fear Finn had run off, perhaps in search of Duncan. She went back into the cave for the cloak Maeve had lent her, and by the time she came back out, the men had all mounted and were trotting away.

It was easy for her now to see Finn struggling to saddle an older mare who continued to chew grass unconcerned. Catherine approached, but didn't try to stop the boy. It took three tries for Finn to put the saddle on, only to have it fall onto the far side.

Finn cursed well, in the manner of the clansmen he'd spent so much of his time with.

"Finn," Catherine began gently.

Finn briefly rested his forehead on the mare's flank, saying fiercely, "I should be there! They'll be frightened."

She put a hand on his shoulder and he shrugged it off, retrieving the saddle to try again. He got it on this time and began to tighten the girth.

Over his shoulder, he said, "Ye've done yer best to help me, mistress. Can ye not help me do the same for the others? Help me repay the kindness of Clan Carlyle."

Biting her lip, she looked down the trail where the men had just gone, then back toward the cave. Angus wasn't watching her—he'd gone with the men. No one seemed to have remembered to look out for her. And there was Finn, staring at her earnestly with big blue eyes, so sensitive to the plight of others, when he could have turned inward, angry and defensive at all he'd experienced in his life.

"Very well," Catherine said firmly. "I'll accompany you. The children need us. But we must hurry if we're to follow them!"

CASTLE Kinlochard was the main seat of Clan Duff, home to the Aberfoyle earls for generations—except the current earl, who normally preferred to meddle in Scottish politics and line his pockets from a distance, at his English estates. But to Duncan's surprise, the earl's banner flew atop the castle, signifying the earl's presence. Duncan stared up at the towers and walls, knowing he was about to enter the home of his enemy. At one time he might have feared losing his temper over the deeds of Aberfoyle, but his mission to discover the mysteries of Catriona overrode his anger.

The castle looked as impregnable as if it had been built this decade, rather than centuries ago. But dozens of people and several horse-drawn carts came and went beneath its open gatehouse, so Duncan crossed the arched stone bridge spanning the moat. To the guards, he claimed himself a McDonald, a traveler seeking hospitality for the night. He hadn't been sure his ruse would work, but apparently even Aberfoyle still believed in the generosity that Highlanders were known for.

Duncan caused no great concern, since he only wore a sword and dirk—the Disarming Act passed by the British after the last uprising had made them all hide their firearms away. He felt naked without his pistol, but was glad not to call attention to himself. He was an outlaw, after all, with a price on his head. He wasn't certain who would know his face after these years in hiding, but he had to proceed with caution.

The courtyard was large, with a separate training yard where men fought with swords, protecting themselves from blows with a targe, a round shield on their arms. It seemed a routine practice day, men drinking from ladles in buckets, talking among themselves and laughing. Other men and women moved between workshops and barracks, going on about their errands as if nothing was amiss. It seemed . . . strangely calm, and only increased Duncan's unease and curiosity. He asked for a night's stabling for his horse, Arran, and was shown a corner stall where he could curry and feed the chestnut gelding.

He'd timed his arrival well, and when he entered the double doors at the far end of the great hall, servants were already preparing for supper. Above a massive hearth at the far end was a warlike display of claymores and targes. More than one person gave him a skeptical look at his threadbare coat.

He found a bench to sit upon at a table not too close to the dais. He didn't expect Lord Aberfoyle to be in attendance in the great hall, with all the "common" people, but Duncan wanted to be certain he could overhear any conversations without being too obvious. Someone brought him a tankard of ale without lingering to answer questions, so Duncan sipped and studied the people around him. There were good-natured expressions upon almost everyone he saw—how was that possible when living beneath the thumb of one of Scotland's most hated chiefs?

Several other people sat down at the far end of his table, no one close enough for conversation, as bad luck would have it. He would bide his time.

A serving woman brought around a platter of bannocks, and as he took one, she eyed him from beneath the cap perched on her frizzy gray hair. "I don't think I've seen ye before."

"I'm a traveler granted a night's hospitality," he explained. "Duncan McDonald is me name."

"And I'm Rona. If ye be travelin', ye must be hungry." She placed another bannock on his plate. "I'll be back with mutton and cabbage."

"Ye have my thanks," he said, offering a faint smile.

He broke apart the warm bannock and chewed thoughtfully. When Rona returned, he helped himself to a slice of mutton and said, "I never thought to be sittin' in an earl's great hall."

She braced the platter on the table. "Aye, 'tis a fancy title, and though the man himself has his polite, distant ways, he is kind."

Kind? He schooled himself to hide his doubt.

"Now his wife, she's a more informal lass."

"Lass" seemed like a generous way to refer to an older woman. "Then she's a good mistress."

"Aye, that she is. Though a McCallum, long a Duff enemy, she's been part of the new peace between our clans. Surely ye must have noticed that in yer travels."

Duncan frowned, but before he could ask anything else, the maidservant moved off with her platter of mutton. A new peace? He didn't know what to think.

But regardless, no one here was worried about Catriona being missing, so all must have assumed she'd be gone at least a fortnight. The old earl hadn't yet started missing her, hadn't yet felt the suffering of the parents he'd taken children away from.

All around him, people suddenly rose, and Duncan followed suit. A man and a woman were now filing onto the dais. Both were close to his own age, and he had to wonder if the man was Owen Duff, the future earl. The man nodded to the great hall, offered a rousing, "Sit down and eat!" that was met with cheers.

Rona came by with cabbage this time, and as Duncan spooned some onto his plate, she said, "Now don't ye see such love shining between them? How could there not be peace?"

Duncan was confused. This was the marriage Rona had first meant, between Duff and McCallum? This woman was their new mistress? Or perhaps she was the lady of the castle because the old earl and countess never put in an appearance.

"So he's the next earl?" Duncan asked, trying to sound suitably awed.

Rona shot him a surprised smile. "He's Himself, the Duff chief, these last few months." Shaking her head, she moved on, saying something under her breath about how ignorant country folk could be.

But Duncan was no longer listening. This man was the new Earl of Aberfoyle. The old earl who'd dominated this part of Scotland and allowed families to be destroyed so he could profit—that man was dead and buried, gone to the devil where he belonged.

But Duncan hadn't known, because he'd taken a risk to keep his people safe after he'd almost been recaptured. He had tightened their patrols around the encampment, hadn't risked sending anyone beyond their glen.

Did the new earl know what his father had been a part of? Did he condone the same injustices? Duncan watched the man sit beside his wife, and they smiled into each other's eyes in a lovesick fashion. As far as Duncan knew, this man didn't even know his sister was missing, and certainly didn't need to suffer for it—if he was innocent of his father's evil deeds. Duncan couldn't know that, not yet.

But without proof one way or another, Duncan's revenge felt hollow. And how was he to proceed with Catriona?

Was he supposed to return her to her home?

Everything inside him rebelled at the thought. She didn't remember this home or these people. She was bringing along Finn, working with the lad and helping him in a way she probably never did as a fine lady going to balls and concerts.

But through Duncan's own failings, she knew too much about his clan and their activities. Her knowledge could prove dangerous to so many people—and to his family.

But all of that hid the truth he knew was deep inside him—he didn't want Catriona to leave. Selfishly, he wanted her for himself, and as long as she didn't remember, he had her.

But could he live with that?

He mused over the thought, staring off to the side into the hearth fire.

"Good evening," said a voice, right in front of him.

Startled, Duncan saw that Lady Aberfoyle herself stood there, regarding him quizzically from two very different colored eyes, one blue, one green. It gave her an arresting, unusual appearance, making her handsome features even more striking.

"I do not ken that I've seen ye here before," she said pleasantly, but pointedly.

Duncan rose to his feet and bowed. "My lady, I am but a traveler passing through on my way to Glasgow. Duncan McDonald."

"Sit, please, eat," she said, motioning him down. "A pleasure to meet ye, Mr. McDonald."

"Ye're kind to offer hospitality to strangers, my lady."

"A tradition in the Highlands, as ye surely know."

He briefly bowed his head.

"So ye're heading to Glasgow. My sister by marriage is there even as we speak, visiting friends."

"She's surely enjoying herself." Duncan was shocked that she'd brought up Catriona so easily, but he'd take the good fortune. If he'd chosen another city, Catriona's name would never have come up. He'd been incredibly lucky. But if they thought she was just visiting, surely after two weeks, they'd expect a letter from her, a response to one they must have sent. He didn't have much time before this new earl put all his efforts into finding her.

He realized that Lady Aberfoyle was still regarding him with friendliness, but also a certain scrutiny.

"Ye seem . . . familiar to me," she said slowly.

He let himself take a sip of ale, even as he leaned back and regarded her curiously. "I've never been here before."

"And ye've never been to Larig Castle, the main keep of the McCallums? My brother is chief."

"Nay, my lady."

Though she smiled, she cocked her head and continued to study him with those unusual, piercing eyes. "I know ye from somewhere. Maybe it came to me in a dream."

Was he supposed to take that as a joke? A threat? Did she suspect he was an outlaw? He gave her another rusty smile. She only nodded her head to him and moved on down the table to converse with other guests.

Duncan kept to himself for the rest of the evening, standing near groups of drinking men, as if he was a part of them, so he didn't look so out of place. He'd debated leaving Castle Kinlochard right after supper, but knew that might appear suspicious, since Lady Aberfoyle was already curious about him. Several times he thought he felt her watching him, but he didn't risk looking her way.

He spent the night rolled up in his plaid on the floor near the hearth with several other travelers. When the castle doors were opened at dawn, he started to leave before even waiting for a meal.

"Mr. McDonald!" came a voice just as he reached the doors.

Everything inside him urged an escape, but he forced himself to turn around. It was the maidservant, Rona, from the night before.

"Mr. McDonald, my lady bid me prepare ye food for yer journey," she called, holding up a satchel.

He let out his breath. "'Tis kind of her. Please give her my thanks."

"If ye wait but a moment, ye can do so yerself."

"I cannot. My journey today will be long."

This time, she didn't try to stop him, and he reached the courtyard without any sense of relief. He wasn't free of the castle yet. Several people moved through the courtyard with purpose, but it was obvious that many more were heading inside to break their fast. Inside the stables, a groom lazily shoveled out a stall, ignoring Duncan. The marshal of the horses was nowhere in sight.

Duncan found his saddle and other gear in the corner of the stall on the floor, not where he'd left it. As he bent over to see if anything was missing, he heard voices as someone else entered the stable.

A man said, "We cannot interrogate a guest simply because ye might've had a dream about him, Maggie."

Duncan froze, staying well hidden in the shadowy rear of the stall, with Arran between him and the visitors. It was the earl and his countess. Why did she keep bringing up a dream?

"I didn't just dream about *him*, Owen, but your sister, too. And ye know my dreams come true."

"Not always," said her husband, his voice goodnatured.

Duncan didn't think he could be any more shocked, and didn't know what to make of this unreal discussion.

Lady Aberfoyle's response to her husband's skepticism was an unladylike snort.

"What happens in this dream of yours?" he continued.

"I . . . well, nothing much," she conceded. "I just see them talking together, and she's happy."

Duncan squeezed his eyes shut. *Happy.* As if he could ever give a woman that.

"Happy to be with a McDonald?" Lord Aberfoyle said, then added with amusement, "Now there's no need to get physical."

"And who'd have ever thought ye'd be happy with a McCallum, Chief of the Duffs."

"Aye, who'd have thought," he murmured.

And there was a conspicuous silence.

"I think we've missed Mr. McDonald," Lady Aberfoyle said with regret. "I wanted to ask if he knew Cat."

"He's on his way to Glasgow—perhaps he'll meet her there."

"I'll write to her about him. Och, don't be giving me that look. I'll not interfere. She doesn't need to know there was a dream involved." She paused. "I've not received a letter from her since she's been gone. Have ye?"

"Not yet, but she loves her parties and balls. Too busy to write to us, I imagine."

"Hmm."

And then there wasn't a sound for a long few minutes, except a shovel's scraping. Duncan slowly got to his feet, peering around his horse. They were gone. He crept out the stall gate, only to see them walking arm in arm across the courtyard, their heads together as they spoke. There was an ease between them, a sense of love and acceptance that seemed foreign to Duncan.

He saddled Arran and rode sedately across the courtyard, letting out a sigh of relief when he passed beneath the gatehouse. As he crossed the arched stone bridge over the moat, he passed several dozen people on their way inside the castle.

"Your lairdship?"

The tension that had slowly been leaving Duncan's body now surged back. He knew Aberfoyle hadn't left the courtyard, and how many lairds could there be on the bridge? He was tempted to gallop wildly away, but the man had used a hissing whisper, as if trying to draw little attention to himself. Duncan couldn't help pulling up and looking back.

A roughly dressed man stood alone, clutching the bonnet from his bald scalp.

"I don't know ye, sir," Duncan said coldly, hand on the hilt of his claymore.

"Nay, ye don't, your lairdship, but ye saved my sister's child, and I wanted ye to know I'd never forget it."

Duncan nodded, uncomfortable about being thanked for something any honorable man should do. "Have you spread the word about what evil is being done, so that families are on guard to protect the children?"

"We have, your lairdship. 'Tis a terrible thing that a man such as yerself is being hounded for doin' what's right."

Duncan thought one of the guards was looking at them with the beginning of suspicion. "I must go."

"Fare well, your lairdship."

Duncan didn't look back as he trotted away. Everything in him wanted to gallop as if chased by redcoats, but that would only prove suspicious.

Throughout the day, he resisted the urge to push his horse harder than he needed to. He was unsettled by his meeting with the earl and countess, confused about Catriona's role in his life and what he was supposed to do about her.

And yet part of him longed to be with her, with an urgency that was foreign to him.

When he arrived at the cave by one of his many

circuitous routes, long after dark, he saw most of the horses gone. He unsaddled Arran, gave him the most basic rubdown, then hurried past the guard and inside the smoky cave. There were only a few men, the four Carlyle women—and no Catriona.

Maeve greeted him with a calm reserve that ratcheted up his worry.

"What has happened?" he demanded.

"We had word of a shipment of children last night," she said. "The men set out as quickly as possible."

"Last night? And they haven't returned?"

She shook her head.

He looked about, then strode across the footbridge, through the passage and to his chamber. Empty. It was dark in the cave pool. Emerging into the great hall, he asked harshly, "Where are Finn and Catherine?"

Brows drawing together, she let out her breath in a rush. "They're gone, your lairdship. We assume they followed our men to be of assistance to the rescued lads."

"But ye don't know?" he demanded, knowing his voice was harsh, but unable to help himself.

"The mistress's favorite horse is gone. Torcall went after them, and his orders were to send word back or come himself if he didn't find them with our men. Otherwise, we were to assume they were all together."

"Assume?" He pivoted away from her, running a hand harshly through his hair, dislodging his queue. "Do ye even know where the shipment was headed?"

She shook her head. "We couldn't leave the cave undefended," she added quietly.

"I know." He gritted his teeth and forced himself to take a deep breath.

It didn't help calm him. He felt panicked, helpless, fearful of what Catriona had gotten herself into. He'd taken advantage of her for his own ends, manipulated her emotions. By allowing her to think he trusted her, that he was completely open with her—had he just been creating some kind of fantasy where they could be together, even after all he'd done? He was merely lying to himself. She was an innocent, who'd be with her family if Duncan hadn't taken vengeance into his own hands.

CHAPTER 13

Duncan passed one of the most tormented nights of his life. Catriona was out in the world, possibly alone, risking herself for his mission—without his protection. How had such a monster as Aberfoyle raised such an incredible woman? Or perhaps he'd been a neglectful, remote father, and she'd been all the better for it. Or maybe her head injury had changed her into the woman she'd always been meant to be. Duncan had rescued her, aye, and they'd grown close, though he'd resisted. But he hadn't resisted hard enough, and now he felt trapped, his insides twisted with emotions he hadn't felt in a long time—if ever.

He cared for the children he rescued, had been appalled that anyone would kidnap innocents. He loved his sisters, and lived in fear that his exploits would bring harm to them. But none of that compared to this all-encompassing obsession with Catriona.

It was well after supper when a guard returned

with news of a party approaching. Duncan strode toward the cave entrance.

"Laird Carlyle," Maeve called, "ye should wait to be certain 'tis our men."

Though she was right, he couldn't wait. He went out into the cool night, the sky pink and purple above the absent sun. With his arms across his chest, he waited until Torcall, the advance rider, came through the trees.

Duncan caught the horse's harness to keep him still, then confronted the panting man. "Is Mistress Catherine with the riders?" he demanded.

Torcall nodded. "She is, your lairdship."

Duncan told himself his relief was only so great because Catriona was his responsibility. By ones and twos his men came through the overgrowth which hid the entrance to the cave. Near the end was Ivor, with Catriona and Finn beside him. He expected Catriona to look embarrassed, but instead it was Finn who met his gaze briefly, uneasily, before looking away.

Catriona dismounted with the grace of a born horsewoman, rushed toward him, her smile exuberant, before coming up short.

"Duncan, the most wonderful thing happened," she cried, then briefly covered her mouth before lowering her voice. "We rescued three children and have already returned them to their families."

He felt a chill, imagining what might have happened if she were recognized.

"I didn't get to see the reunion myself," she said, her expression growing shadowed as if a cloud had crossed it—and as if she'd read his mind. "Ivor insisted I remain well away. I was very safe," she added. Eyeing him, she hurried on. "It wasn't a whisky shipment, of course. Ivor told me he'd never take me to where they store the casks, even if I was curious." She finally broke off.

"Are ye done babbling?" he asked coolly.

She swallowed, then looked around and realized that they were almost totally alone. He could still hear the men at the paddock, and the last of them took the mare's reins right from Catriona's hand and headed toward the path.

"I can take care of him," she called.

"Nay, ye cannot," Duncan said. "Ye'll be speaking with me for a good long while."

Instead of getting abashed or defensive, she linked her hands together and regarded him calmly. "Would ye like a report from me, rather than Ivor?"

Again, he noticed the Scottish creeping back into her speech, and imagined two days with his men had contributed to that. Two days alone with a group of rough men. He could have shaken her.

Of course, she'd spent two weeks in a cave with a group of rough men. But he'd been there to watch over and protect her. But he hadn't protected her from himself.

"Nay, I'll leave the report to Ivor," he said. "'Tis words of explanation I need to hear from ye."

At last she lowered her lashes. "In my excitement at the success of the rescue, I forgot . . . the circumstances."

"Aye, the circumstances. What could possibly have made you and a boy follow my men on such a dangerous mission?"

He didn't even realize he was towering over her, his voice rising, until she was looking up at him, lips pressed tightly together.

She raised both hands. "'Twas wrong, I know."

"Ye'll only concede 'wrong'?"

Those golden eyes gleamed in the last of the day's light, and seemed to beseech him. He didn't want to fall under their spell. Right now he was her chief.

"Yer lairdship, 'twas all me fault."

Duncan and Catriona both turned to see Finn emerging from the shadowy path that led to the paddock. The boy's features were stark with apprehension and fear. Though Duncan hated to inspire such a thing in a child, it was sometimes necessary to keep them safe.

"Finn," Catriona began.

"Nay, mistress, ye cannot protect me. 'Twas I who needed to help others like me, my laird. Mistress Catherine tried to stop me, but I would not listen to her. She came along to protect me in my foolishness."

Catriona frowned at the boy, but did not contradict him.

"Ye did not consider that you could endanger my clansmen?" Duncan said. He was no longer quite so angry, but he couldn't let them see that.

Finn swallowed audibly, then shook his head. "Nay, I wanted to help. I remembered how afraid

I was of yer men and what they meant to do to me. I thought I could ease their fears."

"And did ye?"

The boy's chin came up a bit. "I did, my laird."

"Then go off and see to Mistress Catherine's horse, as well as your own, and think on how ye could have handled your wish better."

Looking abashed, the boy led his mare away.

Duncan turned back to Catriona. The rising moon touched her with a glow, altering her homespun clothing. She looked remote and beautiful, and it took everything in him not to draw her into his arms, to kiss her with passion, with regret, with confusion. He didn't know what he was supposed to do with her now, and couldn't face how that made him feel. So he focused on keeping her safe. "And how should ye have handled *yourself* better?"

Taking a deep breath, she boldly said, "I don't know what I could have done differently. If it had been whisky, Ivor assured me he wouldn't have taken me along. He said I'm not to know such things, that it would be dangerous. He says the Earl of Aberfoyle is involved, that it's his whisky we steal, because of what he's helped to do to the stolen children."

The moment she'd mentioned her father's name, Duncan had drawn a deep breath, waiting for her to say that the name had triggered her memory. Had he not made it clear to Ivor that she was to know nothing? But she still looked at him with earnestness, no revelation of awareness about her identity. Her father's title meant nothing to her, and the constricting feeling of dread slowly loosened its hold on him.

But he couldn't stop thinking of the danger she'd been in, following his men, maybe not even alerting them of her presence immediately.

"You seem upset," she said, her voice pleading. "Finn needed me. He wanted to be of use, to help children like himself, aye, but he also wanted to repay ye for all ye've done for him."

"Try not to make me feel so bad for wanting to keep you both safe," Duncan said dryly.

She came closer in the darkness, and put her delicate hand in the middle of his chest. He willed his heart not to beat faster—he didn't want her to know how easily she affected him, but he might as well have asked an eagle not to soar.

"I care about him, Duncan, and I know how he feels. Finn and I just want to be . . . a part of something, to know we matter, that we can help rather than just sit uselessly in the cave, sheltered and fragile."

"Ye've hardly been useless," he said gruffly. "Ye're our guest, yet ye've been working harder than many a man."

She rolled her eyes. "Now ye're teasing me."

He wanted her to say his Christian name again. Hearing it on her lips, in her sweet feminine voice, fooled him into thinking he was just a man, alone with a woman in the night, two people with possibilities and a future that might arise between them.

Damn, but he was a fool.

"Ye're scowling so," she whispered.

When she reached up and touched his forehead, he inhaled and couldn't seem to breathe again.

"I wish I just could soothe these lines—"

He shuddered as she skimmed her fingers on his suddenly hot flesh.

"—soothe your soul from tormenting you."

He closed his eyes, unable to bear looking at the beauty shining from within her like a beacon that called him home.

But such a light should warn him away, as if he were a frigate heading toward the shoals of disaster. She'd grown to mean too much to him. His thoughts of her were wild and dangerous, of the life they could have together if her memory never returned. It was a fantasy, impossible, but now that there was no more need to punish her father— Duncan had to trust in God's justice now—could he focus on clearing his name?

But even that wouldn't allow him to be with a woman who wasn't his, whose family would never accept a marriage between them after what he'd done to her.

Catriona now cupped his face with both warm hands. He'd been cold and dead inside until she'd come to him, confused him, made him want things he shouldn't have.

He gripped her wrists in both his hands, intending to remove her touch. But she dropped her hands to his shoulders, slid them along the width, then down across his chest. He held her wrists helplessly, unable to stop what she was doing to him.

He hadn't been touched with gentleness, with

innocent curiosity, in a long, long time. Her touch tormented him, aroused him, then inflamed him with a need that suddenly felt overpowering. He hated himself for craving it—he wanted to hate her for inspiring it. He should frighten her away.

He gripped her wrists harder, forcing them behind her back. This arched her against him, hip to hip. He pulled her closer, so that her breasts tormented his chest. He needed her to keep away from him, because he was no longer certain he trusted himself.

Instead, she looked at him boldly in the near darkness. "Ye want me to be afraid, but I'm not," she whispered.

He gave her a little shake, leaning down into her face. "Ye should be. I am no tame suitor."

"I would be disappointed if ye were."

"Your brazen talk will bring ye trouble someday."

"Not from you. Ye've been nothing but good to me."

Good, he thought bitterly. "This isn't 'good,' how I hold ye now, how I've kissed ye, how I want ye."

"I want ye, too, but I know I cannot give ye anything, not with my past an impenetrable darkness. I am a risk to hurt ye."

He let her go, disgusted with himself. Instead of retreating, she slid her arms about his waist and clung to him.

"But oh, Duncan, ye make me feel such wondrous things. My body feels like a candle flaring to life only when ye're near."

He closed his eyes, struggling hard for control,

when her breasts, round and soft, pressed into him, her warm breath fanned his neck. He felt her gentle hands beneath his coat, exploring his back.

And then he crushed her to him, kissing her hard and open-mouthed, her head pressed into his shoulder. He kissed her as if he could devour her, bring back hope and peace, all the things he'd denied himself. He touched her body as if it were his, created only for him. A possessive urgency made him pull her away from the entrance and into the cover of the trees. She moaned as their legs entwined together. He cupped her ass and held her against him.

"That," she whispered, "what I feel beneath your plaid. Is that what I do to ye?"

"Do ye remember being with a man?" he asked, thinking he'd heard no word of a husband, but suddenly uncertain.

"Nay, but I'm not blind to what animals do."

Squeezing the globes of her ass, he leaned down and gave a gentle bite where her neck met her shoulder. "I feel like an animal," he said hoarsely.

She laugh softly. "I make ye feel wild, now do I?"

He kissed her lips again, let his hands roam from her hips around her torso and up to cup her breasts through her stays. "Aye, wild."

She gave a little gasp and then a groan. "I am so shameless. I wish my clothes could be gone so ye could touch me there."

"Nay, I'll no wish for that. I'm a weak man where ye're concerned, lass, and ye mustn't forget it. But . . ." He let the word trail off, even as he reached down and began to bunch up her skirts in his hands.

He heard her gasp in a breath and not release it, as anticipation built between them. At the first touch of her bare thighs, it was his turn to release a shuddering breath. He let his hands span the roundness of her ass, his fingers meeting at the cleft, and she gave a choked whimper. He slowly moved forward around her waist, until his thumbs met at her navel. She was trembling.

"Should I stop?" he said against her hair.

"Nay, oh, no, please don't."

In the darkness, her features were indistinct, but he kissed her nose, her lips, her chin, even as he let his thumbs travel a slow journey down into the curling hair between her thighs.

Her breath came faster, mixed with these little sounds of pleasure that were almost his undoing. He wanted to lift his plaid and bury himself within her. Instead, he moved his thumbs deeper, where it was warmer, slicker, until he found what he was looking for and stroked.

She cried out into his shoulder, then whispered, "God, I want, I want—what do I want?"

"This," he said with certainty, turning his hand so that he could caress her with his fingers.

She clutched his plaid to hold herself up, shuddering with each stroke. He tipped her head back and took her mouth deeply, using his tongue to mimic what he truly wanted. Sweet girl, she spread her trembling legs wider, and he moved deeper, caressed her but didn't force his entrance. He wouldn't risk her maidenhead.

Her little cries grew higher, gasping now, and he held her with his free arm as she shuddered through her climax.

At last she sagged in his arms, her head tipping back to rest on his shoulder, and he knew she was staring up at him as if to read him in the darkness. With great reluctance, he removed his hand and let her skirts drop like a veil between them.

"That was," she began, but didn't go farther, because he was kissing her gently, upper lip, lower. Her tongue touched his with sweet exploration, before she at last pulled back. "That is . . . how it is between men and women?"

"Some of it." His voice was husky with restraint.

"Can I touch ye as ye touched me?"

"Nay," he said quickly.

"It doesn't feel good?"

To his surprise, a chuckle escaped him. When was the last time he'd laughed? "The pleasure ye just felt, so would I feel. But I cannot risk it, lass."

"Why not?"

"Because I'd take your virginity."

"Or take what is my husband's by right—if I have one," she added sadly.

"Ye don't."

"What?" she demanded, stiffening.

"I felt the evidence of your virginity. Do not torment yourself with guilt, Catherine. 'Tis not yours to bear."

"I'm not married." Her voice was full of tentative relief. "And yet I could be betrothed."

They stood entwined for a long moment, as his

guilt seemed a live thing, hovering about his legs like a fog about to rise and swallow him whole.

"Duncan, ye made me feel great pleasure. Can I not do the same for ye?"

The thought of her touching him that intimately—

"Ye're not breathing," she said with doubt.

"Because I'm trying not to imagine ye naked, letting my mouth taste your body as I wish."

"Ye would . . . taste me?"

"Everywhere."

Hesitantly, she said, "I would like to do the same."

And without warning, she put her hand on his plaid and boldly touched him through it. He quickly pulled her hand away and held it to his chest.

"Can I not give ye the pleasure ye gave me?" she asked.

"I beg ye don't ask again, or I might not be able to resist. Ye're not my wife, Catherine, and 'tisn't right for me to pretend otherwise."

"We're not hurting anyone."

"Ye're a sly wench." Her words weren't true. He was hurting *her*, though she didn't know it. The more intimate he allowed their connection to be, the more she'd hate him someday.

If she got her memory back. It was beneath him to wish she wouldn't, to imagine some kind of normal life they might share. He could never have that. But he found himself asking, "If ye knew who ye were—"

"I'd stay here with ye," she said with quiet certainty.

Any response was knocked clear from his mouth by a feeling of unworthiness.

"Go back to the cave," he said harshly.

She turned away, then looked back at him. "Are ye afraid of me, Duncan Carlyle?"

He said nothing.

"I know your secrets now, and I intend to be a part of it all."

He turned his back on her, resting a hand against the tree, head bent as he tried to control himself. His secrets—she didn't know the worst of them. And yet he kept tying her closer to him, with his mission, his good people, his selfish need. There was a foolish part of him that wanted to believe that things between them would somehow sort themselves out, and they could be together.

THOUGH she was exhausted, Catherine had a difficult time sleeping that night. She'd been thrilled to be away from the cave, to see if being on the road made her remember something. It hadn't, but after little time to be disappointed about it, she'd faced Duncan and his wrath.

But oh, the way his wrath had changed . . .

He'd been afraid for her. Following Finn had been a reckless thing to do, but the little boy had been so determined, so endearing—and correct in his worries about the kidnapped children. Those children had been in terror when they'd been rescued, and it hadn't helped when Ivor was forced to kill one of the villains, and had seemed quite frightening himself. The presence of a woman and another child had done much to calm the children, to convince them they were now safe. Catherine had been excited by the adventure, relieved it had gone well, yet hesitant to confront Duncan. And she'd been right.

But beneath his bluster and scowls and remoteness was a man who'd been injured by life, who was only protecting himself from being hurt again. Yet he still cared about stolen children, even with a price on his head.

And he cared about her—cared about giving her pleasure anyway, she tried to remind herself.

With a sigh, she clasped her hands to her hot face in the darkness of the cave and at last gave the memories free rein to envelop her. She hadn't imagined being touched intimately could feel so incredible. She let her hands cup her breasts, touch between her thighs, but it didn't feel the same as when his big rough hands had done it. He'd known just what to do, had known her body better than she had.

He must have done such things before, she reminded herself—but since she'd been the recipient of his knowledge, she didn't care. Her skin still seemed sensitive, her body full of a peace she hadn't imagined. It seemed forever until she could sleep, and even then her dreams were of the future they might have together. But to be with him, she would risk anything . . . Was she falling in love with him? And how could she trust her emotions, when she had no past experience to base them on? After all, Duncan had saved her life—maybe she was mistaking gratitude and lust for something more. All she could do was be patient with herself, take things slowly.

In the morning, it was laundry day. Maeve and the other women were still inside, gathering the clan's garments. Outside near the giant cauldrons that were slowly coming to a boil, Catherine brought the saddlebags that Duncan had taken on his trip. She felt almost like a wife, going through them for any soiled laundry. She'd never even asked where he'd gone—they'd been too busy, she thought with a blush.

At the bottom, something pricked her finger, and she drew in a sharp breath. Pulling out her hand, she saw blood welling on her fingertip. Frowning, she wiped it on her apron, then used her other hand to pull out the soiled shirt. She looked inside the bag and at the bottom, something gleamed. More carefully this time, she reached in and removed a brooch. It was in the intricate design of a clan crest, she thought, but it wasn't the Carlyles', which she'd seen on a brooch holding Duncan's plaid across his shoulder.

This brooch suddenly seemed familiar, as if part of her brain had been illuminated. Her awareness sharpened into focus that blocked out the trees and the cauldrons, and the autumn wind that teased her.

The brooch—it was hers, her family crest. Relief made her stagger as a rush of memories washed over her. She'd chosen Catherine as a name, not even realizing how similar it was to her own.

Though everyone called her Cat, she was Lady Catriona Duff.

CHAPTER 14

$\mathcal{D}$esperate to remain alone before the women emerged and asked questions, Cat staggered away from the cauldrons, clutching the brooch and the bag. Her mind became a torrent of pictures and memories, first from when she was a child and then swiftly moving forward. She saw her brother Owen's beloved face. Tears of relief came to her eyes. They'd shared the misery of parents who kept them from their homeland as much as possible, who tried to turn them into English aristocracy, and who'd almost succeeded.

Her father had offered her in marriage at birth to bring peace between the Duffs and the McCallums. Cat hadn't known about it until her father had changed his mind and deceived the groom into kidnapping the wrong bride, her dear cousin Riona. Riona and Hugh McCallum had fallen in love, to Cat's relief, but their marriage hadn't satisfied the contract between the two families. Owen had offered to marry Hugh's sister Maggie instead. She'd thought her brother so brave and honorable—although it had taken a while to convince Maggie that they could really have a good marriage.

But it had strangely left Cat feeling on the outside. Much as she'd been relieved not to marry a stranger, all around her people were falling in love, marrying, and now both couples were expecting babies. She was happy for them all, thrilled to be an aunt, but . . . there'd been no one in her life. She'd felt it was time to begin finding her own happy ending, and the only way to do that was to meet new people. So she'd decided to travel to Glasgow to visit friends, with the vague future plans of going to Edinburgh and maybe London itself.

As each new memory unfolded, she at last began to remember that final journey, taken with the two clansmen who'd always traveled with her, more like friends than guards. Her eyes welled up as she remembered the storm's approach, the way they'd been caught off guard at its intensity, her men trying to get her to safety—the collapse of the ground beneath their feet. She didn't remember anything right after that, including waking up to find her friends dead. But waking up in Duncan's arms—*that* she remembered. It seemed her brain was either damaged, or trying to protect her from the trauma of her friends' deaths.

Duncan.

She took a deep breath, wiping away the sad memories, and absorbing the knowledge that she knew who she was, that she was free of doubts and indecision. She wasn't married, she wasn't betrothed. She could come to Duncan with honesty, and surely she could find a way to help him escape his past. They could be together, they could marry—

And then she stared down at the brooch still clutched in her hand, as doubt and growing fear assailed her. Something was wrong. The brooch—it had been in Duncan's saddlebag. She *always* wore the brooch when she traveled, a mark of her clan, of her pride.

Duncan . . . he must have taken it from her, hid it away. She feebly tried to tell herself that perhaps he meant to research it, discover where she came from.

She covered her mouth with her free hand, tears welling up. She moved farther into the trees, away from the cave, from what she knew to be true.

She could no longer make feeble excuses for Duncan. He wouldn't have forgotten something so important as a clue to her identity. He had deliberately hidden it away, kept her from knowing her true self. Her breath was coming fast as she fought not to sob, bracing her arm against a tree to hold herself up beneath this terrible weight of shock, disappointment, grief . . . and anger. Oh God, she let that anger well up inside her, burn hotter and hotter, blasting to cinders any thoughts of affection and love.

She'd nearly fallen in love with a man who was holding her captive, scheming against her and her family. He wasn't just a smuggler—he was a thief and a kidnapper!

And she'd helped him.

She felt sick, and leaning back against a tree,

clutched her stomach and tried to quell her nausea. She knew her father was guilty and deserving of punishment—he'd been a cruel man who'd let her innocent cousin Riona be kidnapped so Cat wouldn't be surrendered in marriage to a "savage Highlander"—she remembered those words well.

And it was her father who'd profited off the sale of innocent children, torn from their families and abused. She'd seen the sorrow and fear in young, innocent eyes, the rope marks on their wrists. Finn had been unable to find words at the terror he'd experienced. She leaned against the tree, heaving up her breakfast in horror.

At last she wiped the back of her hand against her mouth and sank down against the base of the tree. She'd known the extent of her father's cruelty. She would have done anything to make up for that, would have helped Duncan, but he hadn't given her the chance. He'd kept the truth from her, had seduced her into caring about him. She shuddered.

She would have given herself to him if he hadn't stopped her. She didn't know if he'd felt guilty, or had worse plans for her. It didn't matter. Her grief and disappointment seemed too great a load to bear.

What was she supposed to do now?

DUNCAN wasn't surprised when, after most of the men had left the cave that morning, Ivor came and stood before him.

"Aye, Ivor?" Duncan said.

"I have news. One of the villains implied that

there might be other children ready to be transported."

Duncan cursed. "Did he know specifics?"

Ivor shook his head. "He might have just been saying what he thought we wanted to hear, to keep me from breakin' his *other* leg."

"Perhaps. Tell the patrols to be extra vigilant."

When Ivor continued to stand before him, shoulders stiff, expression sober, Duncan frowned. "Is there something else?"

"I went against yer orders, Laird Carlyle."

Duncan arched a brow. "Which orders?"

"To keep Mistress Catherine safe." Ivor let out his breath and met his gaze. "I should have sent her back immediately once we discovered she and the lad followin' us."

"Why did ye not?"

"We had the kidnappers in sight, and I feared we'd lose them, if I sent men to escort the lady away."

Duncan put a hand on the man's shoulders. "Ye did what ye had to, my friend."

He felt the tension leave Ivor, who ruefully shook his head. "She's a willful lass, that one."

"Aye." Duncan could have joined him in the head-shaking.

"Ye sure ye ken what ye're doin' with her?"

Ivor was no longer speaking as his war chief, but as a friend.

Duncan hesitated, then admitted softly, "Nay, I'm not certain I ken anything anymore."

"She's a gentle one, but . . ." Ivor trailed off, and rocked once on the balls of his feet. "But made of steel when she wants her way. And perhaps . . . she wants *you*."

Duncan sighed.

"I don't mean to intrude," Ivor added quickly.

"Ye're not intruding. I appreciate your concern. And I'm too susceptible by far to the lass's charms. Don't blame her for my inability to keep away from her."

"I understand that your sister has offered to take her in."

"Muriel told ye that, did she?"

Ivor only cleared his throat.

"Catherine is my responsibility," Duncan said. "If I order her to Muriel's, I think I'd have to tie her up to keep her there. I'll keep better watch on her here from now on."

"I vow we all will," Ivor said.

"Have ye seen her?" Duncan asked.

"Before we spoke, I thought she was with you. Maeve said she began doing laundry with the other women, but now they don't know where she went."

"I'll find out."

"And keep her tied up in the cave?" Ivor asked, wearing a lopsided smile.

"God, no." Duncan grimaced, forcing away the erotic images that evoked.

Outside the cave, he saw Maeve, Janet, and Sheena stirring cauldrons full of soapy wet clothing. The hair curled on their damp foreheads and their faces were flushed with the heat.

"Ladies," Duncan said, to get their attention.

They all paused in unison to stare up at him.

"Where can I find Mistress Catherine?"

"She was supposed to help us, your lairdship," Sheena said, "but she's disappeared. Sometimes she's no a very hard worker."

Maeve frowned at Sheena before saying to Duncan, "This is the first time she's ever missed work she *volunteered* to do."

It was Duncan's turn to frown. He went back into the cave, across the little footbridge, and into his own chamber. It was messy, as she always left it, but quite empty. He followed the passageway to the pool cave, but it was inky black.

"Catherine?" he called, just in case.

His voice only echoed.

In the great hall, several men sharpening dirks at the table looked up as he strode past them. Whatever they saw on his face, they only swallowed and went back to their tasks. At the paddock, Catriona wasn't there, but at least the horse she usually rode was.

When he returned to the cauldrons, Maeve held up a shirt. "I believe this is yours, my laird."

He frowned. "Aye, and what of it?"

"I found it on the ground, and none of us brought it out, so we assume Mistress Catherine did."

His faint feeling of unease was growing stronger. Catriona might leave his chamber a mess, but her work on behalf of the clan was always precise. "Was she feeling well this morn?"

The women looked at each other and shrugged in turn.

The only place left was—he glanced up at the

turret that seemed to straddle the cliff. He left the curious women and found the hidden path, heading up it a little faster than he might. Would Catriona have gone up to the ruins again, when he'd warned her she shouldn't go alone?

At the top he was heading directly for the gate-house when movement caught his eye. He saw Catriona silhouetted against the morning sky of orange and pink, standing so close to the cliff, she seemed like she stood at the edge of the world. The wind whipped her skirts and tangled strands of her long dark hair around her head.

On one hand he was relieved—why had he thought she would leave the encampment alone?

But on the other hand, she stood so still, so near the edge, that his heart skipped a beat as he hurried to her. He feared calling out her name would frighten her, so he deliberately kicked a few rocks together. He saw her start and look back over her shoulder, her expression stark and impassive.

Turning fully toward him, she said, "I know I should not have come up here alone."

Something seemed . . . off as she spoke, and he realized that her brogue had gone away again. He'd liked how she'd sounded like one of his people instead of the aristocratic daughter of his enemy. Perhaps it was better this way. He needed to remember she wasn't for him.

"Why did ye then?" He stepped up beside her, not touching her, and they both looked out over the Highlands, where the barren mountains rose and fell, and the tallest was touched with winter's first frost.

She gave a long sigh. "I don't really know. I suddenly felt like I needed to see the land as a pure thing, where villains who kidnap children—who kidnap women—don't exist." Her voice rose on the last phrase.

Her words echoed into the sudden silence. And he knew, without a doubt, that she remembered who she was, that she comprehended everything he'd done.

He clenched his jaw and braced himself, as if he'd lost something precious—something he'd never had, he reminded himself bitterly. "Ye've remembered."

"Yes, I've remembered," she said with a sneer. "I'm Lady Catriona Duff, and you knew it. You lied to me; you took my brooch and hid it, all to keep me in the dark and dependent on you." Her voice broke, and she covered her face with both hands while her shoulders shook. Her whisper was agonized when she looked up at him with wet eyes. "You let me depend on you, care for you, desire you, and all along you were using me."

Her words cut him, but he deserved the pain. "Aye, it started that way, but it's not how it ended," he said roughly. "I blamed your whole family for what your father had done; I wanted to despise ye as an arrogant aristocrat with no idea what it was like to suffer as my clan has suffered. Instead, I found a woman who treated everyone the same, who felt each person's pain as her own, who tried to help everyone she met."

She slapped him hard across the face, her eyes suddenly blazing within the sheen of unshed tears.

"You made certain I was a dependent, naïve, pliable creature so frightened of the strange world that I never left your side."

"That was never how I saw ye," he insisted. "I saw ye as courageous and optimistic. Ye could have sunk into a corner in fear, but that is no the woman ye are."

"No, it's not me—I'm a woman who doesn't forget the evil done to her and to her whole family."

"Evil done to *your* family?" he shot back to her. "Ye don't think your father deserved far worse than he got, the reward of dying an old, rich man in his own bed?"

"Yes, you've opened my eyes," she said bitterly. "You showed me what kind of man my father was. I knew he was a bastard, but to find out he was a monster . . ."

She shuddered, and he wanted to comfort her, but he'd lost that right—he'd never had that right.

She gathered herself together, and though a tear fell down her cheek, she ignored it to say with sarcasm, "And yet you still needed your revenge."

He could make no rebuttal, for that was the truth.

"What was your plan? Go ahead, explain it to me. Did the brooch show you who I was, daughter of your enemy?"

"I'd seen ye before," he said, "riding through Edinburgh once, in your silks and finery."

"Oh, of course, I deserved to be punished for that."

"Nay, I never thought that. But your father, aye, *he* deserved to be punished, to know what it was like to be missing a child. *His* child was perfectly safe, not sold to agents who planned to use that child until he was crippled or worse."

Though her face blanched, she spoke coldly. "So I was betrayed by the man who I thought had saved me, used to punish a man who was already dead. When did you discover *that* little truth?"

"I went to Castle Kinlochard."

She drew in a sharp breath. "You saw my brother? Is he worried about me? Is his wife full of anxiety? It's not good for the babe she carries."

"They don't believe ye're missing at all. Apparently everyone is used to ye getting so caught up in your social life that ye sometimes forget to write."

She winced, but let out her breath. "At least they're not suffering—yet."

"Aye, and I know they don't deserve to suffer. I knew my vengeance didn't matter anymore. But now ye know where my clan lives, where my faithful men hide; I let ye find out too much."

"So what now—you'll kill me for what I know?" She stiffened her shoulders, lifted her chin. "Do you want to throw me off this cliff right here?"

She gestured wildly toward the glen below, and his stomach twisted as if with vertigo.

"Kill ye? Have ye seen any evidence that I'm a murderer?"

"Fine, you're not a murderer. But you've told me lie upon lie, most especially about myself. You let me think—"

Her voice broke then, and her pain shamed and hurt him.

She steadied herself. "You let me think I might have a husband somewhere, while you . . . made my body feel—" She couldn't go on for a moment, her expression full of grief and disdain. "I agonized over the fear that I was betraying a man I loved with what I felt for you. I lay awake at night in desperation, giving myself headaches trying to remember my life, when all along, the man who'd *saved* my life, who claimed to be protecting me, could have spared me the pain."

"I regretted keeping the truth from ye, but there was nothing I could—" He stopped.

"Nothing you could do?" she finished for him with an ugly laugh.

"Not and protect my clan, which already suffers from stolen children, and a rash chief who got himself outlawed instead of solving their problems."

There was a long silence, during which she turned back to the view of the glen, arms folded over her chest.

Stiffly, she said, "My father is dead, and my brother knows nothing about any of his crimes."

"And ye're sure about your brother?" When she whirled on him, he said, "I had to ask. Although I could see for myself that your clan is at peace under your brother's rule, and that he and his wife seem happy."

"My brother is a good man. He would never condone children being—" She pressed her lips together as if to master herself. "As for the whisky smuggling, I don't know. He only just inherited the earldom a few months ago. That didn't give you justification to steal it."

He leaned closer and spoke coldly. "Nay, your father's crimes made me justified in supporting my clan any way I could."

They glared at each other before Duncan realized what he was doing.

"Arguing about this makes no sense," he said stiffly. "Ye know everything now. What do ye want to do?"

"I want to leave!" she cried. "I want to get as far away from you and your twisted sense of honor as I can. I want to go back to my life." Her voice wobbled, and she gave him a mutinous glare.

"Are ye going to tell my clan everything?"

"Of course not. They *worship* you," she said sarcastically. "They wouldn't believe you could do something like this to me deliberately. I'm a Duff—I know how they'll look at me when they find that out. I'm the *enemy*."

"They won't hate ye."

"No? You did. You had to hate me to do what you've done to me."

"I hated your father."

"Believe whatever lets you sleep at night."

"Ye cannot leave alone. Ye're a vulnerable woman."

"As if I don't have ample proof of that after how you betrayed me."

He took a deep breath. "I've regretted keeping ye here from the moment I realized ye weren't a spy, but I couldn't stop."

"A spy? What are you talking about?"

"I'd never heard of such memory loss. Ye could have been sent here to find out everything about us, to lead your father's men here—anything."

"My father would never—" And then she stopped. "I want to leave. Now. Give me supplies and a horse."

"Nay, I'll not allow it."

"And I won't let you run my life ever again!"

"It has nothing to do with trying to control ye. But I won't let ye put yourself in danger because ye're angry with me. I'll take ye back myself. But I cannot do it yet. There've been rumors of another child kidnapped, but I have no clues yet. I cannot be absent."

She breathed deeply, quickly, as if she would protest, but she didn't. "I don't want to be here," she whispered forlornly, closing her eyes. "I want to go home."

He said nothing, and hoped her good sense would win out so he didn't have to tie her up.

"Very well," she said at last. "But I won't wait long."

"I understand. And what will ye do at Castle Kinlochard?"

"What business is it of yours?"

"Do I need to evacuate the village and the cave, find another place of safety for my people when ye lead your brother to this glen?"

She gave him a look of disdain. "Do you think I'm like you, ready to use innocent people for my revenge?"

"I think ye're a better person than I will ever be," he said quietly. "But I need to make my plans."

"My brother will learn what you've done, but I'll be too confused to lead him back here. Will that satisfy you?"

"Aye, it's more than I deserve."

For a long moment's silence, they simply looked at each other.

"Why are you still here?" she demanded.

He hesitated, then said slowly, "I want to apologize for what happened in the woods."

Her glance was cold. "I'm not going to thank you for being decent by stopping what we did."

"I never meant to frighten ye, or overwhelm ye."

"Don't come near me again, or so help me, my scream will let everyone know what kind of man you are."

He knew when he'd succumbed to his desires that it couldn't last. But now that he'd touched her, kissed her, aroused her, those memories would never leave him.

He took a fortifying breath. "Shall I escort ye back to the cave?"

"Back to my prison, you mean? I hadn't realized how much I've been feeling trapped there, until I followed Ivor and the clansmen."

"I wanted ye to feel safe, not trapped."

"Safe, that is laughable. I thought I was so incredibly lucky to find someone who protected me and didn't try to take advantage of my confusion. I was such a fool."

The stab to his conscience was as if a sword

pierced him. But he'd borne it this long, and would continue to do so until he returned Catriona to her family without betraying his clan's secrets.

She turned and walked away, and Duncan looked once more over the cliff. Perhaps he was just as much of a monster as her father had been.

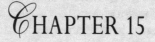HAPTER 15

As Duncan left her with the women, Cat fisted her hands to stop the shaking. Sheena seemed far too aware of Cat's stifled emotions, and it seemed to give the girl pleasure, though she quickly turned away when she saw Cat glance her way. Cat didn't care—the girl could have Duncan.

She felt so very alone, trapped with the knowledge of the truth, but unable—unwilling—to confide in these women, her companions these last weeks. If everyone knew she was a Duff, she'd lose their friendship, perhaps even their respect. And if she had to be with Clan Carlyle for several more days, she didn't want to see that wariness, maybe even disdain, in their eyes.

When Cat had been up on the cliff and seen Duncan for the first time since her revelation, she'd been a cauldron of roiling emotions. To her surprise, after the sorrow and anger had almost strangled her, it was the disappointment that lingered like a bad aftertaste. She'd trusted Duncan, had been so very vulnerable, lost, and alone with no memories—and he'd betrayed her. Deliberately, coldly, cruelly. Yes, he was a man who believed in a good cause—but his methods tarnished his motives. And she'd almost convinced herself she loved him. She shuddered.

As she began to stir one of the cauldrons with a long stick, Cat let her thoughts wander. When she'd first gotten her wild emotions under control, she'd debated stealing a horse and riding away. But it was a long day's journey, perhaps two, to Castle Kinlochard, and without guards and no supplies, she'd be putting herself at risk.

And she'd be running away, something that seemed too cowardly, and easy on Duncan. He'd deserved to know what she thought of him and his betrayal. And besides, he would have figured out the truth and tracked her down. And then where would she be—tied up?

She'd thought about revenge, too—she could have stayed silent, perhaps found out the secrets of their whisky smuggling and stopped it on behalf of her brother, or led her brother there to set a trap. But what would that have accomplished? These people needed the coin that her father and his cohorts had deprived the Carlyle clan of earning, with their chief a wanted outlaw. She knew these people now, and couldn't deliberately hurt them. They were as innocent as she was.

But oh, she wanted to leave. Duncan had insisted she needed an escort, as if he only wanted to protect her—*ha!* she thought bitterly. He wouldn't be protecting her, but protecting his secrets, making sure she told her brother nothing that would harm his people.

When Owen discovered the depth of their father's sins, he would feel guilty, as if he should have stopped the crimes he hadn't known about. She felt the same way, much as her logical self argued against it.

Did Duncan really feel any shame about what he'd done to her? After all they'd shared . . . She turned her head away from the women, as if looking into the distance, so they couldn't see her face. The redness she could blame on heat from the cauldrons, but if she looked like she was going to cry, she'd have to explain.

She could not forget the intimate things she'd allowed Duncan to do to her; she'd even asked him to sleep with her! She shuddered. At least he'd had some bit of decency inside him, and he'd refused. But maybe he'd forget that after a while. She'd grown up hearing that men could be uncontrollable animals when their passions were high. Not that she'd believed her mother, who looked the other way at whatever their father did, so she could continue her carefree, wealthy life. And Cat didn't believe a man like her brother Owen, so scholarly and in control of his emotions, would ever be overcome by anything. But then she'd once glimpsed a glance he'd shared with Maggie, and the heat in it—Cat had blushed and quickly looked away. He was her brother, for heaven's sake.

But if passion could consume a man like Owen, then she didn't know what might happen with Duncan. And she wasn't going to risk finding out. She couldn't stay alone in his chamber for another night. What if he snuck in there and tried—something? He could overpower her, he could—

Or worse, his caresses might overtake her reason and she might very well submit. She hated to admit such a weakness, but she never lied to herself. She despised him for how he'd deceived and used her, preying on her memory loss, watching how much she struggled with it and saying nothing.

And yet when he'd come up to the castle ruins, broad-shouldered and powerful, his dark eyes so intent as if she was the only woman in the world, she'd remembered how he'd brought her body to life, making it hum with pleasure, bringing about a little explosion of passion with just his fingers. Her body remembered, damn him. And lusted. If anyone had ever told her she could be overcome like this, she wouldn't have believed them.

She was not going to stay in his private chamber any longer. She needed the protection of the women around her—these women she was going to lie to. She swallowed hard.

When they took a midday break to serve a simple meal, Cat pulled Maeve aside while the other women refilled the men's tankards of ale from pitchers.

Cat wet her lips and looked earnestly into her friend's concerned eyes. "I'd like to begin sleeping in the great hall, with the rest of the women."

Maeve blinked at her for a moment. "Is there a problem?"

"I don't like being treated differently than everyone else." True enough.

"Himself doesn't mind ye usin' his chamber."

"I know. He's said it over and over again, but I'm growing more uncomfortable with that. It feels like special treatment, makes it seem like there is . . . an understanding between us."

She hadn't meant to say so much, but Maeve had this encouraging, sympathetic way about her.

"And is there?" Maeve asked quietly.

Cat let out a long breath. "There mustn't be. Because of my . . . situation. And I'm worried that because I'm alone, we'll both get . . . ideas."

Maeve nodded. "Very well. Ye're our guest."

No, Cat was a captive—but Maeve didn't know that. What would loyal Maeve, or any of the clan, think of their laird if they knew what he'd done? Cat reminded herself that she was their enemy, and they wouldn't believe her anyway. "Thank you," she said sincerely. "After dinner I'll gather my things."

"I'll give ye the pallet his lairdship has been usin', and he can go back to usin' his own."

Cat wanted to groan, but held it in. Wonderful. She'd be sleeping in his bed yet again. She wasn't going to think about it.

During the afternoon's continuation of the laundry—and after Cat had managed to put Duncan's saddlebag back in the cave, including the brooch, for where else could she keep it hidden?—the women began to discuss a harvest festival to be celebrated in the village the next day. Cat's ears pricked up, and she listened carefully as they discussed attending, and the precautions of having to hide where they were coming from. They spoke with adoration of Duncan, who they felt had saved the village with the barley and other seeds he'd been able to purchase in the spring.

Purchase with money from the sale of Duff whisky, Cat realized. She certainly wanted the price lifted off Duncan's head, so he could help his people by legal methods. Cat wasn't going to condemn the clan because of their chief's method of vengeance. She wasn't going to be like Duncan—or her father.

But a harvest festival would be a chance to escape the cave, even if only briefly. It would remind her of her old life, where she was free to attend parties and balls, where men bowed before her rather than held her captive. But none of those men had been special to her; she had no place to call her own, to nurture. She'd have to build such a life for herself, and she couldn't do that until she went home.

But for now, the harvest festival would distract her. She had to figure out how to get herself invited, and convince Duncan it was safe to allow her to attend.

Cat used Duncan's absence to remove her clothing from his chamber, then hung them where Maeve indicated, on pegs driven into the cave wall. Sheena watched her with her mouth agape, before her expression turned triumphant.

Ignoring her, Cat went to find Finn. She stood with her arms akimbo, blocking Finn's escape from the great hall. "I hear the harvest festival is tomorrow. You are not attending unless you bathe."

The boy mutinously crossed his arms over his chest. "Nay, I'll not. The pool is freezin'."

"You wouldn't know, because it's been so long since you've been in it."

He scowled.

"Very well, I'll tell Himself that you've chosen to stay here tomorrow."

She turned around, and didn't have long to wait before Finn grumbled, "I'll do it."

She hid her smile of satisfaction. It drained away when she saw Duncan enter the cave. Giving him her back, she said to Finn, "I'll accompany you and make sure it's done."

"I don't need a nursemaid!"

"I do believe you've totally ignored Maeve when she's requested the same. I'll make sure you actually bathe this time, rather than wash around the edges. Go find a change of clothing, and I'll bring the soap and towels."

Finn stomped away and she hid a smile, in case he saw it and was offended. Normally, he was such a mild-mannered boy, that his attitude surprised her. He seemed almost afraid.

Her hunch was correct. By the time Finn joined her in the cave pool, after carefully laying a shoe in the passageway—"Are ye certain no one will come in?" Finn kept asking—Cat felt like she could see the whites of his eyes, the way he stared so hard at the pool.

"No one has ever bothered me," Cat said patiently. "Isn't the waterfall beautiful?"

But Finn only stared at the dark pool. He crossed his arms over his chest. "I'll not go in there."

Cat withheld a sigh. "You have to, Finn. You smell. This is your chance to be seen by a nice family."

She thought he might revolt against that part, but he ignored it altogether.

"I cannot swim—I'll drown!"

"It's not over your head, I promise. Shall I go in first and prove it to you?"

He frowned uncertainly. "Ye'd do that?"

"If you don't mind seeing me in my chemise."

"What is a chemise?"

"The undergarment beneath my gown. It's as thick and sturdy as a nightshift."

Still looking suspicious, Finn only nodded. Cat thought he might be using any means to procrastinate, but she was willing to take the chance. Turning her back, she unlaced the bodice of the gown, set aside the stomacher resting behind the laces, and peeled the bodice over her shoulders. After untying the laces of her skirt, she let it fall to the floor and stepped out of it. Her stays unlaced in the front, and she took a deep breath when they were gone.

When she turned around, Finn was watching her with bewilderment. "Why do ye wear all that? Surely 'tis uncomfortable."

She smiled. "It is what a woman wears. I've spent my whole life like this."

"Ye remember something?" Finn asked eagerly.

Her smile faded as once again she was confronted with the knowledge that she'd have to lie to all the friends she'd made in Clan Carlyle. When she wavered in her resolve, she imagined their reactions upon knowing it was *her* father who benefited from the sale of Carlyle children— who didn't care about hurting a little boy like Finn. She felt like a coward, protecting herself. But perhaps she was also preventing strife within the clan, which might happen if they had to take sides against each other over her. And all of this was because of Duncan Carlyle and his dishonorable behavior toward her.

For just a moment, she thought about having a measure of revenge by revealing to his people that he'd known who she was from the beginning. He deserved anything she'd do to him.

But she looked into the sweet—but dirty— face of Finn, and knew she couldn't destroy Clan Carlyle. That's what might happen if they knew the truth and lost all respect for Duncan. He was lucky she was a better person than he was.

Cat touched Finn's chin. "Sadly, I have no new memories." Which was true—they were old memories that kept coming back to her, scenes here and there kept popping up while she'd helped wash clothes, from the shocking time her mother had explained what men wanted on their wedding night, to the charity ball in London where she'd first realized she might be attractive enough to find a husband someday. It was as if, now that her memories were free, they tumbled over each other in a hurry to surface.

Finn heaved a sigh. "Ye're so brave. Tell me again how it felt to wake up and not know yourself."

"You're putting off the inevitable. Into the pool we go. I'll go first."

She stepped down onto the first ledge of the pool, and the water was frigid. Her chemise caught in the little current that expanded out from the base of the waterfall, billowing out around her. Feeling with her toes, she found the next ledge and sank deeper, to just above her knees. One more step found her up to her waist, and she tried not to let her teeth chatter. For a moment, she thought of the bathing tub that was brought right to her bedchamber, the line of servants carrying buckets of hot water, the piles of soft, expensive towels, and the finest soaps.

"See?" she called. "It's not bad."

She turned to see if Finn was undressing, only to stumble back in shock as Finn came barreling toward her, fully clothed but for his shoes. He jumped from ledge to ledge until he reached hers, crouched until the water reached his neck. After scrubbing his face hard with both hands, he jumped back out again, streaming water.

Cat could only gape at him for a long moment, as he shivered and looked proud of himself. She stepped up from ledge to ledge until she faced him head-on.

"Finn, it's obvious you don't want to undress in front of me, and I understand that. But you have to take off those terrible clothes and put on new ones. I can turn my back."

Then she frowned and peered down curiously into his small face, free of dirt. A spasm of alarm widened the boy's eyes, and he tried to turn away but she caught his chin.

"Finn, what is your name short for?" she asked softly.

He said nothing.

"Fiona?" Cat whispered.

"Nay, say no more!" The blue eyes flooded with tears.

"Tell me. I'll tell no one else."

"Finola." The word came out full of misery and despair. "Ye'll tell Himself and the clan, I know ye will."

"I will not." Cat had her own secrets, after all. She stared down at the girl, her heart aching for her. It was terrible enough to be an orphan in the dangerous parts of Glasgow, but to be a little girl must be far worse. "You must have had a good reason to hide your true self."

At first, Finn said nothing. Cat remained silent.

The little girl's shoulders slumped. "Me mum was dying. 'Twas her idea, because I would have no one."

"How long has it been?" Cat asked gently.

Finn shrugged. "Many years."

Cat put a hand on her shoulder. "You're not alone now."

Finn hesitated, then shrugged it off. "I was safe this way."

"You were very brave and resourceful. I'm sorry your mother passed away."

"I—I barely remember what she looks like," Finn admitted, her voice breaking.

"Our memories can play tricks on us."

Finn searched Cat's face, and Cat felt herself blush.

"You don't need to see your mother's face to feel her love inside you," Cat said gently. "And you're not in Glasgow anymore. You're where people want to take care of you."

Finn stiffened. "Tryin' to push me off on someone else, ye mean."

"They want to find you a good home."

"*This* can be me home. Tell them. Himself listens to ye."

"That is not true. Maeve is the one—"

"He doesn't look at Maeve the way he does you."

Cat flushed. What had the little girl seen—and what did other people surmise?

"Finn, Duncan wants you to have a new mother and father, not a group of people living a dangerous life."

"If havin' a mother and father means leavin' here, I don't want it." Finn's lower lip trembled as if she fought to control herself.

Cat looked down at the water that still dripped from the girl's garments. "We don't need to discuss it now. It's more important that you wash and then change your clothes before you catch your death."

Finn blinked. "Me mum used to say that."

Cat suddenly had another flash of memory. Her mother, who was once so focused on her British aristocracy, had apologized to Cat's cousin Riona for saying nothing while her husband had allowed Riona to be captured. Lady Aberfoyle had wanted a new start with her children, and Cat had been grateful and willing to believe things could change. Without thinking, Cat mused aloud, "People can change."

Finn frowned her confusion at the change of topic. "People don't change," she said firmly.

The girl's lifetime of experience had made her bitter; changing that would be a long process. "Then they can change their clothing. Go do so— but wash up first."

The little girl went to her pile of fresh garments and gave Cat an almost fearful look over her shoulder that nearly broke her heart. Cat turned her back and hugged herself, giving the girl privacy as she began to splash in the water.

As Duncan crossed the great hall toward the footbridge, he saw Maeve give him a concerned look. When he turned toward her, she waved him away and went back to her work table, shaking her head.

He didn't know what that was about, but if she didn't need to talk, that was fine with him. Unless Catriona had confessed what he'd done to her. She'd promised she wouldn't, but Maeve was her closest friend here. He couldn't blame her if she needed to talk. But he imagined she would keep her word. It meant much to her—and his meant so little.

How had he come to this?

As he entered his—and now Catriona's— chamber, he came to a halt, frowning. The usual mess of women's garments, shoes, and hair fasteners was gone, and the book she'd been reading was closed upon his trunk. He stormed back into the great hall, and Maeve was watching as if waiting for him. She pointed to pegs in the wall, and he recognized Catriona's garments. Maeve shrugged as if clueless; Duncan nodded, then returned to his chamber.

So Catriona had relinquished her privacy, but didn't seem to have told Maeve why. He should be relieved to have his *own* privacy once again, but he hated the thought that she might be afraid of him, afraid that he might try to seduce her. How could he blame her?

There was a commotion in the passageway, and Finn raced past. Duncan leaned out into the hallway to see the boy carrying a bundle of clothing that dripped on the cave floor. Duncan looked back toward the pool cave, saw that a light still flickered, and went to investigate. He drew up short in the entranceway, stunned to see Catriona standing next to the pool in a chemise that was wet to her waist. She froze when she saw him, and he looked his fill like a man starved for the sight of a woman. This particular woman. The chemise was made of linen rather than the silk she was probably used to, but the sodden fabric clung to her thighs and calves. Without the bulk of gown and petticoats, she looked small and delicate, so beautiful and forbidden to him that he ached. He thought of all he could uncover and touch and kiss. She didn't hide herself in embarrassment, but stared at him, her face pale and disdainful.

The air between them seemed heavily charged, as if a thunderstorm were imminent, the kind that would crackle through the mountain, start floods that would alter the very landscape itself.

He briefly bowed his head. "Mistress Catherine."

As if he didn't know her real name.

It was a long time before she took a deep breath and arched a brow. "Did you need something from me?"

She didn't say his Christian name, and he missed the sound of it on her lips.

He cleared his throat. "There was no shoe outside, and Finn went rushing past with dripping clothes. I was curious."

"I made him bathe for the harvest festival," she said coldly, "and he was not happy about it."

"I see. And did he wash his clothing, too?"

"He decided to bathe wearing them."

Duncan simply blinked at her for a moment.

Catriona looked away. "It's a long story, and not mine to tell. Finn will be fine for the festival."

"Do ye wish to attend?"

Her piercing gaze returned to him. "You would allow it?"

"You already know everything. And ye've given your word ye won't reveal where my people are."

"You trust me?" she demanded.

"I do."

"You think you know me so well?" That ugly disdain he well deserved had returned.

"I'd never doubt your word."

He found himself missing the easy way they

had been together, the way her eyes had lit with excitement and eagerness when they talked. He only had himself to blame for its absence.

"I imagine it would be safer for your secrets were I to stay hidden," Catriona mused, eyeing him.

He crossed his arms over his chest. "My people are vulnerable because of the price on my head. I'd rather stay away myself, but they continue to insist they need me to make the occasional appearance, and they've decided an official assembly is necessary."

She frowned. "You'll hold court, then, make decisions on behalf of your clan?"

"I will. But ye'll not have to sit through such things. There'll be booths with items for sale and contests of skill."

"And I can just wander freely?"

"Not alone, no. Ye'll be with someone. Ye must understand that my people are vulnerable. I've not told them all where our encampment is. They know about the children, but not the smuggling of whisky. I protect them, but they don't need to suffer for what I've had to do, any more than they already are."

He'd kept her trapped here so long, it had to be a relief to soon be out among people again.

"What have you told them about me?" she asked.

"Very little. I didn't want people assuming ye're my—" He broke off.

"Whore?" she said starkly.

"Ye could never be that," he said between gritted teeth. "Since the men know ye've lost your memory, I've given permission for their families to know. That should protect your reputation."

She gave a bitter laugh. "My reputation? I live in a cave with dozens of strange men. I imagine I'll have no reputation left when people find out the truth."

Another thing he'd done to her with his plot against her father, another thing she had every right to hate him for.

"I am sorry." The words were gruff and inadequate.

The silence between them grew, and he couldn't help continuing to stare at her.

She licked her lips and looked away. "I wish to dress."

"Of course." He paused in the doorway. "Ye didn't need to leave my chamber. I would never force ye to be alone with me."

"I cannot take that chance."

Her eyes betrayed a stark angst as she turned away. He left to give her her privacy. She'd brought such grace into his life. Being with her had given him back a part of himself that had seemed dead for a long time. But it had only been a cruel illusion of his own making.

CHAPTER 16

Cat was able to distract herself the rest of the day, but that night, when she huddled on her pallet, unable to sleep because of the grunting and snoring of dozens of men beyond the screen, her mind kept betraying her by returning to the moment she'd faced Duncan in the pool cave, wearing naught but a chemise. She hoped she'd portrayed calm indifference, but underneath, she'd been aghast that her body didn't seem to care that Duncan had betrayed her. Her skin had felt flushed, her breath had been shallow, her breasts had ached to be touched, and between her thighs—oh, she wasn't going to remember how that felt, didn't want to admit she was desperate to experience that moment of pleasure again.

She tried to think of something else—stirring the hot water in a laundry cauldron, kneading bannock dough, pulling weeds in the vegetable garden, all chores she'd never done before she'd come to Clan Carlyle.

She'd never lain with a man, either.

This was what her giggling friends had meant by being attracted to a man who wasn't good for you. Your brain wouldn't listen and your heart heard only its own, desperate beat.

She rolled onto her back and flung her forearm over her eyes in disgust.

In the morning, at least Cat had something else to concentrate on. She was more excited by the harvest festival than she wanted to be. She didn't like being beholden to Duncan, when she should have been free all along. But her anger couldn't hold a candle to her curiosity. Though she'd had a hard time sleeping, now she felt awake and eager. She mounted her horse and tried to avoid Duncan, but he rode up beside her with Finn at his back. Sheena rode her own horse just behind. The rest of the men dispersed then, disappeared through woods or along the cliff or past the paddock.

Seeing Cat's frown, Duncan said, "My people don't know where our encampment is. We try not to be seen coming from the same place, even by Carlyles."

She nodded and said to Finn, "Neither of us will breathe a word."

Finn shook her head solemnly, while Sheena rolled her eyes, as if they lacked all good sense.

Duncan glanced over his shoulder and said to Finn, "This is a chance for ye to be seen. There are families considering bringing ye in, so take every opportunity to show yourself for the good lad ye are."

There was a determined look in Finn's eyes that made Cat uneasy, but she kept quiet. She

looked back and saw Maeve standing at the cave
entrance, waving.

"Why isn't she coming with us?" Cat asked. "I
heard the men say they were taking turns guarding the cave. She isn't needed here."

Duncan nodded. "She'll come. In her own time."

"But—"

"'Tis her choice, Catherine."

Cat nodded, but didn't feel convinced. With a
last wave, Maeve retreated into the cave. Cat eyed
Duncan, and didn't like feeling that they had
something in common, a guilt they shouldn't feel
but couldn't control regardless. Every day, Duncan had to remember that his mother disfigured
Maeve to punish her husband. Cat would always
live with the knowledge that her father had allowed Riona to be kidnapped, when it could have
ended badly. And now she knew he'd allowed
children to have the same fate, torn from their
families, never to return.

After an hour's ride, they followed a path
around the side of a hill, and the glen was laid out
before them, the reds and golds of autumn like
a painter's palette. The village itself was smaller
than any Cat had seen before, only a dozen stone
cottages with tall thatched roofs that sloped near
to the rocky, uneven ground. There were vegetable fields nearby, and in the distance, shaggy
cattle roamed the bare hillsides.

Dozens of people were gathered in clumps of
twos and threes. They didn't seem to care about
the mud or the overcast sky. Though it seemed
like a sparse, barren existence that made her feel

uncomfortably privileged, Cat could hear music being played, and the sounds of laughter and singing. There were booths set up, their tables guarded against the rain by makeshift pavilions. A young man was juggling, a young woman called that she had venison pasties for sale.

Cat saw the first person notice her, and then heads seemed to turn in an undulating wave of curiosity. She glanced at Duncan, but he didn't seem to be at all worried, as if he knew that these villagers, in such a remote part of the Highlands, would never have seen her before.

It was . . . odd to draw attention because she was a stranger, rather than because she was the daughter of an earl. Wherever she'd lived or visited in her lifetime, everyone knew her. Her father, her family, were the subject of awe. Even in England, their title and wealth made them a favorite at every salon and ball. Here in the Highlands, it was Duncan who was the subject of awe, the one who protected these people, the one who saved them. Perhaps they wouldn't even care the lengths he'd gone to to support them. Whisky smuggling or cattle raiding—it was all a way to get even with your neighbor for whatever had been done century upon century.

Duncan wore a sober expression, a man serious about what he did, who bore the weight of his people on his shoulders and accepted the good and bad that came with it.

Cat's station as daughter of the earl had kept her apart from the ordinary people of her clan, the tenants who scraped by in the barren mountains.

Now as they rode past the cottages, she felt as uneasy as if she wore fine silk instead of homespun wool; she felt like a fraud.

Sheena saw someone she knew and veered away from them. Cat followed Duncan past every cottage to where a little lane lined with flowers led to a small manor. Behind, Cat could see an extensive garden, both vegetables and flowers. The front door opened and Duncan's sister Muriel emerged, carrying a baby and leading a little boy by the hand.

Though Cat was pleased to see the woman, she also realized that Muriel was probably her companion—her keeper—for the day. Cat, Duncan, and Finn dismounted. Another boy, a little older, came around the house and took the horses' reins.

Duncan put a hand on the boy's shoulder. "This is Muriel's eldest, Logan. He's a fine one with horses, and will see to ours this day."

The boy reddened, but gave his uncle a quick, grateful look. Then he stared at Finn, who stared back.

"Ye want to see the stables?" Logan asked.

"Aye," Finn said without hesitation. She didn't look back at Duncan or Cat as she followed the boy.

Duncan was frowning.

"Och, stop that. The boy will be fine." Muriel put the baby in Cat's arms. "This is Alice."

Cat, unused to babies of any kind, gave a little gasp and tried not to stiffen. Muriel didn't even check to see if she was doing it right, just turned to her brother. Cat's eyes must have been wide with uncertainty, because she saw Duncan press his lips into a firm line as if to keep from smiling.

"Support her head—that's the most important thing ye need to know," Duncan said.

He never smiled, she remembered. He'd never had the sort of life that inspired smiling. She forced away a hint of sympathy. He was a kidnapper, no better than the men he pursued.

Well, that was a little harsh . . .

And he knew something about babies. That was more than she could say. Although with both her cousin and her sister-in-law with child, Cat would be getting more than enough experience soon.

When she went home.

"She'll be fine with Alice," Muriel said.

"I will?" Cat asked. "But—"

"Ye'll be spending the day with my sister," Duncan said.

That should have made Cat happy. She wasn't sure why it annoyed her. It was probably because she was suspicious of him, as if he were dumping her onto his sister while he did something secretive.

Alice suddenly arched her little body and, startled, Cat gasped. The baby cupped her head with tiny fists, still asleep, little elbows by her ears.

"Ye've got her just fine," Duncan said.

She realized he looked down on his squirming niece with an expression that bordered on contentment.

"She's a feisty one," he murmured, bending over the babe.

Which put his face far too close to Cat's own.

"I try to see them as much as I can," he said quietly. "They might be the only children of my blood."

She frowned. "Are you trying to say you'll never marry? You're the chief—why wouldn't you?"

He glanced at her, his dark eyes speculative. "I'm a man with a price on my head. I would never offer for a woman and put her in such danger."

"You don't know what the future will bring." Was she trying to console him, inspire him, or alter her family guilt? Guilt—there was enough of that to go around, with the lies she was now telling.

He looked at her, and she just looked back. Lies he'd forced her into, she reminded herself.

"Alice'll want to be fed soon, I imagine." Muriel was on her knees next to her little boy, using her wet finger to wipe a smudge from his cheek while he squirmed almost like his sister. "But we can walk a bit."

Duncan straightened and spoke to Muriel as if his words didn't affect Cat. "Stay within the village."

Muriel rolled her eyes. "'Tis where the festival is, aye?"

Duncan lifted a little purse. "Some coins for the two of ye to spend."

Money from her family whisky, Cat knew. But she'd come prepared. "I have my own coins," she insisted. "They were hidden within my clothing when you found me."

Nodding, he glanced at Cat, then cleared his

throat. Alice was rooting at Cat's breast, and Cat looked helplessly at Muriel, who smiled with maternal indulgence.

"I guess the bairn won't be waiting. Come here, sweetling." Muriel took her child and retreated into her house, calling over her shoulder. "I won't be long, Catherine."

And then it was just Duncan and Cat—and a four-year-old who'd been crouching in the dirt, but now looked up at her skeptically.

Duncan squatted down. "Robby, did ye catch any worms today?"

Cat grimaced, wondering if he was trying to give the little boy ideas. But Robby held up his grimy hand, and there was something dark and squished there. Wincing, Cat couldn't help staring in shock when Duncan smiled at his nephew.

The tug deep inside her was startling. He smiled in a way she'd never seen on his face before, genuine and full of love. It made him more handsome than dangerous, and she thought that if she'd seen him across a ballroom floor, she would have been smitten.

He nodded at the boy's little fist. "Perhaps next time ye'd best let him go home."

"Papa said I need him for fishing. Fish eat worms."

"They do," Duncan agreed. "Do ye know what else worms are good for? Gardens. Let's put your worm there for today. No time to fish during the festival."

Dumbfounded, Cat watched as Duncan and his

nephew reverently placed the dead worm next to the last roses of early autumn. After washing up in water brought up from the well, they sat side by side, discussing the fish in the local streams. She felt like an intruder, but also a curious observer of this man who was her enemy.

Except he was conversing with a four-year-old about how to catch fish to feed one's family. She thought about Duncan's parents, locked in a private feud that separated them, eventually permanently, from their children. How little softness he'd had in his life, and yet he could spare time and attention to his young nephew. Confusion, anger, disappointment—they were all wrapped up inside her, and she didn't know how she was supposed to feel.

Muriel emerged with the now-sleeping baby. "She's happy now," she told Cat, smiling. "Shall we go join the festival?"

Robby jumped up from the bench and splayed his clean hands. "Uncle Duncan said we put the worm with the flowers, not just the fish."

Muriel smiled at her son. "Your uncle knows what he's talking about."

Cat glanced at Duncan. "Why aren't you coming with us?"

He stood up. "I have the assembly to prepare for."

"Can we attend?"

"'Tis not necessary. Ye'll have a better day with Muriel and the children. I'll find ye later when we leave." With a nod to his sister, he left through her gate.

Muriel looked down at Robby. "Can ye take Mistress Catherine's hand? There'll be plenty of people and horses and commotion—we don't want to lose ye."

Robby impatiently grasped Cat's hand and pulled. She picked up her pace, then looked over her shoulder at Muriel, who carried the sleeping baby and gradually caught up with them. They followed the little lane back into the green at the center of the stone cottages. Cat felt shy and uncomfortable with all she knew and wasn't saying, especially to Muriel. But soon she was tasting the labor of the best cooks in the village, admiring the wax candles and cloth for sale, watching archery contests and rock-throwing, and listening to pipers play. She took turns holding the baby or running after the inquisitive Robby.

Gradually, the villagers became accustomed to her, probably because of Muriel. Their open skepticism and wariness became curiosity, leading to questions about how she fell, how it could be true that she had no memories. Some people talked loud and slow, as if her wits were addled. More than once, Muriel seemed to be overcome with a coughing fit to hide her laughter, which only made Cat feel as if she soon wouldn't be able to control her giggles.

Occasionally she caught a glimpse of Duncan, always on the edges of the crowd, never the center, though he was their chief. Maybe as chief, he felt it wasn't his place to become friendly with his people. She knew how important it was for him to project strength, after his father's failures. Or maybe he simply didn't know how to be among them.

Maeve was just like her laird, a ghost on the fringes, her plaid worn as a hood about her head, draped to hide her disfigured face.

When Cat saw her and raised a hand, Muriel told her, "She's always afraid of frightening the children, no matter how I point out that my own children are used to her, and others could be the same."

"By staying remote, doesn't she inspire more suspicion or fear?"

"Aye, she does," Muriel agreed with a heavy sigh.

"She always seems so confident at the cave," Cat said. "I never would have suspected . . ."

"That she has the same self-doubt as any of us?"

"Not you," Cat countered with disbelief.

Muriel chuckled. "Aye, me. Our older sister Winifred is far more social and dominating than I. After Father killed Mother—"

Cat tried not to flinch at the bald statement.

"—I didn't know if I could ever be normal again. Winifred redoubled her efforts to find a husband to escape, but I was too young—and perhaps too overwhelmed—to do that. My grief and guilt almost disrupted my friendship with Maeve, but she was the one who wouldn't let it. In many ways she retreated from strangers or even acquaintances, but she was fiercely loyal to her friends."

"She took me under her wing."

"Aye, ye were an injured bird, were ye not?

She could never resist someone who needed her help."

At last, Cat and Muriel sat on a rock wall in the shade watching Robby play with the other boys. Muriel was nursing Alice again, and Cat found herself glancing at the other woman with envy. Muriel's little family did not have wealth or fine castles, but she was happier and more content than Cat had ever been. Maybe it was the love of the men in her life, and the children who completed her world. Cat had intended to flee the Highlands and her pregnant relatives, find her own little world. Instead she was here watching another woman have what she herself couldn't.

Cat sighed over the conflicting emotions bubbling inside her.

"Be patient with yourself," Muriel said.

Cat glanced at her in surprise. "I didn't say— well, perhaps I didn't have to," she admitted wryly.

"Whenever things seem to be going badly, I remind myself of the good things, and how it could be so much worse."

"Aye, I could have become a drooling invalid when I hit my head," Cat said.

"And if your memories never return, ye have a chance to begin anew."

"But where? I don't know where I belong." And that wasn't a lie. She did not want to spend the rest of her life in her brother's household, watching his little family grow. She tried to tell herself she could marry, but explaining her attraction to Duncan seemed difficult.

"Ye'll never be alone in the world," Muriel said, her voice suddenly sober. "Duncan'll see to that."

Cat couldn't help the frown that lowered her brows. "No, I will not burden him."

"He is the Carlyle, our chief. 'Tis his duty."

"I will not be some man's duty," Cat insisted angrily.

Robby, on his hands and knees in the dirt, turned and looked at her wide-eyed. She must have spoken too loudly.

With a contrite glance at Muriel, she murmured, "I'm sorry. I know Duncan is a good chief, and that he means well." For others, not her. "I am just . . . frustrated."

When Muriel put a comforting hand on Cat's arm, Cat felt her deception like bile at the back of her throat. Duncan had started this farce, but she was continuing it.

At last she was distracted from her self-absorbed thoughts by a glimpse beyond the cottages of a manor on the far side of the village.

She stood up to get a better look, but the cottages blocked it. "Is that another manor?"

Muriel didn't even bother looking. "Oh, aye. That's the home we grew up in."

"So that's *Duncan's* manor?"

"The one he won't live in?" Muriel asked wryly. "Aye, that one. Right now he prefers the cave, for all the reasons ye already know. But someday . . . someday I hope he'll be able to live a normal life again."

Knowing she should reassure the woman, Cat said, "He will, I'm sure. When this is all over."

Muriel nodded, her eyes a little sad, until she looked down into the face of little Alice, who smiled up at her. Cat suddenly realized that the crowd had thinned, and most of the men were gone. Duncan's clan assembly. She wanted to be there.

She told Muriel she needed a few minutes of privacy, but instead, moved quickly from cottage to cottage until she found the largest one, where people of the clan were entering by twos and threes. It was easy enough to wait until the entrants thinned, then slip in and stand behind them at the back, peering between broad shoulders to see. Melville frowned at her, but he didn't make any move to send her away.

Duncan sat at a table in front, papers and accounting ledgers spread before him. Ivor stood to one side, intimidating with his sheathed sword at one hip, his pistols tucked in his belt. Other young men of the clan either stood behind him or in the first rows. The rest of the benches were filled with villagers, both men and women.

For a long while, Duncan took care of clan business, dealing with tacksmen who oversaw the land leased from the clan, and negotiating the exchange of lands so that everyone had a turn at the best tacks. Then to her surprise, she watched the men begin to line up, and Duncan began to hand out coins to each, while Ivor meticulously recorded everything in a book.

She suddenly realized what was happening— Duncan was partitioning out to each villager a share of the whisky smuggling money—her clan's money. She sat still and shocked, knowing that represented money that her clan had sweated and toiled for—but whose labor had been paid for by her father. This wasn't money out of her clansmen's pockets, but her brother's. Did Owen even know about the illegal whisky, or was it someone below him who managed it?

But here, in Clan Carlyle, the people were able to see up close that their laird provided for them, even though he was a wanted man. It was hard to blame him for helping his people. There was much to be admired about a man who sacrificed his own well-being and comfort to see to the poor and weak.

She wouldn't admire him, but thought grudgingly that he was more than the man who held her captive.

Next there were the disagreements to be mediated, and Duncan showed himself to be a stern but fair man. She remembered someone telling her that Duncan had once been young and impulsive; that man had grown up. He listened to both sides of a disagreement, consulted his gentlemen, and rendered as fair a verdict as he could. Not everyone left happy, she realized, but the respect he was granted was obvious.

She wondered what would happen if she brought her own complaint to the assembly. Who would punish the chief for kidnapping an innocent woman? But she was a Duff, after all, an enemy.

Would he be treated as his father had, as if his verdict was divine, granted from generations of chiefs before him? Didn't Duncan see he was doing the same thing as his father had done? He was taking the punishment of *her* father into his own hands, and didn't care who was hurt as he pursued his vengeance. His blindness both frustrated and exasperated her.

At that point, their gazes chanced to meet. She stiffened. Did he see the irony of what he did here?

She went back outside, leaving him to his lofty position and its responsibilities—including the ones he betrayed.

Out in the dirt lane, she was so preoccupied, she ran right into Finn when the girl went running by.

Cat caught her by the shoulders. "Finn? What—"

"Get back here, ye devil!" someone called.

Wearing a grin, Finn shrugged off Cat and kept running. Cat realized that she was following Logan, and that Muriel and Maeve were bearing down on them behind an elderly woman who was red-faced with anger.

"Catherine," Muriel called with relief. "Take Alice, will ye?"

Cat found the baby in her arms once again, and this time she wasn't peacefully sleeping. She'd been jarred by her mother's abrupt departure, and now she screwed her face into a little red wrinkled tomato and began to howl.

Cat jostled her carefully, up and down, like she'd seen mothers do. "You'll be fine, little Alice, just be patient." She tried to see what was going on in the parade of two children and two adults that had just passed her, but they were already out of sight around a cottage. Cat wanted to follow them, but the baby howled louder, and she didn't know what to do.

"She wants to be up on your shoulder," said a deep, patient voice.

She whirled around to see Duncan straightening after having ducked beneath a low doorway.

"On my shoulder?" she echoed, dumbfounded as to how she could accomplish that and still support Alice's head, as she'd been warned.

Duncan took the baby out of her arms, and put her right up on his chest, where her little face could peek over his shoulder. Alice calmed down immediately, put her fist in her mouth, and sucked.

Cat let out a relieved sigh, then admitted, "She likes you much more than me."

He arched one brow. "Much more than *you* like me?"

She could feel a hot flush of outrage work from her chest up into her face. "A lot better than *she* likes *me*," she quickly clarified. "You know how I feel about you. You may have your people enthralled by your performance at the assembly, but I know what you're truly capable of."

"I enthralled them?" he said, ignoring her condemnation.

"You cannot be asking for a compliment from me."

"Nay, but ye seemed to be offering one."

"Believe whatever fiction you want."

He continued absently rubbing Alice's back. "I was doing my duty to my clan. They deserve the best I can give them."

Regardless of who gets hurt, she thought. But he was standing there holding an infant with the same ease he held a sword. He seemed good at everything he tried—except dealing with his father and hers.

Thinking of his father brought a sudden flash of memory—the letters she'd found several weeks ago in Duncan's trunk. She remembered that bold "A" by the man who'd threatened Laird Carlyle. Now she thought she might recognize the handwriting—and felt a surge of nausea. Did that "A" stand for Aberfoyle? If those threats had been made by her father, those letters were proof.

And then all she'd learned about Duncan's father swirled together in her mind. Duncan didn't respect him—but if he'd read those letters, he would have known his father had tried to stop the kidnapping of innocents, too. Suddenly she knew she needed to see the letters again.

Duncan looked around. "Why do ye have the bairn again?"

Cat was startled back into awareness of the present. "Oh, it's Finn! Something happened with him and Logan and a clanswoman. I have to know what's wrong."

"Catherine—"

Ignoring Duncan, she picked up her skirts and began to run in the same direction that Finn and the women had gone. She didn't see them at first, and passed a second cottage. Upon hearing raised voices, she turned down another dirt path and found a group gathered about Finn, whose folded arms covered her chest, and her head hunched between her shoulders, turtle-like. Logan stood at the girl's side, looking bewildered.

Maeve's expression was patient as she said something to the angry older woman. As Cat approached, she could hear the retort.

"The lads should be switched, and I'm the one who can do it," said the woman, stepping toward Finn and Logan menacingly.

Finn, trapped at the back of the building but still uncowed, stepped forward as if to shield Logan. Muriel tensed, probably wanting to do the same.

"Mistress MacFarlane, it was a foolish prank on the boy's part," Maeve said calmly.

"What foolish prank?" Cat asked.

"And who do ye be?" the old woman demanded.

"My name is Catherine, and I've been taking care of Finn since he was rescued."

"Ye're Himself's fancy lass, are ye?"

Cat stiffened, sensing she wasn't being complimented. She glanced at Finn, who didn't hide her curiosity. "I am a woman who was also rescued by Laird Carlyle, just like Finn."

The old woman snorted, but only turned back to Maeve. "The lads need a switchin'."

"What did he do?" Cat asked again.

Muriel sighed. "They were throwing mud balls at a fence, but overshot the target . . . many times."

"Mud come flyin' all over me fine cloth I'd worked hard to weave," the old woman cried. "No one will buy it now."

Cat winced. "I'm so sorry for the boys' mistake." But was it a mistake? She'd seen Finn tossing horseshoes against the paddock fence and hitting it perfectly every time.

Finn's glance at her was momentarily sly before turning innocent once again.

"The boys did not understand how important the cloth's sale is, Mistress MacFarlane," Cat said. "Finn, and I assume Logan, will wash all of it for you and anything else they dirtied."

Finn frowned, but said nothing.

Cat gave the girl her own frown. "Won't you, Finn." It wasn't a question.

Muriel elbowed Logan, who gulped and nodded, whispering, "Aye, mistress."

Finn's gaze became fearful, leading Cat to turn and see Duncan entering the fray, the baby still on his shoulder. Muriel tsked and went to take her child, leaving Duncan to look more intimidating as he folded his arms across his chest.

"We always repair our mistakes," he said in a cool voice.

Logan and Finn bobbed their heads quickly.

Mistress MacFarlane's expression softened as she curtsied. "Laird Carlyle, yer help is much appreciated."

But not that of his "fancy lass," Cat thought sourly.

"Follow me, lads," Maeve said, her voice brisk but still kind. "We'll see what Mistress MacFarlane needs ye to do." She readjusted the scarf across her face and shooed them before her.

Mistress MacFarlane and Muriel followed behind, and when Cat would have accompanied them, Duncan put a hand on her arm. She pulled away, although she tried not to be too obvious.

"Do not touch me," she whispered, tilting her head to look him in the eyes.

"Fine. But I only meant to say that ye don't think that shower of mud was an accident," he said.

Reluctantly surprised at his insight, she said, "No, I don't."

"Why would my nephew and Finn want to ruin the harvest festival?"

"Not ruin it," Cat pointed out, "but call attention to themselves. Or Finn wanted to, anyway. Logan might have been totally innocent of planning any damage."

"Finn has been a good lad. What has changed?"

Cat debated if she was revealing Finn's confidences, and decided it would all be public eventually. "You want to give him to a strange family, and he doesn't want to go. I think he believes making the village disapprove of him will ensure no one here picks him."

Duncan frowned. "But—"

"Don't you see? He knows all of us now. We've shown him the most security in his young life. He thinks being given to another family is the same thing as the indentured servitude the sheriff's men stole him for."

"I've had much success finding the orphan children good homes," Duncan insisted.

"He doesn't know that—nor does he care. This is all about *him*, a boy who's been alone for several years now." A little girl who hadn't had the protection of anyone. Cat didn't know if she'd really understood how alone and defenseless a woman could feel until she'd lost her memory and been manipulated by Duncan. But now she felt a solidarity with Finn.

Duncan rubbed a hand on the back of his neck. "I cannot excuse what he did."

"Of course not. Actions have consequences."

His expression didn't change, although he did look away.

And she felt childish, though she had a right to her anger. She felt a pang of sorrow that he could do this to her—that her father could have started it all by allowing children to be stolen.

Duncan sighed. "Then let us witness the punishment." He gestured for her to lead the way.

Finn and Logan were ordered to fetch water from the well in many trips and bring it to boil in a cauldron that they first had to wrestle over a fire. While that was going on, they used rags to clean up the mud that spattered not just Mistress MacFarlane's booth, but many others. The afternoon dragged on, the "boys" were the object of much teasing, and Cat thought at least Logan had learned a valuable lesson. She wasn't so sure it had taught Finn anything. The girl seemed far too pleased to be on public display as a scamp.

As if the two children were the evening's entertainment, the men brought forth a barrel of whisky to share, and the merriment increased. Duff whisky, she thought tiredly. Duncan was stoic as the whisky was distributed, as if he knew it reminded her of what had happened the last time she'd over-imbibed, how she'd let him kiss her.

Since she didn't want the clan to know anything was different, she accepted the dram they urged on her. It burned just as much this time. A clansman laughed and nudged her into Duncan. She was his "fancy lass" after all, and she couldn't jump away like she wanted to. Sadly, touching the warm length of his arm muscles did not inspire revulsion, much as she wished it would.

CHAPTER 17

On the ride home, the last climb was in the darkness, and Duncan's horse knew the path as well as he did. Finn slept slumped against his back, and Duncan felt another stirring of sympathy. The boy had worked hard to make his mistake right—although it hadn't begun as a mistake.

What was Duncan supposed to do with Finn?

He'd never had this problem before. Children were always so grateful to be rescued, and if they were orphans, pleased to have a home. But the longer Finn stayed, the more he'd think of this dank cave as home, and that wasn't fair for a little boy to grow up as a fugitive.

Duncan carried Finn into the great hall of their cave complex, where some of the men were subdued after a long day, and others were still gregarious from too much drink. Catriona, who'd been ahead of him with Maeve on the way back, was nowhere to be seen. Probably preparing for bed, he thought, inwardly grimacing as he remembered she slept on a cave floor in a room with dozens of men.

He lowered Finn to his pallet, then tucked the blanket in around him.

Tonight Catriona had pretended there was no distance between them, for the sake of his clan. She'd sat beside him in the village, sipping her whisky as the gentle September wind brought the scents of fish frying and the laughter of his people. Her arm had briefly been against his, and it had taken tenuous control not to slip his arm around her shoulder and bring her more fully against him as he wanted to.

But she wasn't his wife, she wasn't a woman he was courting—she wasn't his "fancy lass." She'd been tipsy when she'd told him Mistress MacFarlane had called her that. He'd been furious, while Catriona had given him an accusing look—he didn't need her to point out that this was his fault.

There didn't seem to be room for any other thoughts in his head but for Catriona, all of them tinged with both guilt and desire. It wouldn't be long before he'd be escorting her home—and she'd be lost to him. *Ye're drunk,* he told himself, disgusted.

Preoccupied, he left the great hall and headed down the stone passageway. There were several boots at the far end, signaling the pool cave was well occupied. He heard deep laughter and splashing and hoped no one was too drunk to swim.

At his bedchamber, he swept the curtain aside— and froze.

Catriona, bent over his trunk, rose up swiftly to face him, her face pink in the lantern light. They were alone, and he couldn't help boldly looking down her body. He'd spent the entire day trying not to stare at her, at the way the laces across her bodice seemed to bring her breasts together and lift them up as if on display. It was nothing overt, but the creamy skin of her cleavage hinted at what was below. Her waist was delicate, and the flare of her skirt only emphasized her round hips.

"I didn't mean to disturb you," she said stiffly.

When their gazes met and held, he reached behind him and slid the curtain closed. He saw her eyes widen.

"Did ye want people to see us alone together?"

She shook her head.

"Why are ye here?" he asked, hearing the roughness of his voice.

He wanted her. The anger and frustration of that made him take a step closer. Lifting her chin, she didn't back away.

She licked her lips. "I thought I left something in the trunk, but . . . I can't find it."

"What was it?" He was another step closer, and he could have touched her if he reached out. It was a daring game he played with himself: touch her or not, test his powers of control or back away.

But she smelled so good. On her, the plain soap the women made seemed somehow enhanced by mingling with her skin. He wanted to bury his face against her neck and inhale.

"It's not your concern," she insisted. "And you're drunk," she added accusingly.

"And ye're blushing." Without planning it, he reached to cup her cheek.

They both inhaled at the touch, warm skin to warm skin. Then she pushed his hand away, but there was no room to step back.

"'Tis just a chemise," she said with exasperation.

He tilted his head. "I do not remember seeing such a feminine garment in my trunk after you moved out."

"It's not there. I'm going to leave now."

He didn't step aside, and she didn't push him away.

Words he didn't mean to say tumbled out in a husky voice. "I know what I've done to ye, and though I've asked your forgiveness, ye haven't granted it, as is your right. But I cannot stop thinking about how it was with ye in my arms. I've never wanted to kiss a woman as I've wanted to kiss ye, never wanted to touch a woman as badly as I want to put my hands on ye."

Her eyes widened more and more with each word he said. For a frozen moment, he didn't have any idea what she thought of him. And then without a word she pushed past him and fled.

Duncan had once deluded himself into believing he could have her; he'd let himself sink under her spell until she was all he could think about. But now that she knew all he'd done to her, there could never be forgiveness between them.

He pounded his fist hard into the rock wall, little caring that he bloodied his knuckles. It was less painful than the way his heart felt, torn up knowing that he'd hurt her, that he could never have her—that he'd fallen in love with her.

He had to take her home the first chance he got. After the assembly, he'd sent even more men to search out this missing child, to see if at last the sheriff had run out of men and was doing his own foul work. The lust for money was apparently too powerful for the man to lie low.

But after that, it was time to take Catriona home and accept her brother's punishment.

Cᴀᴛ stood in the passageway, fighting to control her racing pulse, her uneven breathing. She was disgusted with herself and the way Duncan's words had even momentarily tempted her into forgetting everything he'd done and exploring that dark world of pleasure she'd only ever glimpsed. What kind of person so easily forgot betrayal? Apparently, she did. She'd thought she could control her reactions to the dazzling sensations he invoked in her—she was lying to herself. Regardless of what he'd done, her body still wanted him.

She had to forget about her weakness and think about what she'd uncovered in the trunk—proof of her father's guilt. But there was also a revelation about Duncan's father. After what he'd said of his father's weaknesses and mistakes, she didn't think he knew about the letters. In some ways, even her captivity was because of how Duncan had shaped himself to be nothing like his father. She found herself more curious about the dead man than she wanted to be.

It wasn't until the next morning, when Duncan left the cave with Ivor and many of the men, that Cat slipped back into his chamber. Dropping to her knees beside the trunk, she carefully moved aside his clothing until she found all the letters. Wrapping them into her towel, she ducked back into the passageway with her lantern, left her shoe on the ground and slipped into the empty pool cave. No one would disturb her there for a while. She had to begrudgingly give him credit; he'd kept his men loyal and in line. She sank to the ground, her back against the rough wall, and found the letter she was looking for.

She stiffened as she recognized her father's handwriting. She'd been right; he was "A," making threats he didn't bother to veil against Laird Carlyle and innocent children. Of course, he didn't put it into incriminating words, damn him. He'd always been too smart for that.

Duncan had assured her that his father was a weakling. But if his father had been investigating the missing children, had even connected it to the Earl of Aberfoyle, but had died before he could finish the work—then he was more than the pathetic chief Duncan thought him to be.

Duncan's father had had the same goal as he did. Had Duncan known? She shouldn't care, but . . . she did.

And there was her father, his spidery penmanship reminding her of the evil he wreaked in all the lives he touched. Tears stung her eyes but she wiped them away. Though Duncan had made his own poor choices, he was only desperate to save his people because her father had made everything worse for them.

At a commotion echoing down the passageway, Cat lifted her head and froze. But no one called her name, and the shoe she could see at the edge of the shadows remained undisturbed. She gathered the letters back together, and after tying them up, crept down the corridor, dropped them in Duncan's chest, and emerged into the great hall attempting to look untroubled.

Duncan and Ivor were standing face-to-face, glaring at each other, the rest of the men watching with either curiosity or worry.

"I must go to her," Duncan said coldly. "My sister needs me."

"Muriel?" The name left Cat's lips without her even being aware.

None of the men looked at her, but Maeve hurried to stand by her side.

"Muriel?" Cat whispered again in fear, searching Maeve's face.

Maeve shook her head. "Nay, not Muriel. His lairdship's other sister, Winifred. She sent word that she'd been interrogated by Sir Brendan Welcker, the sheriff of Glasgow, for the whereabouts of Himself."

Cat caught her breath, her gaze rushing back to Duncan. If his sister had been hurt, he'd blame himself forever. "Is she . . . ?"

"She says she's unharmed, that she told the sheriff she's estranged from Himself, and he finally believed her. She wants her brother to continue his work for the children. But he . . ." Maeve's words faded away, her eyes full of helplessness.

"But he blames himself and wants to go to her," Cat finished for her.

Maeve nodded.

Duncan suddenly strode past her without glancing her way, crossed the footbridge and disappeared up the passageway. When no one followed him, Cat did. She didn't know why; it wasn't her place, but—

She found him packing a saddlebag, stuffing things in without even paying attention to what he was doing.

"Duncan."

He didn't look at her. His movements got more explosive, and she thought he'd rip a hole in the bottom of the bag.

She repeated his name more firmly, then put a hand on his arm. He froze. She could feel the terrible tension of his muscles, a faint vibration from holding himself still when she knew he was desperate to do something.

"Welcker hit her," he said through gritted teeth.

She caught her breath. "Winifred? She told you that?"

"Nay, of course not. She thinks she has to protect me, but her servant said she had a bruise on her face after the encounter."

He was still clutching the bag with both hands, as if he needed something to hold onto as he accepted the blame for everything that went wrong.

"I have to go to her," Duncan said.

But he held the bag and looked at it, as if unseeing.

"And then you'll have made her bravery useless, because you'll be captured. This is just what the sheriff wants." The words of advice took even her by surprise.

Duncan bowed his head and shuddered. Hoarsely, he said, "I cannot continue to hide while people risk themselves defending me."

"You're risking yourself for their children. Do you think that means so little to them?"

She took the bag from his hand and pushed him down into a chair. To her surprise he didn't resist, but now that she could see his face, she saw the impassive mask that didn't hide the pain in his dark eyes. Duncan had never known any kind of peace. He'd inherited terrible problems when he'd become chief, perhaps too young to chart the wisest course in solving them. He'd made mistakes when he'd first tried to save the children, and he'd learned from them. He suffered for what those mistakes had cost his family and friends. She would admire any other man who'd accepted such responsibility, grown in wisdom, and never surrendered. But none of that excused how he'd used and betrayed her.

With his elbows on his knees, Duncan put his face in his hands and just sat there. She imagined how she'd feel if someone harmed her brother because of her.

She put her hand on his back. He felt so stiff and unyielding, but after a moment, he let out a heavy sigh. She didn't know how long they remained like that, didn't understand her own emotions that twisted between pity and the simmering anger over his betrayal.

At last he sat up, and she let her hand drop away, tempted to look at her hand as if it didn't belong to her.

She had to distract herself. "The sheriff discovered nothing from Winifred."

"So it seems."

"Is Winifred's husband strong enough to protect her?"

"He's a lawyer for the town council. He has power in his own right."

"Then that's what you have to focus on. Winifred wants to protect you and your mission."

"If only children could feel safe," he said with frustration. "Then we could live in peace."

"It will happen. When you've caught the sheriff in the act of stealing children, what will you do?"

"Take him to the High Court in Edinburgh, where he has no influence, no support from the magistrates. I have many witnesses, even children, ready to tell their story. Until then I cannot stop—"

"Winifred doesn't want you to stop."

Stoically, he said, "I know how terrified the bairns feel; I know what it's like to think no one can help ye. At least I was fed and housed. To be taken away from all ye've known, barely fed, fearing to be thrown into a world without sympathy—" He stiffened. "Aye, I cannot stop. If it takes the rest of my life, I'll make the children of my clan feel safe."

She knew he'd allow himself no softness, no comfort, no peace until then. But if he took her home, and she told her brother what had happened, Duncan might be accused of yet another crime. The twinge of guilt she felt angered her. She wasn't going to have him thrown in gaol, but she wasn't going to let him suffer nothing for what he'd done.

"So what will you do about Winifred?"

She saw his jaw clench, but his voice was almost mild as he said, "I will write to her and thank her for her bravery." He glanced up at her. "But I won't risk her sacrifice by going to her. My thanks for your wise words."

"I said nothing that Ivor did not say, that you did not know yourself."

It made her feel uncomfortable that her opinion could sway him. Suddenly, she felt strange knowing that she'd seen his father's papers, that she'd committed her own indiscretion. She wanted to ask if he knew the contents—if he knew he might have some evidence against her father, vague though it was. But it wasn't her place to talk to him about something so personal. They weren't going to have that kind of relationship anymore. Awkward and unsure, she left him alone.

She was still lost in thought when she wandered back into the great hall. As if she'd been waiting for Cat, Maeve met her when she crossed the footbridge.

"Well?" Maeve asked anxiously. "Did ye convince him to stay?"

Cat blinked at her. "I don't think I had the power to do that. He realized the truth himself."

Maeve let out her breath. "'Tis good that ye're here."

"I don't understand."

"I've never seen him react to anyone the way he's done with you."

Cat felt herself flushing with heat. "I think that's overstating things."

"Nay, 'tis not. Just promise me that if your memory returns, or if ye think ye have to go, try to spare him if ye can."

The woman was uncomfortably close to the truth, and Cat couldn't even meet her always direct gaze. Again, she felt the sting of guilt, knowing she was lying to this kind woman, even if it was for the clan's benefit. But she could get one thing off her chest.

Cat looked past her, to see if they were alone. "I must confess something, Maeve, and I need your advice."

"Confess?" Maeve echoed, her frown distorted by a scar snaking up from her cheek.

"When I was storing my clothing in his lairdship's trunk, I found letters to his father."

The woman's wrinkled forehead smoothed out. "Ah, yes. Himself had a . . . complicated relationship with his father. It often brings him pain to remember. I urged him to throw those letters out—"

"But it's good he didn't. Maeve, they might be proof that the Earl of Aberfoyle was involved. And they also show that his father had known about the missing children, and had been pursuing justice in his own way. He'd died before it could happen, but . . . perhaps Duncan should know that his father wasn't as weak as he'd thought he was."

Maeve studied her closely. "Ye care much for our laird."

Cat wanted to deny that outright, but it would make her friend suspicious. And that was the *only* reason she stayed silent.

"Why did ye not tell him yerself?" Maeve continued, with a teasing edge to her voice. "Ye were just alone with him."

Cat hoped she was suppressing a blush. "We've both agreed not to pursue this attraction we feel. And to tell him something so personal—not to mention admit I read them . . ."

"Very well," Maeve said kindly. "I'll pick a good time to tell him. I'll even say me own curiosity made me ask ye to read me the letters. I cannot read, ye know," she admitted matter-of-factly.

"No, I will not let you lie for me." Cat was aghast.

"'Twill not be much of a lie. I've always been curious. Just let me take care of it."

"Maeve—"

But with a wave, the other woman walked away.

And Cat let her, because she was far too confused about her own motives.

CHAPTER 18

Taking comfort from a woman—a woman he'd wronged, no less—only confused and irritated Duncan. Aye, it had been necessary to hear the words of truth about Winifred's situation, and his own responsibilities, but he didn't like how easily he wanted to revert to the youth he'd once been, the one who acted first and worried about the consequences later. He thought he'd left that fool behind, but apparently, one threat to his sister and he lost himself again.

Catriona had come to him, offered advice, listened to the worst of his fears, and calmed him. Was it such a weakness that a woman he loved could do such a thing? Especially when he knew she didn't want to have anything to do with him. But he couldn't let himself grow accustomed to her counsel. He'd be taking her home, and her family would make certain Duncan never had anything to do with her again.

Walking through the great hall, he saw more than one of his men watching him with wary sympathy, though none bothered him. Finn wasn't within the cave, and he found the boy at the paddock, brooding as he watched the horses graze.

Though Finn stiffened, Duncan leaned on the fence beside him and said nothing. It was a cold, misty wet day, and even the ruins towering on the cliffs over their heads were hidden within a dreary fog.

"Ye're disappointed in me," Finn finally said in a low voice.

"Are ye disappointed in yourself?" Duncan asked.

The boy hesitated. "Do ye want me to be honest?"

"I do."

"Then, though I disappointed ye, I would not do anythin' different."

"So ye'd still make it difficult for poor Mistress MacFarlane to earn her coin."

Though Finn was in profile, Duncan could see his young brow furrow.

"Nay, I wanted to cause trouble, not harm an old woman," he admitted in so soft a voice that Duncan barely heard him.

"Then what do ye want, Finn?"

"I don't want to be foisted off on people who resent havin' to do ye a favor."

"Ye don't think I know what I'm doing? That I've found good homes for orphaned children before? That there are families who could not have children, or perhaps only one, and have love to give to more?"

"Is it love, Laird Carlyle? Or is it the need for a laborer?"

"Everyone works in a family, Finn," Duncan said patiently. "I certainly put ye to work here."

"'Tis not the same," Finn insisted. "I *want* to be here."

"Ye could want to be in a family, too. Don't ye want a mum again?"

"No one can take me mum's place!"

The shout was sudden and cracked with emotion.

Softly, Duncan said, "Just like having another friend doesn't make the first one any less to ye, 'tis the same with parents. Ye can love them in a different way than your own mum, but it can still be real and important to ye eventually."

"Not to me. I'm different than other boys."

"And how is that?"

Finn said nothing.

"Ye like Mistress Catherine, do ye not?"

Mutely, the boy nodded.

"And ye like Mistress Maeve, too. That's two women ye like, not one at the expense of another."

Instead of answering, Finn dashed an arm across his eyes and ran back toward the cave.

Duncan leaned back against the fence post and watched. He'd never had such a challenging lad before, and was beginning to fear he'd need to force the lad into a new home for his own good.

And that meant that Duncan had to find just the right home. There was one he'd considered, visited, but they already had four children, and he feared Finn's assessment of needing another laborer would have been true with that family.

But there was something about Finn that made

Duncan feel even more protective than he normally did. Perhaps it was simply because Catriona was so fond of the boy, and he didn't want to disappoint her.

As Cat helped serve the midday meal, she noticed Finn's dejection as the girl squatted near the burn, half hidden by the footbridge. It seemed to give her some feeling of safety, and Cat thought again of the bridges in Glasgow that might have once meant the same thing to Finn. Since the other children had gone, Finn had taken to building elaborate little villages out of the stones in the burn, stacking the flat ones as little houses, using sticks as people, and round stones as animals. Cat often saw her lips move, as if she gave voice to her little creations, ruler of their world when she could not rule her own.

When Cat approached, Finn jumped to her feet.

"I saw you run in from outside," Cat said hesitantly. "Are you well?"

Finn didn't meet her gaze and said nothing.

"I saw Laird Carlyle head out just before. You spoke?"

"I don't want to talk about him. He thinks only he knows best, and that I have to do anythin' he says."

Cat didn't point out that those things were most likely true. Instead, she sat on a rock beside Finn and spoke quietly. "Perhaps you'd have better luck reasoning with his lairdship if you told him the truth about yourself."

Finn crouched back over her little stone village,

shoulders hunched, as if she could protect her entire little stone world. "I cannot. He'll be mad and send me away even sooner."

"I think he'll be sad you didn't trust him sooner."

"Are ye going to break your word and tell him?" Finn accused.

That angry look pierced Cat like an arrow. "No, I promised I wouldn't, and I won't. But the lie must surely be eating at you, and grow more and more difficult to hide. You cannot make water against a tree like the boys."

"I've spent years gettin' around that," Finn said with scorn.

"When summer comes, they'll all swim without their clothes, and you won't be able to."

"I can't swim."

"You have an answer for everything," Cat said with a sigh. "But trust me, I have a secret, too, and it's tearing me up inside."

Finn stared at her, wide-eyed. "You, mistress?"

"Me. I will tell you, and though I won't swear you to secrecy, I ask you to allow me to tell everyone in my own way, as I've allowed you the same courtesy."

"Of course," Finn said eagerly, sitting on another rock across from Cat.

Cat guessed the girl was desperate to find someone else trapped in lies, just like Finn herself. And maybe this was a mistake, but perhaps sharing her own mistakes would help the girl see that lies only tangled a person the longer they went on.

"A couple days ago," Cat began softly, "all of my memories began to return."

Finn's mouth dropped open, and she leaned forward. "Ye remembered yer life!"

Cat nodded.

"But . . . ye told no one."

"I told Laird Carlyle."

Finn frowned. "He must be glad for ye."

With a shrug, Cat said, "It is not so easy. If everyone found out who I am, it might cause . . . hard feelings."

"But . . . ye're a woman alone."

"I am, but I'm of the Duff clan, Finn, and we've been enemies of the Carlyles."

"Oh." Finn may have lived in town rather than the Highlands, but she obviously knew of the great clan rivalries and the feuds that could last centuries. "His lairdship is protectin' ye. He's a good man."

Protecting her. Cat could have choked. "It's not just that. Everyone here is doing good deeds for others. Finn, I am the sort of woman who takes the wealth of my family for granted. I have done very little except enjoy my life while others are struggling to survive, or risking their lives on behalf of children."

"Like Himself," Finn breathed.

Cat nodded. "It makes me feel . . . ashamed." She bowed her head.

Finn's dirty hand touched her knee. "'Tis not yer fault yer father coddled ye."

"I know, but . . . it's sad that I did not see it as such, even when I looked out my carriage window and saw that others did not live as I did. I helped my mother with charities, but nothing compared to the sacrifices that the people in this cave make every day."

Finn said nothing, and Cat was wondering if confessing her own secret had been the right thing to do. She glanced up to see the little girl pondering her village.

"I've told his lairdship," Cat said, "and he doesn't hate me. You could tell him your secret, too."

Finn gave her a piercing look, then said sadly, "I'll be . . . a girl with boys, weak." Her thin shoulders hunched again. "I don't know."

"Think about it." Bracing her hands on her thighs, Cat stood up. "I'll leave you to your make-believe. Pretending everything is okay can be a lot easier than facing the truth. We both know that."

Cat felt a little disoriented as she left the burn. She saw the women working together, and just couldn't face pretending nothing was wrong. She donned her cloak and went outside. The mist hadn't dissipated, and the chill dampness made her hug herself. As she always did when she needed to think, she went toward the paddock, but before she reached it, she heard a thunder of horses' hooves and saw two clansmen duck past the trees and ride into the clearing, pulling up short when they spied Duncan. She hadn't even realized he was out there. She moved deeper into the trees, intending to leave them alone, when she heard a breathless Angus speak as he dismounted.

"Laird Carlyle, ye're needed for a newly arrived shipment."

Cat froze.

"Whisky?" Duncan asked quietly.

Both men nodded.

"I'll go," Duncan said. "Get some food and rest."

Duncan saddled his horse, but instead of going back inside the cave, he mounted and departed. Cat realized that the whisky shipments must not be hidden very far away, if he didn't even bother with supplies. Feeling bold and deserving of the truth, she quickly saddled the mare she preferred and rode off after him.

DUNCAN rode several hours, lost in thought about Catriona, about Finn, about the decisions that weren't so easy to make. But he was aware that a solitary horseman was following him.

As the ground began to level out, and the trees grew thicker the closer he got to Loch Lomond, he led the man away from his true destination and looked for a place to surprise him. The dense trees near the loch made that relatively easy, and soon he was hidden behind a tree, still mounted on Arran, his sword drawn, ready to run down the villain from behind.

The horse cantered past him down the path, its rider leaning forward, obviously looking for him. And then he saw the dark hair of a woman piled high, her cloak falling back from her shoulders to cover the horse's flanks. Since she straddled the horse, her skirts were lifted, displaying supple calves.

Catriona.

She came to a stop in the clearing beyond the trees, swiveling her head in confusion.

"Looking for me?" Duncan asked, urging his horse out of the trees.

She twisted in the saddle, her eyes wide.

"Why have ye been lurking behind me for hours?" Duncan demanded.

"Because I wasn't certain it was you," she said, her expression an attempt at seriousness.

"Try again," he commanded coolly.

She wet her lips. "Duncan—"

"Dismount."

"What?"

"Get off your horse."

"Are we here?" she asked quickly, looking around.

Through the trees, they could glimpse the smooth surface of the loch, but nothing else.

"Are we where?" he asked, eyes narrowed. "Where did ye think I was going?"

She didn't answer, just dismounted, her leg sliding over the mare's saddle, her skirts bunching but revealing only a wool-covered ankle. Where Catriona was concerned, that was almost as tantalizing as bare skin.

He walked his horse closer, still towering above her, and raked her saddle with a withering glance. "You have no supplies at all, not even water."

"Why would I need supplies? I thought you were just going for a ride to exercise your mount."

He dismounted and stalked toward her. "Do not be foolish, Catriona."

She flinched as he used her Christian name, and he thought perhaps it was the first time she'd heard it in a long while.

"Tell me why ye were following me."

"Because I had something to discuss with you, and I was hoping to do it in private. We seldom have any privacy."

He stood with his hands on his hips, looking down at her. "Very well, if ye need more privacy, then by all means, let's have some." He took her elbow and began to tug.

"Where are we going?" she asked sharply.

"Ye followed me about the countryside, a woman alone, risking yourself. I'm damned sure ye must be out of your mind with curiosity. And we need privacy, of course, as ye've so smartly pointed out."

"Duncan—"

"Be quiet, woman, or ye'll risk our lives."

Her mouth snapped shut. At least she could be smart about some things. He gathered the reins of both horses and began to pull them along as well.

"I can walk on my own!" she whispered.

But he didn't let her go, although he did take her hand instead of her elbow. He tugged her and the horses along behind him, then at just the right spot, ducked beneath a spray of ferns, to a hidden path down toward the water. He heard her suck in a breath in surprise. The horses followed them easily, this being well-known to them. The path grew muddy, their footsteps causing ripples along the shore of the calm loch. Her foot slipped once and he pulled her upright, catching her around the waist. Her hands flat on his chest, she stared up at him in shock.

"Should I not have touched ye, *my lady*?" he said emphasizing her honorific title.

"Ye're a Carlyle," she shot back.

They both knew that wasn't the reason. Yet her Scottish lilt was back, and foolishly he rejoiced, even though it should mean nothing. But it made her seem of the Highlands, as if he could have her forever.

A warning bell sounded somewhere distant in his mind, but he ignored it.

She pushed at his chest, and for just a moment he kept his arm around her narrow waist, looking into those flashing golden eyes and thinking how much he admired her. At the outset she'd been calm and sweet, then gradually revealed her hidden fire and outrage, unafraid to speak her mind, though he was the chief of her enemies. He desired her more now that there were no lies between them, a powerful yearning he had no answer for.

But he let her waist go, kept hold of her hand and continued on the narrow muddy path, still hidden by the trees, and the growing size of boulders strewn along the loch, a giant replica of Finn's stone village. Past the last boulder, he saw the tiny house, built into the rocks themselves. It could have been a fisherman's home, and most who came upon it would think it that. But it wasn't.

At the door, he pushed Catriona to the side and put a finger to his lips. She nodded, looking to the door with eagerness. She was brave and fearless, his Catriona.

Not *his*, he warned himself.

He knocked a specific beat, and when the door opened, he was staring at a cocked pistol. Catriona gasped, and the pistol turned toward her.

Duncan stepped between her and the barrel. "'Tis me," he said softly.

The pistol lowered, and out of the gloom stepped a short, hulking man who always seemed ill-at-ease and lumbering on land, but moved with surprising balance and agility on his small sailing vessel.

"Carlyle," Reid said. "It took ye long enough."

The man stepped back as Duncan looped the horses' reins around a tree branch, and pulled Catriona inside with him. It wasn't as dark as it had first seemed. Reid turned up a lantern and added peat to the low fire. He saw Catriona glance around curiously, and understood what she saw. The front of the little building seemed sparse, with a neatly made box bed built into a wall near the hearth, a table and two uneven chairs, and a cupboard with shelves holding the barest necessities with which to cook meals. Along one wall were stacks of wooden crates piled to the ceiling.

"I came as quickly as I could," Duncan said.

Reid looked at Catriona with lascivious interest. "And who be you?"

"She's with me," Duncan said coldly. "She'll keep silent. Now tell me why ye insisted I come?"

After a suspicious glance at Catriona, Reid said, "My ship has been followed. I cannot deliver your cargo, and I don't know when I'll next return. I can't risk sailin' at night for they'll mark me as a smuggler. I might be stopped leaving Loch Lomond regardless, and I want nothing suspicious aboard."

Duncan scowled. "Then ye didn't load the cargo?"

"Nay, 'tis all yours. I'll send word when I can next sail." He leered at Catriona, then insolently tugged his bonnet. "Mistress."

"Reid," Duncan called when the man reached the door.

Reid glanced over his shoulder and paused. "Aye."

"Be safe."

He flashed a smile, where several teeth were missing. "That I will." Then he went out the door and closed it behind him.

Duncan turned and regarded Catriona, who looked at the closed door as if disappointed.

"If ye miss him, I can make him return," he said dryly.

"'Tis true, I had questions for him."

"None he would have answered."

"He smuggles the whisky?"

"That's none of your concern."

She frowned and looked around. "But . . . this is only a fisherman's cottage. Where are all the casks?"

"Ye know I'll not answer that—for your own protection, of course."

"Of course," she repeated dryly.

"But I do have questions for ye."

He stepped closer, her skirts swirling around his legs. They would have touched if she hadn't stepped back.

"Are ye afraid of me?" he demanded, more harshly than he'd intended. He'd spent weeks protecting her, and the thought of being the cause of her fear both infuriated and saddened him.

She drew herself up and leaned toward him, pointing a finger for emphasis as she said, "*You* don't frighten me. I followed ye, didn't I?"

"Why? Does it have something to do with your snooping in my trunk?"

He couldn't tell if she was blushing, in the low light.

"Aye, ye didn't hide that from me."

Stiffening, she said, "When ye gave me space for my garments in the trunk, I saw letters."

"So ye found my father's papers. Nothing in that trunk is a secret to me."

"And have ye read them?"

He frowned. "Ye read them?"

"Have *you*?" she demanded.

"I read the first few, and they're inconsequential. I don't need to read another thing related to that man. He gave up on me, our family, this clan, a long time before he died."

"Ye think so?" Now she pointed her finger in his face. "If ye believe that, it's obvious ye didn't finish the letters; ye don't know what kind of a man your father was."

"I know he was the kind of man who killed my mother."

"So when it's convenient, you refer to her as your mother, rather than the woman who spent her life making you miserable, who tortured poor Maeve?"

"Convenient?" he yelled. "You think because she was a monster, she wasn't my mother?"

"I'm not saying that. This is about your father. Though ye think ye know—and disdain—

everything about him, he had his own secrets, just like *you* do."

Secrets? He took a breath to calm his frustration and steady his thoughts, even as uneasiness began to kindle inside him. "Speak plainly."

"Your father knew about the stolen children, and was actively working to right that terrible wrong."

He stiffened. "What are ye saying?"

"I read his letters, some even from the Earl of Aberfoyle, your enemy—"

"Your father."

"—who was threatening *your* father because of what he knew. Oh, Father didn't say it outright, but I understood what was happening."

His mind spun as he tried to resettle this new picture of his father, but it was like a globe that circled and circled, never settling back where it had started.

Catriona lowered her voice and spoke calmly. "Your father had his beliefs, Duncan. He was fighting for them in his own way, not with his sword, but with letters."

And for his part, Duncan had charged off, speaking rashly until it had gotten him imprisoned. He shook his head, forcing aside his own mistakes. "Ye didn't follow me to tell me this. Ye could have said it right in the great hall."

He glimpsed panic in her golden eyes before she replaced it with deliberate confusion. "I said I needed to speak with ye in private. I had no idea we were going to ride for hours. I lost ye at one point, but luckily I found ye again, and then it was too late to go back."

"Ye've an answer for everything."

That seemed to touch something within her. "Excuse me?" she said quietly, formally.

"Ye did not follow me to talk about letters. Ye could have caught up to me anytime, but ye hung back so ye could see where I went, where the whisky is hidden. With your foolish curiosity, ye put yourself in danger—"

He saw the moment something snapped inside her.

"*I* put myself in danger?" she cried, throwing her arms wide.

"Aye, ye did, at every turn. Do ye believe yourself so above the hazards of the road? Ye traveled to Glasgow with only two guards—"

"Two strong, talented soldiers!" she cried.

"Ye went up to the dangerous ruins of my castle—"

"I had to, or I'd never have left the cave!"

"And now ye followed me on treacherous paths where outlaws could have been hiding—"

"Outlaws like you!" she cried.

They were leaning toward each other, hands on hips, both furious.

"Aye, I'm an outlaw," he said gruffly, "and outlaws take what they want."

He pulled her to him, relishing every curve of her body pressed hard to his, and kissed her.

CHAPTER 19

Cat had been full of righteous indignation, fury that he'd spurned her news about his father's letters, accused her of being reckless—

And then he kissed her, and every reckless impulse of hers came true. It was as if her mind turned off, and her sensual emotions, long denied, just took over her body. She flung her arms around his neck, as if desperate to get closer. He lifted her right off the floor, and she hung suspended against him, the hard muscles of his body an agony and a temptation all at once. Their kiss was hot and wet and rough, his whiskers scraping her chin—she couldn't taste enough of him, moaned when she lost his mouth, only to fling her head back when he gently bit her neck. She held his head to her, pulled the queue from his hair so that she could grasp the wavy locks.

He roughly set her on the ground, unhooked her cloak, and started pulling up her skirts, as he had the last time. She began to tug at the laces keeping her bodice together.

Duncan froze and watched her, his eyes hot with desire, their darkness full of temptation. When her laces were gone, and the stomacher fell away, he grabbed the edges of her bodice and held them together.

"Stop me, Cat, if ye must, but do it now."

"If ye stop now, I'll scream," she said.

He let her go, and she staggered. Every part of her burned for him, burned for the pleasure he'd showed her, burned to see what she'd been missing. But if he didn't want her—

"Take it off," he said harshly, hands fisted at his side, every line of his body tense. "Take it all off before I tear it off."

A wildness seemed to sweep over her at his rough words. She didn't think about what he'd done to her. Nothing mattered but this room, this dark place, and the passion that felt like it might consume her.

She tugged at her tight sleeves, and her bodice fell to the floor. She untied the tapes holding her skirt and petticoats and kicked them away from her. All that was left were her stockings and shoes, her stays and chemise. The laces on her stays opened in the front, and her fingers fumbled with them, but he was patient, standing as still as a statue but for his harsh breathing, which made his chest rise and fall rapidly. She couldn't seem to get her own breath, frustrated, until he pushed her fingers aside and his big hands deftly untangled and unthreaded the laces. She took a deep grateful breath when her stays fell away—and she let the past do the same. She couldn't think about all the reasons not to do this. She wanted every pleasure she'd denied herself.

"Now *this* is the chemise ye wore when I found ye," he said in awed husky tones. "Shiny silk, so fine it shows each delicate curve of ye, and your pretty nipples."

He tweaked one gently and she shuddered.

"I wondered often if beneath the simple woolen gown, ye still wore this, all feminine and desirable. Let me see ye, Cat."

She could only nod, trembling as she loosened the drawstring at her neck and shrugged her shoulders to start the downward slide of the garment. It caught briefly at her breasts, and he groaned. She suddenly felt powerful, capable of affecting this man in a primitive, sensual way. If he had a hold over her, then she had one over him.

And then the silk slithered down her body and she was naked.

He stared at her as if he'd never seen a woman before, when she knew that couldn't be true. He was a man who did what he wanted, who'd once been wild, or so Maeve had told her. He reached out and cupped her right breast with his rough hand, and she closed her eyes and experienced the deep pleasure of it, which expanded outward from her breast and made the center of her thighs hot and yearning. She was trembling, and didn't know how much longer she could stand to be on display for him.

"I'm on fire," she whispered.

She felt him shudder through his hand.

"Take off your clothes," she said.

It was an order, and he obeyed. After removing his sword belt and tossing onto the table his pistol and sword, he unpinned the plaid from his shoulder, and the folds fell to hang at his waist. He peeled off his jacket, his waistcoat, his neck cloth, with such speed that she could have laughed if she wasn't so breathless to see him completely nude. He unbuckled his plaid and it fell down to the ground, leaving him in just his shirt, loose through the sleeves, long to his thighs, tented forward by the male part of him she was so curious to see. She thought he ripped a button at his throat opening his shirt, and she put her hands on his chest to stop him. She felt his racing heart, heard his frantic breathing, knew he wanted this joining as much as she did.

But she didn't want it over so quickly.

"My turn," she murmured, then began to pull up his shirt as he'd once done to her skirts, and slid her hands beneath.

His breathing seemed to come at a rasp, and then he wasn't breathing at all, just standing all taut as a bowstring ready to let fly. She put her hands on his hips and found them hot and smooth, devoid of the hair that was on his legs. Looking up into his face, she braved a teasing smile and let her trembling hands slide back to find his backside, the muscles hard and twitching, as if he were a great horse held still when it wanted to gallop.

Leaning against his body, she felt the long length of his arousal against her stomach through the folds of his linen shirt, the only thing that separated them. Part of her wanted to rip it away, the other part of her wanted to explore, without all of his nakedness to overwhelm her. Their gazes locked, she let her hands explore him beneath the shirt around to the front. His chest had hair that dwindled as she followed the ridges of his abdominal muscles down. She took his penis in her hands, hot and smooth and hard, saw the pleasure change his expression into a grimace.

"Am I hurting ye?" she asked, loosening her hold.

"God, no." His words were guttural and strained.

"Take off your shirt."

He pulled it off over his head while she still held his erection. They were two naked people facing one another in the faint firelight. While she looked down in fascination at the maleness of his body, he reached up and began pulling the pins from her hair. The long locks fell down around her shoulders, brushed her breasts.

"Ye're such a beauty," he murmured. "I've longed for ye from the moment I first saw ye."

There was nothing she could say to that that hadn't already been said—and besides, she didn't want to think about conflict when she could have this moment of passion. She explored him with her fingers, delicately at first, then with more confidence.

"If ye've satisfied your curiosity, I'll take ye to bed, aye?"

It was another moment where she could change her mind, but it was too late. She wanted what he offered, wanted to think of nothing but satisfying her body's carnal demands. She wanted something that was hers, now, this experience, these memories, for she didn't know if she'd ever have others like it.

Still holding on to him, she drew him back toward the box bed and sat down. He loomed above her, over her, and she let go as she fell back. Her hair spilled out around her, even as he braced himself above her and looked his fill with such admiration. Then he bent his head and kissed her mouth, her nose, her chin, moving ever downward, to the hollow of her throat, the wings of her collarbones, between her breasts. He teased her unmercifully then, kissing patterns up the swell of her breasts without ever quite reaching the peaks, until she was shivering and on the verge of begging him to touch her.

As if reading her mind, he licked across her nipple and she cried out at the absolute pleasure of it. He did the same to the other, before meeting her gaze and drawing her nipple deep into his mouth to suck. She shuddered and moaned.

"Don't stop," she begged.

When at last he did, she caught her breath in disappointment—until his kisses moved lower, and his body spread her thighs. He lingered at her belly, and she couldn't even breathe.

"Duncan—" His name was a broken plea.

He murmured into her curls, "Should I stop? Or can I show ye what pleasure can be?"

She hadn't imagined there could be more, that he would be so bold—but then he was her Scottish outlaw. She gave a nod, and he used his tongue in ways she hadn't imagined a man would do. He pleasured her, he licked her, he suckled her, and she made the wildest gasps and moans as she felt that intense pleasure taking hold inside her again, tightening everything she was, focusing all her concentration, until the cataclysmic release had her shaking beneath him.

And then he came down on top of her, all hot hard muscle, and kissed her mouth until she could taste herself on his tongue. It seemed both embarrassing and exciting all at once. She held him to her with her arms, her thighs at his hips, felt the hard length of his arousal along the sensitive swollen flesh he'd just pleasured.

"I'll make the pain quick and brief," he said against her mouth.

When he slid deep inside her, she gasped at the sting, the uncomfortable intrusion.

Holding himself still, he asked. "Are ye all right?"

She nodded. "I was led to believe it could be worse."

He smiled, that rare smile that made her see how he could have been if his life had been easier, a man who'd never take happiness for granted.

"I'll make it even better," he promised.

He slid partially out, then back inside, and those feelings that had just subsided now rose up again.

"Oh!" she gasped.

And then he was riding her, sliding against her, and she gradually changed from awkward to graceful as she learned how to move with him. In the shadowy darkness of the box bed, hidden away from the world, only he existed with her, his hard body that was made to bring her pleasure, his groans that told her she was all he needed, the damp heat of his skin, the salty way he tasted when she kissed his chest. The climax swept over her again, sudden and swift and welcome.

When he suddenly pulled out of her and thrust against her belly several more times, she wasn't sure what was happening. He went still, braced on his elbows so he didn't crush her, his chest heaving against hers. He rolled off, grabbed something off the floor and wiped her stomach.

"What are you doing?" she asked.

"Using my shirt to clean ye. Unlike some, I packed supplies for this journey and brought an extra," he added.

The hint of amusement was rare, and made her smile. Then she frowned. "Clean me of what?"

"My seed. I didn't spend it inside ye."

Her eyes went wide, but he only lay on his back, forearm across his eyes, his chest still rising and falling. A baby. He'd thought to protect her from that scandal, but she hadn't thought of anything except desire, so overpowering that even now she wanted more of it.

Coming up on her elbow, she looked down at herself, glistening with perspiration, with faint pink spots from passion. Yet instead of exhausted, she felt rejuvenated, aware of her body and the wonderful secrets it had been holding all this time. Then she turned to look at Duncan, and the firelight danced across the beautiful muscles that made up his form.

He peered out from beneath his arm. "Aye?"

A feeling of shyness swept over her—they were completely naked. She'd given in to passion, lost her virginity. She should feel upset and guilty, but didn't. What would happen when they left this cottage, she didn't know, but right at that moment, she didn't want to think about any of it.

"Ye must be cold," he said at last, then rose up to tend the fire.

That was when she saw the scars crisscrossing his back, and couldn't help her gasp. But squatting down before the fire, he hadn't heard her, and she was able to watch him move with grace, with power under control. She'd never imagined a man's body could be so beautiful to her.

But those scars . . . surely he'd gotten them in gaol, and her father had helped put him there. How would she feel, what would she do, if someone had done such a thing, harmed innocent children, almost destroyed an entire clan?

Duncan's faint smile faded as he came back to the bed and saw her expression.

"Your back," she whispered.

He lay down on the bed, then pulled her up to rest within the crook of his arm, his shoulder pillowing her head.

"'Tis the past," he said quietly. "It doesn't matter between us."

"Everything matters, Duncan. All of it is how I came to be living at the cave."

His heart beat strong and sure beneath her hand.

"The first time I tried to escape the thieves' hole,

they caught and punished me. Let us not talk of it now. Tell me of your girlhood."

"What?" She tilted her head up so she could see his face. "Ye want to discuss something so unimportant?"

"It formed ye. How can it be unimportant?"

Those dark eyes were serious upon her, and his fingers began to comb through her hair. The gentle tug, the occasional brush of his fingers on her back or shoulder, were strangely comforting.

"Ye know who my father is," she said softly. "He could be a monster to others, but he was not to me."

"I am glad for that."

"Truly?" she whispered. "It makes me feel . . . spoiled, useless, this precious object on his shelf."

"It makes me glad to know ye were happy, that ye had the best your father could provide."

Her throat was tight. "I never understood how he treated those who weren't family. Oh, he was brusque with the servants, but Mother assured me he was only busy thinking about the weighty matters of the world. I was able to travel in fine carriages, dress in the best clothing, socialize in Edinburgh or London, and I thought I had the pick of men for my husband." She gave a sad laugh. "It turned out that Father was manipulating me from the moment of my birth. I was betrothed to the heir of the McCallum clan when I was but a babe, but he never told me."

He stiffened. "Ye're betrothed?"

"Nay, it ended this past summer."

He let out a breath.

"Do ye think I'd have done this with ye if I was promised to another man?"

He met her gaze. "Nay, I assumed ye'd have told me something so important when your mind cleared. But to hear the words on your lips . . ."

She gave him a gentle bite on the chest. "Ye deserved it."

He nodded. "Your father was thoughtless and cruel. Betrothals often happen to repair clan ties, but to not tell ye . . ."

"Do ye know how I found out?" she whispered, her throat tight. "When my betrothed, Hugh Mc-Callum, came to meet me in York, Father refused him, sent me out of town oblivious, put my dear cousin Riona in my place, and manipulated Hugh into kidnapping her. And it worked."

His chest lifted in a great sigh. "I'm sorry."

"Poor Riona must have been so frightened. Hugh thought he was only doing what he'd been forced to by my father. Riona and I have the same name, Catriona—our fathers were competitive in *everything*—so Hugh thought Riona was trying to elude the marriage, just like my father had done."

"I did not hear of a scandal."

"Nay, ye didn't, because they fell in love and married. My brother Owen agreed to wed a Mc-Callum to keep the contract between our two families whole. He and Hugh's sister Maggie were lucky enough to fall in love, too. Everyone is happily married, bairns on the way. I thought it was my turn to find my own life, my own happiness. 'Tis why I left for Glasgow."

"And then I kidnapped ye," he said, his voice flat, yet with undercurrents of anger and frustration.

Cat boosted herself up on one arm and looked down at him gravely. "Aye, it was an awful thing, using me to punish my father. He used me, too. I don't know if I can ever forget what ye did."

It was a strange conversation to have when they were utterly naked, their legs touching. But without clothes, after such an intimate act, there seemed to be no barriers between them and facing what he'd done to her.

"I trusted ye, Duncan. Ye'd saved me. I thought ye were so noble."

"I have no claims to nobility," he said hoarsely. "At first, I thought I was justified—not that it makes what I did right. Guilt about what had been done to my clan was its own powerful weapon that let me deceive myself, that let me ignore that ye weren't your father, that I was punishing ye."

"And when ye discovered my father was dead, when your plan no longer mattered? Ye didn't take me back."

"I couldn't," he said hoarsely. "Ye mattered too much to me. And in my selfishness, I still kept the truth hidden from ye, as if I could find a magic potion to make it all work out."

"But instead ye lost me, Duncan." Her words were solemn.

"I knew that, and yet it did not stop me from seducing ye, another wrong I have done to ye."

She stiffened. "Nay, not that. I wanted this as much as you."

He sat up on the edge of the bed, his profile somber. "I've kidnapped and then taken the innocence of an earl's sister. I have no life to offer in a cave, though honor demands I wed ye."

She moved away so they weren't touching. "I don't want to marry ye, Duncan. I went off to search for a man I trust—and you can never be that man."

He said nothing, because it was her choice, not his.

"As for why I offered myself to ye . . ." She looked away. "It was passion, not love, a fire that burns quickly, and just as easily burns out."

He nodded silently.

"But, Duncan, the whisky smuggling—it has to stop, for the safety of both our clans, or it'll only worsen the feud."

Now he looked at her from beneath lowered brows. "When the children are safe, and my people can earn their living without fear, *then* it'll stop."

"We'll just have to make it all happen then," she said briskly. "Ye'll capture the sheriff, then we'll take him to my brother, who'll see that true justice is done."

He eyed her. "*We'll* do that? Did I not just have a discussion with ye about putting yourself in danger?"

"Was it a discussion?" she asked primly. "I seem to remember being yelled at."

He harrumphed, but didn't look away. They stared into each other's eyes for a long moment, their words outlining the reality of their relationship— their lack of one. But they were still naked, and his gaze seemed to go all hot as he looked at her. That gaze drifted down her body—

He stood up. "I'll fetch ye some water to wash before we leave."

As he reached the door, she said, "Ye'll go out without clothes?"

"Who's to see me? And then I'll go for a swim."

"A swim!" she repeated, shocked. "Duncan, it's freezing."

"Good."

Confused, she could only stare at the door as it closed behind him.

CHAPTER 20

Duncan rode silently beside Cat the entire way home, and thought of the words she'd used to condemn him. *I went off to search for a man I trust—and you can never be that man.* She was right. Over the several-hour ride home, every time he glanced at her, she looked nothing but calm, even serene.

Those emotions would forever elude him. He had to end an injustice to his people, and then afterward . . . he'd have to return Cat to her brother and face the consequences. No punishment could be as severe as losing her. He hadn't realized how much he counted on seeing her lovely face each day, watching her interact with his people, never seeming above them. And then there was how she was with Finn. She would make a fine mother, and make a husband proud.

But not him.

They reached the cave after sunset, when the few men not out patrolling were gathered around the fires to relax. Maeve rushed toward them, her expression filled with relief.

"We were so worried, Catherine," she said, taking both of Cat's hands in her own and squeezing them. "But we realized ye'd taken yer favorite horse, and since none of the patrols had seen ye, we hoped that meant ye were well."

"I went after Himself to ride with him, and never thought to let anyone know. Forgive me."

Maeve waved a hand. "'Tis good ye got away from this damp old cave. Come, I've saved ye some supper."

Duncan had Cat precede him to a table. After Sheena studied the two of them, her shoulders drooped, and she turned away. Much as he knew Cat would never make it obvious that they'd been intimate, it was better that Sheena understood that he was not drawn to her.

Their homecoming obviously made Cat nervous. She sat on the opposite side of a table, down a bit from him, though they were the only two people there. She didn't meet his gaze, and talked pointedly to Maeve as she brought them roasted plovers, carrots, and cheese. Duncan didn't want to make Cat feel uneasy—didn't want her to have any regrets. He had enough for them both.

Ivor proved a good distraction as he updated Duncan about the patrols searching the southwestern Highlands. Another child had gone missing, and his every instinct told him that the sheriff was going to try another run to the coast, with less children this time, in hopes of slipping through the web of Duncan's men. One by one Duncan had incapacitated the sheriff's men, leaving less to do his bidding. The people of the countryside had risen as well, searching high and low for the children. He felt like he was so close to ending this scourge on his people, to proving he could keep them safe at last—to catching the sheriff at his evil deeds.

He retreated to his chamber after the meal, not so much for Cat's benefit as his own. Looking at her made him feel a mixture of pleasure and pain, all of which had to remain hidden behind his usual somber façade. He'd never thought it was difficult to project strength, command, and certainty to his people; he was their chief, and confidence was a duty he owed them. He'd learned to hide his more conflicted feelings since childhood.

But not Cat. From the moment she'd arrived, her sweet face projected her every emotion, at first fear, then gratitude and contentment, then even the happiness of helping the lost children. And this day, when she'd lain beneath him in bed, her face had been a reflection of wonder and desire, urgency and fulfillment.

But not love. She would never love him. And he didn't think it fair to her to make her suffer through this evening struggling to hide whatever she felt: shame, guilt, or perhaps even regret. Much as she'd insisted the choice had been hers, she could be regretting it now.

Duncan ran a hand through his hair, uncertain what he should do. He'd thought making love to her might have cured him of his desperate need, but it only seemed worse now that he knew what he'd miss for the rest of his days. Every time he closed his eyes, he could see the wild way she'd thrown her head back in exultation, her dark hair cascading across the bedding. He relived the eager and unashamed way she'd touched him, and the feel of her soft, sweet skin beneath his mouth, the hard little nipples, the sensitive, wet folds of her womanhood.

With a groan, he stumbled away from his pallet, the one she'd spent so many nights in—and saw his trunk. Cat had reminded him of his father's letters, and he pounced on the distraction with relief. He'd read the first few before, had seen only a chief dealing with rent and taxes and farming. Duncan hadn't gone further, for he thought his father had buried himself in the mundane details of his lands, rather than overcome the shame of his sins to be the leader his clan needed.

This time Duncan kept reading, saw with disbelief that his father had known of the kidnappings. The man had never been a warrior, had not hoped to defeat this evil with sword and pistol, so he'd tried to use his pen and his intellect—neither of which had worked against the sheriff and the hidden support of the Earl of Aberfoyle.

But he'd tried.

For the first time in his life, Duncan could see through his bitterness and find a kernel of strength in his father. The man had been more than what Duncan, in his youth, had thought of him. Like his father, Duncan had done things he wasn't proud of, but he wouldn't abandon his people—and neither had his father, until an explosion of temper, and then guilt and shame, had worn him down.

Duncan had let *revenge* wear him down, cloud

his thinking, until he'd believed that holding an injured, innocent woman captive was something necessary, imperative even. He'd been such a fool. Much as he was a chief, he wasn't God, sitting in judgment over all the world. If he wanted the respect of his clan, he had to deserve it. Cat was right—the whisky smuggling, much as it helped his clan now, would only lead to further problems. He would stop it as soon as he could.

He couldn't imagine a day when he would be a normal man, overseeing his clan, searching for a wife. That woman could never be Cat; she'd made that clear. Though he didn't deserve her, he wanted to be worthy of her, wanted to earn her respect.

But would the ache of regret and lost love ever ease enough that he could court another woman?

"Laird Carlyle?"

Duncan stiffened at the sound of his name. He slid open the curtain to find young Finn standing there, hands twisted in his coat, eyes wide, then quickly downcast.

"Aye, Finn?"

"Might I speak with ye, Laird Carlyle?"

"Of course." Duncan stepped back, and when he felt like he dominated the chamber by towering over the nervous boy, he sat down and regarded him. "What might I do for ye?"

Finn took a deep breath, then spoke quickly, "Mistress Catherine thought I should tell ye all the truth, so I'm here to do that."

Duncan's own lies felt a sword to the gut when

looking at this boy's innocent, smudged face. He frowned. "And why did ye feel the need to with-hold something from me?"

"There's only been me to protect meself since me mum died. And if those on the streets knew the truth . . . it wouldn't go well for me."

"I'm glad to have your trust then, Finn. I won't betray it."

"Hope not, sir. The thing is . . ." The words trailed off, Finn closed his eyes, then said in a rush, "I'm a girl, not a boy." Finn peered at him worriedly through narrowed, frightened eyes.

Duncan blinked for a moment, as everything he thought about the lad—lass—rearranged itself. "I can see why ye kept that a secret on the streets of Glasgow."

Finn's thin shoulders sagged. "Mistress Catherine . . . she said ye knew the truth about her, and 'twould be all right if I told ye about me. Is it, sir?"

Duncan briefly touched the girl's arm. "I am honored that ye shared your secret with me, Finn. What did Mistress Catherine say about her secret?"

"About her memory comin' back? Och, she's worried what people'll think about her, a rich, fine lady that she is. I think she was unhappy before. She didn't say it," Finn added confidently, "but I think she's happier here."

"A cave is no place for a lady," Duncan said with solemnity. "Or a young lass either."

"There's other women here," Finn insisted.

"With their menfolk."

Finn sighed. "I thought sharin' the truth with ye would make ye change yer mind about findin' me a family."

"Finn—is that short for Fiona?"

"Finola," Finn said glumly.

"And what is your surname?"

"Hume."

"Finn, I hope that someday ye're proud of your name and can use it freely. I won't make ye do so here. And I won't tell your secret until ye're ready."

"Thank ye, sir."

"But I'm glad ye told me the truth, that ye trusted me. Now trust me with your future, and know that I will do my best for ye."

Finn nodded, but didn't meet Duncan's eyes. After she left, Duncan regretted that she looked so dispirited. He vowed not to disappoint her.

CAT spent an awkward evening considering everything she'd done. Once again, she'd rushed heedlessly into a decision, chasing after Duncan, without giving thought to the consequences—one of which was losing her virginity, she thought wryly. She'd made the decision herself, but still . . . did that mean she trusted him? No, she refused to consider that. She'd shared an intimacy with him, but it had ended. She wasn't entrusting him with her life.

The other consequence of her choice to be with Duncan was that everyone knew they'd gone off for hours alone. She felt like they all knew that she'd given herself to their chief.

Sheena knew. Cat had never seen a woman mope around so much, dispiritedly helping clean up the last of the dishes, slinking off to sit by herself with her father, Melville, who patted her shoulder and glared at Cat.

Cat knew she was hot with a blush, and leaned closer to the cauldron of hot water, hoping everyone would think that was the reason.

And then there was Finn, who seemed just as depressed. When Cat finally confronted the girl, she only said that she'd told Duncan the truth, and though he'd been kind, he hadn't changed his mind about finding her a home. Finn pulled a blanket over her head on her pallet and fell asleep early. If she actually slept, Cat couldn't be certain.

Cat herself found her pallet soon after, and almost wished she could hide under a blanket, too. She imagined people staring at her back, thinking her a harlot—or a "fancy lass," she remembered with faint amusement.

And she was, in truth, Duncan's fancy lass, and had been quite willing about it, too. As she lay dozing, images came to her of the afternoon lying beneath him. Her breasts were still sensitive, and between her legs—oh, she still blushed to remember what he'd done to her, how he'd pleasured her. She was no longer a virgin, had nothing to offer her husband on her wedding night.

Any man who cared about that wasn't worth marrying, she told herself sternly.

But beneath her bluster was a creeping undertone of doubt. Never before had she met a man she'd even wanted to risk her reputation on. Oh, she'd snuck away for an occasional moment alone at a ball, had even been kissed before—and liked it.

But only Duncan, a Scottish outlaw who'd betrayed her and held her captive, had made her pull off her own garments in her haste to be with him.

And it had been worth it.

What was she supposed to make of that?

At last she fell asleep, and it seemed little time had passed at all before she was awakened by an odd sound. She rolled over onto her back and heard the snores of a handful of men—all the others were on patrol looking for the kidnappers. A few torches still burned on the walls, but the peat fires were nothing but embers. She lifted her head, listening, and at the narrow opening between two screens, saw movement at the entrance to the cave—a person sneaking past a dozing Melville. A small person.

Finn.

Cat quietly put on her shoes, pulled the laces of her gown tighter, and followed the young girl. Most likely she was going out to tend the horses. Now that she'd been taught to work with them, Finn seemed to have found a measure of peace with the animals.

Melville made a snorting noise as Cat passed by. She lifted a torch from the wall, said quietly, "I'll be with the horses," and he nodded and lowered his chin to his chest again.

But Finn wasn't with the horses, who crowded toward her eagerly for treats. She patted noses and necks as she looked around, but there wasn't a sound. Apparently Finn did not want to be found, and Cat had a prickly, uneasy sensation spread across her skin. Dawn was beginning, a gray smudge in the eastern sky. After one of the guards gave a nod as he went past, Cat put the torch out in a bucket and began to roam the area outside the cave, from the woods to the paddock, to the burn Duncan used for his bath. At last she looked straight up, at the towering turret of the Carlyle castle on the cliff. Would Finn really have gone up there, when she'd expressly been forbidden?

Letting out a sigh, Cat picked her way up the path in the gloom, glad that each passing moment brought more and more light. Her skirts caught on bushes, she tripped once over a rock that blended in to the dirt, but with every step climbed, she felt more confident. She came up at last to the open area in front of the gatehouse, lifting her skirts, ready to march in there and drag Finn back by the ear if necessary—

And then she saw Finn running straight toward the path, toward her. The terror on the girl's white face made Cat's lungs seize, her heart kick in to a wild beat. She only had a moment to realize she would protect brave, wonderful Finn until the day Cat died. Then the true danger revealed itself. A stranger on horseback galloped behind Finn, his cloak swirling in the wind, his head lowered over the horse's neck, one arm reaching for the girl.

CHAPTER 21

Cat wasn't in the cave when Duncan appeared for breakfast. It was Melville who told him that Cat had followed Finn to the horses some time ago.

"It's barely light out," Duncan said, frowning. "How long is some time ago?"

Melville swallowed hard. "'Twas dark outside, sir. And I might have . . . closed me eyes a bit."

Or perhaps not cared much, since in the older man's mind, Cat was competition for the foolish dreams he was encouraging in his daughter.

Duncan gritted his teeth. "Do not allow such a thing to happen again."

The man gave several bobs of the head as Duncan strode past him outside. The night guard confirmed that Cat had gone to the paddock, but Duncan couldn't find her there, and her favorite horse—all the horses—were accounted for. Had she gone for a stroll in such dangerous times? He searched the entire outdoor encampment and found nothing. He had to have missed something. Back inside, he tried the pool cave, where he surprised Torcall floating contentedly on his back, naked. Upon seeing Duncan, Torcall flailed and sank beneath the surface.

But no Cat. Maeve was waiting in the great hall when he returned.

"I cannot find Finn, either," Maeve said in a low voice, twisting her hands in her apron. "Mistress Catherine has disappeared before, Laird Carlyle."

"Aye, but usually with me or the men. There are no missing horses," Duncan added with frustration. "I cannot believe they would just start walking to the village." And then he stiffened. "The castle."

Outside, he hurried up the steep jagged path, then jogged across the open grounds and through the gatehouse.

"Catherine?" He wanted to call her by her real name, as if that would make her appear faster. "Finn?"

There was no answer but the wail of the wind through the reeds. Cat and Finn were gone.

He went back through the gatehouse and, to his surprise, saw fresh hoofprints. He didn't know when the last time he'd ridden here had been, and no one else came this way. The hoofprints seemed to head right for the path, which no horse would have an easy time of—and then he saw a woman's shoe lying in the mud.

The shot of fear was almost shocking, paralyzing. Cat's shoe. Or was it? He picked it up and began to run down the path, jumping over bushes, climbing through rocks, sliding through scree near the bottom, anything for a more direct trail straight down. He ran into the cave, holding the shoe high.

"Maeve!" he barked.

Everyone jumped and froze.

"Is this the shoe ye gave Catherine?" he demanded.

Maeve began to nod before he even reached her. "Where did ye find it?"

"Up at the castle. She and Finn are gone." He looked at Torcall and Angus. "Pack provisions for a several-day journey. I'll ready the horses."

He turned.

"Laird Carlyle," Maeve called.

He glanced over his shoulder.

"Do ye think someone took 'em?"

"Aye, I do."

Her look of fear only echoed his thoughts. Had someone realized who Cat was and took her for ransom? He told himself that since they hadn't killed her, they surely had no plans to. But since Finn was also gone, he had to consider that Sheriff Welcker and his men might have succeeded in stealing another child right out from under his nose.

He and his two men rode off, knowing there was only one road up to the castle—only one way down for horses. The kidnappers couldn't have much of a start, and they had two very unwilling prisoners.

Cat never would have been exposed to such danger if he'd just taken her home right from the beginning. His selfish need for vengeance might have put her in the path of a man so bloodthirsty he didn't care what happened to children, as long as his pockets grew heavier with gold.

And Finn—the little girl so afraid of the world she'd had to pretend to be a boy. Duncan hadn't kept her safe, had let her be plunged back into her worst fears.

Duncan knew the sheriff's men made occasional forays to the castle ruins to look for him, and he'd always been well-prepared. But this night raid had been a new tactic, and it had caught a helpless woman and child, instead of him. But at least he knew the sheriff never bothered to disguise his tracks, had always felt superior to the "savages" of the Highlands. Duncan reached a main horse trail, where tracks were obscured by others, and then he had to make a choice. The sheriff wouldn't head deeper into the Highlands, nor would he go to Glasgow. If the rumors were true, he had three children now, at least—and a woman—and it would be the coast he'd aim for. There were two paths to Loch Lomond, while Duncan had only two men. The extra man would have to serve as the go-between. It was only a several-hour journey to the loch, but where along its coast would the men await the next stage of their journey?

And what would happen to Cat while they passed the time?

His stomach tightened, and he fought back his fear. It wouldn't do her any good, and would only impede him. He'd spent a lot of years mastering his emotions, and he fell back on that experience now.

In the end, the two clansmen saw signs of them first, and one doubled back to find Duncan.

By the time the three of them trailed the group to a hidden bay of Loch Lomond, where barren mountains rose above the tree-lined coast, it was obvious a rescue attempt couldn't easily be made. Duncan and his men worked their way through trees at a crouch, and then on their bellies until they overlooked the rocky coast. Duncan took no satisfaction that at last Sheriff Welcker himself was there, since there were five other men with him. It was obvious by the weapons on their belts, and the way they carried themselves, that these were no mere clansmen but mercenaries. Duncan and his two men might attack six, but the odds were they'd lose, or some of the captives might die. He couldn't take such a risk.

When he saw Cat, alive and unharmed, he thought he'd feel a measure of relief. And he did. But he hadn't imagined how his gut would clench, his fear would threaten. She sat with three children gathered around her skirts, a young one literally clinging to her, though Cat's hands were tied together in her lap. Finn sat nearby, stiff with trying to look brave, though she, like the other children, was bound. Cat herself, though white-faced, exuded calm.

Duncan signaled his men, and they all crawled backward, away from the sheriff's encampment on the beach, until it felt safe enough to speak in low tones.

"Angus, you gather our patrols and bring them here."

Angus grimaced. "I know the paths, aye, but to track them all down could take through the night."

"I know, which is why I want Torcall"—he turned to the other man—"to go to Castle Kinlochard and tell the Earl of Aberfoyle that his sister, Lady Catriona, is in danger."

Both men gaped at Duncan.

"Lady Catriona . . . ?" Angus began. "She's Mistress Catherine?"

"Aye. We'll discuss it later. Tell the earl to bring all the men he can spare." Duncan glanced grimly back through the trees toward the loch. "I'll do my best to delay them until ye arrive."

"But how will ye—"

"There's no time for discussions. Go!"

Crouching, the two men headed back toward the horses. Alone, Duncan crawled on his belly to take the measure of his enemies. He spent a long time estimating their strengths and weaknesses. The sheriff paced as if on edge, and the mercenaries calmly talked among themselves. The littlest child cried against Cat's breast on and off.

And then a small two-masted fishing lugger sailed into the bay just before dusk, and Duncan's hopes sank. They would smuggle a human cargo at night, because once they reached the river, there'd be more traffic, more questions during the daylight hours. The darkest part of night was creeping on them, and the moon that rose was only a sliver, which would aid the kidnappers but delay his reinforcements.

Duncan didn't have much time to act. Slowly, he backed up through the brush, then came down to the shore of the loch beyond the bay itself. He stripped off his garments, hefted his dirk, waded into the freezing water, and began to swim around the point, only slowing when he knew his vigorous strokes might be seen. Head barely out of the water, arms moving beneath the surface, he swam to the back of the ship, where it loomed up out of the dark to protect him. He could hear the men on the shore now, saw the cook fire. Some of the sailors had rowed a small boat ashore, but there was probably still a man or two aboard.

Very quietly, Duncan explored the hull, until he found a weak spot near the surface, where a hole had already been patched. Several times he took in a mouthful of water and fought not to cough. With his dirk, he pried a hole between the narrow boards and slowly widened it. Occasionally he had to take a break from bobbing by holding onto the anchor chain. But eventually, when he put his fingers into the carved slit, he could feel water seeping in. He slowly swam out of the bay and around the point. After drying himself off with his plaid, he dressed again and made his way back to his hidden overlook.

CAT forced herself to eat some of the rabbit meat her kidnappers offered, though she didn't feel at all hungry. They didn't untie her, and though she could have fed herself, they took turns putting their fingers to her mouth and laughing with each other. She shuddered.

It had been a long, terrifying day, starting with the horror of watching a stranger lean over and grab a running Finn around the waist and swing her over the front of his saddle. Cat had chased after them, screaming, flailing her arms, but she needn't have worried about being left behind as a witness. A second man had done the same thing to her, as if she weighed no more than Finn. It seemed like hours passed as she'd lain on her stomach across the horse, every pounding hoofbeat jarring her, bruising her ribs. Her kidnapper seemed quite happy to keep a hand on her backside, giving an occasional squeeze. She couldn't see where they were going, because she couldn't keep her head arched up long enough to find out.

When they'd at last stopped behind a copse of trees for a midday meal, Cat had fallen forward when the man pulled her off the horse, because her legs wouldn't support her. She'd come up on her elbow, every gasp for breath making her ribs ache, and saw Finn. The girl had been cowering in a heap, arms covering her head as if to block out what had happened to her—again.

Though one man had stood guard by Finn, the other two had looked Cat over and spoken with coarse English accents. For the hours leading up to the stop, she'd frantically debated: should she reveal her identity and attempt to negotiate their release, or pretend to be a simple Scottish house-wife. In the end, the latter had won out, and she figured she could always change her mind later. Luckily, they were more interested in getting back to their leader, who, she was told, would deal with her.

But on the shores of Loch Lomond, their leader, Sheriff Welcker, a thin, nervous-looking man, seemed glad that she could talk calmly to the children and keep them under control. Finn was the oldest, the only girl. One child couldn't have been more than three years, and spent the rest of the day clinging to Cat and crying in ragged outbursts that only subsided to whimpers when Cat comforted him. They didn't bother to tie up the littlest one. The other boy, six or seven years old, sat stiff and wide-eyed, and didn't even seem to notice the food she awkwardly tried to put into his fingers. She got the name Adam out of the littlest boy, but the other wouldn't speak at all, poor thing.

When Cat had seen the small ship sail into the bay, she'd begun to let go of the last tenuous hope that someone would find them. "Let me keep 'er," one of the mercenaries said again.

Cat shuddered. This debate had been going on all day. She thought being with the children protected her some, but now that they were encamped on the shores of the loch, she could be dragged off into the woods at any time.

"Nay, she'll fetch a pretty penny on a plantation," the sheriff insisted.

He seemed to be enamored of the fact that he might earn more with her, as if he was only now considering expanding his commerce into the sales of women. She shuddered. When several men had come from the ship to join them, she'd tried to keep her face averted.

But then there'd come a shout from the ship itself, and the captain rowed his small boat back. Cat could hear the cursing from shore. The sheriff waited, practically on his toes as he craned to see what was going on at the ship, but the night was too dark.

The boat returned, the captain got out and swore again. "There's a leak in the hull. We'll no be goin' anywhere until it's patched, and we cannot see to patch it. We'll be spendin' the night pumpin' her out to stay afloat."

The sheriff cursed, the children whimpered, and the mercenaries turned to look at Cat, as if they needed some amusement. She shivered, but again the sheriff overruled the men, who bedded down around the fire, muttering. There were no blankets to spare for Cat and the children, so they huddled together and tried to keep warm as an autumn wind came down the loch and swirled around them. It was hard to hold them all within her arms when she was still tied up, but little Adam crawled up within the circle of her bound arms, Finn leaned against one side, while the other traumatized boy didn't protest when she looped her bound hands around him and pulled him against the warmth of her body.

"Mistress?" Finn whispered.

"Aye?"

"Can I run for help?"

"Nay!" she practically hissed. "Ye'll not risk yourself in these woods when ye don't know where ye are."

"But—"

"Don't give up hope that we'll be found."

Finn remained silent, and the flickering firelight showed the doubt in her expression.

By morning's light, Cat could see that the boat

hadn't sunk, and that the sailors who'd kept it afloat now worked to repair it. Hours passed, bringing her closer and closer to setting sail from the Highlands, perhaps from Scotland forever. When the captain appeared on deck and saluted smartly from across the water, Sheriff Welcker jumped up.

It was now or never, Cat thought. She'd hoped through the night that the Carlyle clansmen would find them, and it was her own fault they hadn't. She had to do what she could for the children.

"Sheriff, I wish to discuss the possibility of ransom," she said coolly, using her most aristocratic British accent.

The sheriff stiffened and turned slowly from his view of the ship and studied her from beneath raised eyebrows. The three mercenaries who weren't patrolling the beach and the woods did the same.

"Ransom?" the sheriff echoed.

He sounded as if he wanted to scoff, but she knew her cultured voice had made him wary.

"Yes. My true name is Lady Catriona Duff, sister to the Earl of Aberfoyle."

The mercenaries looked interested but unaware, while the sheriff narrowed his eyes at her. "What would the sister of an earl be doing near the ruins of Carlyle Castle?"

"I fell from my horse and hit my head, which left me incapacitated and unaware for some time. When I came to my senses, I could not yet be returned to my home. But I am who I say I am. Ask me any questions you would like."

For several minutes, he asked about her father and his land holdings, the castles and properties of her clan. They were easy for her to answer, and the bored mercenaries watched her with little curiosity. The little boy in her arms kept his face against her chest and stared up at her, her flow of words hushing his whimpers. Even Finn looked at her with wonder.

The sheriff became more and more intrigued and narrow-eyed with calculation. At last, as she was reciting details of her brother's Edinburgh townhouse, he held up a hand.

"Just stop. I believe ye."

"Then you comprehend that my brother will pay handsomely for my safe return." She glanced at the ship.

"Aye, he likely will. But then he'll also know all about my private venture."

Cat felt her simmering fear begin to rise again, and she struggled to keep it from her voice. "Why would I tell him this, if you returned me and the children safely to my brother?"

"Because ye're just a woman, and won't be able to keep your mouth shut about anything important," he said, giving her a friendly smile. "I'll not lose the sure profit from the children on the chance I might receive a ransom, which will certainly lead to too much notice from Aberfoyle. Your father, now he was a man who understood the value of coin."

She offered a look of distaste. "My father believed himself all powerful. My brother is a far more practical man, a man of science, rather than a warrior. He will negotiate in fairness—"

"Stop, there'll be none of that. 'Tisn't worth the risk."

"But—"

And then he rose up above her, hand raised as if he'd hit her. The children shrieked, Finn tried to jump to her feet, and Cat had to restrain the girl.

"Touch her and ye'll die."

The deep, cold voice rang across the beach.

CHAPTER 22

Catherine closed her eyes in a brief prayer of thanksgiving at the sound of Duncan's voice, before it dawned on her that he didn't appear—which probably meant he hadn't come with a large contingent of men. Or was it a trick? She couldn't know—and the sheriff couldn't know, either. The two mercenaries who hadn't gone on patrol drew their swords and pistols.

Sheriff Welcker's smile grew slowly. "Why, Carlyle, is that yourself, come to me at last? I couldn't have used the girl for any better result."

"Let her and the children go and I'll let ye live," called Duncan.

The sheriff chuckled. "Show yourself and we'll discuss it like gentlemen."

Finn slid her hand into Cat's, and they glanced at each other with worry.

"Throw down your pistols," Duncan demanded. "I don't want a stray bullet harming your captives."

As the sheriff began to laugh, a shot rang out, so close that he ducked.

"Or the pistols of my men can harm ye," Duncan added.

The sheriff tossed aside his pistols, then nodded to the mercenaries, who reluctantly did the same.

Duncan appeared from between two trees, his claymore ready but held relaxed. The sheriff drew his sword.

Cat met Duncan's gaze across the expanse of the beach, and she felt something swell up inside her—gratitude, surely. He wore only his belted plaid and his shirt, as if his coat would hinder him. The wind caught his sleeves, and the folds of plaid, but Duncan himself stood like a rock, tall, masculine, determined. She might not trust him about some things, but she knew he would never abandon her and the children. His glance for her was brief and betrayed no emotion, but something passed between them and she was grateful for it.

Duncan eyed the sheriff. "I thought I'd lure ye into the open, and it happened at last."

The sheriff threw his arms wide. "This is the open? I see a deserted beach with my men all around."

"I see ye with your hands dirty in the ugly theft of children."

"'Ugly theft?' What harsh words—and untrue."

Cat gasped.

"I'm *saving* these children," Sheriff Welcker insisted.

"Saving them?" Duncan repeated in disbelief. "Are ye trying to make noble your greed?"

"No doubt the money is welcome, and I damned

well deserve it after the poverty-stricken childhood I had. But who better to know what these
children are suffering here, than me? In America,
they'll only be indentured for seven years. They'll
learn a trade, have a chance to better themselves,
far more than they ever would in the Highlands.
Ye think returning them to their cursed families
is better?"

"Ye're mad," Duncan said bitterly. "I have witnesses as to what ye've done, but I didn't have
your participation. I do now."

"Ye won't live long enough for that to happen."

"And *you* think ye'll kill me?" Duncan scoffed.
"Without your pistol, ye're not even a man."

The sheriff's sword came up. "I can defeat a
coward skulking in the brush easily enough."

"Do ye think so?" Duncan asked softly. "Shall
we see what ye can do?"

Cat wanted to call his name, warn him about
how many sailors were on the ship, how many
mercenaries lingered in the woods. This was mad-
ness. There were surely no other clansmen, and
the sheriff knew it as well. He was simply toying
with Duncan. She wanted to believe that Duncan
was toying with *him*, but couldn't let herself. Even
the children were silent, watching the tableau.

Sheriff Welcker impatiently waved back his
men as he approached Duncan across the rocky
beach. The well-trained mercenaries didn't leave
Cat or the children, frustrating her chance to lead
the children into the woods. Instead, she watched
the sheriff and Duncan circle each other. The sheriff was lean, but there was a wiry strength to him,

and without any sense of decency or a conscience, he might be a formidable opponent.

But Duncan was a Highlander, a warrior who believed in defending his people more than benefiting himself. As an outlaw, he could have fled to the continent, sold his sword arm as a mercenary, lived a better life than here. But instead, he hid in a cave near his people so that he could keep them safe. Much as Cat detested what he'd done to her, she knew and appreciated his strengths.

When the sheriff thrust out his sword, and Duncan parried it and slid to the side with the skill of a dancer, she took a gasping breath. For long moments, she didn't even hear the sound of breathing, only the clash of metal and the grunts of the sheriff as he tried to parry Duncan's slashes. Duncan's face showed narrow-eyed concentration, and his claymore flashed reflections of sunlight as he moved it with precision. Slowly the sheriff gave ground. When the man fell to one knee, Duncan waited. With a grimace of anger, the sheriff came up thrusting low. Duncan jumped over his blade, slashing sideways in a move that the sheriff barely repelled before it could slice off his arm.

One sound at last broke Cat's concentration on the fight: the swish of swords leaving their sheaths as the mercenaries moved closer to the children and her. She didn't dare cry out a warning, for fear of distracting Duncan. But the children pressed ever closer to her, even the mute boy. She wished she could gather them all within her embrace, but with her hands tied together, all she could do was hold little Adam against her chest while he trembled.

And then one by one, as if in a dream, men began to step out of the trees to line the beach, five, ten, a dozen, then more than she could count. Finn gave her arm an exultant squeeze, and they shared a hopeful glance. Out on the loch, the ship's anchor began to rise out of the water, even as the first sails unfurled, as the captain prepared to abandon Welcker.

At the sight of her brother, Cat drew in a sharp breath, and tears flooded her eyes. She felt like it had been forever since she'd last seen him. The mercenaries dropped their weapons and stepped away from the children and her.

But the sword fight went on. Why did the sheriff not surrender? It was apparent he'd seen the number of his enemy, and knew he could never go free. He was slow in lifting his weapon, his arms shaking from exhaustion. But still he fought, his desperation rising as he took wild swings. Duncan was impassive and calm, though sweat dotted his face with the exertion.

At last, Duncan slipped past the sheriff's defenses, thrusting his claymore deep into the man's chest. For a moment, the two men stared at each other over the killing blow, and the entire beach was silent. Welcker looked as shocked as if he'd never experienced defeat before. With a scream, he crashed to the ground.

Little Adam began to cry again, the mute boy just stared, but Finn raised a fist triumphantly.

Cat desperately wanted to press their little faces against her so they could not see such ugliness. She could only hope that the vanquishing of their captor would at least help them sleep easier at night.

"'Tis all right now," she said to the children. "We're safe and unharmed. Ye'll go home soon."

The rest happened quickly. Duff and Carlyle clansmen poured onto the beach and the mercenaries surrendered, protesting loudly that they'd only recently been hired and hadn't hurt anyone. Shuddering at her memories of what they'd wanted to do with her, Cat struggled to her feet, Adam still clinging to her. Owen strode toward her, and she would have flung her arms around his neck if her hands weren't still tied. But Owen dragged her into his embrace.

"I was so worried," her brother whispered against her hair. "No letters came from ye, I thought ye were just enjoying yourself, and then this news—" He shuddered as if unable to say more.

"'Tis all right," she murmured, "but I'm starting to lose my breath."

She smiled as he quickly loosened his embrace, but Owen wasn't smiling. He pulled out his dirk and began to work at the bonds restraining her and the children.

"Where have ye been? How did this"—he spread his arms as if encompassing the whole beach— "even happen?"

She realized he didn't know anything except that she'd been kidnapped by the sheriff. She looked past him at Duncan, who wiped the blood from his sword across the sheriff's plaid before drawing the loose ends over the man's contorted, frozen face.

Then Duncan met her gaze, sheathed his sword, and walked toward them. Cat felt a terrible anxiety seize her. She'd wanted Duncan to pay for what he'd done to her, how he'd betrayed her by taking advantage of her weakness for his own ends. But suddenly she didn't want any of it to come out at all. He'd just challenged and slain the sheriff, risking his very life for her and the children. There were many sides to Duncan, and she feared she might love them all. She was so confused.

Duncan formally bowed to Owen. "Lord Aberfoyle, I am Duncan Carlyle, chief of Clan Carlyle."

"Ye were the one who sent for me," Owen said slowly. "Ye've saved my sister's life."

"'Tis not that simple. Ye need to hear everything."

Flustered and worried, Cat put Adam into Finn's arms and said to the girl, "Take the children to my brother's men. They'll feed ye."

Finn hesitated, but the mute boy seemed to swallow excessively, as if beginning to come out of his terror. The three-year-old squirmed.

Finn looked from Cat to Duncan, who nodded to the girl, and said kindly, "Go. I'll speak to ye after the earl and I talk." He put a hand on her shoulder. "Ye were very brave, Finn."

Finn reddened, but nodded, and with a last anxious glance at Cat, walked down the beach with the other two children. That left just Cat, her brother, and her lover alone on the beach, tension rising to crackle between them.

Owen folded his arms over his chest and regarded Duncan impassively. "Explain to me what I need to know."

"This is my tale to tell," Cat found herself saying, even though she'd had no idea what she intended to say at all. But she felt a desperate need to forestall whatever was about to happen.

"Nay, this is my tale, all my responsibility." Duncan removed his sword belt and laid his sheathed sword at Owen's feet, along with his pistol. "Your sister has been living with my clan for the last three weeks."

Owen rounded on Cat. "But you were heading for Glasgow. My men were escorting ye there."

Tears returned so quickly. "A terrible storm rose up and we fell down a ravine. When I awoke, they were both dead, bless their souls, and I . . . I couldn't remember who I was."

Owen's mouth tightened. "What are ye saying?"

"I had no memories at all. I didn't know my name or where I was from or if I had any family. My head was badly injured, and I probably would have died in the wilderness except . . . Duncan found me."

"I knew who she was," Duncan said coldly. "And I didn't tell her."

Owen stiffened.

"I make no excuses for myself," Duncan continued, "but ye should know the truth. Your father was my bitter enemy, a man who countenanced children being stolen from their families and sold to the colonies. My clan's children—those children." He pointed to Finn and the others, who were now sitting in a little circle eating.

Cat saw Owen's mouth move, but he couldn't seem to find words.

"Welcker, the sheriff of Glasgow, had me imprisoned when I tried to stop it. My people have been rescuing the children when we can, but we weren't able to reach the sheriff himself who organized these crimes with the backing of your father and some of the magistrates. At last both men are now dead, the magistrates defenseless. I'm grateful my people will no longer suffer. But when I found Cat—Lady Catriona—I thought your father lived, that perhaps she was part of his plan. But then when it was obvious she really had no memory, I wanted him to know what it felt like to have a missing child. So I used your sister for my own ends, and put her in terrible danger."

No one said anything for a long moment. Owen, usually so logical and impassive, wore a variety of emotions that paraded across his face as if he didn't know which to feel first: confusion, sorrow, fury. Cat had felt all of those, and more, since she'd first met Duncan Carlyle.

"Ye held my sister captive," Owen said coldly to Duncan, then turned to Cat. "But ye didn't know it?"

She shook her head. "I was well treated by him and all of his people."

"Ye cooked food and cleaned laundry," Duncan shot back. "That's treating the sister of an earl well?"

Before Owen could say anything, Cat rounded on Duncan. "What else should I have done? I wanted to contribute, because I was being fed and clothed and housed."

"Housed in a cave!"

Owen's eyes went wide but she brushed those words aside with a swipe of her hand.

"We all lived in the cave. Even if I'd known my identity, I would have wanted to be of help. What should I have done, sit in a chair and find something to embroider?"

"I could have told ye the truth, but I let ye worry about the family ye couldn't remember," Duncan said tiredly. "I denied ye that." He turned to Owen. "Lady Catriona can verify that my clan knew nothing about this. To them, she was a vulnerable woman in need. Do what ye wish with me, but don't take my crimes out on them."

Owen frowned at Duncan for a long moment, then turned back to Cat. "When did your memories return?"

"Four days ago. Duncan had promised to return me when it was safe, but I saw poor little Finn being kidnapped, and I tried to help, and only found myself in the same trap."

"I think ye're leaving much out of this story," Owen said at last, then faced Duncan. "But none of that matters compared to what ye've done to my sister. Ye'll answer for those crimes." He gestured to one of his men, who approached. "Take him, but allow him to ride his own mount. If he gives ye trouble, rope him across the saddle."

Cat had to stop herself from protesting—then examined her own conduct in shock and confusion. Duncan *had* committed crimes against her. She couldn't deny that. But he walked away from her so calmly, perhaps returning to gaol once again without protest. He'd made it possible for the children of his clan to play freely, without fear. And now it was as if he didn't care what happened to him. Would she ever rid herself of the terrible ache of frustration, sorrow, and regret?

CHAPTER 23

The journey back to Owen's castle lasted most of the day. Cat knew that Duncan was somewhere among the soldiers, but she never saw him. He'd sent his own men back to the cave, and though they'd been confused, they'd obeyed him. Cat kept Finn with her, knowing the girl would probably follow them on her own.

Cat busied herself comforting the children, to whose families Owen had already sent word—with Duncan's help. She knew her brother was still outraged, frustrated, and sad that he'd known nothing about the kidnappings, that their own father had been capable of such deceit.

But they couldn't talk about it in front of the children, and she was almost glad. She didn't want to answer Owen's questions about what had happened to her. She was still trying to accept that she was never returning to the cave, that she might seldom see Maeve and the other friends she'd made. Maeve and Muriel had felt as close to Cat as any friendships she'd ever had, except for her close bond with her cousin Riona. Oh, she knew she could visit them—and she wanted to see Maeve in her own home again, now that the sheriff was dead and his evil deeds would come to light. Though Owen would feel guilty over what their father had done, he wouldn't hide from it.

But what would happen to all the Carlyles if Duncan languished in gaol once again? Would his tanist seek to have his chiefdom revoked? She'd never met the man who would become chief if Duncan died without an heir. She'd once asked about him, only to be told the man was supervising the move of clan cattle from their summer pasture.

She must have looked worried and confused as she rode, because Owen kept glancing at her. To avoid him, she'd kiss little Adam's head as he slept against her, or lean in to say something to Finn and Calum, riding together on another horse. Calum had finally awoken from his fear to speak his name.

Castle Kinlochard was such a welcome sight that she had to blink away tears. Finn kept sneaking awed glances at her now, as if knowing she'd grown up lavishly changed what Finn thought of her. After crossing the arched bridge over the moat, they found the courtyard full of men dismounting. She saw Finn's expression when the girl caught a glimpse of Duncan, with two men holding his arms as if he'd flee after coming here willingly.

Between Adam holding onto her neck and Finn suddenly gripping her hand, and battling her own need to see what was happening to Duncan,

Cat felt pulled in so many directions she was a little panicky.

"I'll fetch Mrs. Robertson to help ye," Owen said, giving her a dubious look.

"Nay, 'tis all right," Cat murmured. "The children are just frightened. The housekeeper can meet us at supper, then show us to rooms for them." She hesitated, then whispered, "Duncan?"

"I'll put him in a bedchamber under guard."

Cat's shoulders sank as she let out her breath.

"Ye look very relieved for a woman who was wronged. I could put him in a cell."

Again, she caught Finn's swift look. "Nay, let's discuss this later."

They entered the great hall through the double doors at the back, and Owen's wife, Maggie, was the first to meet them, throwing her arms around Cat's neck, then pulling back in surprise at the sleepy toddler she'd disturbed. Maggie's unusual eyes, one blue, one green, were narrowed with curiosity.

Cat gave her a smile. "It's a long story."

"But ye're safe," Maggie said. "Relieved I am, especially when that messenger said ye'd been kidnapped. Ye must be hungry. Mrs. Robertson and I have been ready to feed everyone all day." And then she gaped as Duncan was escorted past her toward the stairs. "I—he's been here before! Owen, ye remember that traveler last week?"

Owen's frown grew even darker. "I'd been so concerned when I found Cat, that I hadn't even realized that's where I'd seen him before. I just assumed at a Highland assembly or festival. He's

Duncan Carlyle, chief of the Carlyles." He lowered his voice. "He had Cat all this time, including when he was here spying on us."

Cat winced, though she appreciated he was keeping the truth just between them. "Aye, he told me he came here."

"Then I was right!" Maggie exclaimed triumphantly.

"Right about what?" Cat asked.

Maggie leaned close. "I saw ye with him in my dreams, and ye were both so happy."

Cat gaped. She knew of the rare dreams that Maggie had, the ones that usually came true. She glanced at her brother, who only frowned at his wife.

"Aye, well, we're hungry," Owen grumbled.

Maggie was overly cheerful as she saw to the children's comfort, calling for baths to be prepared while they ate. She would be a mother herself soon, and it showed in the tender way she coaxed traumatized Calum to eat, and the way Adam agreed to sit in her lap and suck his thumb.

At last Mrs. Robertson said the children's rooms were prepared, and the three women began to lead them away.

Cat looked over her shoulder and called to her brother. "Stay there. We have things to discuss and I won't be long."

As she helped with the children, she couldn't stop thinking of how Maggie had seen Duncan happy in her dreams. Cat had only seen that sweet emotion on his face once, after they'd made love, but even then it had been brief, because nothing had been settled between them. He was not a man who'd ever been allowed to be happy as a child, and had never had cause to be so as an adult.

Duncan hadn't just been happy in Maggie's dream—he'd been happy with Cat. They'd been together, and she didn't see how that could come true.

DUNCAN was surprised to be left alone in the bedchamber, though he knew a guard was stationed in the hall. They brought him a tray of food—no knife, of course—and left him to his own devices. He found himself standing at the window as the sun set, watching the courtyard activities wind down. He could see the glow of fire diminish in the blacksmith's shop, saw the last horses put into the stables at dusk. This had been Cat's home— one of many. In days to come, he would be able to picture her here, happy and cared for. He felt as if he was memorizing how everything looked. It was good to think about anything other than losing Cat.

He'd already lost her.

He could be honest with himself about his relief that she was home, that she'd be safe. When he'd watched her trying to negotiate with the sheriff, he'd stepped out to defend her, though he hadn't known that Aberfoyle and his men were nearby. He'd only been concerned with keeping Cat safe.

And she *was* safe. He braced both hands on the window frame and lowered his head to breathe a sigh of relief. Whatever happened next, she and the children would be well. He knew she and her brother would pick up where Duncan had left off, see that there were no more kidnappings.

Someone knocked at the door and entered before he could respond.

The guard said, "Ye're to come to the great hall and wait to be heard."

Duncan nodded. He hoped his fate would be decided sooner rather than later. The longer he was here, the more Cat would suffer. And he didn't want that.

Once again, the two men did not bind him, allowed him to walk on his own down through the castle to a corridor outside the great hall.

"Wait here," one said.

And then he heard Aberfoyle's voice. "Cat, tell us everything."

It echoed in the great hall, but Duncan heard no whispered voices or movement, and thought there weren't many people deciding his fate. Perhaps Aberfoyle did not want many witnesses to what had happened to Cat. Duncan had brought shame upon her; he would do anything, even lie, to make sure her reputation did not suffer.

"I told ye about my accident," Cat began slowly. "I learned about Father's involvement before I even knew he was my father."

"How do ye know he was involved?" Aberfoyle demanded. "Just the word of an outlaw?"

"At first I took his word. Someone important had to be behind the scenes to permit this level of crime to happen, to try to bury it by discrediting a clan chief—that is not an easy thing to do. But I read the letters our father sent Duncan's father after the old Laird Carlyle had made inquiries about the missing children. There were threats there, Owen. Our father knew what was going on."

There was a long tense silence, until Aberfoyle spoke. "I always knew he could be a cruel man. Betrothing ye as a bairn, but never telling any of us, then trying to dishonorably break the contract—none of that spoke well of him. But to allow and encourage *children* to be sold . . . to know some of my wealth came from cruelty and heartbreak . . . I cannot countenance it. I will work on behalf of those desperate families, see if I can find the children and have them returned, even if I have to buy them back."

Duncan's relief was so overwhelming that he dropped his head back and closed his eyes. He hadn't had the resources for that, had only hoped to stop the practice. But Aberfoyle had the power and wealth to make things right.

"But now I have to deal with Laird Carlyle," Aberfoyle continued, his voice growing cold. "Aye, he tried to help children—"

"Owen, ye make it sound like he sent some men or called in some favors," Cat said. "Put aside what was done to me—"

"I cannot."

"Not forever. Just . . . hear me. Duncan tried to stop the theft of children, and to cover their crimes, the sheriff and his men threw him in gaol. The scars on his back, Owen . . ." She trailed off, her voice hoarse.

"And ye've seen his back?" Aberfoyle demanded.

Duncan stiffened, praying she'd come up with something that would not damage her standing with her brother. He ran both hands through his hair, briefly cupping his head. He'd caused all this. He turned to enter the hall, but the two men stopped him.

"We lived in close quarters in a large cave," Cat said carefully. "People bathed outdoors, or in a pool within the caves. I saw many men's backs."

She was cleverly using the truth, Duncan thought with admiration.

"Ye lived in a cave with lots of men?" Lady Aberfoyle asked with curiosity.

"And women," Cat hastily added. "Duncan gave me his private chamber as my own."

"Chamber? Ye mean cave." Aberfoyle's voice was flat.

"I had a bed and table and chest. There was furniture."

To Duncan's surprise, she seemed to be defending him.

"Why were they all in a cave?" the countess asked.

"Because Duncan is an outlaw. He had to stay hidden to help the children—otherwise he'd have been imprisoned again. Many of his clansmen stayed with him, because they, too, believed in the importance of the mission. We rescued nearly a dozen children while I was there, returning them to their families or finding the orphans new families. Our father was part of a terrible crime, Owen. Duncan's only crime was trying to make things right. And for that he was outlawed and banished, his people shunned. The village I saw was so poor, and that was only one of them."

"You forget his crime of kidnapping ye," Aberfoyle said angrily.

"I'm not forgetting it. But I don't want his people to suffer anymore. Duncan's father was a weak chief, easily swayed by others. But Duncan has been an honorable leader. Those people trust him; they need him."

"What are ye saying?" Aberfoyle demanded.

"Help him be free of the bounty on his head," Cat said.

Duncan couldn't believe what he was hearing. After all he'd done to Cat, now she was helping him. Apparently her brother couldn't believe it either.

"Cat, I cannot forget what he's done to ye!" His voice rose.

"I'm not asking ye to forget. I won't. But his people need him. He's done a brave, noble thing sacrificing his own freedom for them. He defended me when his own life was at risk from the sheriff and his men. I need ye to see that the sheriff is vilified, his crimes exposed and ended, Duncan freed. Ye can do that, Owen, I know ye can." Her voice grew softer, yet more urgent.

Duncan didn't deserve such selfless kindness. He felt like the worst sort of monster, that the generous woman he'd betrayed could defend him after he'd taken her innocence.

Aberfoyle raised his voice. "Send for the Carlyle."

The guards prodded him around the corner and into the great hall. At the dais, only three people were seated: Aberfoyle, his wife, and Cat.

Aberfoyle's eyebrows rose. "How are ye already here?"

"I thought he needed to be available," Lady Aberfoyle said smugly.

Duncan's gaze met and held Cat's. She flushed red as she realized he'd overheard everything. He expected her to look away, but she didn't. Those amber eyes glittered by torchlight, and her expression was a little haughty with discomfort. He almost wanted to smile. Instead, he bowed to her. She looked away.

Aberfoyle rose slowly to his feet, as if gathering his thoughts. "Carlyle, there's been much wrong ye've experienced, and ye've done well protecting your people and stopping a vicious crime. For that, I'll see that the bounty on your head is dismissed, and that ye'll be free to return to a normal life. But for what ye've done to my sister, I want ye gone. I never want to see ye in this castle or on any property I own. Ye can spend the night, but at dawn, take your horse and your weapons and leave."

Duncan took a deep breath and nodded. "Thank ye, Lord Aberfoyle."

It was far more lenient than he deserved. And it was all because of Cat. He stared at her too long, he knew. Her complexion was white, her eyes grave. He tried to memorize her features, her eyes that reminded him of the finest Scottish whisky, the mouth that had been sweet beneath his. He would never taste that mouth again, or bask in her gentle smile. It was a punishment all its own.

He bowed to her. When he spoke, his voice came out rough. "Lady Catriona, deceiving ye has been the greatest regret of my life. I do not deserve your forgiveness or the kindness ye've shown to me tonight. The best thing I can do to make up for what I've done is vow that ye'll never see or hear from me again. Ye have my sincere apology."

With another bow, he turned and left the great hall. One guard still trailed him and remained outside his door, but he wasn't surprised. Duncan had spent too many weeks denying Cat the right to her own life. It was time to give it back to her in truth. Even if he could not imagine going back to a life without her. He'd never thought he'd have the kind of happy marriage he'd seen in others. It was just difficult to have glimpsed such a thing, experienced a moment of heaven with Cat, and know it could never be his future.

CHAPTER 24

Cat spent another restless night because of Duncan Carlyle. Her sister-in-law had arranged for Duncan to overhear everything Cat said about him.

She rolled over and pounded a pillow, trying again to remember just how she'd phrased things.

Oh, what did it matter? It had worked, hadn't it? She'd persuaded her stubborn, arrogant brother to free Duncan, to even help him with his legal troubles. And she didn't regret it. She'd made clear to Duncan that there could be nothing more between them. He'd betrayed her, and she could never forget that, however wonderful he was as a clan chief, however much his people admired and were devoted to him, however much seeing him hold infants and talk to four-year-olds had made something twist painfully in her chest—however much she wanted to picture his face with a smile.

She would just have to tell him this when he came to her. Because of course, he would not leave without speaking to her.

So although she only dozed through the night, no one knocked on her door; no one snuck in and put a hand over her mouth to keep her quiet; no one wanted a last kiss. She felt like a princess in a tower, alone and unloved.

At dawn, she was left standing in her window, watching Duncan mount his horse in the muddy courtyard below. He pulled Finn up behind him. The girl had come to Cat crying an hour before, saying she missed her friends in the cave, and she couldn't let Duncan be alone.

And the unspoken chastisement was that Cat was letting Duncan go.

Letting him go? Cat had never had him! Their relationship had been nothing more than captor and captive—she just hadn't known it until it was too late, until she already had feelings for him. And those feelings had taken her over, leading to one night of lovemaking that she'd never forget.

But that was all she could have of him, because trust was one of the most important things about a marriage, and how could she ever trust him again?

For several weeks, she tried to resume her old life. It felt strange to have so much room to move around, a bedchamber that felt nearly as big as the cave's great hall, and a real great hall that rose several floors high and was filled each night with nearly a hundred clansmen. None of them knew all the details of her adventure with Clan Carlyle. Perhaps Owen thought he was sparing her, when in truth it made her feel even more different and alone.

Now that she knew what it was truly like to have so little, Cat made it a point to visit all the villages she could, bringing baskets of treats, and mostly being there to hear the good and the bad, and bring things to Owen's attention.

Maggie, the sister-in-law she'd only just gotten to know before her accident, now seemed a refuge. She wanted to hear all about Cat's adventures, and never tired of asking questions. She seemed to know when Cat couldn't sleep, and would come into her room, curl up near the fire, and they'd talk.

Three weeks after her return, Cat was standing at the dark window, hugging herself, seeing nothing, when she heard Maggie's familiar knock, a couple quick taps.

Maggie ducked her head in, wearing a hopeful smile. "I can't sleep." She touched her finally noticeable belly. "I get queasy when I lie down."

Smiling, Cat gestured her in. "Then come sit with me."

Two chairs were before the fire, and they each curled up in them, blankets over their laps for warmth, as autumn nights in the Highlands foretold the approach of winter.

"Ye looked . . . far away," Maggie said.

Cat bit her lip, then gave an embarrassed smile. "I was. I was thinking how glad I was that the Carlyles no longer have to live in a cave. Ye're sure Owen said everything was taken care of?"

Maggie nodded. "Several of the sheriff's men even agreed to testify as to what was done, in exchange for leniency, all to ensure Duncan's freedom. He's back with his people, clear of any crime."

Cat let out a breath. "I'm so glad. I feel guilty being warm each night knowing winter will soon come to those caves. Maybe now he can be the chief he was always meant to be."

"And that's . . . what?"

"Ye know," Cat said with a shrug, "living in his family manor again, helping his people improve their lives—"

"Finding a spouse?"

Cat was surprised that she actually jerked in response. She forced a laugh. "That's what people do, do they not?"

"I don't think ye're doing that. Ye know Owen would take ye wherever ye want—with more guards this time."

"The number of guards didn't matter," Cat said sadly, remembering the men who'd died. "I don't know if I'm ready to tell a stranger, some man, what has happened to me these last few months."

"That's all that's worrying ye?" Maggie asked with gentleness.

Cat bit her lip, and was surprised when her eyes flooded with tears. She sniffed and dabbed at them with the edge of the blanket. "I'm such a fool. Ye'd think I'd be happy to be home, to get back to my old life. But . . . I always felt like this fragile doll on a shelf, existing only to look pretty at balls, to shine on behalf of my overly proud father, to find the perfect husband to marry. But . . . I never felt like I had a real purpose"—she put a fist to her chest—"in here."

"And the Carlyles gave ye purpose?"

Cat nodded desolately.

"The Carlyles . . . or Duncan."

To her utter shock, Cat burst into tears. She covered her mouth, eyes wide and streaming as she stared at Maggie. "Oh, forgive me, I never do this sort of thing!"

"What, cry over a man? As if your brother hasn't made me cry plenty of times?"

Cat felt a giggle well up inside her. Crying and giggling at the same time felt ridiculous, but also . . . good.

"Ye're being very kind to me," Cat murmured as her smile died.

"And why would I not? Your brother's been worried for ye, says ye haven't been yourself. Blames the Carlyle every time we're in private, like only a man can cause our problems," she added, scoffing.

"A man did cause my problems this time." They were quiet for several minutes, as Cat looked into the fire. "I mattered to the Carlyles, and aye, to Duncan. Of course, when I felt like I most mattered was when he was lying to me about who I was. Maybe that's why he was also so kind to me in his gruff way. It . . . hurts to know that when I was trusting him, growing . . . fond of him, he had ulterior motives."

"Sounds like it started that way between ye, but maybe it didn't stay that way?"

Cat shrugged. "Of course it did. He didn't tell me who I was until I discovered my brooch—the one he hid from me! Then all my memories rushed back at having something familiar, something that was mine."

"Maybe he didn't know how to tell ye what he'd done, now that ye were both . . . fond of each other." Her voice grew teasing.

And Cat blushed. "Maybe. I don't know."

Even after she'd known the truth, she'd given herself to Duncan—she couldn't say that to Maggie. But the woman was perceptive, wasn't she?

"Ye once said," Cat began tentatively, "that ye saw us together in your dreams. Happy."

"Very happy," Maggie admitted, watching her too closely.

"Was he . . . smiling?"

"Grinning."

Cat caught her breath. "I've always wanted to see him happy."

"It's not too late."

"But . . . how can I trust him?"

"How can we trust anyone?"

And then Cat realized she was talking to a woman who'd agreed to marry to save the peace between their clans. "Oh—forgive me! How dare I act like I'm the only woman who's ever . . ."

"Think nothing of it. I did know your brother a long time ago—not that we parted on the best of terms. I wanted to trust in him. And between us, we found trust growing. I think that's true of any marriage. We cannot know what's inside a person, but we have to have faith that between us, we can cherish each other and work hard to grow together in love. Do ye love him?"

"When I didn't know myself, I thought . . . maybe. Now I don't know."

"Ye were still the same person, even without your memories. Maybe ye have to trust yourself first."

WHEN Finn came riding into Castle Kinlochard the next day, Cat was in the stables, grooming her horse. She saw the little girl first, and went running into the courtyard, expecting to see Duncan following behind. But Finn was alone.

The girl threw a leg over the saddle and dropped to the ground, taking off at a sprint toward Cat. They collided in the center of the courtyard, hugging each other.

"Oh, Finn," Cat said, "ye're alone? Ye know how dangerous the countryside can be."

"I was careful."

Cat pushed the hair out of the girl's face. "Look how long your hair is growing."

"The better to wear a queue," Finn insisted, then grinned.

"Ye're still wearing boys' garments." Cat clucked her tongue.

"Ye'll be happy to know I've told Maeve about myself. I've been living with her."

"I'm so glad. But I thought ye'd be with Laird Carlyle until he found ye a family."

"He seems to have forgotten that, thank the Lord."

"Nay, he'd never forget ye."

"Aye, well, maybe."

Together they walked slowly down the court-yard toward the great hall.

"So . . . how is Laird Carlyle?" Cat finally asked.

"Not good."

Tension coiled around her. "I'm sorry to hear that."

"He won't go live in his manor house."

"Why not?"

"We don't know. He's stayin' at the cave or up in the castle. It's his ancestral home, he says. I know he's started workin' on it himself, clearin' stone. He says he has more time now."

Because he's alone, Cat thought. "I don't like to hear that he's hiding away from his people."

"Sometimes he's with us. He is doin' his duty by the entire clan. I want to be with him, but he says 'tis not 'seemly.' Another reason I don't like bein' a girl." She hesitated, then glanced up at Cat. "Do ye miss him, my lady?"

It all came down to that, didn't it? "Aye," she answered, then with more firmness. "Aye, I do."

Finn didn't ask any more questions, but practically skipped along happily at Cat's side.

After the midday meal, Cat waited until the servants had gone. Owen and Maggie were talk-ing with their heads close together, chuckling, and she saw her brother put his hand on Maggie's belly with a sweetness that made Cat ache.

"Can I talk to ye both?" Cat asked.

Finn was seated at a lower table, still eating a leg of mutton, but looked at them with interest, as if she were a spectator at a play.

Owen regarded Cat warily, but he nodded.

"I want ye to know I've tried to return to my old life," Cat began slowly, "but . . . I haven't been happy."

"Well of course not," Owen said a bit too heartily. "Ye need to be in Edinburgh or London, where all the eligible young people are. Ye need society and parties."

Next to him, Maggie almost seemed to roll her eyes.

"I don't need any of that," Cat said with gentleness, knowing that her brother would take this hard. "I've experienced it all, and I'm grateful. But I want to be needed, Owen, and I felt needed with the Carlyles—with Duncan."

He stiffened. "That outlaw."

One corner of her mouth tilted up. "Well, he's not an outlaw anymore, is he?"

"Catriona."

He only called her by her full name when he was playing the part of the clan chief, her lord. She wasn't having it. "Owen, my life had more meaning when I was with them. They're a poor clan, and I can bring much to them."

"Especially your dowry. Did Carlyle demand it of ye?"

She tamped down her anger, knowing he was simply worried. "He doesn't know anything about my dowry."

"But he's not stupid—he can guess, can he not? 'Tis rumored to be the largest dowry in all of Scotland—maybe even England."

"I doubt that. But who better to make use of it than the Carlyles, for perhaps they contributed to it most unwillingly."

And there was nothing he could refute about that. Then all the breath left him and he seemed to sag. "He didn't ask if he could marry ye."

"Nay, but why would he have thought he could?"

"Did ye talk about marriage?"

"Never."

"Then how do ye know?"

"I have faith."

Cat and Maggie shared a gaze, and she thought her sister-in-law's eyes grew misty.

Owen saw where she was looking. "It's that dream again," he said, but without anger.

"I love him, Owen. Regardless of what he did to me, I saw the man he was to his people. I know he regrets his mistakes. And I think he loves me. He offered to sacrifice himself to save me."

"That could be guilt."

"Maybe. But I have to find out. Finn and I will leave together tomorrow. Somehow I have to find a way to convince Duncan that love is more important than the mistakes we've made."

Finn cheered, then subsided when Owen glared at her.

"I'm worried for ye, Cat," Owen said gruffly. "Now his whole clan knows who ye are. They might blame ye because of our father. 'Tis hard to forget such pain."

"I know. But maybe Duncan and I can be the bridge to heal the pain between Duff and Carlyle,

just like the two of you were a bridge to peace between Duff and McCallum. Let me go, Owen."

He sighed. "Aye, go with my blessing. But if it
isn't what ye think, know that ye can come home
anytime."

She leaned forward to kiss his cheek. "Thank
ye." But this wasn't her home anymore—it was
Maggie and Owen's. She wanted to make her own
home. With Duncan.

DUNCAN had spent a long day, touring outlying
farms, feeling free to be seen in broad daylight
with his people. He should have been rejoicing.

But he was miserable. And when he was miserable, he went to the castle, working in silence,
knowing it was better than inflicting his misery
on anyone else. He'd cleared the rubble from the
great hall, and soon he'd need equipment and oxen
to move the larger stones. It would take perhaps
his lifetime and more to make the castle habitable
and defendable again, but he wanted to try, for his
sisters' children. Maybe for his own someday, if
he could find a way to do his duty to his clan and
marry to produce an heir. He couldn't think about
that.

"Laird Carlyle!"

At the sound of Finn's voice, he straightened
and wiped the sweat from his brow with his forearm. Damn that girl. Maeve had sent word that
Finn had gone to visit Cat, without waiting for his
permission. Walking toward the doorway, Duncan knew he'd have to explain that they had to

leave Cat alone, now that she was Lady Catriona, not Mistress Catherine—

Words died in his throat. Lady Catriona, robed in silk, rode toward him on her horse—sidesaddle, like the elegant, stunning lady she was. He couldn't seem to find his breath, thought his heart had shattered, filling him with regret and the ache of love lost. Finn rode beside her, grinning. Cat was as regal as a queen, her garments hugging her waist, embroidery spilling down her underskirt, and up her bodice. No fichu blocked his gaze from the upper slopes of her breasts and her delicate collarbones.

She was smiling at him. "So will ye help a lady dismount?"

He went to her, not sure how it felt to be so blinded as if by the sun. When he would have reached for her hand, she simply fell toward him, and he was forced to grab her waist and steady her as she touched her feet to the ground. She looked up at him from beneath the brim of her hat, that smile softening.

The ache of what he'd lost was almost too much to bear.

He stepped back. "My lady, what brings ye to Carlyle Castle?"

"Finn tells me ye've begun to work on the place. Show me what ye've accomplished."

He cleared his throat. "Little enough. It'll take time."

"Aye. But show me."

She stretched her hand out in a ladylike gesture that he remembered from long ago. He found himself putting out his arm for her to rest her hand upon it as he escorted her inside.

He heard Finn snort behind him, but the girl didn't follow them.

"Ah, I can see a difference already," Cat said.

He tried to see the great hall as she might see it. The floors were clean of broken furniture and dirt, but the hearths were empty, the stone walls bare of tapestries.

He frowned at her. "Ye're just being polite, my lady."

She suddenly rounded on him. "Stop that nonsense at once."

"What nonsense?" he asked, arching one brow.

"Ye're my-ladying me as if ye don't know me, as if I'm not Cat, as if we'd never—" She broke off, glancing at the doorway as if Finn might appear.

But the lass had wisely left them alone.

"Calling ye by your title reminds me that ye can't be just Cat to me," he said quietly.

"I want to be."

It was a whisper, and he wasn't certain he heard her correctly. "What did ye say?"

"I want to be Cat—your Cat. I liked who I was, what I was doing, when I was with ye."

He had no response. No words came to him for a long moment, and he squashed some unnamed emotion as it struggled to surface. "Ye're just unhappy right now," he finally said. "When ye go off to Edinburgh—"

"I've been to all those places. They're fine, but . . . they're not here."

Shocked, he spread his arms wide. "Here?"

"Aye, here. Your castle. Or your manor near the village."

He stepped closer, frowning. "Cat, are ye with child? Is that what this is about? I never wanted a child of mine to be as unwanted as I felt, in a marriage that wasn't about love."

"Nay!" she cried, putting both her hands on his chest as if she would push him over. "Why cannot it be about love between us? Do ye love me, Duncan?"

He opened his mouth, but again, could find no words. She was full of surprises, his Cat.

His Cat.

"I've promised your brother I'd never see ye again," he said stonily. "'Tis not my place to—"

She slid her hands from his chest to his face, forcing him to look down upon her. "Do ye love me?" she whispered, her voice an ache that pierced him.

He gripped her upper arms, as if he'd shove her away—but he couldn't. "Aye, I love ye. I've loved ye, maybe from the moment ye opened your eyes and stared at me as if only I could save ye. And then I betrayed ye. What does my love matter?"

She closed her eyes, as everything in her seemed to relax. A smile spread slowly, and when she looked at him again, he was struck by the tenderness and thankfulness.

"And I love ye, too, Duncan."

He let her go, backing away, realizing he could not bear to hear this, only to have it snatched away, as it must.

"Don't say that," he ground out. "We both know

it can never be. 'Tis best if ye go back to your real life."

"This could be my real life."

"Ye don't know what ye're saying! Look at this place—as much a wreck as I am. Ye could have any lord, any gentleman ye want."

"I want the chief of the Carlyles."

The first bit of hope hurt almost as much as the pain of losing her. "Stop, Cat, don't do this to both of us."

She approached him, and he saw a lone tear track down one cheek. It undid him, unmanned him.

"Ye can never trust me," he insisted with the last of his desperation.

She stopped right in front of him and took both his hands. Her skin was warm from her ride, while his was the deep cold of the stone he'd been working with.

"I was worried about that," she admitted softly. "But I gave myself to ye, Duncan. How did I not see that that was a form of trust? How does anyone learn to trust another except through faith? And how many women get to see proof of their man's deeds? How many men would risk imprisonment, even death, for a stranger's child, night after night?"

"Don't make me out to be better than I am," he insisted. "I was righting a terrible wrong. Any man would—"

"Nay, they would not," she said forcefully. "I don't know many men who'd live in a cave, rather than lead danger to his own people. I've decided I know enough about ye to wed ye. Now will ye ask me properly, Duncan?"

He realized they were still holding hands. He lifted hers and stared at them. They were delicate within his. Slowly, he kissed her knuckles, first one hand, and then the other. "Cat . . . will ye be my wife?"

Another tear fell, but her smile grew broad. "Aye, I will, Duncan."

She might have coaxed him to propose, but no one had to force him to kiss his Cat.

EPILOGUE

"They're coming!" Finn came running into the great hall of Carlyle Castle, holding up her skirts.

Maeve, their housekeeper whether in the manor or castle, made a halfhearted attempt to slow her down, then laughed.

Cat watched her daughter fondly, knowing the girl was still getting used to skirts, but at least she didn't trip this time.

"Nothing's finished," Duncan grumbled.

"It'll never be truly finished," Cat said, her usual reply in this last year since they'd become man and wife. "But we'll make do. My brother, your sisters, all the rest of our combined families will be pleased to see the great hall looking so magnificent."

And it did. The stone walls soared up to a beamed ceiling. Banners and tapestries hung everywhere, as did the ancient weapons of Clan Carlyle. She stood with her hands on the rail of the cradle where their infant son lay sleeping, and admired it all. Much of her dowry had gone to help the Carlyle people, to buying new cattle and horses, replenishing seed, refurbishing the manor house that Duncan had grown up in, making it truly homelike.

But not home. Carlyle Castle connected Duncan to his family and his past. It would be their home permanently someday soon. For now, home was this man, their daughter, their new son.

Duncan came to her, and put his large, rough hand on the downy black hair of their bairn. And then Duncan looked up at her, and the smile he gave her burst with so much joy, that once again, she had to blink back tears.

This man could always make her cry. And they were tears of happiness, contentment—and faith.